A WHISPER OF PASSION

"My lord, this takes my breath away."

Nicholas smiled as if he was quite pleased and reached for her hand. The heartache that had been troubling her for two days eased. She allowed him to take her trembling fingers in his hand. He gently slipped the ring onto the third finger of her left hand. It fit perfectly.

"Are you chilled?" he asked, looking up at her suddenly. "Your hand is cold and you're shivering."

"Oh, no," Dorian protested. "Not at all. I'm—I'm just overwhelmed by the generosity of this gift."

"Am I allowed the privilege of kissing my betrothed?"

"Of course, my lord."

His lips touched her briefly, airily, lightly brushing against them. Then he clasped the back of her head in his hand and with a low moan, pressed his lips to hers more urgently.

With a thrill of excitement, Dorian opened her mouth to him. All the fear that she'd lost him seeped away. She applied herself to kissing him with all the yearning and care she truly felt.

A WHISPER OF VIOLETS

Linda Madl

Zebra Books
Kensington Publishing Corp.

http://www.zebrabooks.com

ZEBRA BOOKS are published by

Kensington Publishing Corp.
850 Third Avenue
New York, NY 10022

First Printing: April, 1997
10 9 8 7 6 5 4 3 2 1

Printed in the United States of America

To my husband Ron

ACKNOWLEDGMENTS

I would like to say thank you to Karyn Witmer-Gow, Lynne Smith, and my agent, Evan Marshall, for their help and support on this project.

Kristine Hughes also deserves a thank-you for her excellent help with research.

Special thanks go to Jan and Betty Kenny who are friends, readers, and exceptional critics.

Love's Philosophy

The fountains mingle with the river
And the rivers with the Ocean,
The winds of Heaven mix forever
With a sweet emotion;
Nothing in the world is single;
All things by a law divine
In one spirit meet and mingle.
Why not I with thine?—

See the mountains kiss high Heaven
And the waves clasp one another;
No sister-flower would be forgiven
If it disdained its brother;
And the sunlight clasps the earth
And the moonbeams kiss the sea:
What is all this sweet work worth
If thou kiss not me?
—Percy Bysshe Shelley

Chapter One

London
Spring 1807

The peacock feather on the lady's bonnet trembled. She turned ever so slightly, peering around her bonnet brim to search the crowd seated behind her for her opponent.

Without shrinking from her gaze, Nicholas studied her. She was unlike any opponent he had expected to find in a room of Sotheby Parke Bernet's auction house.

She was too tastefully stylish from her feather-trimmed bonnet to her indigo silk boots. Too soft and sweet in a room full of bewhiskered, pipe-smoking collectors and greedy dealers. Too young and fresh in her blue velvet cloak to be collecting anything but admiring looks and beaux.

When the lady did not spot him, she abruptly faced the auctioneer and increased her offer.

Nicholas didn't much appreciate the fact that she'd just forced up his bid on the item he sought by five guineas.

Next to Nicholas, his uncle harumphed.

''I say, St. John will be fit to be tied when he finds out his twin sister is here without a proper escort,'' Uncle George whispered with relish in Nicholas's ear. ''He and I belong to the same club, you know.''

Nicholas gestured to the auctioneer that he would top Miss St. John's bid. He wondered just how far she'd go. She'd shown no interest in any item but this one. Now she was watching the auctioneer with intense interest, clearly eager to win the exchange.

When the auctioneer announced the new price her head turned, not too quickly, but just enough to let Nicholas know that she had spotted him at last. Over her shoulder her violet eyes flashed, rich and dark. She lifted one winged brow. Her generous mouth pursed in annoyance, giving the hint that it might bow quite deliciously in a kiss.

Nodding slightly, Nicholas acknowledged her gaze. She faced the auctioneer again; the feather in her bobbed bonnet violently. With a small gloved hand she brushed the brim of her hat.

The genteel auctioneer's face betrayed no emotion, but his voice rose a key and almost broke. The price of the music fragment on the table before him went up ten guineas.

A low murmur ran through the crowded room.

Uncle George sucked in his breath. ''Well, she certainly isn't going to let you get by cheaply.''

Miss Dorian St. John, Nicholas knew, had something of a reputation among the *ton*. One nearly as notorious as his own, in fact, though of a different nature. It appeared her reputation might be well earned.

Nicholas grimaced to himself, grudgingly pleased with her challenge, despite the elevated price. Her obvious determination amused him more than he'd been amused in a very long time.

With a barely raised hand Nicholas indicated he was still in the bidding. The auctioneer practically crowed the new price. Jaded bidders, seasoned collectors and merchants all turned to look at each other in surprise.

Uncle George nudged him. "Nick, what on earth are you doing? That's an outrageous price for that dead Hungarian's music. What is his name?—Franz Chamier. Only namby-pambies and brokenhearted women collect sonatas and such."

"I told you, that's what we've come for." Nicholas just hadn't expected to have any competition for the stuff. It wasn't even a complete page of a song. He'd expected some stuffy gentleman collector to bid against him, but he'd certainly never anticipated opposition from a fashionable young lady of the *ton*.

"Well, of course I didn't believe you," George added unnecessarily. "But it appears Miss St. John has an abiding interest in it also. I doubt her brother is going to appreciate her frittering away the family fortune on dusty, sentimental music."

"That's not my problem," Nicholas said, seeing that Miss St. John had raised her bid once more. Without hesitation, he topped it. A general drone of astonishment filled the room.

Uncle George leaned closer. "At the club I've seen Davis St. John in his cups and quite weeping in frustration. It seems his sister fairly cuts dead every suitor he brings home and he fears he will never get her properly married. She's very nearly past marriageable age as it is."

Nicholas made no reply. He and every other collector in the room awaited Miss St. John's next response. She sat painfully still, facing the auctioneer's podium looking neither to her right nor her left. The peacock feather in her bonnet seemed to droop slightly. Though she continued to hold her head high, her shoulders sagged a bit.

Finally Miss St. John gave a subtle shake of her head, one only a veteran auctioneer—or another experienced bidder— would perceive. A pang of disappointment stabbed through Nicholas, catching him by surprise. Why he should want their contest to continue he didn't know. Even another glare cast at him over her shoulder would have been more satisfying than this sudden end to their exchange.

The auctioneer's voice resumed its normal pitch as he called for other offers. A hush filled the room disturbed only by a low murmur of amazement. At last he declared the shred of music Nicholas's for an astronomical price—one that made even Nicholas wince. But he had no regrets. The message the sheet of music carried, or the fragment of a message, should be worth every penny.

General pandemonium broke out in the room as he, Uncle George and Miss St. John rose to leave. The lady swept out the door before anyone else. A maid and a footman hurried along in her wake.

At the clerk's desk Nicholas arranged for payment and delivery of his purchase. That business concluded, he was about to put on his hat to leave when a footman wearing the St. John gold-and-green livery approached him.

"My lord, the Earl of Seacombe," the footman inquired, bowing as was appropriate.

"What's this?" Uncle George asked, pointedly surveying the footman from head to toe. "St. John's tiger. I must say, impressive. A well-trained fellow, I think."

The footman's respectful but haughty gaze remained on Nicholas as though Uncle George's comment had gone unheard.

"I'm Seacombe," Nicholas said, still uncomfortable with the title that had been his for almost two years.

"For you, my lord." The tiger presented a letter with Nicholas's title carefully lettered across the front.

Nicholas accepted it. "Thank you."

The footman stepped back but made no move to leave. "Miss St. John asked me to await your reply, my lord."

"Miss St. John?" Nicholas repeated, surprised and amused—and more pleased than he cared to admit.

"So she didn't give up after all," Uncle George chortled. "Well, open it, my boy."

Uncle George leaned over Nicholas's shoulder, clearly as curious as he. Nicholas quickly scanned the brief document. "It's an invitation to a musicale at the St. John town house."

"When?"

"At the end of the week."

"I say, rather short notice, isn't it?" George sniffed at the impertinence of the late invitation and turned to glare at the tiger as if the servant was personally responsible for the slight.

"I don't receive many invitations these days," Nicholas reminded his uncle, "late or otherwise."

"Humph. The ones you do receive you don't accept." Uncle George squared his shoulders. "Society is made up of a lot of fools, if you ask me."

Nicholas thoughtfully folded the invitation. He appreciated his uncle's loyalty, but the fact was that the unsubstantiated rumors of his treason had made him something of a social outcast. Though his seclusion was largely self-imposed, the turn of society's cold shoulder had left him cynical, if not a little embittered. No doubt the only reason Miss St. John requested his presence at her party was to pursue the matter of his purchase.

He had no intention of giving up the music. Aware of that, he should refuse her invitation; yet the flash in those rich violet eyes had intrigued him. He knew why he wanted the fragment, but why was she so determined to acquire the Hungarian composer's work? Why not find out? Engagements hardly crowded his calendar and the company might prove entertaining.

He turned to the footman. "Tell your mistress that I am delighted to accept her invitation and I shall look forward to enjoying her hospitality at the musicale."

Uncle George remained blessedly silent.

"Yes, my lord." The tiger bowed again. "I will inform Miss St. John of your acceptance."

When the footman was gone Uncle George and Nicholas put on their hats and stepped out onto Yorke Street. Under the gray March sky they glimpsed the St. John carriage as it disappeared around the corner.

"The St. Johns are an unusual family," Uncle George commented, obviously angling for his nephew to reveal his reason for accepting the invitation.

"So I've heard," Nicholas said, disinclined to tell Uncle George how fascinating he'd found Miss St. John. He signaled for his carriage to be brought up.

"Yes, rich as King Midas. Mrs. St. John died giving birth to the twins and James St. John himself never remarried. Then he was lost at sea not too many years ago. Since then I've heard Davis continues in the importing and exporting business and is doing very well," George went on. "And they're considered stylish. His twin sister's, Miss Dorian that is, good taste is greatly admired. Money and taste—irresistible to the *ton*, you know—everything they admire, adore and long for."

Nicholas remained silent, knowing that Uncle George required little prompting.

"Of course, there was that scandal about their aunt, Charlotte St. John, and her unfortunate affair with some foreign patriot fellow. But Society overlooked that. Wealth is useful that way. Nearly as useful as a title. And Davis St. John is very ambitious. Hopes to acquire a title himself. Knighthood or a baronetcy. That's the word out at the club."

The open Derrington carriage arrived at the curb.

"Then he won't appreciate having me as a guest in his house." Nicholas climbed in after his uncle and instructed the coachman to drive them across Town to the London docks. He was ready to quit Society and intrigue for the day. He wanted to see what ships lay anchored in the Thames. Captain Gavin Trafford of the *Dauntless* was expected to sail into Deptford any day now, and Gavin was Nicholas's only friend these days besides Uncle George.

"I can't imagine why you accepted the St. Johns' belated invitation," Uncle George persisted, clearly unready to give up the subject. "However, I do think Davis is too well-bred to make a scene. And Dorian St. John . . . well she's not inclined to give a fig about reputations. In fact, she's probably going to try to buy that piece of music from you."

"I suspect as much." Amusement twitched at the corner of

Nicholas's mouth, and the memory of the challenge in the lady's violet eyes strangely lightened his heart.

Out of habit, he looked up at the lowering sky to read the weather signs. The gray clouds offered no evidence of anything more than the usual British dreariness. The customary prevailing breeze from the river caressed his cheek and flaunted the dank smell of rotting garbage and dead fish.

Still he could feel the difference in the air, subtle and indistinct. The tiny crackle of energy. The airy lift of momentum on the breeze. He now possessed one piece of the evidence he needed to clear his family's name. More was required, but at last he knew it was possible to vindicate himself and the Derringtons.

With an instinct born of years at sea, he knew the wind was about to shift. A radical shift. One bringing heavy swells and hard sailing.

A smile of anticipation—and satisfaction—spread across Nicholas Derrington's face.

Dorian softly closed the workroom door, careful not to wake the lady dozing in the fireside chair.

Thankful for the few moments in which to think how she was going to tell Aunt Charlotte that she had failed, Dorian tiptoed across the room. Without a sound she bent over the sheets of music scattered across the table and examined what her aunt had accomplished. Compiling Franz Chamier's works was a slow, painstaking project. The slower the better, as far as Dorian was concerned, especially after her unsuccessful bidding at Sotheby Parke Bernet.

When she had set out for the auction house she'd thought her errand a simple one. Then Seacombe had turned up—where he'd never been before. Dorian couldn't put the memory of his face from her mind: the short dark hair that curled over the edge of his crisp white neckcloth and his sharp, piercing blue eyes and cruelly sensual mouth. If she wasn't mistaken, the man had had the gall to offer her a mocking smile when he'd acknowledged her stare. Then he'd topped her bid.

He collected nothing as far as anyone knew, but the blasted man had bid relentlessly. Who would have thought a Derrington and a former navy captain would have any interest in music?

The mantel clock began to strike. Aunt Charlotte started in her chair, and her eyes fluttered open.

"Oh my, Dorian dear, there you are." She struggled to sit up, and as soon as she succeeded, she tugged at the lace cuff of her violet-colored gown. Aunt Charlotte always wore violet, and for good reason. It flattered her pink complexion and enhanced the pure whiteness of her hair. "I just sat down for a moment to rest. I didn't mean to fall asleep."

"That's all right, Aunt Charlotte," Dorian said. "I see you were busy today. You have arranged the set of etudes we talked about yesterday."

"Yes. I think that's the order in which Franz wanted them." Aunt Charlotte leaned forward in her chair, her face alight with excitement. "I found one piece that I'd quite forgotten. Would you like to hear it?"

Before Dorian could reply Aunt Charlotte rose, went to the pianoforte, and began to play. Notes floated through the room: light, trilling, and lyrical. So magically rendered by her aunt that Dorian closed her eyes and imagined Franz himself, his head of dark curly hair bent over the ivory keys as he performed music only a genius could compose.

Dorian dismissed the memory of her trying afternoon in the smoke-filled auction house. Such a small annoyance hardly mattered in a world where music like Franz Chamier's existed. When the piece ended she sighed, reluctant to part with the delight and balm that it brought to her soul.

Her aunt sighed also.

"Did you get it, Dorian?" Charlotte broke the spell. "Were you able to get the fragment of Franz's song that was up for auction?"

Pulled abruptly back to earth, Dorian faced her aunt across

the piano and summoned her courage. "Aunt Charlotte, I'm afraid I wasn't able to acquire it. I didn't anticipate how high the bidding would go."

"Oh." Dismay stole the light from Charlotte's eyes. She suddenly seemed to shrink as she sat on the piano stool. "My funds are limited."

"Funds aren't the difficulty," Dorian said, careful not to betray the flutter of panic in her stomach. She silently berated herself for not going to the auction house better prepared. Her aunt's health was so delicate; it seemed to ebb and flow with the number of pieces of Franz Chamier's work Dorian could supply her. Dorian would do anything to keep her aunt—the woman who had been like a mother to Davis and her—healthy and well. "I'm not giving up, Aunt Charlotte. I believe I can still get that piece of music for you. It will just take a little more time than I anticipated."

"I hadn't thought obtaining it would be difficult," Charlotte began. "Perhaps you should leave well enough alone. You should be spending your afternoons in the company of friends and meeting young men. This is the time in your life when you should enjoy yourself, Dorian. You should be finding a loving husband."

"But of all of Franz's works he wrote this song, 'A Whisper of Violets,' for you, Aunt Charlotte."

"Yes, I admit I would like to have it, but not at the expense of your happiness, dear." Aunt Charlotte seized Dorian's hand and pressed it between her own gnarled but nimble fingers. "Promise me that you will not hide yourself away, but will seek out your heart's true, loving mate. True love, Dorian: That's what life is all about. And it is better to have had it for only a brief time, as I did, than to never have known it at all.

"Promise me, dear that you will seek out your true love and wed him if possible."

"Of course, Aunt Charlotte, I promise." Dorian tried not to sound too cavalier in her promise. She believed exactly as her aunt did about love. It was precious and elusive and unlikely to be found in the cold, carefully arranged marriages of past generations. But, at the moment, her aunt's health and future was of more importance to her than the pursuit of true love. "My search for love doesn't have to exclude finding the song Franz wrote just for you and intended you to have."

"Who did purchase it?" Charlotte ventured.

"The Earl of Seacombe."

"Seacombe? Seacombe?" Concern furrowed Aunt Charlotte's brow. "That would be a Derrington—oh, there is a new earl of Seacombe. Let me see, wasn't he one of Admiral Nelson's chosen captains?"

Aunt Charlotte's faded blue eyes grew wide. "Oh, not the one who betrayed us at Trafalgar . . . ?"

"So some say," Dorian admitted, less impressed with the accusations of treason against the earl than with the fact that he possessed a piece of music she wanted. "However, not all is lost. He's accepted an invitation to our musicale. I shall see that he's well entertained. Once he's at ease, I shall persuade him to come to some arrangement with us."

Charlotte's face brightened once more. "Of course. Seacombe is sure to be a gentleman. The Derringtons are a fine old family. Once he understands that we are trying to compile Franz's work as a tribute he will surely hand over the fragment."

"I'm sure he will," Dorian said, less confident than her aunt. Seacombe's mocking smile had not been reassuring. The uncompromising navy blue of his coat and breeches, the hard line of his jaw and his strong aristocratic nose bespoke a dark, intense man. Even if his size did not intimidate Dorian—he had loomed head and shoulders above the crowd in the auction house—there was a self-assured arrogance about his manner that left her cautious of him.

But strangest of all was the enameled ring he wore. She'd heeded little of the whispers about it. But to see the gleam of a gold-and-black skeleton mourning ring on his hand when he'd raised it to acknowledge the final bid had sent chills down her spine. No one knew for certain whom he mourned.

She knew little about him except that he was never seen in Society these days. Inviting him to the musicale would raise brows and feed the gossips, which had never troubled Dorian in the past. And it didn't now. It seemed the only thing to do if she wanted to keep a door open for acquiring the music.

She wished she knew why Derrington wanted the worthless scrap of Chamier's music. Whatever his reason, she suspected the stern, cool Earl of Seacombe would not yield possession of it for less than a costly price.

The afternoon grew darker. Outside, in the London streets, lanterns glowed on the hansom cabs. By time the servants brought a tea tray generously heaped with sandwiches and cakes, the footmen had begun to light the drawing room lamps. Dorian had established the daily ritual of tea and sandwiches in order to keep flesh on Aunt Charlotte's thin frame and color in her cheeks.

Dorian had just begun to pour when she heard the commotion of Davis's arrival home. Paying little heed to her brother's return, she offered Aunt Charlotte a cucumber sandwich. Her brother seldom paid his respects to the ladies until dinnertime.

But today Dorian heard him come pounding up the stairs instead of retiring to the library. Certain that he'd heard of her trip to the auction house, Dorian took a sip of tea to fortify herself. When he burst into the drawing room, a frown marring his handsome face, she was prepared.

''Good afternoon, ladies.'' Davis paused in the doorway, almost as tall as the Earl of Seacombe but of a slighter, more youthful build. A lock of his fair hair drooped across his forehead and his violet eyes narrowed when his gaze lit on Dorian. His tone was courteous and pleasant as always when addressing Aunt Charlotte, but his lips were thin with anger.

"Davis," Aunt Charlotte said, a smile of pleasure spreading across her gentle face. "How thoughtful of you to join us."

"Yes, indeed." Dorian smiled at her twin, knowing he dare not cast loose his outrage on her in the presence of Aunt Charlotte. Upsetting her was too risky. Their aunt's welfare was the one thing Dorian and Davis agreed upon. "I'll ring for another dish."

"No, thank you, Aunt Charlotte," Davis said. "That won't be necessary. I must go out again this evening—a business meeting. But I must speak with *you,* Dorian."

"Yes, of course." Dorian rose slowly from the tea table. She'd hoped to put off this confrontation until Davis's anger had cooled a bit, but she'd deal with it now if she must.

Distress clouded Aunt Charlotte's face. "Is something wrong?"

"No, nothing at all, dear," Dorian said, patting her aunt's hands. "I'll be right back. Do have another sandwich."

Davis closed the door quietly. Then sister and brother confronted each other in the hallway. "How could you? It's all over London already. They were laughing at me by the time I reached the club this afternoon."

"How could I what?" Dorian had learned long ago that it was best to define exactly which infraction she was being taken to task for before she undertook her defense.

"You went to the auction house without a proper escort."

"I took my maid and footman."

"Going to an auction house is hardly the same thing as a stroll in the park." Davis threw up his hands. "You know you should have had a gentleman with you."

"I prefer riding in the park to strolling."

"That's not the issue," Davis said. "You went to Sotheby Parke Bernet, and if that wasn't bad enough, you had some communication with that traitor, what's-his-name."

"The earl of Seacombe," Dorian supplied. "I thought you'd be better informed about a titled gentleman."

"You know whom I mean." Davis glared at her. "What

kind of note did you write him? Everyone saw our tiger deliver it."

"I merely invited him to the musicale on Friday," Dorian said, as if her brother could expect nothing less from her. Davis had a penchant for titles. "The earl had just shown an unusual interest in Franz's music, and I thought he might enjoy hearing Aunt Charlotte play."

"You invited Seacombe here?"

"Yes, and he accepted," Dorian said, unable to suppress her own sense of victory. When she'd dashed off the invitation in the coach she'd expected the man to decline. "Honestly, Davis, he appeared quite respectable. Not like a traitor at all."

"What did you expect a traitor to look like?" Davis sputtered. "He'd hardly be wearing a French uniform."

Dorian ignored her brother's remark. "I understand the accusations of treason are unproven, are they not?"

"Formal charges have never been brought." Davis appeared mollified a bit by that thought. "Nevertheless, everyone thinks the man was responsible for hundreds of deaths. There are people who refuse to remain in the same room with him. I can only imagine what Elizabeth will say. If the *ton* takes offense, they'll snub us."

"Ah, that's what concerns you. Lady Elizabeth and her father, the Duke of Eastleigh," Dorian said. Davis was inordinately sensitive where that particular dark-haired lady was concerned. She also knew that the *ton* protected its best interests above all else. Too many members of Society could ill afford to ignore the St. Johns. "I sincerely doubt anyone will snub us. And if you think I'm going to withdraw my invitation, you're mistaken."

Davis glared at her, frustration clear in his violet eyes.

"It's only an informal musicale, hardly the social event of the year," Dorian appealed to her brother. "A few hours of music. Some sherry for our small group of guests. Mayhap a little dancing. A light buffet, and everyone will be gone before you know it. What harm could that do?

"By the end of next week there will be something infinitely more scandalous for the *ton* to gossip about than the appearance of Seacombe at our town house."

"The *ton* may have a longer memory than you credit them," Davis said, his frown growing deeper. "I suspect Seacombe would agree with that."

"Perhaps." Dorian offered her brother a charming smile. "But I sincerely doubt his brief appearance will cause much of a stir in this instance."

"Perhaps not. But see that he's not invited again." Davis assumed his gruff, lord-of-the-house demeanor. He tugged at the hem of his embroidered waistcoat to smooth the wrinkles from it.

"We'll see," Dorian said, reluctant to give way to her brother. There was no way to know how difficult obtaining the music from Seacombe might be.

"We won't see," Davis corrected. "This is a one-time-only invitation. That's final."

Davis turned away and strode down the hall, demanding no further agreement from Dorian which was a good thing, because she would have not given it.

Chapter Two

Carriages crowded the street outside the St. Johns town house by the time Nicholas arrived at a stylishly late hour when most guests had already arrived. For the St. Johns' sake he'd decided to avoid calling attention to himself by being either too early or too late.

The house fulfilled the *ton*'s every requirement of a domicile. Situated in fashionable Mayfair, it was appointed with a myriad of servants, marble floors, imported carpets, lustrous wood furniture and gleaming brass lamps. From what Nicholas glimpsed of the rooms as the footman ushered him down the hall, the house was more than just the traditional showplace. Salon, library, dining room—each offered a curious but appealing air of exquisite good taste warmed with the unexpected charm of comfort—pillows, plants, footstools and books. Dorian's touch, no doubt.

In the drawing room the furniture and carpets had been removed. The doors between the rooms and into the garden had been opened to allow the guests to circulate. Nicholas only recognized a few of the guests, including the Duke of Eastleigh and his pretty brunette daughter, Lady Elizabeth. According to Uncle George, the gossips connected Davis St. John with the duke's only daughter and heir. Though everyone knew the young man had no need of money, a match with a prestigious house would make him eminently eligible for a title.

One or two heads turned to offer Nicholas polite but distant greetings. A servant appeared to offer him sherry, which he accepted as he scanned the room for his hostess. It took him only a moment to spot Dorian standing over a pale older woman seated on a sofa.

Miss St. John wore a high-waisted gown of a delicate pink stuff that clung to her figure and brought out the roses in her cheeks. Blond curls swept up from her temple and crowned her head in Roman goddess style, enhancing her long, elegant neck. Pink roses decorated her coif and added an aura of femininity, a contradiction of the determined young female Nicholas had glimpsed in the auction house.

Almost as if Dorian felt his gaze roaming over her, she turned to face him. A smile lighted her features. Merely a hostess's smile, Nicholas told himself. Nonetheless, his gut twisted in an odd way that he knew was more than simple desire.

She excused herself and moved toward him across the room, speaking briefly to her guests as she wove her way through the crush. When she reached him, she held out her hand.

"Lord Seacombe, how good of you to come," she said. "I hope I'm not being presumptuous. But you showed such interest in Franz Chamier's music at the auction that I thought perhaps you'd be interested in hearing his work."

"Miss St. John, I hadn't given presumption a thought." Nicholas took her well-shaped hand and marveled at how small and fragile it seemed against his palm. Defying the urge to grasp her and not release her for the rest of the evening, he bent to kiss her hand. The gesture seemed so natural that he was pleased to find his manners had not entirely deserted him over his last year in seclusion.

She snatched her hand away, too quickly to be courteous.

Nicholas caught her gazing at his mourning ring, but he pretended not to notice. "My aunt is quite devoted to Franz Chamier's music and has agreed to play for us this evening."

"How nice," Nicholas said. "I've only just begun to learn of Mr. Chamier's work, and what I have learned is fascinating."

"Yes, he was a man of many facets," Dorian agreed. Nicholas wondered how much she truly knew about the Hungarian's music and his last days in prison.

"Who do we have here?" A blond young man with features as well-proportioned as Dorian's appeared at her side. "Am I to assume you are the Earl of Seacombe?"

From the young man's fair coloring, Nicholas could only conclude that this was Dorian's brother, Davis. Still, the gentleman's brusque attitude annoyed him.

"Davis, where are your manners?" Dorian chided, blushing ever so charmingly. "Of course this is Lord Derrington, the earl of Seacombe, the gentleman who also has an interest in Franz's work. I believe I mentioned him to you."

"My lord." Davis bowed, coolly polite. "Also known, I believe, as Captain Derrington of the *Dauntless*."

Nicholas never permitted his annoyance to alter his expression. Over time he'd become inured to most insults—the hinted allusions as well as the outright ridicule and hostility. But he found himself indignant with this young pup for bringing up his career in front of Dorian—though surely she knew his reputation.

"Davis!" Dorian turned on her brother before Nicholas could make a suitable reply. "Would you be so kind as to make certain all of our guests have comfortable seats? I believe Aunt Charlotte is nearly ready to perform."

Davis departed, but not without throwing Nicholas a glare first.

"I'm sorry," Dorian began. "He fancies—"

"Not at all," Nicholas interrupted, touched by her embarrassment. "He's only being a brother. So your aunt is going to play for us?"

Dorian's face cleared. "Yes, she was one of Franz Chamier's best piano pupils, you know."

"I see." The connection between Dorian's interest in the music and her aunt's relationship with Chamier dawned on Nicholas at last. Of course, she wanted the music for her aunt.

Strains of piano scales reached them from the music room.

"There, she's warming up now." Dorian put her hand on his arm and smiled up at him. The beguiling spontaneity of the gesture warmed his insides. He smiled in return. "I know you will enjoy hearing her."

"Then let's go do just that, shall we?" At her nod, Nicholas couldn't resist placing his hand over Dorian's as he escorted her toward the music room.

Aunt Charlotte performed splendidly on the pianoforte. Nicholas listened to the music, enjoying it in a way that he'd never bothered to even pretend before. There was no doubt from the dreamy expression that came over Dorian's face that she loved the melody and the rhythms that her aunt drew from the instrument. The Hungarian musician must have relished the attentions of these two ladies before the poor soul got himself locked away, Nicholas thought. When the sound faded away he was sorry Aunt Charlotte had concluded her performance.

As the musicale progressed, Nicholas found himself the special guest of his hostess. She practically never left his side, but she never neglected her other guests either, talking freely with both ladies and gentlemen. Her easy conversation brought smiles to faces and polite greetings from the lips of people Nicholas knew would never have spoken to him under other circumstances.

He had expected her to bring up the topic of the music he had won away from her at the auction house, but there was hardly a private opportunity for that. By the time the buffet was served she had not uttered a single word about the music. He was beginning to think he'd become too cynical and wondered if he'd been unfair to think Dorian's invitation held a deeper intention. She excused herself for a moment to see to a crisis in the kitchen.

Nicholas took another glass of sherry from a footman's serving tray and stood back to survey the guests once more. The general atmosphere was cordial and relaxed, and he understood why initiations to affairs at the St. John town house were much sought after.

"Nick, old man," came a hearty greeting from behind him. He recognized the voice immediately and turned to greet his friend. "Gavin, when did you drop anchor?"

The two men exchanged a warm, handshake.

"Just last night," Gavin Trafford said. "I heard you were looking for me, but I didn't expect to find you here."

"Nor I you." Nicholas envied his friend his wind-burnt complexion and sun-bleached hair. How he longed to be on the deck of a ship again.

"I happened by my club this afternoon and ran into young Davis, who nearly begged me to stop by." Gavin snagged a glass of sherry from another passing footman. "I thought you weren't going out in Society these days."

"I discovered a good reason to reconsider my decision," he said.

Dorian emerged from the kitchen and smiled across the room at Nicholas before she joined a group of guests. He knew with pleasurable satisfaction—which he didn't care to examine too closely—that she would find her way to his side again.

Gavin's gaze followed Nicholas's. "Miss Dorian St. John? Bloody hell, man. You don't want to travel down that road. I say, Davis is a nice chap, but I hear his sister can be a real she-dragon."

"I find her amusing."

Gavin eyed him closely as he sipped from his glass again. "Does your interest in her have to do with your investigation?"

"Perhaps," Nicholas said, knowing that Gavin was asking about his personal inquiry into the treason rumors. He was unwilling to share his growing suspicion that Dorian St. John might hold a key to the mystery.

"Wouldn't that beat all?" Gavin said. "The St. Johns involved in something like that."

"I don't think it's as simple as you might think," Nicholas said. "Let's have something to eat and you can tell me about your voyage."

As Nicholas listened to Gavin, he began to think the evening was going to be a pleasant success—until he looked into a familiar face across the buffet table. Gavin had turned away to greet a friend, leaving Nicholas alone for the moment.

Across a cold plate of sliced tongue, a fellow ship's captain, John Kenwick, stared boldly at Nicholas. After two years of living with rumors sometimes muttered just beyond his hearing or more often to his face, Nicholas steeled himself against the ugly distaste that contorted the expression of a former friend.

"What are you doing here?" Kenwick demanded, his round, weather-creased face a mask of cold hostility. "I'd have thought someone such as you would have had the good sense to stay out of Society."

Nicholas stared at the man he'd always thought of as a friend. They'd been shipmates on the *Sparkwell*. As he recalled, John had left His Majesty's Navy shortly after Nicholas himself had resigned his commission. That hardly prevented the man from believing all the sordid things that had been rumored about Nicholas and his last battle at sea.

"I have no reason to hide from Society." Nicholas helped himself to a slice of tongue. His seclusion had been primarily for the purpose of investigating the source of the rumors of betrayal that had sullied his family's good name. He felt he owed no apology for his presence to Kenwick or to anyone else at the musicale.

Gavin nudged Nicholas to move on down the table. "Hello, Kenwick. You aren't going to spoil a nice evening, now are you?"

"How can you stand there next to a traitor, Trafford?"

Kenwick slammed his plate down on the table. "I for one refuse to dine in the same room with him."

"Is there some trouble, Captain Kenwick?" Dorian appeared at Nicholas's side. "Perhaps I can order something special for you from the kitchen?"

"No," Kenwick snarled. "No offense, Miss St. John, but it's the company that is not to my liking. Perhaps you are unaware of Captain Derrington's past deeds."

A rose petal in Dorian's hair quivered. Nicholas knew instantly that she was about to wage war—astonishingly, on his behalf. He opened his mouth to head off an embarrassing clash, but he was too late.

"I am offended, Captain Kenwick." Dorian's violet eyes flashed. "I select my guests for their common interest from the best of Society. It occurred to me that the chosen ships' captains of Admiral Nelson such as Lord Derrington, Captain Trafford, and yourself, would have a great deal to share. Especially your concern over the ungentlemanly spread of rumors discrediting His Majesty's Navy and Lord Seacombe's family."

Conversation died in the dining room. Nicholas knew there wasn't a guest present who wasn't holding his breath and stretching his ears to catch the next word.

Harsh disapproval froze on Kenwick's face.

Nicholas leaned toward Dorian. "It's all right, Miss St. John. Captain Kenwick is entitled to his opinion."

"Perhaps." Dorian's voice rang with skepticism. "But that does not entitle him to express it in my drawing room to the discomfort of my guests."

Kenwick turned a deep, angry red, but he inclined his head in Dorian's direction. "As you say, Miss St. John, I overstep my place as your guest. I do apologize for that. However, many suffered because of the man who stands next to you, and I do not apologize for my opinion."

"Your apology is accepted, Captain Kenwick," Dorian began. "However, I believe—"

"I am quite satisfied with Captain Kenwick's apology to

you.'' Nicholas betrayed no emotion and purposely ignored the opportunity to challenge Kenwick to a duel. Putting a lead ball through a man who clearly believed in the same rumor scores of others accepted as truth would hardly clear the Derrington name.

At that moment Davis swept into the room with a big smile on his face and eddies of energy and excitement swirling around him.

''We've just begun a new table of card games in the front salon. Come one, come all. . . .'' Davis stopped and stared at the grim faces in the dining room. Some of the guests took the opportunity to slip out. ''Is something amiss?''

''Nothing at all,'' Dorian said, with a cool glance in Kenwick's direction. ''Captain Kenwick was just bidding us farewell.''

''So soon?'' Davis asked. ''I'd hope to challenge you at the gaming table, Kenwick.''

''Not tonight.'' Kenwick glared at Nicholas, then made a curt bow in Davis's direction. ''Perhaps another time.''

He turned on his heel and left the room.

Davis turned to Dorian. ''What did *you* say?''

''Your sister was very gracious,'' Nicholas said, surprised to find himself ready to return the favor of his fiery hostess's defense.

''No, I was not,'' Dorian said, frowning as though she was displeased with herself. ''I reminded Captain Kenwick of his manners and he was annoyed by my bluntness. So he made his excuses.''

''As I fear it is time for me to do also.'' Nicholas reached for Dorian's hand, intending to leave before his presence caused any more disturbances—among the guests or between brother and sister.

''Oh, no you don't.'' Dorian pulled away. ''We have yet to discuss something.''

''What's this?'' Davis asked, clearly suspicious of his twin's interest in Nicholas.

"Nothing you need concern yourself with." Dorian gave his arm a comforting pat. "It's just a little business arrangement between Lord Derrington and I."

Davis cast a wary frown in Nicholas's direction. Nicholas shrugged, though he knew that Dorian was about to bring up the issue of the Chamier music at last.

"There you are, Davis," Dorian said with a laugh and a dismissive wave of her hand. "It's so unimportant, Lord Seacombe doesn't even know what I'm talking about. Pray see to our guests and I'll join you soon."

Davis's frown turned to one of warning. Nicholas would expect nothing less from Dorian's only male relation. He suddenly pitied Davis. The poor young man must be torn between the desire to see his sister safely wed and keeping at bay the unprincipled wolves who might take advantage of her.

As soon as Davis had departed, Dorian led the way into the empty music room and closed the door.

The evening had grown late and the candles burned low, casting soft shadows across the gleaming wood floor. Nicholas admired the slight figure that crossed the room and gestured to a pair of chairs by the piano. Though he expected her to drive a hard bargain, he was prepared to offer his own deal.

"I will not mince words, Lord Seacombe." Dorian settled onto the chair, arranging the soft pink stuff of her skirt. "I was terribly disappointed in not being able to acquire the Chamier fragment at the auction."

"I was aware of that." Nicholas turned a chair around and sat in it, facing the lady secure in his determination to win this round also. But she had a charmingly direct way of laying her cards on the table, and he intended to enjoy it. "And of course I was sorry to have caused you distress, but I also wanted the music."

"Yes, well, but do you realize what your determination to own the Chamier fragment has done?"

"My determination?"

Dorian went on as if she'd not heard his question. "The price on everything remotely connected with Franz Chamier has become monstrously expensive. Already there's hardly a shred of Franz's work to be found in London at any price. Those silly collectors and dealers thought you knew something they didn't."

"Me?" Nicholas watched Dorian, who now seemed totally preoccupied with her skirt. "I seem to recall you taking an active part in bidding up the price."

"Just what is your interest in Chamier's work?" she demanded, as though she'd not heard his point. "You're hardly the sort to be collecting an obscure composer's sentimental work."

"Nor are you," Nicholas pointed out.

Dorian chewed her lip nervously. "I have been helping my aunt with her compilation of his work. As you might have gathered, she holds his talent in high regard."

"Yes, I suspected as much after I heard her play."

"I invited you here tonight so that you could see and hear for yourself the care and devotion with which Aunt Charlotte approaches his work. She worships his memory and wishes to honor him with a complete compilation of his work."

"Admirable," Nicholas admitted. He'd heard of Charlotte St. John's scandalous affair with the Hungarian musician before the Hungarian patriot's imprisonment. He chided himself for not realizing that affair might play a larger part in the mystery than he'd first suspected.

"I appeal to you to sell your music fragment to me," Dorian continued. "You will be making a sweet lady very happy while also making a great contribution to the music world."

"Indeed, a magnificent opportunity." Nicholas shook his head, impressed and amused with her earnest appeal. There was no denying the issue lay close to the lady's heart. "I'm sorry, madame. I cannot part with the music."

Dorian blinked at him.

''Let me explain, my lord,'' she began again patiently, as if he were an uncomprehending child and she was going to make him see the error of his ways. ''I was not properly prepared to pay any price when I went to the auction house. Since then, I have arranged to offer whatever sum you name.''

''Whatever price I name?'' Nicholas repeated thoughtfully, allowing his gaze to take in the creamy whiteness of her throat and the soft fullness of her breasts, so neatly tucked into the scoop of her gown. Her naive offer brought delightful fantasies to mind, tempting things he'd like to demand of so lovely a lady.

For the first time in years he let a true smile spread across his face. He wished he was more of a sailor and less of a gentleman.

''Unfortunately, price is not an issue.'' Nicholas tried to ignore the uncomfortable stirrings of desire in his body. ''I intend to keep the fragment for myself, for my own use.''

Dorian's dark eyes widened in surprise; then a puzzled frown turned on her lips. ''But why? What need have you for a piece of a sentimental love song?''

''Just let me say I have my reasons. In time perhaps I will be able to reconsider your offer.''

Dorian shifted impatiently in her chair. '' 'In time' is not good enough, Lord Seacombe. I need the complete manuscript at the earliest possible opportunity.''

''I regret that is impossible,'' Nicholas said, troubled by her agitation but careful not to show it.

She gave an unladylike huff of annoyance and rose to stare down at him. ''Just what do you intend to do with the fragment?''

''I have my purposes.''

''Well, it seems quite useless to me without the other pieces to make up the whole.''

''Believe me, I understand the problem.'' Nicholas regarded her more closely, the thought dawning that she might know more about Chamier's music and imprisonment than he first thought.

"Good. Then you understand why you might as well sell your fragment to me." Dorian leaned closer and spoke very slowly, as if she suspected he might be hard of hearing. "Aunt Charlotte and I already own one of the three pieces."

Chapter Three

Nicholas sat very still, careful to keep the surprise from his face. Dorian watched him intently, and he didn't want her to know it had never occurred to him that she might possess exactly what he wanted.

He'd been searching for over a year for this piece of Chamier's music and found nothing. He'd uncovered few rumors and had developed several theories as to who possessed the other fragments of music. The St. Johns had never figured in either rumor or theory. But of course their connection made sense. A paramour would seek out the last writings of her lover, and her lover might well try to get them to her. Nicholas suppressed the excitement that threatened his composure.

According to Uncle George's remarks, London society had gossiped of nothing but Charlotte and the composer for weeks. Gossips whispered about wild, passionate love trysts between the lady of Quality and the foreign composer.

Nicholas had paid little heed to the tales at the time. The Derrington name had still been untarnished. Jonathan Collard had still been alive, and Nicholas's brother had still been reigning as the Earl of Seacombe. Gossip had held no fascination for him. He'd been promoted to captain of a second-rater, a ship of the line, the *Dauntless,* and was about to set sail on another voyage.

Yet Nicholas did remember that what had seemed to shock the gossips and Uncle George the most had been the St. Johns' refusal to dissemble about the love affair.

Now that he'd met Dorian, he understood perfectly. She would never attempt to sweep such a thing under the rug. She would help her aunt with a compilation in the Hungarian patriot's honor rather than pretending, while red-faced, that the whole business had never happened. He glanced up at the lady pacing the floor before him.

"You didn't know we had a piece, did you?" Dorian smiled and looked absolutely triumphant.

"No, I did not."

"Will you reconsider then? Surely you understand that Aunt Charlotte and I will never give up what we have. Franz's music is too dear to her. Your fragment is useless alone. Put with ours, it might be possible to reconstruct the whole melody."

"The music is not what is important," Nicholas said, forgetting what he might be revealing. A thousand new possibilities assailed him.

"What do you mean, the music isn't important?"

"Do you have any idea who possesses the third scrap?"

"The third?" Dorian strolled to the piano, thoughtfully striking middle C. "What if I did know?"

Nicholas's restraint broke. He was off his chair in an instant. "If? If you did know, I'd insist on knowing, too."

"I don't know." Dorian turned on him.

Nicholas regarded her for a moment, relieved by her admission because he was certain she had no idea how dangerous this search for the music of Franz Chamier could become. "Then I'm afraid I can't be of help to you."

Dorian regarded him in apparent disbelief before turning away. "I'm sorry you feel that way. I can find it on my own."

Nicholas didn't like that thought, and the suspicion lingered that she might know still more that she was admitting. "Perhaps we should work together."

"Just how would that be of benefit?" She eyed him with skepticism.

"Together we could investigate the most likely collectors."

"My plan exactly," she said. "Why would I need your help?"

Nicholas attempted to look as innocent and reasonable as possible. Now that he knew she had a fragment, he couldn't afford to lose track of it—or of her. "Two sets of eyes, ears, and hands will find the last piece all the sooner."

Her elegant winged brows drew together and she made no reply. Nicholas knew she needed more convincing.

"If we each proceed on our own, we might defeat each other's purposes." He took a deep breath, the wisdom of his own proposal just occurring to him. "Working together, we can build on each other's intelligence and learn facts the other might not so readily discover. And you'll know if I find the music and I'll know if you find it."

She folded her arms across her breasts and her bottom lip took on a childish, stubborn fullness. "Then what?"

"If—when you find it you must lend your fragments to me to copy," Nicholas offered, with no intention of fulfilling his part of the bargain. A copy would never serve his purposes. "And if I find it, I'll lend my pieces to you and your aunt will likewise transcribe a copy."

"Aunt Charlotte and I would prefer to have the original."

"I understand, and so would I," Nicholas agreed, a gratified smile coming to his lips. He was rather pleased with the apparent success of his offer. How could she refuse? "But we can't both have the original. So we must compromise."

Dorian tapped her chin with a slender finger, then shook her head. "No, I don't think so."

"No?" Nicholas peered more closely at her. "What do you mean, no?"

''No. Just as I said.'' Challenge rang softly in her voice. ''Why should I work with you? I've done well enough on my own so far. I want the real thing. I want the original. Why should I settle for anything less?''

''Indeed, why should you?'' Annoyed with her refusal, Nicholas stepped away from Dorian. No wonder her brother drank himself into his cups and wept over her future. She was entirely too headstrong for her own good.

''You will not sell your fragment?'' she asked once more.

''No, madame, I will not sell,'' Nicholas said.

''Then it seems we have come to an impasse.''

''So it seems,'' Nicholas agreed with regret. He longed to linger, to inhale more of her scent and feel the softness of her skin beneath his hands again. He moved closer, standing so near he could smell the fragrance of the fresh roses in her hair. She refused to look up at him.

''Well then, our discussion is over.'' Dorian offered her hand in farewell.

Nicholas took it and pulled her to him, giving in to the unexplainable but demanding urge to kiss her. Before she could protest he slipped a hand around the back of her neck and covered her full lips with his mouth.

To his satisfaction, she yielded after a brief resistance, spreading her hands across his waistcoat and leaning against him. He savored the delicate tremor that ran the full length of her body. She was soft and pliant in his arms. His need for her grew strong and painful; he was certain she could feel it through her thin gown. He wished he'd locked the music room door behind them.

The kiss he'd intended to be brief deepened. He tasted her wine-colored lips and the corners of her mouth, soaking in her warmth and seeking the deeper intimacy of her mouth. When he parted her lips she stiffened in his arms and pushed him away. He held her a moment longer, then released her.

''Sir!'' She was breathless, blushing and vulnerable. Her violet eyes had darkened to purple and grown wide in confusion.

Nicholas struggled against the desire to seize her again.

"I think we've said all there is to say to each other," she gasped.

"I agree, for now." Nicholas bowed, said his thank-yous, and bade his hostess farewell.

In the hallway as Nicholas accepted his cloak from the footman, the Duke of Eastleigh and Lady Elizabeth appeared, offering their farewells to Davis. Nicholas noted that Dorian had followed him.

"Shall we see you at the house party at Thorpe Hall week after next?" Elizabeth was saying after she thanked Dorian for the evening. "Lord Halthorpe will not stop bragging about his new pianoforte."

"Yes, we plan to be there." Davis took Lady Elizabeth's pelisse from the footman and draped it over her shoulders.

Nicholas would have thought nothing of the conversation except for Dorian's nervous glance in his direction. She did not want him to know something about Halthorpe.

"Halthorpe wants us all to admire the changes he's made in Thorpe Hall," Davis continued, allowing his hands to rest lightly on the lady's shoulders for a moment. "I think it should be a fine party in the country and I look forward to it."

"Yes, I do also." Lady Elizabeth clutched her pelisse closer.

Nicholas busied himself with his gloves, his memory nagging at him all the while. He seemed to remember something about Lord Halthorpe being a musician and scholar—fairly common occupations in genteel circles. The elderly earl was just the sort who would think nothing of spending a fortune on Chamier's music if it was something to show off to his friends.

In the carriage on the way home Nicholas could hardly believe his good fortune. Uncle George had received an invitation to the Halthorpe house party, a particular social entertainment Nicholas had never been fond of. House parties meant exhausting balls, tedious dinners, riding to the hounds, long picnics, and silly games—kissing games.

A country house party with Dorian St. John in attendance

took on a new appeal. She had a delicious, truculent lower lip. And there would be old Halthorpe's collection to inspect.

His failure to enlist Dorian's help was a bit of a disappointment, but thanks to her, he now knew who owned one of the three pieces of the music. One way or another Dorian would lead him to the third—and give up her own as well.

Idly watching the passing street lamps, Nicholas wondered whether the headstrong Dorian St. John could be seduced. An even more intriguing thought: Was she a virgin still? She had passed the age of dewy innocence, if he recollected rightly— a full five and twenty. Yet in his gut he was certain of her virginity. She was too unaware of her effect on men to have been introduced to passion. No sweet-talking rogue had breached Miss St. John's defenses, yet. She might smile at a pretty speech and flutter her fan, but mere words would make no fool of her. He'd discovered that for himself.

Nicholas suspected beneath her sensibleness lay a warm, soft, generous heart. Once touched and charmed, she would prove loving and selfless—and, he liked to think, gloriously passionate.

For once he was tempted to think of seducing a virgin. He normally took the gentlemanly view that virgins were off limits, but with Dorian—

Nicholas smiled to himself. It wouldn't be long now before he possessed the evidence he needed to prove his innocence— and he'd do it with Miss St. John's willing help or without it.

Nicholas tapped the ceiling of the carriage. He'd share his new discovery with someone who would appreciate the information.

The tiger opened the small door. "Yes, my lord?"

"I've decided not to return to my uncle's town house just yet," Nicholas said. "To the London docks. I'll have a nightcap at the Blue Mermaid."

"Yes, my lord." The door snapped shut and the carriage took the next turn toward the river.

* * *

Merchant seamen, midshipmen, and sea captains crowded the smoky taproom of the Blue Mermaid. Under the smell of tobacco smoke floated the ripe scent of ale.

Nicholas had left his greatcoat, neckcloth, and tall crowned hat in the carriage. The pub owner and numerous regular customers knew him and would only be surprised by the formality of his dress, not by his appearance in the taproom. But he saw no need to call undue attention to himself.

The Blue Mermaid was one of the few pubs Nicholas had frequented regularly over the last eighteen months, and the only one where he still felt safe. He took a seat at an empty table and nodded to the barmaid, who brought him the ale he usually requested.

He'd nearly finished his first drink when one of the midshipmen at a neighboring table left his comrades. With his tankard in hand, the young man strolled to Nicholas's table and sat down next to him.

"You're near ready to crack that stern face of yours with a smile tonight." The blond young man, tanned from long days at sea, eyed Nicholas closely. "You've found it, then?"

"One part of it." Nicholas allowed himself to smile at Jamie Collard, the one man who would be as pleased as he that parts of the puzzle were falling into place. "I feel as though a bit of a joke has been played on me."

"I told you the best I knew, Captain."

"No, Jamie, I didn't mean that." Nicholas grinned reassuringly at the younger man. "Your information was good and it has helped me learn more."

Jamie shyly peered into his drinking glass. "Glad to know that, Captain. I want to learn the truth behind my brother Jon's death as badly as you do."

"I understand," Nicholas said. "That's why I wanted to let you know that we're getting closer. I only need to see the other two parts to know who betrayed us at Trafalgar. You'll inform me about anything more you learn?''

"Be assured of it, Captain," Jamie said, rising from the chair. "Watch your back. Whoever the music names will be after the pieces, too.''

Nicholas nodded; he didn't have to be warned. He'd done what he'd come to the Blue Mermaid to do, but he was in no hurry to leave, so he caught the eye of the barmaid again. She brought him another glass of ale.

He downed his drink more slowly this time, though he sat alone. Solitude had never troubled him. He needed no one to talk to, but he enjoyed hearing the boisterous conversations of the seamen, listening to their ribald jokes and observing the ebb and flow of their fellowship. They were as likely to break out in song as erupt in a fistfight.

Their earthiness was an antidote to the cool, poisonous sophistication of the *ton*. The sea and her men gave no sly looks or clever cuts. The sea was the sea, churning in a storm or calm as the doldrums. And the men who rode her were survivors.

Suddenly Nicholas longed to be a sea captain again, though he knew it was impossible. Why he should prefer being the commander of a ship at sea to being the earl and holder of vast estates was impossible to explain, but he did. Suffice it to say, the privileges of earldom seemed overblown and overrated.

Yet fate had contrived this difficult course for him, and follow it he must. Follow it he would, until he could at least set straight what was within his power to rectify.

Nicholas drained his tankard then laid enough coins on the table to cover his bill and bring a smile to the barmaid's lips. He decided to walk up the street to the carriage rather than trouble someone to fetch the vehicle.

He left the light and warmth of the Blue Mermaid, stepping out the door into a fog so thick it obscured the light of the street lamps. Though the deserted street was narrow, Nicholas could see no farther than a few steps ahead of him.

The dampness settled in tiny droplets on his shoulders, and the chill penetrated his coat. Quickening his steps, he regretted leaving his greatcoat behind in the carriage.

He had not gone far before he heard the footsteps of someone walking along behind him. He thought little of it until he rounded a corner. The footsteps behind him speeded up, as though the man was running to catch him.

Nicholas flattened himself against the wall and waited for the man to pass, but no one appeared. The steps stopped in line with the corner of the building. In the fog Nicholas could see nothing. No sound reached him, but he sensed someone standing just beyond him in the street, waiting.

The carriage was still too far away for him to enlist the aid of the coachman. Touching his side, where once he had carried his officer's saber, he suddenly realized how defenseless he was—no saber, no pistol. Because he'd dressed formally for the evening at the St. Johns' he'd not even worn the small knife he usually carried. Strategy and bluff was all he had at his disposal.

He stepped away from the stone wall, feeling safely concealed in the fog. "Hello. Who goes there?"

A shot rang out. The ball whistled past Nicholas's ear. He threw himself against the wall. He knew all he needed to know. With a noisy groan for the benefit of his assailant, he dropped to the pavement stones.

Silence followed. Then footsteps approached him with caution, the sound of boot heels ringing cold and deliberate in the mist. Nicholas lay still, taking no breath, listening.

The footsteps stopped near his left hand. He could hear the click of the second pistol being cocked. Without hesitation, Nicholas seized his attacker's ankle his fingers sinking into soft expensive boot leather, and yanked the man off his feet. With a yelp, the man thudded against the wall. The pistol clattered to the pavement out of reach and flashed as it misfired.

Nicholas jumped to his feet. The one thought in his head

beyond surviving was to identify his attacker. He grabbed the man's coat lapels and hauled him up off the pavement.

The weight was so much greater than he expected, he was nearly pulled down again. When he finally pulled the attacker to his feet Nicholas discovered the man was well over half a foot taller than he and probably two stones heavier.

The man's face was purposely streaked with stove black, making his features impossible to recognize or recall. And the fellow possessed all the power his size promised. With a snarl, he struck a vicious blow against Nicholas's arm. Nicholas expected to hear the bone snap. Before he could fend off another blow, the miscreant landed a punch against the side of Nicholas's head.

He staggered to the side, but not before he managed to strike his giant attacker in the ribs, sending the man spinning away and groaning in agony.

''Lord Seacombe?'' The coachman called from the top of the hill. Nicholas was unable to see the servant in the fog, but he sounded only yards away. ''My lord, is there some trouble? I heard a gun discharge.''

''Here, Bigsby.'' Nicholas turned to pursue his attacker, but the monster in Hessian boots and a blackened face had already disappeared into the fog.

Bigsby, carrying a lamp, appeared out of the mist. ''My lord, what happened? Footpads? Are you all right?''

Nicholas rubbed his sore arm to make certain it wasn't broken; then he touched the knot on the side of his head where the man had struck him. ''I'm fine.''

''Your uncle will never forgive me for letting you go out to a place like this alone,'' Bigsby lamented.

''Uncle George will not hold you responsible, Bigsby, have no fear. I'll see to it.'' Nicholas took the lamp from the coachman and paced along the pavement in search of the pistol. It was nowhere to be found.

Nicholas held up the lamp and peered into the fog hoping for answers. Ordinary footpads seldom carried pistols, and they certainly did not wear Hessian boots of the quality leather his assailant had worn. The man who had shot at Nicholas was a paid assassin. The true traitor had finally shown his hand, whoever he was. But why now? Because Nicholas had revealed himself to the St. Johns? Because Jamie Collard had told him too much? Because Davis St. John did not like the way he looked at Dorian? Nicholas rubbed the growing knot on his head. He was not thinking clearly after the blow.

But he smiled with grim satisfaction. He had a nemesis, and the man had made his move at last, after two long years of silence.

The dust tickled Davis's nose until he sneezed and closed the carriage window. Across from him, Dorian stared out at the passing countryside with the same sober distraction that had dominated her mood since their last musicale.

"I do hope you're going to pull out of this gloomy temper before we get to Thorpe Hall," Davis said. No gentleman was going to take an interest in a Friday-faced lady with a far-away look in her eye. "You look as if you've lost your best friend."

That brought Dorian around. Her eyes snapped with defiance. "I do not. I'm just disappointed about not getting the music for Aunt Charlotte."

"I'm glad to hear that's all."

The vehicle lurched across a rut in the road, throwing both of them against the velvet-lined walls and making Davis wish he'd ridden on horseback. He could have let Dorian make the grand arrival at Thorpe Hall and ridden his new hunter to show off for Lord Eastleigh and Elizabeth. But then he wouldn't have this opportunity to speak to Dorian before they arrived.

"Algernon is going to be there, you know."

"Algernon Halthorpe?" Dorian straightened in her seat. "I thought he was betrothed to the Margaret Maidwell."

"Oh, no, it was never made official," Davis said, pleased

that Dorian seemed to know so much about the heir to Thorpe Hall. "I understand he's still quite interested in you."

Dorian uttered something that sounded suspiciously like an oath. "The interest is not mutual, Davis. You know that. I'm you're elder sister; don't forget that you have no right to agree to anything on my behalf."

"Elder by only six minutes," Davis countered. "I hardly think that relieves me of my responsibility as your protector."

She uttered another sound that did not bear translation.

When they'd first received Halthorpe's invitation some weeks ago Dorian had thrown it down on the hall table and positively refused to go. Why the change of heart, Davis had no idea, but he intended to make the most of the opportunity. "Algernon Halthorpe has always had a soft eye for you."

"Algernon is a bore," Dorian said. "I have no more interest in him now than I've had in the past."

"You and Algernon would make a fine match," Davis persisted, mystified as to why Dorian had accepted this invitation. "You'd eventually become the Countess of Halthorpe."

"I'd be married to a man who talks of nothing but horses and hounds," Dorian pointed out with her usual unerring accuracy. "He detests Town and would never sit still through a play, let alone a musicale or an opera. A match between us would be an unholy disaster."

Davis said nothing, though he silently agreed with at least part of Dorian's argument. The heir to Thorpe Hall could be quite a bore about his hounds.

"Indulge him," Davis suggested with little hope of changing his sister's mind. "You know enough about horses and hunting to entertain him. I'm sure he'd love to hear the story about how you seized the carriage reins from me in Green Park and outraced Lord Benton's famous team of grays."

"I thought you didn't like me to tell that story." Dorian grinned at him, the teasing light of a irascible sister gleaming in her eyes.

"All I ask is, don't repeat it within Elizabeth's hearing," Davis pleaded. " 'Twould be damned embarrassing."

"And how does it stand with you and Elizabeth?" Dorian asked, seemingly preoccupied with her burgundy gloves, which perfectly matched her fitted traveling gown. The rich color deepened the gold of her hair and the wine color of her lips. "Will you be speaking to her father soon—about marriage?"

"Speak to the earl?" Davis delayed answering the question by repeating it. He was uncertain in his own mind about how to approach the earl—and when. "I think it's too soon."

"You're not sure of Lady Elizabeth?"

"No, that's not it," Davis said. He and Elizabeth enjoyed each other's company, and he was fairly sure that she found him attractive. He'd certainly done everything in his power to make himself presentable to the earl's daughter, even to the point of hiring a new, meticulous valet and submitting to Dorian's critical but unfailing eye for flattering fashion.

Still, there were moments when he detected in Elizabeth a distance that he must attribute to the social gulf that lay between them. She came from an old, aristocratic family, while the St. Johnses were mere merchants, upstarts whose name could be traced back only a century or so.

But the fact remained, Elizabeth would make a wonderful hostess, as excellent as Dorian herself. The Eastleighs were well connected, and Elizabeth's family name would add prestige to the St. Johns' fortune.

And if Dorian married an earl, the St. Johnses and their descendants would join the ranks of the aristocracy. It was a goal that required planning and patience. It was a goal that allowed for no mistakes.

"I just believe that the time is not right yet." Davis hoped Dorian would accept his answer without asking more questions. The lift of her brow revealed her skepticism.

Yet, instead of arguing with him, as she was wont to do, Dorian merely said, "Patience is wise, I think. You are only twenty-five, Davis. There's no reason for you to rush into marriage.''

''While you, dear elder sister, are also five and twenty and nearly on the shelf,'' Davis reminded her. ''Time is of the essence.''

''That's not fair,'' Dorian said, the hint of a pout returning to her lips.

''But it's a fact,'' Davis said. ''I would like to see you settled and happy.''

''I am settled and happy,'' Dorian said. ''The only thing that would make me happier would be to marry a man I loved and whom loved me. That is the promise I've given to Aunt Charlotte.''

She would hold out for just that, Davis feared. Their father had been equally generous with his twin son and daughter, leaving Dorian as wealthy as Davis, and therefore rich enough to remain independent if she chose. She'd somehow gotten it into her head that she wouldn't marry if it didn't suit her. Who had ever heard of such a thing? Marriage was a woman's fate, and only ugly, poor relations or selfless dears like Aunt Charlotte remained spinsters.

''Marriage is not a matter to be decided on the basis of fleeting emotions, Dorian. Don't delude yourself with some fantasy that Aunt Charlotte and Franz Chamier's grand passion would have lasted over time had they wed.''

''That shows just how little you understand about the strength and power of love,'' Dorian said, her lips pressed in a stubborn line.

Davis shook his head as he studied his sister. She had grown up sheltered. She knew how to find the right fabric for a chair and how to select the right girls for a household staff and how to cajole the butcher into providing the St. Johnses with the best cuts of meat and fattest poultry. She could arrange a table seating with diplomacy a king's butler would envy.

But the fact remained, she knew little of the seamy side of passion. She understood nothing of the way a night's all-consuming lust could wither and die in the first light of dawn. How reason and plans all fell blessedly back into place after they'd fallen asunder during a wild night of passion. But Davis was ashamed of those dark hours of pleasure, when his body dominated the logic of his mind.

He frowned. Not that he'd experienced that side of life so often himself, but he'd lost himself a time or two in gratifying his carnal desires. He was hardly proud of his weakness. Perhaps he should ask for Elizabeth's hand in marriage soon.

Once committed to a betrothal, it would be difficult for Elizabeth to cry off. Once committed to a betrothal, the future would be secure.

"We're passing through the Thorpe Hall gates," Dorian said.

Davis opened his carriage window and stared out at the well-kept grounds of Halthorpe's estate. The turreted old house that Halthorpe was rumored to have spent a fortune on sat majestically on the hill in the center of a large hunting park. Below the turrets it boasted Elizabethan half-timbered walls and a purely gothic stone entrance. As the St. Johnses' carriage rounded the drive, they caught a glimpse of tennis players and spectators on the lawn.

"I see Lord Eastleigh is here already with Lady Elizabeth," commented Dorian, casting Davis a sly, teasing glance. "But I don't see a single hound or hare of Algernon."

Davis leaned toward the window, eager to note who the other company might be. "Yes, so I see, and there are Lord and Lady Symthe. They are old friends of Halthorpe. What? Is that . . . ? That's Seacombe on the other side of the court!"

"I believe so," Dorian said with a puzzled frown.

"What on earth is he doing here?" Davis demanded, still displeased about the fellow's presence at the musicale. He'd never understand Aunt Charlotte and Dorian's penchant for adopting disreputable people.

"I suppose he's come in response to an invitation from Lord

Halthorpe.'' To Davis's satisfaction, Dorian looked as unhappy about Seacombe's presence as he was.

"I don't recognize the others," Dorian said, still frowning. "Who is that pretty little redhead standing next to Halthorpe?"

"I don't see a redhead," Davis said, still too annoyed about Nicholas Derrington to take note of the other guests. "What's Seacombe doing talking to Elizabeth?"

"How should I know?" Dorian leaned forward to peer out of the coach window once more. "I've never seen the redhead."

"I'm sure I wouldn't know her." Davis slumped in his seat, apprehension worming uncomfortably in his gut. He would delay no longer. He must ask for Elizabeth's hand this weekend—before anything happened to complicate matters—or embarrass Davis and Dorian.

Chapter Four

Dorian barely had time to change from her traveling clothes into an afternoon gown so she was presentable for the serving of tea and claret on the terrace.

With a dish of tea in her hand, she wasted no time in learning what she wanted to know—other than what Nicholas Derrington was doing at this house party. The redhead's name was Susanna Sunridge, and she was a young widow just out of mourning for Sir Roger Sunridge, of Ridgemont. The fact that the girl was landed gentry, not of the aristocracy, bothered Dorian not one wit. She liked Susanna immediately.

"It's such a pleasure to meet you, Miss St. John." Susanna offered her hand, blushing and curtseying all at once. "You are just as beautiful as people say."

Dorian accepted the girl's hand and squeezed it warmly, trying to smooth over Davis's cursory greeting. She knew her brother wanted to be done with the obligatory introductions so he could attach himself to Lady Elizabeth. "Forgive my brother, Lady Susanna. He is eager to find out when the first hunt will be going out."

"But of course, the gentlemen are all looking forward to riding to hounds." The young widow had a sunny smile, a sweet heart-shaped face, sincere brown eyes, and a wealth of warmth in her husky voice.

With a cool, objective eye, Dorian noted that Susanna had yet to learn how to make the most of color and fashion to flatter her luscious figure and the red tones of her thick hair. Though her manners were a trifle countrified, Dorian thought that with a bit of polishing Susanna would make quite a success of the Little Season when it came round. Being all things that fashion frowned on seldom kept a worthy gentleman from seeing the true value in a lady.

Making a note to lend aid to Lady Susanna should she ask, Dorian set about mingling with the other guests. The company pleased her. It was beginning to look like a delightful stay in the country when the earl and his countess, a tiny, meek, gray-haired woman, informed her that their son, Algernon, would join them on the morrow. Dorian smiled, holding back a sigh. He was to return from a trip in search of a blooded hound to add to his kennel.

"He is so looking forward to seeing you," the countess cooed, squeezing Dorian's hand.

"That's very kind of him." Dorian looked in Davis's direction for help, but her twin brother had already wandered off with Lady Elizabeth. Only Nicholas Derrington smirked at her over the earl's head.

She turned away immediately. Though she hadn't seen him since the night of the musicale, the man and his kiss had bedeviled her thoughts and haunted her dreams. He was hardly the first man she'd allowed to kiss her. Yet the memory of his demanding touch and masculine scent had invaded her waking hours and insinuated itself into her nocturnal fantasies. She resented his intrusion. She could concentrate on nothing, not even on the plans she should be making for acquiring Franz Chamier's music for Aunt Charlotte.

"But Algernon's absence is no reason not to give all of you

a peek at the improvements we've made here at Thorpe Hall,'' the earl said, gathering the guests together for the traditional tour of the house.

"Yes, that would be lovely," Dorian agreed. Despite Algernon's professed interest in her, she'd never been to Thorpe Hall. "I've heard you have added an extensive library and a wonderful new music room."

"Indeed, we have," the earl said, a proud smile on his round face. "And a new pianoforte. Come, my dear."

Like a great many country homes, Thorpe Hall was richly furnished with both new acquisitions and old heirlooms. The gothic entrance offered a collection of shiny but dented suits of armor. The newly decorated salon was furnished with lacquered cabinets and inlaid tables in the Chinese style favored by the Prince of Wales. The earl even threw open the narrow back passages to the new kitchen wing to show his guests the sophisticated system of call bells he'd had installed.

"No more servants lingering just outside the door to overhear things they have no business knowing, say what!" the earl exclaimed to the approval of his guests.

"Very innovative." Davis murmured a few more approving phrases to Lady Elizabeth, who appeared unimpressed.

In the gallery where the portraits of the great Halthorpes were displayed the earl stopped below the portrait of a round-faced man wearing a long Elizabethan robe and glittering jewels. "Dorian, dear, come let me introduce you to the Halthorpe ancestors."

Dorian put on a gracious smile—which didn't waver even when Davis gently thrust her to the front of the tour group. She joined the earl below the portrait of his bejeweled ancestor. He launched into a detailed history lesson as to how he had become the seventh Earl of Halthorpe.

Dorian smiled weakly at the others in the group, who had lost interest in the earl's story, but were more interested in the fact that he'd singled out Dorian St. John for the lesson. Such recitations of lineage were usually reserved for the young ladies in the party, especially young ladies considered eligible for marriage into the family.

When the earl was finished Davis drew him into a further discussion of the Halthorpe ancestry. Rescuing her from the earl was the only decent thing he'd ever done for her as a brother, Dorian thought as she gratefully slipped from the center of attention. The earl took Davis by the arm, obligingly answering his questions, as he led them toward the garden.

"I didn't realize you had ambitions to become the eighth countess of Thorpe Hall," a low voice murmured over her shoulder.

Dorian started and whirled to find Nicholas Derrington grinning at her. Until this moment he had made no effort to seek out her company. She frowned at him over her shoulder. "I have no such ambitions, I assure you."

Now that he stood so close to her again every part of her body was warmed by his nearness, his overwhelming size, his unrelenting focus on her. The memory of his kiss brought heat to her cheeks. Dorian feared her fascination with him might be more difficult to cure than she'd first thought. "What on earth are you doing here? I thought you didn't go out in Society."

"Uncle George received the invitation but could not accept. I've come in his place." Nicholas stood aside to allow her to step through the doorway into the garden ahead of him. "The invitation to your musicale made me see the error of my ways. For which I'm most grateful, I might add. I intend to thoroughly enjoy my first house party in several years."

Dorian huffed and marched into the garden. Nicholas followed her, seeming to take no offense at her reaction. She knew why he had accepted the invitation; he wanted Chamier's fragments.

Nicholas continued unfazed. "And where do you think he keeps his music collection?"

"The music room certainly didn't offer much, did it?"

"Not a single cabinet in it," Nicholas agreed. "The few instruments looked as though they'd been acquired for display rather than for performing. Whatever made you think the Earl of Halthorpe had what we wanted?''

''What makes *you* think he has what *you* want?'' Dorian countered. He was acting as if she'd agreed to work with him. ''He has a library also.''

''True enough.'' Nicholas touched the small of her back, urging her to move on. ''Let's not fall behind.''

Seeing the group disappear around the corner, Dorian decided not to protest and hurried to catch up with the others.

The garden was a lovely affair laid out by 'Capability' Brown, but the library proved to be the best feature of the house. A new addition to Thorpe Hall, the large chamber soared two stories, brightened by high windows and warmed by rich oak paneling and bare shelves.

The aroma of freshly sawn wood and drying lacquer tickled Dorian's nose. White furniture covers had been draped over a long table and a massive desk. Sawdust crunched beneath her slippers as she walked across the black-and-white marble floor.

''I planned to have it completed for the party.'' The earl's voice echoed through the lofty room as his guests edged their way inside through the French doors from the garden. ''But the workmen just would not be rushed.''

The earl chattered on about his plans for the room, the medieval hangings he had ordered for the walls, the library of rare books he had directed be sent from London, the collection of rare music and manuscripts that he was preparing to display in the cabinets along the wall.

''I've spared no expense on the library or my new collection.'' The earl gestured toward the crates and trunks stacked in the room. ''Some of it has arrived already, as you can see.''

Nicholas and Dorian shared a knowing glance. They'd found it at last. If the music was anywhere in Thorpe Hall, it was in one of the many crates in the library. Dorian managed to keep her excitement from her face. She didn't want Nicholas Derrington to realize that she had every intention of getting to it before he did.

* * *

In truth Nicholas thought it unlikely that Lord Halthorpe possessed Franz Chamien's music in a collection that had been purchased as a lot in London.

He had doubted that Dorian would lead him to her best prospect first—until he saw her smile falter when the countess had informed her Algernon would be arriving soon. Dorian St. John held no great affection for Algernon Halthorpe. She was at Thorpe Hall for a purpose.

"It appears you'll have a fine collection," Dorian was saying as the earl gestured toward the books and crates. "I'll be eager to see the library when it's completed. But it will take forever to go through all of these crates."

"Not that long." The earl waved his hand in the air, dismissing the thought of any work on his part. "I've engaged a clerk just for the purpose of keeping the library in order and the manuscript displays in good condition."

"How clever, my lord." Dorian gave the earl a smile of admiration.

"Do you think we could ask for the benefit of a clerk to help us?" Nicholas whispered into Dorian's ear.

"We?" Dorian never deigned to look in his direction. "I don't know what you are referring to, my lord."

"Then, if we find it—no, no—*when* we find it, what do you propose we do?" Nicholas leaned close, inhaling the scent of violets that seemed to drift around Dorian. "Do we steal it?"

Dorian frowned. "If one found a piece of Franz's music, then she—or he—would offer the earl a fair price."

"Do you actually think he'll settle for that, seeing as how Chamier's work has become nearly priceless now? Thanks to you, bidding the price through the ceiling at the auction house."

"I did not bid it through the ceiling—"

"Miss St. John, did I hear you ask a question?"

Nicholas looked up to see the earl gazing at them over the heads of the others.

"Oh, no, my lord," Dorian sputtered. "Lord Seacombe and I were just exclaiming at the beauty of the room. So well proportioned and richly appointed. You must be pleased with the outcome of your project."

"Yes, as a matter of fact I am." The earl beamed with pride. "But enough of this. You must be exhausted and ready to freshen up and change before dinner."

The earl led the way out of the library, his guests still murmuring over the fine detail in the woodwork and the glass of the skylights above.

"Should we begin our search tonight?" Nicholas asked.

"We are not going to start anything tonight," Dorian snapped.

"You won't start the search without me?" He was certain Dorian was playing for time to put him off.

The last of the guests filed out of the library, leaving them alone. Dorian turned on him. "As I recall, I never agreed to any search with you."

Nicholas pursed his lips and stepped back from her, his hand over his heart as if he was wounded. "Could it be you were truly serious in you refusal?"

"You mean you actually believe I might join you in this . . . ?" The thought was apparently too horrendous for Dorian to even finish aloud. "Sir, the night of the musicale I told you I had no interest in your proposition."

"I know. A partnership with me is too appalling to contemplate." Nicholas assumed as serious an expression as he could manage, considering the fact that he was thoroughly enjoying baiting her. "But think of the advantages. I have your expertise; you have my protection."

"Protection! You have your nerve, my lord, after kissing me like that in the music room." Dorian's brow furrowed in a frown of outrage. "I'm not in any danger, and I don't need your protection."

She turned to follow the other guests as they quit the library.

"Then consider this." Nicholas caught her arm before she

could get beyond his reach. He played one last card in his game to secure himself a place in her search. "I realize my traitorous reputation dims my luster as an escort, *but* I'm not looking for a rich bride. Unlike a certain son of an aristocratic father impoverished by the improvements made to his country house who will be arriving on the morrow."

To his satisfaction, Dorian stopped and regarded him over her shoulder. "You consider your disinterest in fortune hunting a redeeming quality?"

"That is for you to decide." Nicholas admired her careful response. "My presence at your side would dampen the enthusiasm of unwanted suitors."

"I daresay I can manage my suitors, thank you." With a twitch of her skirts, Dorian swept out of the library as if she were true mistress of her fate.

Algernon Halthorpe arrived the next day to the delight of his parents and all the house guests, except Dorian.

"Dorian, look who has joined us at last." Davis drew her to his side as he shook hands with the heir to Thorpe Hall and the earldom.

Dorian cast Davis her best you-will-regret-this look, but her brother ignored her.

"Dorian, my dear, I'm so glad you accepted Mother's invitation," crowed Algernon. He was a tall, thin blond man of about seven-and-twenty, with a long face and wet, fleshy lips. He seized Dorian's hand in the presence of the entire company gathered in the drawing room and laid a wet kiss on her knuckles.

Dorian smiled thinly, withdrew her hand, and resisted the desire to wipe Algernon's kiss off her hand. "It is a pleasure to be here. Thorpe Hall is such a lovely house."

As she spoke, Nicholas caught her eye and gave an imperceptible shake of his head, as if she should be ashamed of herself. The man was incorrigible. To her relief he turned away.

"You like it?" Algernon giggled shrilly and possessively tucked Dorian's arm through his. "I'm so glad to hear that."

From that hour on Dorian's time was taken up either by Algernon or the ladies. Dorian was immensely thankful that social tradition divided the ladies from the gentlemen from time to time.

The house party proceeded with a tour of the home farm for the gentlemen interested in agriculture and a trip to the village on market day for the ladies. They took morning horseback rides and picnicked—an activity Dorian especially favored, though Algernon insisted on playing children's games during the outing. Dorian would have enjoyed the play if there'd been children included in the party, but the company was entirely adult.

One evening Algernon arranged a clandestine trip for the gentlemen to a cock-fighting establishment. Davis went, but Nicholas declined. He quietly mentioned something about having seen enough blood running across the deck of the *Dauntless* to last him a lifetime. Then he proceeded to make himself a congenial partner in a card game with Dorian, the old earl, Lady Elizabeth, and the countess.

The next evening, after supper, Algernon bolted from the dining room, where the men had been drinking port and smoking cigars, and burst into the drawing room. The ladies at their tea and sherry looked up in surprise.

"Let's play children's games again." Algernon giggled. The shrillness made Dorian shiver. She looked up from a book, wondering if he had drunk too deeply of the earl's port.

At her side Susanna Sunridge sniffed and whispered, "Games now? I thought we were going to have a round of country dances."

"So I thought." Dorian searched her mind for an excuse to retire early, but nothing acceptable came to mind. Not that she didn't enjoy carefree games, but there was something hidden behind Algernon's interest in them. She didn't quite understand what it was or why she felt that way, but his insistence on the games made her uneasy.

"What great fun!" Davis seemed to find the idea to his liking, as did several of the other gentlemen. Dorian thought his color a trifle high, as it was when he was foxed. No doubt he'd imbibed more port than was good for him and now deluded himself into hoping the game would benefit his pursuit of Lady Elizabeth.

"Now this is a jolly good one." Algernon gave his high-pitched giggle once more, less inane but more naughty than usual. "Gentlemen, you will love this. Each of the ladies will remove her right shoe—after the gentlemen have left the room, of course—then place it in a basket.

"When the gentlemen return each will take a shoe from the basket. Once he finds the owner she will owe him a kiss, or . . ." Algernon paused for dramatic effect. "Or any other liberty she would care to bestow on him."

"Algernon, we'll have nothing improper going on here." The earl looked to his wife for a nod of agreement.

"It's all in good fun, Father," Algernon protested. "It's just a kiss, no more than a gentleman might claim beneath the mistletoe at Christmas time."

"Oh, well, I see no harm in that," the earl said. The countess seemed to find the game innocent enough.

Dorian looked to Davis, but he was smiling at Lady Elizabeth. She knew exactly what was going on in her brother's mind. He had every intention of winning Elizabeth's shoe and claiming a kiss the lady seemed none to free to give.

"I knew I should have developed a headache after supper," Dorian murmured to Susanna.

"Me, too," the widow sympathized. "Where did he learn these games? There's hardly a soul here I'd like to kiss."

Dorian glanced away from Davis just in time to find Algernon's gaze fixed on her. His expression was even more greedy and calculating than her brother's.

Gooseflesh prickled down her spine. The last thing she

wanted was to have Algernon smack his fat wet lips against hers. What if he used his tongue, as Nicholas had?

With the memory of Nicholas's intimate kiss, the bottom dropped out of her belly. Her whole body warmed at the thought of tasting Nicholas again—and of being tasted. She could not keep herself from scanning the room for him.

He was there, standing in a far corner with a small, amused smile on his lips. Clear-eyed and quiet, he appeared completely in control of his faculties. He was watching her with an odd expression on his face.

Dorian decided that it was time for someone to raise an objection.

"But, Algernon, nearly every lady here is wearing black slippers—velvet or satin. How are you going to be certain whose is whose?"

"Oh, a gentleman knows such things." Algernon giggled with maddening self-assurance. "I, for one, would know a piece of your apparel anywhere—anytime—Miss St. John."

The guests laughed at his obvious confidence and clear intentions.

Dorian did not join in the laughter; her sense of humor had deserted her.

"Whose shoe will you be seeking, Algernon? Wouldn't be Miss St. Johns's, would it?" called Lord Carrington-Smith.

A breath of dismay escaped Dorian. Clearly she could not object again without making a she-dragon of herself or embarrassing her host and hostess. "How flattering, my lord, but I do believe you will need to trust the ladies in claiming their shoes."

"We shall see." Algernon winked at her and emitted that annoying giggle again. "I believe the gentlemen will fare quite well in this game."

That was exactly what Dorian feared as the men left the room and the countess came around collecting ladies' slippers in a basket brought in by a footman.

The ladies laughed and chattered; apparently none of them

was as apprehensive as Dorian. She untied her shoe reluctantly. As she dropped it into the basket, she tried to tell herself that she was being foolish about a simple kiss from the son of her host. It meant nothing.

The problem was, she suspected, that Algernon felt otherwise. Not that she had given him any reason to think so. She'd merely been polite and kind—a gracious guest. But kissing her in public, even in an innocent game, she feared would give the impression that they were near betrothal. An impression he undoubtedly wanted to promote. Rumors had spread in Society with less evidence.

The countess and the footman disappeared through the door into the next room to the welcoming cheers of the foxed gentlemen.

"It's just a childish game," Susanna reassured Dorian, patting her hand.

"Of course. A silly, ridiculous game, and I pray everyone here believes it so." Dorian reached for her glass of sherry and finished it in one gulp.

Algernon burst through the door first, waving a black beribboned slipper over his head and giggling. "I have it, Dorian. I have it. Where is your foot?"

Dorian shrank back in her chair.

Algernon stumbled to his knees before her and grasped her ankle, his fingers stretching higher on her calf than Dorian thought necessary.

"Get ready to pucker up, my dear. I'm going to put this shoe on your foot." When he shoved the slipper on Dorian's foot she shuddered with repulsion. With a quick wiggle of her toes the slipper fell off.

"Much too large." Dorian was so relieved, her voice was barely audible.

"No, it is not." Algernon picked up the shoe and tried it again. Once more it dropped off her foot.

"I'm afraid it's not my slipper." Dorian was so relieved, she was ready to giggle herself.

"I don't believe it." Algernon turned to Susanna, on whom Lord Carrington-Smith was trying to fit a shoe. "It's yours then, Lady Sunridge."

"I don't think so," Susanna said. "Nor is this one."

The shoe on her foot dropped to the floor with a thud. The two gentlemen eyed each other, then scrambled on their knees to exchange places and frantically tried to fit the slippers on Susanna and Dorian's feet, to no avail.

Over the men's heads, Dorian caught Susanna's eye and realized the little widow could barely hold back her own mirth.

Still unsuccessful, the two men struggled to their feet and moved on to other ladies.

Susanna leaned close. "Perhaps our shoes were lost in the confusion."

"I'm afraid we won't be so blessed."

A shadow fell over Dorian and she looked up to see Davis standing over her with a black satin slipper in his hand.

"Surely I couldn't be this unfortunate." He scowled at her. Dorian peered around him at Lady Elizabeth, who seemed to have found her slipper in Algernon's hands. "I'm not kissing my own sister."

Dorian understood Davis's disappointment, but considering what she'd been faced with, there were far worse misfortunes in life.

"I think it goes like this." Nicholas loomed behind Davis and nudged him toward Susanna. "Try your shoe on Lady Sunridge's dainty foot. I believe I have your sister's slipper."

Dorian laughed aloud at last, allowing Nicholas to slip the satin shoe on her foot and lace up the ribbon. His touch was warm and efficient and even made her tingle a bit—ever so much more pleasant than Algernon's fondling.

"To watch you, one would think you laced up a lady's shoe every day." Dorian smiled at the top of his head of dark, short cropped hair, completely forgetting about the company in the room.

"Life in His Majesty's Navy requires many skills." Nicholas

finished with her foot and released it, but remained kneeling before her. He gazed up at her.

Dorian searched his unreadable face for a clue to his feelings. "I don't know what you did or how you did it, but thank you, my lord. I *owe* you a kiss."

"Only a kiss? Have I not demonstrated the benefits of agreeing to my proposal?"

"Well, yes, I suppose you have, but I . . ."

"Now is the perfect time to leave a lasting impression for Society to savor." She could feel his eyes lingering on her lips.

"But I'm still not certain . . ." Dorian glanced across the room in time to see Lady Elizabeth give Algernon a peck on the cheek. He did not loiter in the lady's company, but turned immediately and started in Dorian's direction.

"All right, I concede, but do hurry."

Nicholas waited for no more conditions on his proposal. He curved his hand around her neck and pulled her close to meet his lips.

Their mouths melded in a hot exchange of attraction and desire that Dorian felt only when this particular man touched her. She knew the world was watching, but she was too lost in the wonder and the need of his touch to care. She tasted his tongue and sought to offer hers, but he refused her.

Gently he pushed her away. Confused and bewildered by his denial, she opened her eyes. Promise glimmered in the blue depths of Nicholas's gaze.

Sudden applause startled Dorian and she looked up to see that everyone in the room was standing and applauding her and Nicholas's performance.

She'd tasted so sweet and so willing—that's what Nicholas remembered of the kiss. Much as he ached to take what she offered, he could not allow her to forget herself before her hosts or her brother.

Over the next few days the busy schedule of events had

prevented Dorian from returning to the library after the tour; Nicholas was certain of that. As far as he knew, Dorian spent all her time in the presence of the ladies or the company in general, or with her brother in an apparent attempt to avoid finding herself alone with Algernon.

Nicholas thought it unlikely she had made any nocturnal or daytime trips to the unfinished room. Nor had anyone else. He'd been watching. The grit on the floor and the bareness of the shelves discouraged the guests from seeking reading material there.

It wasn't until the fifth day of their stay, after luncheon had been served, that he was able to stray into the unused library to visit with the clerk. Nicholas wanted to learn what precisely was in those crates and trunks.

Each morning he'd seen Mr. Hadley, a thin, wan man with long arms and skinny thighs, scuttle up and down the hallways to the library like a pale, loose-jointed spider.

Though the day was a bit overcast, the ladies had decided to take a turn in the garden while the gentlemen traipsed off to inspect their horses for the next day's hunt. Nicholas wandered off aimlessly with the library his true destination. As expected, he found Mr. Hadley bent over a crate of books at the far end of room.

"My lord, you startled me." Mr. Hadley dropped the book he was thumbing through and bowed to Nicholas. "I tend to become so engrossed in my work."

"Easy to do." Nicholas offered the man the kindest smile he could manage. "Just what the earl would like to see, I'm sure. I was looking for something to read, actually. I thought you might know of something that has been unpacked that I might spend a few short hours with."

"I'd be more than happy to suggest something," Mr. Hadley said, bowing once more. "Something in the line of military or naval history, perhaps?"

"Actually, I was thinking of broadening my horizon a little with something on music; Hungarian music or Hungarian composers?'' Nicholas lied. His usual reading material consisted of physics books and design plans for ship hulls.

"Music?" Mr. Hadley looked around at the mountain of crates stacked in the corner behind him. "I haven't unpacked those yet. I'm not even certain which one contains music or what composers' manuscripts it contains."

He leaned toward Nicholas to offer a confidence. "Some of the manifests were quite vague about what the earl purchased. A good many of these tomes were bought in a lot from one old house or another. I fear the earl didn't care to spend much time making the selections himself."

"Is that so? Perhaps we could take a look into those crates together," Nicholas offered. "I don't mind giving you a hand."

"Oh, no, my lord." Hadley gasped and clutched his midsection as if he'd been mortally wounded. "I couldn't allow that. This is my responsibility."

Nicholas inclined his head. "I meant no offense."

"Oh, none taken, my lord," Mr. Hadley hastened to reply. He reached for the crowbar that lay atop a neighboring crate "Allow me to begin unpacking the music immediately. I should have opened this crate sooner. You aren't the first guest to ask about music."

Nicholas hid his surprise. "Oh? Who else has been inquiring after the music?"

"Why, Miss St. John." The crate creaked as Mr. Hadley succeeded in prying away the top. "She is quite musical, you know. Of course you know. You heard her play last night, just as the rest of us did. The servants couldn't resist turning an ear in the direction of the music room. That was the first time anyone has touched the fine pianoforte the earl purchased for Thorpe Hall."

"Is that so?" Nicholas could hardly keep his surprise and annoyance from his voice. So Dorian had already been seeking out the music. She'd eluded him at some point in the past few days. He should have known. She was hardly one to let grass grow under her feet.

What a fool he was to think she'd hang back. This was the lady who had dared to invade the male-dominated auction house to get what she wanted. Why would a dusty library daunt her?

"I'll have something unpacked for you in no time, my lord." Mr. Hadley huffed and puffed as he pried the top off another crate. "Perhaps, if you'd come around later this afternoon, my lord . . . ?"

"Yes, I'll return then," Nicholas said. He threw open the French doors and headed out into the garden to find Dorian.

Dorian knew exactly what brought Nicholas into the garden the moment she saw him burst from the library. He was bound to learn that she'd been asking about the music at some point. She watched him pause on the doorstep, scanning the garden for her and twisting the black-and-gold skeleton ring on his finger. Instantly she regretted that she had picked this particular moment to stroll away from the other ladies to have a minute to herself.

She turned in their direction, but Nicholas's long-legged stride carried him too swiftly toward her to allow her to reach the safety of their company.

"Miss St. John." His voice was even, but no pleasure gleamed in his eyes.

"My lord." Dorian curtsied. "To what do I owe this attention?"

"Well, did you find anything?" he demanded.

Dorian glanced at the others to see if they had overheard him. Thankfully, they were still talking among themselves. She opened her mouth to speak.

"Don't be coy with me, lady." A glint of warning flashed in his frosty blue eyes.

Dorian hesitated, deciding that with the ladies strolling in the garden it was best not to incite his anger. "Nothing yet, but I hardly had a chance to look at any of the music. You've seen for yourself it is still crated."

"Mr. Hadley is supposedly unpacking it now." Nicholas took her arm and urged her to walk at his side. "You might have told me that you'd already asked about it."

"Did you inform me that you had planned to visit Mr. Hadley just now?"

Nicholas's eyes narrowed. He glowered at her.

"You see, there is no way for us to be partners." Dorian glanced around at the ladies, who were watching them, as curious and wide-eyed as a herd of deer.

Nicholas's grip on her arm tightened and his steps quickened as he dragged her toward the arbor at the far end of the garden. "Just when did you plan to have a look at the music manuscripts? One hardly has a moment to himself at one of these damned house parties. Even after everyone has retired to bed, the hallways echo with the sound of footsteps and giggles."

"So you heard them, too," Dorian said, hoping to change the subject. "I think the duke is having an affair with the countess. And the earl is—"

"I don't care who is doing what." Nicholas's face turned hard and cold.

Dorian looked back at the ladies and forced a smile to her lips, as if she was perfectly delighted to be disappearing into the arbor with the scandalous earl of Seacombe.

In the shaded privacy of the arbor he released her, his face softening a bit. "I *will* see what is in those crates of music. Tell me your plan. I feel certain you have one."

"Tonight is best." Dorian rubbed her arm and stared at him, astonished at his vehemence. Franz's music seemed to mean a great deal to him.

"Why tonight?"

"The ball is this evening," Dorian said.

"I don't understand. The house will be even more full of people than it is now."

"Exactly, and there will be nothing exceptional about finding someone in the library," Dorian explained, "or anywhere else in the house. There will be games and dancing, eating and drinking. If one isn't dancing, one might be anywhere, playing cards or billiards or taking fresh air in the garden. Hadley will be occupied with enjoying himself belowstairs.''

"I see." Nicholas appeared to be turning her words over in his mind. "I believe you have a certain talent for subterfuge, Miss St. John. Did you have a specific time in mind?''

"After supper is served," Dorian said, a bit offended by his reference to her strategic abilities. She was hardly a schemer. "You're not searching through the crates without me.''

"Likewise. You're not rummaging through them without me," Nicholas countered, his voice and expression implacable. "Do we have an understanding?''

Dorian frowned and nodded.

"Yoooohoooo." Susanna Sunridge peeked into the arbor.

Nicholas slipped his arm around Dorian's waist and pulled her closer. Dorian started to resist but realized that the appearance of an assignation between herself and Nicholas was the simplest disguise for their relationship. The possessive strength in the arm around her made her heart beat a little faster.

"Hello, you two." A charming blush stained the pretty widow's cheeks. "So sorry to intrude, but the countess wanted me to invite you to join us for a tour of her woodland garden. The daffodils are in bloom and her Dutch tulips show great promise.''

"But, of course, we'd be delighted," Nicholas said, before Dorian could open her mouth to refuse. Much to her annoyance, he took her hand and led her out of the arbor and toward the curious ladies. "I've always admired Dutch tulips.''

Chapter Five

Only a single branch of candles lit the empty library when Nicholas entered after supper. Softly he closed the door on the music and laughter of the ball going on elsewhere in the house. In the ballroom he'd claimed one dance from Dorian early in the evening. Just before supper he'd glimpsed her playing whist with Davis and Lady Elizabeth in the drawing room. But that was all he'd seen of her since the tour of the woodland garden.

Stacks of music books and manuscripts stood on the library table draped with a dust cover. Mr. Hadley had indeed begun to unpack. Nicholas started across the room to the table when Dorian opened the door and swept inside.

"There you are," she said. With the light from the ball behind her, Nicholas once again admired the cling of the Bishop blue and silver gown she wore. She closed the door. "I should have known you'd be here first."

"I've just arrived."

"Of course you have." Dorian obviously didn't trust him anymore than he did her. "Found anything yet?"

"No." Nicholas idly shuffled through the stacks. "I don't

know much about collecting music, but little of this looks like anything special to me.''

Dorian crossed the library to the table and began to peruse the stack next to his. ''I agree.''

Her scent filled his head and distracted him so that at first he could hardly make sense of what he was looking at.

They worked side by side in silence for some time before Dorian spoke up again. ''Susanna Sunridge tells me the gossip's mouths have been flapping since this afternoon.''

''What happened this afternoon?'' Nicholas asked, moving away to begin searching another stack.

''Us,'' Dorian said. ''You and I in the arbor. If we aren't careful, we'll create a scandal.''

''I think it's too late to prevent that,'' Nicholas said, amused by Dorian's belated concern.

She laughed, a soft, delightful sound that made Nicholas feel lighthearted, though he knew her brother would surely never approve of the two of them. ''Perhaps you're right about it being too late to prevent it,'' she agreed.

He was glad the thought of scandal did not trouble her greatly. He rather relished the picture of shock unfolding on righteous faces as the news buzzed through the rumor mill. Seacombe and Dorian St. John!

The library doorknob clicked ominously. The murmur of voices drifted through the door. Dorian froze.

Nicholas took action. It would be damned difficult to explain why they were digging through the earl's collection on the night of the ball, even if Dorian was a musician. He grabbed her arm and pulled her down behind the dustcover-draped table. The noise of the guests grew louder as the door opened wider.

''No, it's empty,'' a feminine voice whispered.

''Good. We can talk in here,'' a male voice murmured in reply. The couple entered. The sound of footsteps tapped upon the marble floor. Nicholas yanked up the dustcover and shoved Dorian under the table. He followed her as quickly and quietly as possible.

The door clicked closed.

Dorian rolled her eyes in disbelief. Nicholas could hardly believe their bad luck himself, but he put his finger to his lips to remind her to remain silent. Maybe after a few stolen kisses the couple would depart.

Sighs and the rustle of clothing intruded on the quiet of the library. Then a soft moan could be heard, followed by a lady's whimper and whispered words. "Touch me there. Oh, yes, like that."

Dorian cocked her head, as if to hear better. With each sigh and moan her eyes grew wider. A virgin was hardly well acquainted with the sounds of lovemaking. Nicholas briefly considered covering her ears before she heard more.

A masculine groan of eagerness rumbled from the man.

"No, that's enough," the lady insisted. "You are going to muss my hair."

Nicholas listened to the lady's slippers slap on the marble as she moved away from the man.

"Now, Davis, just what is it you had to talk to me about this evening?" the lady said, the edge of demand in her voice.

Nicholas saw Dorian's eyes grow wide.

"Elizabeth, I think it's time I—well, that I declared my feelings for you." There was no mistaking Davis's voice.

Dorian clamped her hand to her mouth as if to prevent some exclamation from escaping.

Nicholas cursed inwardly. Of all the trysts that had to be going on during this house party at Thorpe Hall, why did they have to become unwitting witnesses to Dorian's brother and his lady love?

"And what are those feelings?" Elizabeth asked.

Nicholas thought her voice deuced cool under the circumstances. She had to know what was coming.

"I've been calling on you for some months now, and over time my feelings for you have grown." Davis's voice was husky with emotion. "I believe I love you and—and I hope you return those feelings."

An awkward silence followed Davis's declaration.

"I have enjoyed these past few months," Elizabeth said. "I've grown to—well, to care for you, too, Davis."

"I can't tell you how much it pleases me to hear you say that." Genuine relief rang in Davis's voice. "Then I'd like to ask you to consider being my wife."

Quiet swelled in the lofty library.

"I realize asking this question now might be a bit of a surprise." Davis's words were hurried, as if he sensed the need to fill awkward the silence. "Of course I would speak to your father. I'd do everything in my power to win his blessing. I know you wouldn't be happy without the duke's approval."

Nicholas watched Dorian's shoulders slump in dismay. She covered her face and shook her head.

"I do admit, Davis, you have taken me by surprise with your proposal at this very moment," Elizabeth said. "I think perhaps you misunderstood what I meant to say earlier. I'm very fond of you, Davis, but marriage . . . I'm not sure."

When Dorian took her hands away from her face Nicholas saw tears of sympathy for Davis welling in her eyes. Unaccountably, he longed to seize Lady Elizabeth by the throat and shake her, for Dorian's sake, if not for Davis's. Had the woman no heart?

"Of course you want to think about it," Davis said, the pain in his voice barely disguised by a tone of nonchalance. "I don't expect you to give me an answer this very moment."

"I think it would be best if you waited until the end of the season to ask me that question," Elizabeth said, her intention clear to Nicholas, if not Davis. She still hoped to find someone else to take as a husband—someone better.

Tears rolled down Dorian's cheeks, and she hastily brushed them away with the back of her hand. Nicholas studied her. It was hard to think of her as a scheming she-dragon when she wept so easily for her brother. She sniffled noisily. Hastily, Nicholas shoved his handkerchief into her hands, praying she hadn't been heard.

"So be it then," Davis said. "At the end of the season, when we both know our own feelings better, I will ask you again to be my wife. Until then I will live every day with the hope that you are growing as fond of me as I grow daily of you."

"We should get back to the dancing before Papa misses me," Elizabeth said. Her slippers clicked across the floor. The door snapped open and the tap of the slippers faded away.

"Bloody hell," Davis muttered.

Dorian reached for the dustcover, obviously determined to go to her brother. Nicholas grabbed her arm and shook his head.

"He needs me," Dorian mouthed to him silently.

"Leave the man alone," he mouthed back. "That's what he needs. To be alone."

Dorian frowned but remained where she was.

After a moment the solid thud of Davis's leather shoes followed Elizabeth from the library.

Dorian released a weary sigh. "Poor Davis. He told me he was going to wait until he could be more certain of Elizabeth's feelings."

"Can a man ever be certain of a woman's feelings?"

Dorian stared at him in wide-eyed astonishment. "My lord, you are cynical. Of course he can, provided he listens to more than just her words. I'm afraid Davis wasn't listening to Elizabeth or to his own heart. Oh, Davis, what am I going to do with you?"

"I suggest you leave him to lick his wounds in private." Nicholas pulled aside the dustcover and crawled out from under the table. "With all due respect, your brother's romantic life is the least of my concerns right now."

Nicholas gave Dorian a hand as she climbed out from under the table.

Sawdust clung to her crumpled gown and the blue feathers in her hair had been twisted askew. Soft golden curls drooped from her coif. She looked as though she'd been shamelessly mauled by some man deep in the throes of passion. The thought aroused Nicholas.

"I assure you I do not need you to be concerned about my brother." Dorian bent over to brush the sawdust from her skirt, unintentionally giving Nicholas a delicious glimpse of her breasts.

When she straightened, Nicholas couldn't keep himself from reaching to right the feathers in her hair. "I'm afraid the gossips may keep prattling if you go out there like this."

"I'm sure I'm not very concerned about the gossips," Dorian said, stepping away from Nicholas, to his regret, and trying to repair the damage herself. "There. How does my hair look?"

She still looked disgracefully debauched, and Nicholas rather liked pretending he'd committed the debauchery. "Much better," he lied.

"Well, then, let's get back to the music."

Nicholas did not argue with her.

The house grew quiet.

They spent another two hours, uninterrupted, sorting through the stacks, followed by a quick assessment of the crates to determine that Mr. Hadley had unpacked all the music and manuscripts.

"I doubt what we're looking for is here," Nicholas said, brushing dust from his hands.

"I quite agree," Dorian said, leaning against the edge of the table and blowing ineffectually at the feather drooping over her brow.

"I say we strike Lord Halthorpe from our list of suspects."

"Yes, I believe we must," Dorian agreed.

"Who does that leave?"

Dorian eyed Nicholas in skeptical silence.

"I know you were reluctant to work with me in the beginning," Nicholas said, "but look how well this worked out. With two of us searching we went through the music stacked here in half the time. If you were doing this alone, it would be dawn and you'd still have half the music to look through."

"Your point is well taken," Dorian said, but Nicholas knew she was not yet convinced.

He walked around the table toward the French doors, where the glimmer of dawn could be seen. "I've heard Lord Tewin is having a musical weekend at his country house in a fortnight."

Dorian gasped. "How did you know about that? It's a small party, mostly for musicians."

"Let's just say your confession about owning one of the pieces inspired me to develop some new sources of information," Nicholas said. "However, Lord Tewin's family and mine have seldom socialized, so I cannot count on Uncle George for an invitation this time. Can you help me?"

"That would set the gossips on their ears," Dorian said.

"Has that ever stopped you from doing as you pleased?"

"You are beginning to sound suspiciously like Davis," Dorian grumbled. "The fact is, I expect the situation at Lord Tewin's house party to be quite different from the one we found here."

"You mean you think we're more likely to find what we're looking for there?"

"I did not say that." Dorian frowned. "I'm saying I simply will not agree to this partnership idea of yours. If you're so certain that Lord Tewin might have what you want, get your own invitation."

"I take it Algernon Halthorpe is not going to be there."

"Just what are you implying?"

"That you have used my company to keep the gentleman at bay. Now that you are finished with me, you are ready to toss me aside."

"And if I am I thought you at least gentleman enough—"

"And so I am. However, I am exceedingly disappointed that you feel no obligation to grant so small a favor as using your influence—"

"Enough. I see your point."

"And since we work so well together I see no reason not to continue."

''That remains to be seen.'' Her bottom lip took on a pouty fullness. ''I shall do what I can about the invitation.''

Nicholas reached for Dorian, but she sidestepped him once more and eyed him suspiciously. ''No kissing.''

''Forgive me. It was just a spontaneous gesture of gratitude,'' Nicholas said, disappointed but not surprised.

''You will get your invitation.''

''For that I am most humbly grateful.'' Nicholas bowed his head in appreciation and hid his smile of victory.

Dorian never uttered a word to Davis about his unhappy interview with Elizabeth, though she considered bringing up the topic during the carriage ride back to Town. But something innately honest about Nicholas's advice kept her mouth shut. Though she didn't agree with him about leaving Davis to ''lick his wounds alone,'' she did understand that her twin might need some privacy. Besides that, she didn't want to explain to Davis how she came to overhear him and Elizabeth.

So she left her questions and advice unsaid and concluded to herself that she had never really liked Elizabeth in the first place. The elegant brunette had always seemed a bit cold-blooded. If that was a quality of good breeding, then Dorian was quite content with her less illustrious status. Davis deserved better than an icy duchess-in-training.

By the time they reached the outskirts of London what became even stranger than Davis's silence about Elizabeth was his lack of interest in Dorian and Algernon Halthorpe. For that Dorian was tremendously thankful. She wasn't about to mention Algernon or Nicholas either, though the latter was constantly on her mind.

She found her own preoccupation with him irritating, and to her surprise it made her snappish. There was absolutely no reason why she should cooperate with a man who would take for his own selfish purposes what Aunt Charlotte so desperately needed. But he had succeeded in making Dorian feel guilty for refusing to cooperate. And she disliked him for manipulating her.

Aunt Charlotte appeared rested and in good spirits when she greeted Dorian and Davis upon their return. Dorian suspected she'd spent most of her time playing and replaying Franz's music for her own amusement. Whatever kept her aunt alive and happy was fine with Dorian.

Satisfied with the state of her aunt's health for the time, the next day Dorian set out to procure Nicholas's invitation to Lord Tewin's house party. The matter required a few tactfully written notes, some gracious social calls, the right names dropped.

By the end of the following week a brief note arrived from the Earl of Seacombe. Davis recognized the crest on the stationery lying on the hall table before Dorian did.

"Just why is Seacombe corresponding with you?" Davis demanded without preamble.

Dorian cringed. She wasn't the only one in the St. John household who had turned snappish since the Halthorpe house party.

"A courtesy note," Dorian replied as lightly as she could manage as she broke the seal and read the bold handwriting. "He's going to be at Lord Tewin's house party."

"He has nothing more to say? He seems to be taking a mighty interest in Society all of a sudden," Davis observed, shuffling through the other correspondence lying on the silver salver.

"Why should he not?" Dorian said. "He's a free man with no charges brought against him."

Since her return from Thorpe Hall she'd made a trip to the lending library and taken the time to read some past issues of several newspapers and the penny presses. She'd uncovered some interesting facts about Captain Nicholas Derrington of His Majesty's Navy.

"Did you know Lord Seacombe and Sir Trafford were childhood friends?" Dorian asked, pretending to be interested in another invitation on the table.

"Gavin told of it," Davis said.

"I believe the name of his ship was the *Dauntless.*"

"I couldn't say," Davis said, still occupied with the post. Another tense second or two ticked by.

"Despite the headlines in the newspapers, one can read in the stories that Lord Seacombe's officers and crew speak highly of him." Even Dorian knew such loyalty was unusual. A captain was God aboard his ship at sea and entitled to mete out justice in whatever manner he chose. Flogging and keelhauling were still practiced. Few sea captains, even under Admiral Nelson, earned accolades from his sailors.

"How nice for Seacombe to have such a loyal crew. See that you don't let him occupy all your time at Tewin's party so that a truly eligible suitor is discouraged."

"Truly eligible?" For some mysterious reason the slight to Nicholas annoyed Dorian—in addition to the fact that she was sick of Davis's matchmaking. "Nicholas is an earl, and a wealthy one at that, if the gossips are to be believed."

"And a man of questionable reputation and allegiance, Dorian," Davis added. "Herby Dashworth is going to be at Tewin's."

She should have known where Davis was headed with his plotting. "Herby is merely the Viscount of Corywood—"

"And heir to a dukedom."

Dorian shut her mouth. It was time to change the subject. "Will Lady Elizabeth be attending?"

"I'm sure I don't know," Davis snapped and threw the post down on the table.

Dorian instantly recalled the painful silence in the Thorpe Hall library after Elizabeth had walked out on Davis's impulsive proposal. She regretted her hasty nettling of her brother. "I hope we run into Susanna Sunridge again. She is so very nice and lots of fun. How comical that it was her shoe that you drew in that silly game."

"Who? Oh, you mean the little redhead." Davis turned

toward the library. "She should really do something about that hair. It looks so common."

As her brother disappeared into the library, Dorian sighed. If she hadn't been mistaken, Susanna had developed something of a soft eye for Davis during the house party. The sad thing was that Davis barely remembered who she was. A widow of landed gentry hardly merited notice in her brother's view of the world.

Dorian tapped Nicholas's note against her hand, which brought her back to her original problem. Odd; she looked forward to seeing the exasperating man again. His note had been short, and he'd not repeated his offer of working in cooperation. However, over the last few days she'd come to understand what he'd been telling her all along. If she worked alone, she might find the fragment of Franz's music, but if he found it while working alone, she might never know he had it.

He certainly was under no obligation to inform her of the find, and he'd made it clear that he wanted it for his own purposes. Whatever that was.

Which led to the next question: was his offer to cooperate sincere? The fact was, he had to be just as concerned as she that she might be first to find the music. If she did, would he try to buy it from her, even though he knew she would refuse to sell? Or would he attempt to take it from her?

Dorian found herself disinclined to believe the accusations of treason leveled against him. There was no logic in a peer of the realm—and a respected navy captain—selling out to the French.

But that didn't mean the man might not take the upper hand to get what he wanted. The best course of action, Dorian decided, was to behave as if she was cooperating while doing her best to find the music before Nicholas did.

And if he found it first—she'd just have to deal with that when and if it happened.

* * *

Nicholas sipped the amber liquid Gavin had just poured for him and let it roll along his tongue and trickle down his throat, savoring the rich flavor and the warm sting. It was good to enjoy the company of an old friend and imbibe the best liquor again. He hadn't realized how much he'd missed both pleasures over the last year.

"Fine stuff," Uncle George said, holding his glass up to the candlelight in the drawing room of the Derrington town house. "Good of you to bring it along, Trafford."

"My pleasure." Gavin seated himself beside the fire and took a sip of the cognac himself. "One of the good things about still going to sea is enjoying the bounty of other ports and bringing it home to share with friends."

"And your wife. Eleanor is well and glad to see you, I trust?" Nicholas asked, careful not to think too deeply about something that still had the power to hurt him.

"Eleanor is fine but prefers the country to Town." Gavin shook his head. "Are you still searching for the source of those ugly rumors?"

"I've found nothing significant as yet," Nicholas said. "But the trail has taken a turn I never expected."

"Is that why you are going to all these house parties?" Gavin asked.

"Can you believe it?" Uncle George said, stretching his feet toward the fire. "Nicholas Derrington playing the gentleman at Quality house parties. Now he has an invitation to another. Where is it you're going, Nick? Tewk Abbey?"

"An invitation from his lordship, the Duke of Tewin? How did you manage that?" Gavin looked absolutely astonished. "Moving in exalted circles, aren't you? Doesn't appear to me that people are taking this rumor too seriously if the duke is inviting you into his home. Give it up, man, and get on with your life."

"I consider accusations of treason against a Derrington, substantiated or unsubstantiated, quite serious,'' Nicholas said, without looking at Gavin. Even when they'd been boys, Trafford had always been one to shrug things off while he, Nicholas, brooded over an offense for days. ''The fact is, if the charges had been brought out in the open, I'd at least have had my day in court to prove them false.''

''Here, here!'' Uncle George said, downing more cognac.

''You're determined to prove them false nevertheless, aren't you?'' asked Gavin.

''That's why I accepted the invitation to Tewk Abbey.''

''Don't believe a word he says, Trafford,'' Uncle George said. ''Methinks Nick's beginning to enjoy social life. I daresay, I suspect some lady of the *ton* has caught his eye.''

Gavin cast a sidelong glance in Nicholas's direction.

''Uncle George entertains several erroneous theories regarding my social life,'' Nicholas confided to his friend.

Gavin smiled with understanding and turned to Uncle George. ''So, tell me who is going to attend this party at Tewk Abbey.'' ·

''I've heard that the Carrington-Smiths will be there,'' Uncle George began. ''Sunridge's charming little widow, the Earl and Countess of Sadder, the Baron Seaton . . .''

Nicholas hardly heard Uncle George's recitation of names; he only cared about the fact that Dorian was going to be at Tewk Abbey. In truth, he'd been quite astounded when the invitation from the earl had arrived at his door, delivered by the earl's own liveried footman. He'd never been certain that Dorian would do what she'd said she'd do. But she had.

Nicholas had immediately sat down to write her a note of thanks and found himself engulfed with the most astonishing longing to see her. The yearning, he feared, had little to do with the evidence he sought. He simply wanted to spend time in her company again, even if it was only to watch her brow furrow in annoyance with him. He quite relished serving as protector, discouraging eager suitors, if need be. It wasn't a role in which he had ever pictured himself, but he quite enjoyed seeing the disappointment, trepidation, and envy in gentlemen's eyes when they saw him lingering near Dorian and assumed he was her escort. It had become something of a game with him. He fully intended to play it once more at Tewk Abbey.

". . . Mr. Davis St. John and his sister, Miss Dorian St. John, and a few more folks, I suppose," Uncle George concluded. "It should be quite a nice group. 'Tis to be a musical week, I understand."

"Music again?" Gavin turned to Nicholas in amazement. "I'm surprised at this new side of you, Nick. Music?"

Nicholas shifted in his chair. He had not decided how much he wanted to tell Gavin about the investigation. "You were at the St. Johns's musicale."

"To humor Davis," Gavin said. "Have I missed some talent you possess?"

"Hardly," Nicholas said, unaccountably reluctant to share with his old friend what he'd learned about Franz Chamier and the composer's life and death in jail. "I don't see why I shouldn't broaden my horizons."

Gavin turned to Uncle George. "I think you're right, George. This must be due to a lady."

"I'll give her a kiss myself as soon as I ascertain who she is," Uncle George vowed. "I am that pleased to see Nick out in Society again."

"Don't talk about me as if I'm not here," Nicholas warned with a half smile.

"There was a time when it seemed that you weren't here in this world, even when you sat before the same fire with us," Gavin reminded him.

"Thank heavens that's over now," Uncle George said rising from his chair. "Forgive me, gentlemen, but thanks to Trafford's fine cognac it is time for me to retire. I bid you both good night."

After the older man had disappeared upstairs Nicholas put another shovel of coal on the fire. Without saying a word, Gavin poured each of them another portion of cognac.

"So you've decided to get on with your search, then?" Gavin prompted as soon as they both had settled in their chairs again.

"Losses must be atoned for," Nicholas said with a shrug. "But then life goes on, whether one's reputation is diminished by rumors or not. The days pass, the weeks, the months."

"Indeed, they do," Gavin commiserated. He took another sip of cognac. "I miss Jonathan, too. But I'm glad you've come to realize that grieving won't bring him back. It's been difficult these past two years to watch you withdraw. But now you're out in society again, I'm glad to know. You'll choose a countess soon."

"Not quite yet," Nicholas said, his mind drifting to Dorian. She'd somehow managed to gain him the invitation to Tewk Abbey. Now how would he get the other thing he wanted from her—her fragment of the Chamier music?

Strange that Gavin would bring up marriage. Nicholas had actually given the institution some thought. Davis's unfortunate marriage proposal had inspired the examination, he suspected— along with his vivid memories of Dorian's delightful qualities. The cling of her ball gown, the swell of her breasts above the scooped neckline, and the eagerness of her kiss. He ached to introduce her to the mysteries of lovemaking.

Matrimony offered him more legal rights than seduction; as his wife, Dorian would be obligated to share her possessions with him. However, technically, the music belonged to Aunt Charlotte. Dorian could claim it was not hers to give up. And wedlock seemed an extreme measure to take, especially when the lady had openly professed resistance to such an alliance.

"Nick, what on earth are you thinking?" Gavin asked, leaning forward in his chair to openly stare at Nicholas. "I don't recall ever seeing such a calculating smile on your face."

"Forgive me." Nicholas sipped from his cognac once more and tried to suppress his picture of Dorian, Countess of Sea-combe, cutting a lively swathe through the quiet life he'd made for himself at Seacombe Manor. The thought was amusing, only because he knew it would never happen. "I was thinking of something else."

"Once you're married—"

"Who is going to allow their daughter to wed a traitor?" Nicholas asked, feeling the old anger rise inside him. The Derrington name had been sullied by this false accusation of treason. Every time he thought of the wickedness behind it, his anger flared, bright and furious.

Gavin sat back in his chair. "Is that what troubles you? Believe me, there are plenty of title-hungry mothers and daughters who will overlook so unfounded an accusation against an earl. Wearing a coat from an unfashionable tailor is more likely to get you scratched from their 'eligible' list."

"I will not have a breath of treason hanging over the Derrington name when I take a wife," Nicholas said in all honesty, though he had more reason than his future marriage for finding the man or men responsible for false charges against him.

"Very noble, Nicholas," Gavin said, "but not necessarily practical."

"Perhaps," Nicholas allowed.

"Some pretty miss will snag your heart and you'll forget all about this ordeal. It will fade into the past. Maybe you'll learn to play the violin." Gavin raised his glass in a toast. "To the lady of your heart, whoever she may be."

"Rest assured, I'll do what I need to do," Nicholas said, grimly knowing he intended to do just that.

Chapter Six

Tewk Abbey was a grand old house built around an abbey that King Henry the Eighth had so generously usurped for his own to bestow on a loyal member of his court. Over the centuries it had grown from a modest country manor to a palatial house worthy of being known as a duke's country home. It featured none of the innovations the Earl of Thorpe boasted of in his renovated manor. Servants lingered in the halls to be of service when hand bells rang. Guests bathed in tubs carried to their chambers; Tewk Abbey offered no decadent marble bathing room.

Dorian rather liked the quaintness of the huge old place with the carved stonework arches, long echoing hallways, and the open cloister that had been planted in roses.

Tewk Abbey did offer one feature that few other English country homes offered: a symphony hall. The previous dukes had been content to use the former chapel as a library. But the current duke wanted a symphony hall in which to perform his works—a mere music room would not do. So the books had been carted out, a dais built at one end for the performers, and the long room filled with chairs for the audience.

The Duke of Tewin wasted no time in showing his symphony hall to his house guests. Some knew of it from other visits, but this was Dorian's first introduction to the hall.

"And for you, Miss St. John," the duke said, turning to Dorian. He was a short man, ample in girth, who wore his graying locks, long and free, in the manner of the great composers. "I just had the pianoforte tuned properly this very afternoon."

"How thoughtful of you, Your Grace." Dorian smiled and bobbed an appreciative curtsy. In the past she'd declined invitations to Tewk Abbey because she'd heard the duke was a demanding conductor of his guest musicians. Only her search for the sake of Aunt Charlotte was enough to make her accept this invitation. "The sound in here must be impressive."

"Yes, indeed it is," the duke replied with a gleam of pride in his eye. "We will begin rehearsals tomorrow."

"You see, His Grace can hardly wait to put all of you to work," the duchess said with a laugh. She was a tall horsy woman, all long limbs and obtuse angles, the antithesis of her short, rounded husband. "The least we can do is feed and entertain you well. If you've seen your fill of the symphony hall, follow me. Dinner is served."

The duke and duchess led the way into the dining room.

Dorian found herself seated at the duke's elbow and across from Nicholas. When she peered down the table she saw that Davis was seated with the duchess.

"I can't tell you how pleased Her Grace and I are that you accepted our invitation to stay a week at Tewk Abbey," the duke was saying to Nicholas as the footmen began serving the meal.

"Thank you, Your Grace, 'twas my pleasure to accept," Nicholas said with a quick glance in Dorian's direction. "I'm looking forward to hearing some fine music."

"And riding to the hounds, too, I hope," the duchess called down the table.

Dorian blinked, surprised that the duchess could hear their words from her end of the table above the clatter of china and the conversation among the other guests.

"Yes, of course," Nicholas added, leaning forward to address the duchess at the end of the long table. "I'm looking forward to the hunt."

"Oh, good." The duchess nodded. She was renowned for her skill as an equestrienne and her enthusiasm for fox hunting. Dorian suspected that was the only reason Davis had consented to come for the week once he learned that Elizabeth would not be present.

"I have a fine stable of hunters," the duchess continued. "You must look over the horses and select just the right mount."

"Her Grace and I did so wish for this opportunity to let you know that we don't believe a word of the things people have been saying about the Derringtons," the duke said, clearly wishing to control the conversation at his end of the table. "I know we never traveled in the same circles, geography being what it is with the Derringtons up north in Lincolnshire and us here in Sussex, but we think it's just dreadful what the gossips have spread around."

"That's very kind of you, Your Grace," Nicholas said, frowning at his plate.

Dorian opened her mouth to change the subject, but the duke, as she'd half expected, did it for her.

"Now, tell me, what instrument do you play?" the duke asked as he applied his knife to the leg of lamb.

Nicholas flung another quick glance in Dorian's direction. Slightly panicked, she cast about for some music-related task to assign Nicholas. She berated herself for not being prepared for his question; she should have known the Duke of Tewin would ask such a thing.

"I'm the page turner for Miss St. John," Nicholas said.

Dorian nearly choked on a bit of mint jelly. She felt a boot toe nudge her slippered feet beneath the table as she gulped down the last of her bite of food. "That he is, Your Grace. Lord Seacombe is so skilled at the task that I can hardly abide anyone else for the job."

"You don't say?" the duke said, turning an appraising eye on Nicholas. "How very interesting. Did you hear that, Lady Lurette?"

Lady Lurette Cushing was a buxom, brunette widow of undetermined years who was reputed to be the finest amateur violinist in all of Sussex. Dorian had heard that though the duchess did not like the lady, she was a frequent visitor to Tewk Abbey. From the way the buxom violinist fixed her hungry gaze on Nicholas, Dorian understood the duchess's feelings about the woman.

"Yes, indeed, I heard, Your Grace," Lady Lurette simpered. "You seem to be a man of many talents, Derrington. Sea captain, rider to the hounds, music page turner."

At the other end of the table, the duchess half rose from her chair. "What is it you are discussing down there, my dear?"

"We are talking of Lord Seacombe's many talents, dearest," the duke called back, as if the long distance conversation were an everyday event.

"I'm also a collector of music just as I hear Your Grace— is," Nicholas said to the duke, clearly not to be deterred by Lady Lurette's flirtations or the duchess' interruptions.

"Are you? I say, I knew that Miss St. John collected Chamier's work especially," the duke said. "But I did not know you also collected. Then you both must see what I have assembled."

"That would be delightful," Dorian said, pleased that Nicholas had breached the subject so successfully. "This evening perhaps?"

"Oh, no, I have other things planned for tonight," the duke said, motioning to the footman to take away his plate. "Tomorrow we begin rehearsals in the symphony hall. I have a full schedule laid out for my guests. No idle visitors here at Tewk Abbey. We keep busy improving our minds—''

''Or our bodies with fresh air and exercise,'' the duchess chimed in from the other end of the table.

''How healthful,'' Dorian said, hiding her dismay.

When she glanced across at Nicholas, he only offered an imperceptible shrug and motioned for the footman to refresh his wine. The tour of the symphony hall and the house had not revealed where the duke kept his collection. Unlike at Thorpe Hall, they dare not try to examine the music on their own. They didn't even know where it was. She could see this was going to be a long weekend.

Davis was in a dour mood when he appeared in the doorway of the breakfast room late the next morning. His tardiness was purposeful. He was thankful to find the sunny room deserted. Everyone had come and gone before him, and he would not be required to make civil conversation. He did not feel civil.

In fact, he was already regretting that he'd accepted the invitation to spend a week at Tewk Abbey. Though he enjoyed hearing Dorian or Aunt Charlotte at the pianoforte, symphony music was not to his liking. The week that stretched ahead promised to be long and boring.

When he'd first agreed to accept the duke and duchess's invitation, he'd thought Elizabeth would also be attending. She loved to sing; her voice was adequate and she enjoyed being the center of attention. He'd thought surely she would want to attend one of the duke's famous musical weeks.

But she had declined, deciding to spend a week at Brighton where Prinny, the Prince of Wales, and his crowd were said to be. Now Davis berated himself for not sending his regrets as soon as he discovered that fact and taken himself off to the seaside resort.

But here he was at Tewk Abbey with Dorian and a houseful of amateur musicians. There was not an eligible, interesting woman among the guests—except the little redheaded widow, Lady Sunridge, whose vivid earthiness might appeal to some but not to him. The truth was, his heart wasn't in finding someone to replace Elizabeth. He harbored hopes that she would see the error of her ways before the season was over and return to him. He planned to be waiting for her.

In the meantime he decided he would attempt to pass the time as pleasantly as possible—at least the week should offer some good riding and hunting. His new hunter had served him well at the little hunt the Earl of Halthorpe had hosted. Now he would have the opportunity to try the horse out on a longer, more demanding course and field.

Davis strolled to the sideboard, where the ever-present footman picked up a plate and awaited instructions. The Duke and Duchess of Tewin were known for their high-quality, well-trained servants. Davis frankly found the staff a bit above themselves, but he had no problem in dealing with them. He had long ago perfected the necessary condescending tone of voice and expression of boredom beyond irritation.

As he scanned the sideboard laden with several egg dishes, cheeses, fruits, breads, jams and jellies, ham, bacon, and kippers, he was only vaguely aware of another guest coming into the room to join him.

"Good morning, Mr. St. John," Susanna Sunridge greeted him.

"Lady Sunridge." Davis spoke succinctly, hoping to discourage further conversation with the lady, though he found her husky voice fell sweetly on his ear. She was wearing a shade of apple green that Davis personally detested and thought entirely too bright for her coloring.

"We seem to be the last ones down to breakfast this morning," she said, annoyingly oblivious to his shortness. She also surveyed the spread of food.

"So it would seem." Davis purposely turned away and addressed the footman. "Give me that last kipper, would you please."

The footman obeyed.

"Ooh," Lady Susanna mewed, peering in dismay at the empty platter. "Kippers are your breakfast favorite, too?"

Davis ignored the lady's distress; he had no intention of giving up his kipper. It was just what he needed on a morning like this and he didn't feel like sharing it with anyone. "I'm sure the footman will order more from the cook for you."

Lady Susanna cast a hopeful look in the direction of the haughty footman. Before she could summon her courage to speak the footman rudely turned his back on her and carried Davis's plate to the table.

Davis, who was about to follow, halted. The servant's indifference to a lady guest, even one of so little distinction, vexed him.

He frowned.

"Really, that's quite all right," she protested, wringing her hands in some confusion. "I don't need kippers this morning."

Davis eyed the offending footman. This was Tewk Abbey, the home of the Duke of Tewin, who was known to be richer than rich. If his lady guest wanted kippers, she should have kippers. No footman should stand in her way.

Clearing his throat, Davis pursed his lips, lifted his chin, and drawled in his best tone of disdain, "My good fellow."

The footman's head snapped up and he turned promptly toward Davis. "Yes, sir?"

"Order fresh kippers from the kitchen for Lady Susanna and for myself as well. Make haste. Don't keep us cooling our heels here at the breakfast table."

The footman bowed and scurried from the breakfast room.

"You!" Davis lifted his chin a bit higher as if to see all the better what was at the end of his nose and waved a lazy but commanding finger in the direction of the second footman standing by the door. "Prepare a plate for His Grace's guest, Lady Susanna. Hop. Hop."

The footman literally leaped toward the sideboard.

"What else will you have, dear lady? I'd offer you my kipper, but it's much too cold by half to be suitable to your delicate palate.''

Lady Susanna blushed.

Within moments Davis and Susanna Sunridge were seated at the table near the window with plates of steaming hot food before them.

Susanna leaned across the table. ''Thank you, sir. That was near miraculous.''

''Not at all,'' Davis said, settling himself at the table and refusing to smile at her expression of gratitude. ''I'm afraid I'm not good company at breakfast, Lady Susanna. That's why I came down so late.''

She sat back in her chair. ''Oh, I see. Of course, I understand. Sir Roger—my late husband—tended to prefer quiet in the morning also. Say no more.''

They both ate in silence until the discourteousness of it nettled Davis. He finally looked across the table at Lady Susanna to find her eating without any expression of vexation or annoyance on her face. The lady really did deserve a better breakfast companion.

''Tell me where you are from,'' he asked, forcing himself to carry on the sort of conversation he detested.

''Devonshire,'' Susanna said. ''Sir Roger, my late—''

''I know, your late husband,'' Davis supplied.

She blushed again. ''Well, he and I ran a modest establishment near Exeter.''

''And did you allow your footman to intimidate you?'' Davis asked, managing a smile.

''We only had a housekeeper who also cooked—and I . . .'' Susanna paused and smiled self-consciously. ''She did run the house much as she wanted.''

''Is the woman still in your service?''

''I had to shut the house and discharge her,'' Susanna said.

''Good,'' Davis said, truly glad to hear it. ''Sounds as if she deserved as much.''

"Oh, there you are, Davis," the duchess nearly shouted from the breakfast room doorway.

Davis flinched and Susanna started.

"I think your quiet breakfast is about to come to an end," Susanna whispered sympathetically.

Davis studied her delicate features as she offered a welcoming smile to the duchess and he regretted that she was right about the end of breakfast.

Dressed in a gold, mud-spattered riding habit, and waving her riding crop, the tall duchess swept into the room. "I've been looking for you, sir. One of my best dams has dropped a fine foal. I daresay this will be a hunter to best that black of yours that you boast about."

Davis reluctantly rose from his place. "Of course, Your Grace. I'd be delighted to have a look at this foal. But I tell you, there ain't going to be another hunter to match my black for another century."

"We'll see about that on hunt day, won't we," the duchess said. "You don't mind if I take St. John off to do the stables, do you, Lady Susanna? He and I have a difference of opinion to settle."

"Certainly not, Your Grace." Susanna smiled graciously at her hostess.

"Please excuse me, Lady Susanna?"

"Of course, Mr. St. John. Thank you for your company." She smiled and touched her fork to the kipper on her plate, reminding him of the true reason for her gratitude.

"My pleasure, dear lady." Davis bowed, then followed the duchess out of the breakfast room with a new lightness in his step and feeling unaccountably like a hero.

Chapter Seven

"Slower, Dorian, dear." The tapping of the Duke of Tewin's baton on his music stand snapped Dorian's attention away from thoughts of Nicholas's splendid physique as he stood beside the piano turning the pages for her. His cutaway coat fit snugly across his broad shoulders and his shiny Hessian boots emphasized the length of his leg.

In a matter of hours during their first rehearsal at Tewk Abbey the Earl of Seacombe had become a tolerably good page turner, picking up quickly on her cues and standing patiently beside the pianoforte while the duke lectured on the nuances of his symphony. He'd also made himself an attentive dinner companion every evening. Dorian was beginning to fear that she liked the man. The problem with that was, she was certain that was exactly what he was after.

"Dorian?" The duke called her name again.

Disconcerted by her lapse, Dorian snatched her hands from the keyboard. "Yes, Your Grace."

"You are playing two measures ahead of Lady Lurette's violin part," the duke said. "Do slow your tempo."

"Sorry, Your Grace," Dorian said, annoyed with herself and impatient with the duke and his musical obsession.

When the duke turned to speak with the violinist, the buxom Lady Lurette Cushing, Nicholas leaned over Dorian on the pretext of arranging the sheets of music.

"Is something wrong?" he asked in a low voice. "You seem distracted."

"Is he never going to show us his music collection?" Dorian whispered in exasperation, fearful that Nicholas sensed he was the source of her distraction. She tucked a stray lock of hair behind her ear. "We've been here three days rehearsing this symphony written by a man who can hardly hear the difference between middle C and F sharp. Every day he puts off showing his collection, as if it is the only reason we are here."

"Well?"

"Well, yes, I suppose that *is* the only reason we're here, but he can't know that."

"But he knows his collection tantalizes every musician in this hall," Nicholas said, leaning so close that Dorian caught the spicy scent of his shaving soap. "This morning over breakfast Lady Lurette told me the duke's collection is housed in the tower room."

"That's more than we knew before now," Dorian said. "We could seek it out ourselves."

"I think we only need to be patient," Nicholas advised.

The rapping of the duke's baton drew their attention again.

"Ladies and gentlemen, my dear dedicated musicians," the duke began. "Lady Lurette informs me that she is quite fatigued and that we should forgo rehearsals for today. I agree."

"Here, here," was uttered by a squire in the horn section and echoed by a baron among the woodwinds.

"To reward you for your hard work," the duke added, "I'm opening my manuscript collection for your perusal right this moment."

Dorian almost stood up and cheered.

Nicholas grinned at her and offered his arm as the duke led his company of guests from the symphony hall.

As soon as the duke's butler unlocked the tower room and threw open the doors, the guests flooded in, each seeking the manuscript they were most curious about.

The room was a round one at the top of the Abbey's only tower. It was more spacious than Dorian had expected, but it was poorly lit, with only one narrow window over which hung a heavy damask drapery that had been tied back to admit the sunlight. Glass cases lined the walls and formed an island in the center of the room, while a sofa sat before the cold fireplace.

"I was just telling everyone that this is one of the most valuable fragments I own." The duke gestured to a glass case in the corner near a window. "A piece of a love song by Franz Chamier. You know, the Hungarian patriot. Naturally, I'm quite pleased with the increase in value of all his works."

Dorian cast Nicholas a look of annoyance to be certain he knew that increased value was his fault.

"But, in truth, its value is of no consequence to me," the duke confessed. "I'll never give it up. I've come to have a great deal of admiration for this musician and patriot. Not many men of culture have the backbone to stand up for their country, too. Look at Lord Byron, out supporting every nation in the world but his own England. A disgrace I say, famous poet or not."

The duke's houseguests crowded around the glass cabinet to examine the famous piece of music, but Dorian and Nicholas hung back, waiting to get a long, close look.

"He keeps it well secured," Nicholas muttered as they waited. "The tower room doors were locked."

"Too well?"

After a moment of thought Nicholas shook his head. "I don't think so."

"Dorian, you must tell me what you think," the duke said proudly as the other guests strolled away to look at other displays in the tower room. "This is the only piece of Chamier's work that I have. I know you and your aunt are something of experts on his music.''

Dorian and Nicholas joined the duke at the glass cabinet and bent over it to examine the fragment.

The paper had yellowed and the ink had faded from being displayed in the sun so near the window. Apparently the draperies were drawn back most of the time.

The duke backed away. ''Look your fill and tell me what you think.''

Dorian leaned over the glass and squinted at the fragment of paper. She longed for Aunt Charlotte's magnifying glass. The blue sleeve of Nicholas's coat brushed against the rose pink sleeve of her gown as he, too, leaned closer to examine the music.

Dorian noted for the first time the distinguished silver hairs at his temple and the fine lines at the corners of his eyes, lines on the face of a man who looked to faraway places. This was the closest they'd been during the three days of the house party. Yet she'd been aware of him constantly near at hand: across the table at dinner; at the next table during cards; beside the pianoforte as she played.

Preoccupied with examining the music, he placed a hand on the glass. The sun glinted off the black enameled skeleton ring on his right hand. Dorian stared at it and shivered.

''What do you think?'' he asked. ''Is it genuine?''

''I'm not certain,'' Dorian said, realizing she'd hardly looked at the fragment at all. ''It's so faded.''

''Can you tell anything?'' Nicholas asked. ''This is important.''

''I know how urgent this is,'' Dorian snapped. ''My aunt's happiness is in jeopardy here.''

''I realize precisely what is at stake.'' Nicholas turned an icy blue gaze on her and spoke in a cold, dispassionate voice that startled Dorian. ''Believe me, it is no game. No amusement for bored young men. I wish you'd leave this search to me.''

Dorian stared at Nicholas, speechless in the face of his sudden vehemence.

After a moment he turned to the cabinet once more. "Would a closer look help you?"

Dorian fingered the lock on the case and stammered, "I believe it might."

"Your Grace." Nicholas hailed the duke, who had just finished a story about a manuscript for his other guests.

The duke joined them at the cabinet. "Special, isn't it?" he said.

"Wonderful," Nicholas agreed. "Miss St. John and I were wondering if we might take a closer look?"

"You mean take it out of the case?" he asked. "Oh, no, I couldn't do that. The fragment is much too fragile. You can see that for yourselves. I'm sure you understand."

"Of course," Dorian said. "It's just that our interest is so keen."

"I appreciate that," the duke said, "but I just can't take the chance, not with it having become so valuable and all. Wouldn't you like to see the rest of my collection?"

Dorian allowed the duke to lead her away to a Vivaldi manuscript he was proud to show her.

After a few minutes Dorian and Nicholas fell behind the group once more.

"We'll come back tonight and give it a closer inspection," Nicholas said.

"But how?"

"Tonight after everyone has retired," Nicholas explained, "we'll return to the tower."

Dorian knew as well as Nicholas did that skulking along the halls of Tewk Abbey at night, unobserved, would be nearly impossible. The hallway echoed with the patter of slippered feet and secretive giggles.

"Not tonight." She would have offered another plan if she could have thought of one. "Remember, the duke is requiring each of us to solo this evening."

"Tomorrow night, then. Yes, after the fox hunt," Nicholas said. "Wear something dark so you won't be spotted easily in the hallway and don't carry a candle. Meet me at the door to the tower."

Dorian agreed, her heart a little chilled by the way he planned their adventure and advised her what to wear. He plotted this nefarious assignation as if he did so all the time.

The morning of the Tewk Abbey fox hunt dawned clear and cool: perfect for riding to the hounds. Davis began the morning in good humor, confident that he and his black were going to show the Duchess of Tewin what a good hunter was made of.

Though it might be slightly unappreciative to outride the duchess at her own fox hunt, he felt his hostess had challenged him to it. And she seemed a good sport.

He was smiling to himself, already basking in the pleasure of being first to the kill, when he spotted Dorian, who was dressed in a blue military-styled riding habit and mounted on a spirited chestnut mare from the duchess's stables. Nearby, Seacombe swung up on a powerful bay gelding.

Davis's mood soured suddenly. He glared at the traitorous earl. The man had continually lurked in the proximity of Dorian throughout the entire house party, ingratiating himself to her with every attention and flattery.

While Dorian didn't appear to be falling for Seacombe's ploys, she certainly wasn't discouraging the man either.

Before Davis's mood could darken more, a horse pranced into his hunter's rump from the other side. He whipped around to glare at the inept rider on the dappled mare.

"Oh, I'm so sorry," Susanna Sunridge said, trying to manage the reins of her horse and hold the hat on top of her head all at once.

Davis stared at her. The dark brown of her velvet hunt coat brought out the peach blush in her cheeks and enhanced her large amber eyes. Davis found his hostile gaze lingering on her body, taking in the trimness of her waist and the firm roundness of her bosom.

She smiled tentatively at him. "I'm afraid this mare is a trifle spirited for me."

A reluctant smile came to his lips. Though he thought her red hair a bit bright and common, he couldn't resist softening at the sound of her husky voice.

"She's just eager to get started," Davis said, surprised at how the widow's voice always fell so pleasantly on his ears. "She'll be fine once we get going."

"I do hope you're right," Susanna said, sawing at the reins to maneuver her mount away from Davis's black hunter.

Personally Davis thought it a great mistake for the ladies to be riding with the hunt; they always slowed up the field. But the Duchess of Tewin was a fine horsewoman and so devoted to her horses and hounds, there was little chance that the ladies would be discouraged from riding if they wished. Dorian certainly never passed up a chance for a wild gallop through the countryside, though she hated riding on a ladies' saddle—and always avoided being present for the kill.

The hunt horn wailed, echoing off the walls of Tewk Abbey and the hills beyond. The dogs raised a chorus of voices and dashed off in the direction of the call, spike tails wagging. The hunt master in his red coat and black jockey cap spurred his horse on and disappeared with the hounds over the first hill. The field, ladies and gentlemen alike, continued to mill about in confusion on the abbey lawn.

Impatient with the disorder, Davis urged his horse through the crowd. As soon as he cleared the field, he spurred the black into a gallop, following the hunt master. He'd win the fox's brush today, he decided, because there was nothing else worthwhile to win at this house party. Though he knew the duchess expected to take home the brush, he'd win it and graciously present it to her. The hunt trophy would be his.

Soon he heard the field of riders thundering along behind him. When he looked over his shoulder he caught a glimpse of Dorian urging her mare to pass his black. Leave it to his sister to turn the hunt into a race between them, but he wasn't too concerned. It was only the exhilaration of the wild ride that appealed to Dorian. To his satisfaction, Seacombe was nowhere to be seen.

The wind in Davis's face and the rhythmic movement of the black beneath him dispelled his ill humor. He settled himself into the saddle, took a firm grip on the reins, and bent his attention on being the first rider to the kill.

On her chestnut mare Dorian cleared the hedgerow ahead of Davis, but by the time they reached the stream at the bottom of the hill, the black surged ahead. With a grin of pleasure, Davis left Dorian behind in a shower of water.

The field of riders spread out as the wily fox's trail lengthened. Davis kept the red coat of the hunt master in view. The master had enough of a head start that catching him was nearly impossible, but Davis was determined. He spurred the black, and the gelding valiantly lengthened its stride.

The few riders of the field who galloped along with Davis broke out of the forest in an open field. They crossed a road, cleared a low stone fence, and scattered a small herd of bleating sheep. When Davis glanced around at his competition, only Seaton and Sadder rode neck-in-neck with him. The duchess galloped well behind. Davis grinned to himself; he had a good chance to win the brush.

When they charged into the next stand of forest Davis was in the lead. He bent over the black's neck, urging the gelding on. The noise of a horse crashing through the undergrowth close behind made Davis look over his shoulder.

A feminine cry of distress reached him. He was about to curse Dorian for following him when he recognized Susanna Sunridge. She was bouncing along atop her dappled mount, her brown velvet hat gone, her red hair flying loose, and her horse chomping the bit between its teeth. The mare galloped alongside Davis on his black and threatened to pass them.

"Help me, sir," Susanna cried, clutching the useless reins in her tiny gloved hands. "I can't stop my horse."

Davis couldn't imagine how she had managed to even stay aboard the runaway this long. She was headed for a nasty fall.

He glanced ahead to see that the hunt master rode only a short length ahead now. Winning the brush was still within Davis's reach; he'd be the lauded rider of the hunt. But he couldn't ignore a lady in distress, even in favor of greater glory.

Davis bit back an oath.

"I'm going to grab his reins," Davis shouted so Susanna could hear him over the thunder of the horses' hooves. "Hold on to the mane."

She did as he told her.

Moving slyly so as not to startle Susanna's mount, Davis reached out to seize the bridle. Despite his deliberateness, the blasted animal shied, threw its head to the side and planted all four hooves. Susanna plunged headlong over the dapple mare's shoulders and hit the ground with a sickening thud. She somersaulted over the edge of the hill and rolled head over heels down the steep slope into the undergrowth below.

Cursing, Davis threw himself off the black before the gelding came to a halt. Tossing the reins aside, he charged down the hill after her. In his haste he nearly fell into a headlong descent himself. He gave no heed to scuffing the shiny leather of his new boots. He just scrambled down the slope with a cold, sinking fear in his gut.

"Lady Susanna? Susanna?"

No answer.

He cursed under his breath again and began to beat his way through the undergrowth with no concern for the nettles snagging the fine wool of his jacket. "Susanna?"

A soft moan from behind him caught his ear and he whirled, lunging back through the spring greenery.

"Here, I am—ooh my—I'm here."

Davis found her, lying on her side on the edge of a rocky

spring, her face smudged, her hair tangled with leaves and twigs, and her skirts rucked up around her knees.

"Don't move," Davis warned, kneeling by her side. He'd seen riders take some nasty spills in his time and he knew he needed to assess her injuries before she tried to stand.

"I think I'm all right," she insisted, raising up on her elbow. Her face was pale, her eyes dilated with fright.

"Let's just be certain of that, shall we." Davis shrugged out of his hunt coat, wadded it up, and put it behind her head. "Lie here until we've confirmed there are no broken bones."

"Not on your coat!"

"Don't worry; my valet can work miracles," Davis said, gently urging her to lay her head on the makeshift pillow. Then he began untying his neckcloth and noted with some concern that Susanna had closed her eyes. He'd seen a fellow do that once before, and the man had never awakened again.

He began to talk, just to keep her awake and alert. "What happened? What made your horse bolt?"

"I don't know," Susanna said. "We started out with the field of riders and next thing I knew she'd gotten the bit in her teeth and there was no stopping her. She took every fence, gate, and hedgerow she saw. All I could do was hang on."

"And good job you did until I interfered," Davis said, wishing he'd considered stopping the horse in another manner. "Why on earth were you on that particular mount?"

"It seemed the most docile in Her Grace's stables," Susanna said, without opening her eyes. "Actually, I was first given the chestnut mare that your sister rode, but Dorian exchanged horses with me because she could see I was bound to have difficulty with it. I'm not much of a horsewoman, but I'm afraid the duchess quite intimidated me into riding today. No one dared refuse to ride with her hunt pack."

"Quite so." Davis dipped his neckcloth into the cool water of the spring and wrung out the excess. "Here, let's wipe some of that dirt off your face."

He touched the cool cloth to Susanna's face and his gaze

met hers. She looked so soft and vulnerable, he wanted to take her in his arms and tell her to ignore the duchess. Silently he berated himself for not seeing what Dorian had seen: that Susanna didn't belong on a high-strung hunter. He would have made the grooms find a mount suitable for her.

Her skin was just as smooth and soft as it looked. Fascinated, Davis stroked away another smudge of dirt.

Suddenly Susanna struggled to sit up once more and put her hand over his. "I can wash my own face; I just need a mir—"

"A mirror?" Davis smiled at her, relieved to see that her vanity had returned. It was always a healthy sign in a woman. "But you don't have one. You'll have to trust me."

She touched her hair. "I must look a fright."

"It could be worse," he reminded her. "You could have broken a bone or even your head. Are you ready to try to stand?"

"I think so."

"Easy now." Davis got to his feet and offered his hand. Susanna put her hand in his and stood slowly.

"Oooh!" She swayed a bit. "I feel light-headed."

Davis pulled her against him to prevent her from falling. Her head fell against his chest, fitting perfectly beneath his chin and resting lightly against his shoulder. Her hair felt like silk against his chin and smelled sweet and spicy, like cinnamon and nutmeg. Slipping his arm around her waist, he steadied her, holding her close for a moment, taking pleasure in the feel of her soft roundness beneath his hands and pressing against the full length of his body.

Lust lanced through Davis. The intensity and urgency of it shocked him. Instantly he froze with Susanna in his arms. His body never failed to react to the nearness of a woman, but this tightness in his loins made him long to bury his nose in her hair and his tongue in her ear, to caress her breasts until she whispered his name in that husky voice of hers.

"This is really very kind of you, Mr. St. John," Susanna

said, thankfully unaware of his arousal. She gently pushed away from him.

Stunned, Davis released her and dropped his hands to his sides. He was suddenly uncertain of himself and so terrified of the power of his lust that he didn't dare touch her again.

She tugged at the bottom edge of her bodice and smoothed her skirts. "I do appreciate your efforts to help me. You have my undying gratitude."

"Do call me Davis," he said, unable to resist taking the liberty of wiping an invisible speck of dirt from her dainty nose. "You owe me no debt of gratitude, Susanna. I apologize that my efforts weren't more successful."

"But you were heroic, Davis." She smiled shyly at him before lowering her gaze with a flutter of dark lashes. At the sound of his name on her lips his heart skipped a beat. He could hear the hint of warm laughter in her husky voice. The ache in his groin grew more painfully sweet.

"If you hadn't stopped my runaway horse, we'd all have been embarrassed when I, the clumsiest horsewoman in England, became the first to reach the kill and win the trophy from the duchess."

"An embarrassment indeed, for the duchess." Davis chuckled, pleased to find himself smiling down into Susanna's amber eyes, completely unable to remember that he'd begun the day in a foul mood. "Let's get you back to the Abbey."

Susanna agreed. Davis led the way up the hill, careful to help Susanna when she needed a hand but still wary of touching her. Lust had nearly scuttled his ambitions once before. He wasn't about to allow that to happen again.

Dorian was there waiting for him at midnight in the dark at the top of the tower stairs. She was cloaked in a black velvet cape just as he'd told her. Her golden hair hung loose across her shoulders and down her back. Nicholas didn't allow himself to speculate about what she wore or didn't wear beneath that cloak.

"I brought a magnifying glass I borrowed from Aunt Charlotte so I can examine the fragment more closely," Dorian said.

"Good." Nicholas handed her a candle. "Hold this while I light it."

"I thought you said no light."

"In the hallway outside the bedchambers." Nicholas found the tinder box in his pocket and lit the candle. "Here I need light to work on the lock."

He knelt before the door and took from his pocket the small, narrow knife he'd brought for picking the lock.

Dorian peered over his shoulder, watching him closely. "Do you do this sort of thing often?"

"More often these days than I like," Nicholas admitted. Just to establish that the door was locked before he began to work, he turned the handle. The door clicked open.

Dorian gasped. "Do you think the duke forgot to lock it?"

"Perhaps," Nicholas said, uneasy with this new development. "Or someone has arrived ahead of us. Wait here."

Nicholas rose and crept slowly into the library. The room was completely dark except for the long rectangle of moonlight that fell on the floor from the tall window. The smell of dry paper, old leather, and wood polish filled the darkness.

Pausing, Nicholas listened intently. The soft snoring of someone asleep on the sofa rippled through the silence. Nicholas tiptoed to the sofa and peered over the back of it to find the duke, sleeping on his back, his mouth open and a down comforter clutched up under his chin. Why on earth would the duke be sleeping in his tower room? Nicholas wondered. To watch over his precious collection? Unlikely.

Nicholas walked quietly back to the door where Dorian awaited him.

"What is it?" she whispered.

"The duke is in there asleep on the sofa," Nicholas said, unable to keep from smiling at the absurdity of their situation.

"But why?" Dorian asked, astonishment in her voice.

Nicholas shrugged. "There is nowhere else to sleep?"

"I suppose every bedchamber in the house is occupied with guests or servants," Dorian mused aloud, "but that doesn't explain why His Grace is asleep on the sofa in his own tower. Surely he has a bed in his dressing room, or he'd sleep with Her Grace."

"Be that as it may, he's in the tower."

"Is he sleeping soundly enough for us to do what we need to do?" Dorian asked.

Nicholas admired her audacity. "I believe so."

"Let's proceed then." Nicholas bent close to Dorian. "Carry the candle so that the light won't disturb the duke, then hold it while I open the glass cabinet. When we have the fragment we'll go to the window and pull one of the draperies across it to examine the music without the duke ever knowing anyone is in the room with him."

Their plans laid, they tiptoed into the room. Kneeling before the cabinet, Nicholas picked the lock. Without a sound, he lifted the glass door and removed the fragment. Dorian set the candle down on the window sill and loosened the tie on the heavy damask drapery, pulling it across the window. Nicholas gently laid the music on the sill. He stood back as Dorian slipped the magnifying glass from the bag that hung from her wrist.

"This really is in poor condition," Dorian muttered as she leaned closer to study the fragment.

"Can you tell anything?" Nicholas asked, impatient now that they had the music in their hands at last. "Is it Chamier's work?"

Beyond the drapery, the duke snuffled loudly. The sound echoed through the tower and brought Nicholas and Dorian up short. Neither of them moved.

The duke smacked his lips, shifted his position on the sofa, and then fell to snoring softly once more.

Nicholas and Dorian looked at each other and released simultaneous sighs of relief.

"Give me a moment to study it, my lord," Dorian scolded, turning back to the fragment. A lock of golden hair fell across her temple as she bent over the music again; distractedly, she tucked the strands behind her ear. "I believe it may be something written by one of Franz's students."

"Is there anything written on the back of it?" Nicholas demanded. That would tell him all he needed to know.

Dorian turned over the fragment. "No, nothing."

"Then this is not what I'm searching for," he said, disappointment and frustration rising in him. If this had been it, the third and final piece, he'd be close to having the information he needed to solve the mystery.

"I don't think this is a an authentic piece by Franz."

Just as Nicholas reached for the fragment to replace it in the cabinet, he heard the tower door latch click. The door was thrown open so violently, the sudden draft fluttered the damask curtain. Dorian blew out the candle and tucked it beneath her cloak. Nicholas pressed her back against the window frame and prayed the curtain would obscure them.

"There you are, Cecil."

Nicholas and Dorian shared a startled glance.

"The duchess," Dorian mouthed unnecessarily for Nicholas.

The duke muttered some sleepy reply.

"I might have known this is where you would have gotten off to," the duchess said, slamming the tower door behind her. The curtains trembled again. "I looked for you in Lady Lurette's chamber first. You can imagine how embarrassed I was to barge in on Seaton and Lurette."

Dorian's brows shot up. "The Baron Seaton and Lady Lurette Cushing?" she mouthed at Nicholas.

He shook his head. He had little interest in the affairs of the other houseguests.

"Katherine, I told you I have no interest in Lady Lurette beyond her skill with the violin," the duke muttered. "What more proof do you want?"

"But the way you stare at her when she is playing the violin . . ." the duchess went on, indignation in her voice. "It's quite embarrassing to me. Cecil, I will not be humiliated."

Dorian's eyes grew round. She clamped her hand over her mouth to stifle her giggles.

Nicholas could not suppress a smile. Lady Lurette's bosom shook quiet thunderously when she played the more lively passages of the duke's music.

"Is that all that concerns you, my dear? The lady plays a fine violin for an amateur." The duke sounded as if he was yawning as he spoke. "Can't we sort this out in the morning?"

"I want your word that you will not humiliate me again with one of your pretty musicians," the duchess insisted.

"My dear, I have done nothing to be of an embarrassment to you for years and years," the duke said, a tinge of regret in his voice. "My interest in my fellow musicians is purely platonic, Katherine. Can you say that of your interest in your fellow fox hunt riders?"

"A fair question," Nicholas mouthed to Dorian.

The duchess paused, too long to be completely innocent of her husband's suggestion, Nicholas thought.

"Yes, I can say my interest in the hunt club has solely to do with dogs and horses. You know that. Few men want to go to bed with a woman who can outride them."

"Well, this bloody sofa is damned uncomfortable and I would gladly return to bed with a lady who could outride me if she'd promise not to spend the rest of the night carrying on about a woman who plays the violin."

Another pause. Nicholas and Dorian held their breath as they awaited the answer.

"You would come back to my bed?" the duchess asked, clearly amazed and disarmed.

"There is no other chamber in the house where I'd be welcome,'' the duke said. ''And I can't get any sleep in my dressing room with my valet snoring.''

Nicholas choked back his own amusement and put a warning finger to his lips to shush Dorian, who looked as though she was about to erupt in more giggles.

''Come along, Your Grace,'' the duchess said. ''Let's go to bed. You'll be more comfortable in my chamber than here in the tower. Remind me to tell the servants to do something with those draperies in the morning.''

Nicholas and Dorian held their breath as they listened to the duke and duchess's footsteps fade toward the tower door. Nicholas heard the door latch but waited several more moments before peering around the edge of the curtain. He wanted to be certain the duke and duchess had left. And he wanted to savor a few more seconds of having Dorian's body pressed against his.

''Have they gone?'' Dorian asked.

''Yes,'' Nicholas confirmed reluctantly. ''Let's put this away and get out of here.''

They made quick work of replacing the fragment in the glass case, locking the cabinet, and then slipping out of the tower. They said no more to each other as they sneaked down the stairs and made their way back to Dorian's bedchamber.

Only after Nicholas had closed the door softly behind them and Dorian had lit a candle did they allow themselves to chuckle out loud.

''Somehow I assumed things were always sedate and orderly between a duke and duchess,'' Dorian said between fits of giggles.

''Do things ever go sedately between a man and a woman?'' Nicholas asked.

''Never between Davis and I,'' Dorian said, placing the magnifying glass on the table by the window and slipping her cloak from her shoulders. Nicholas's mouth went dry. She was wearing a thin green morning gown that revealed the tantalizing swell of her breasts beneath the sheer lawn fabric. It clung sensuously to her hips and thighs.

"You and Davis are brother and sister." Nicholas's gaze drifted over her hungrily. "It's different between a man and a woman who care about each other."

"I suppose so," Dorian agreed without looking at him. "I think he loves her, don't you?"

"Who?"

"The duke," Dorian said, clearly amazed that he didn't know of whom she spoke. "He loves the duchess. Were they a love match?"

"I don't know," Nicholas said, wondering how the Duke and Duchess of Tewin had become the topic of conversation between them. "I suppose they had some regard for one another when they were married, but I doubt it was a love match. Alliances between great families seldom are."

"But he must love her," Dorian insisted. "He has such patience with her fox hunting."

Nicholas stared at Dorian; her logic escaped him. "How does that prove love?"

"He allows her to be what she is," Dorian said, as if everyone knew this fact. "And she accepts him as the aspiring musician and composer that he is, though he's quite tone deaf."

"That's love?"

"A large part of it." Dorian's eyes became dark and dreamy. "Of course, there are other things such as caring, attraction, and passion. What do you think true love is?"

Nicholas cleared his throat, turned away, and tried to think of a way to change the subject. "True love is sheltering, protecting. It is devotion and sacrifice."

"Brave emotions, everyone, but not the tender sort that tug at the heart," Dorian said.

Nicholas frowned, not certain he understood what she meant.

"Let's return to the subject of our search, shall we?" he said. "We are back where we started a month ago. I have one fragment; your Aunt Charlotte and you have one; and we have not found the third.''

"The piece of music in the duke's tower is definitely not an original by Franz," Dorian agreed.

Nicholas sat down in a chair at the window-side table and loosened his neckcloth so he could think more clearly. "Who else might be a collector? Who else might have what we are looking for?"

Dorian stood in the middle of the room gazing off into space as she contemplated Nicholas's question. "It's possible a dealer is holding it somewhere, but surely we'd have heard about that. Aunt Charlotte and I have let it be known that we're interested in Franz's music."

"I know," Nicholas said.

"You know?" Dorian's eyes narrowed. "I suppose you've been talking to the dealers?"

"Of course," Nicholas said. "Not the same elite ones you and your aunt patronize. I investigated dealers of a less respectable standing. But they had heard of the St. Johnses interest in Chamier's music. None seemed to know more about the third fragment than we do."

"What if someone else has put out the same word?" Dorian said. "Suppose they offered to pay the asking price for Chamier's music?"

"When a dealer smells money he goes for the highest bidder. Just like at an auction," Nicholas explained. "If a dealer had come across what we're looking for, he would have contacted one of us looking for a better offer. Unless . . .''

"Unless . . ." Dorian leaned forward, hanging on Nicholas's last word. He hadn't spoken the rest of his thought because he didn't like it.

"Unless he was threatened with the direst of consequences," Nicholas finished.

"Consequences?" Dorian looked puzzled. "What consequences? Who would threaten anyone over a collector's item?

I know some collectors are rather fanatical about their pastime, but surely not to the point of . . .''

Suddenly impatient with Dorian's naïveté, Nicholas rose from his chair and crossed the room to where she stood. He had to make her understand what was at risk. ''There are people who have a lot at stake where this piece of music is concerned. Do not underestimate the lengths to which they might go to get what they want.''

Dorian looked up at him, her violet eyes dark with questions. ''Do these people of whom you speak have anything to do with the skeleton mourning ring you wear?''

It was not the question he'd expected from her, but he had wondered how long he would be able to keep Dorian in the dark about what all of this meant to him. ''Indirectly. I wear the ring as a reminder of something I don't intend to ever forget or forsake.''

She licked her lips. ''You're not going to tell me any more, are you?''

''You don't need to know any more,'' Nicholas said, stepping closer to her and surrendering to the urge to put his hands on her delicate shoulders. He longed to feel her warmth and fragility through the thin fabric of her gown.

''Tell me, at least, should I be frightened?'' Dorian asked, making no effort to move away from him.

''Not when I'm with you,'' Nicholas said.

Dorian neither moved away from him or toward him. ''You know, the people who want—you're going to kiss me again, aren't you?''

''Yes,'' Nicholas said, amused by her directness but undeterred. ''Yes, I think it's about time. Have you any comment before I commence?''

Only the briefest of doubt flickered in her eyes before she answered, ''None.''

Chapter Eight

Dorian lifted her face to Nicholas's, allowing him to spread his hand on her neck. He drew his thumb along her jaw, giving her a moment to change her mind. But she had no desire to change a thing. Closing her eyes, she thrilled to the tenderness of his touch, and the warm promise in it. With his other hand Nicholas spanned the small of her back, pulling her close. She licked her lips in anticipation of the pleasure of his mouth on hers.

"Sweetheart," he whispered against her lips, his breath warm and tantalizing. He pressed her closer. "Feel how your body fits perfectly against mine."

"Oh, yes." The words sighed on Dorian's lips. She slipped her arms around his waist, savoring his solidness, then tipped her head back farther, offering her lips. Was he never going to kiss her?

When he finally bent to brush his lips against hers, she found them hot and passionate. Tantalized, she allowed him to move his mouth across hers.

Impassioned but still in control, Nicholas pressed her closer and sought entrance to her mouth. She yielded, making a whimper deep in her throat. His tongue stroked the corners of her mouth, then plunged deeper. The weakness was on her again, and she leaned against him, depending on him for support.

Nicholas lifted her against him. This time there was no mistaking the bulge of his blatant arousal pressed against her. The knowledge that he wanted her thrilled Dorian even more.

Pressing her backwards, he guided them the few necessary steps to the bed. Pushing her down onto the counterpane, he covered her body with his, never releasing her from the kiss. Lying beneath him, Dorian stroked the cords of his back and moved against him wantonly. Nicholas groaned with pleasure.

He released her briefly to take a deep breath and move from atop her to her side. Then he lifted her chin and captured her mouth again. All the time he caressed the contours of her body: kneaded her breasts, spread his hand across her belly, stroked her hips and thighs. Dorian yearned to feel his long fingers on her bare body.

Then his hand was slipping up along her leg teasing the sensitive skin of her bare thigh above her stockings.

Dorian sucked in her breath. "Nicholas?"

"Have you ever been with a man, sweetheart?" Nicholas whispered into her ear, his hand roving higher beneath her skirt.

Dorian's strength was gone and the urge to part her thighs for his caresses was strong and instinctive. She was warm and pliable under his touch and knew that as long as his hands were on her she could deny him nothing. "Have I what?"

"Have you allowed a man inside you, sweetheart?" Nicholas asked, then gently trailed his tongue along the shell of her ear.

"Oooh, no." Dorian's ability to make sense of words deserted her.

"I thought not." Nicholas's fingers never ceased seeking her most secret places. And she moved beneath his hand, wanting him to find them, though she knew he would discover her disgracefully hot and wet there.

She shivered when he caressed her mound. He moaned when

he delved deeper, his hand slipping beneath the protection of her shift and touching the delicate folds between her legs. The moistness and heat he found there didn't seem to disappoint him at all. His touch was gentle but expert. He seemed to know exactly how to draw unbearably exquisite sensations through her body. Lost in pleasure, Dorian cried out. Nicholas whispered words of encouragement in her ear.

At the sound of a sharp rap on her chamber door his hand went still. Dorian whimpered in frustration.

Nicholas cursed and pulled a corner of the counterpane across her bare thighs. "I should have locked the bloody door."

Just as Nicholas feared, Davis burst into the room. It took St. John a fraction of a second to take in the scene. "What the hell are you doing with my sister?"

"Good evening, St. John." Nicholas got to his feet, tugged his coat closed over his obvious arousal, and offered his hand to Dorian. Beneath the counterpane she attempted to smooth her skirt and petticoat back in place. Then she accepted his help, sliding off the high bed as gracefully as possible.

"I demand an answer right now!" Davis shouted, his face contorted with suspicion and his hands balled into fists at his side.

"Close the door and stop shouting," Nicholas ordered calmly.

Davis complied and dropped his voice. "This is disgraceful. I demand an explanation."

Nicholas glanced at Dorian and squeezed her hand, which he'd never released.

"I was sharing a kiss with your lovely sister," he said, unable to resist grinning a bit. She looked disgracefully debauched and this time it was *his* doing.

"Impose your unwanted attentions on some other female in the house, if you must," Davis said, his eyes flashing with anger. "But not on my sister."

"I invited him here, Davis," Dorian said, shoving a heavy lock of golden hair aside and casting Nicholas an embarrassed smile. He noted with pleasure that her lips were still swollen from his kiss. "It's all right."

"It's not all right," Davis insisted, gasping with indignation. "He's taking advantage of you, Dorian. Don't you understand the man is fortune-hunting? He can't find a wife among the families of quality because he's a traitor, so he'll settle for a rich heiress."

Nicholas released Dorian's hand and frowned at Davis. "Don't ascribe your own ambitions to me, St. John."

"Davis, please." Dorian tugged at Davis's coat sleeve. "I allowed him to kiss me. It was my choice."

Davis shrugged her off. "What do you mean by that comment, Seacombe?"

"Simply that I have no designs on your sister of the nature you describe," Nicholas said, deciding to tread lightly. This was Dorian's brother, and the young man had a right to be angry.

"So you were kissing her for the pure pleasure of it?"

"That's enough, Davis," Dorian said. "You are interfering in personal matters that are none of your concern. I realize this situation is awkward, but no harm—"

"There had better not be any harm done," Davis said, glaring at Nicholas, who met his gaze without comment. "You're using her, Seacombe. You're older, more experienced. You and I both know what it takes to get a woman into a compromising situation. A few sweet words, a caress, a kiss. By the time she's aware that it's time to call a halt, it's too late. And everyone knows Dorian is afraid of becoming a spinster."

Dorian sucked in a shocked breath. "I am not!"

The flames of embarrassment burned in her cheeks and tears of humiliation welled in her eyes.

Nicholas frowned. "I think you've said quite enough."

"I'm not finished," Davis said. "You have put my sister in a compromising position and I demand satisfaction."

"Davis!" Dorian turned to Nicholas, clearly desperate to stop this ridiculous scene. "He's been drinking and doesn't know what he's saying."

Nicholas held Davis's gaze, recognizing the earnestness in the young man's eyes. Despite his heated, careless words, he loved his sister very much. "He knows what he says."

"Your choice of weapons." Davis lifted his chin a notch higher. "Name your second."

"Wait."

Nicholas allowed Dorian to step between them. She placed a hand on the waistcoat of each man. "Dueling solves nothing. There must be another way of settling this."

Davis looked at her as if such an idea was unthinkable.

"If Nicholas and I were betrothed, you'd be satisfied, wouldn't you?" Dorian demanded, peering into her brother's face.

Nicholas started. The idea was absolutely inspired, though not what he'd originally intended. Betrothal would win him exactly what he wanted. Seizing Dorian's hand, he looked down into her tense, pale face. "Yes, Davis, would you be satisfied if I asked for your sister's hand in marriage?"

Dorian blinked at him, obviously speechless.

"Wouldn't you like that?" Davis glared at Nicholas. "Then you'd have what you wanted: Dorian's fortune."

"I have no interest in your sister's fortune," Nicholas said without taking his gaze from Dorian's face. He knew she'd only spoken up to prevent a duel, but he could not let the opportunity pass. "An agreement can be drawn up to ensure Dorian's money remains hers alone."

"You would do that?" The idea seemed to intrigue her.

"Of course, if it would satisfy your brother," Nicholas said, continuing to hold Dorian's gaze. He was astounded that attaining Dorian's hand in marriage was going to be this easy. "And you, too, of course."

Dorian searched his face, finding whatever she sought,

because she suddenly whirled on her brother. "Spinster, indeed. I accept Nicholas's offer of marriage. That should satisfy you."

Astonishment cluttered the emotions on Davis's face. "But you can't accept his offer, Dorian. This is a disaster! What will Elizabeth and her father think? A St. John wedded to an infamous Derrington. What will you tell Aunt Charlotte, when you promised her you'd marry only for love?"

"I don't know what the Duke of Eastleigh and his daughter will think and I don't care," Dorian said, clearly annoyed with Davis and his concern for appearances. "But now there is no need for a duel."

"Dorian?" Davis raked his hand through his hair.

"Was there a reason why you came to your sister's room?" Nicholas demanded as gently as he could and not appear eager to get Davis out of the way.

Davis shook his head, his expression one of confusion and bewilderment. "Nothing that matters now."

"Then good night," Dorian said.

Davis started for the door, then stopped. "When are you going to announce this engagement?"

"As soon as we return to Town, I think," Nicholas said calmly, though he was surprised to find himself planning his betrothal announcement.

Davis glared at Nicholas. "I hope you're pleased with yourself. She had an opportunity to marry higher, you know. Much higher. Dorian could have wed the heir to a dukedom."

Nicholas frowned but inclined his head respectfully. "I am painfully aware of my modest station in life."

Davis nodded righteously as if he was satisfied at last with the Earl of Seacombe's humility, but he lingered at the door.

"Nicholas will be along directly," Dorian said. "If we are betrothed, Davis, what harm can there be in leaving us alone together for a few moments?"

Davis cast Nicholas a suspicious frown but said no more.

As soon as her brother had left the chamber, Dorian turned

on Nicholas. He was aware of an awkwardness between them that had not existed only moments before.

"What have we done?" she asked.

"The only thing we could do, unless there was to be a duel at dawn," Nicholas said, a small smile of satisfaction on his lips. This time he tucked the unruly lock of hair behind her ear. "I for one have never thought that duels settled much of anything."

"I quite agree—" Dorian hesitated, clearly trying to sort through events and emotions. She dropped into the chair at the table.

"Think about it," Nicholas suggested. "Betrothal offers certain advantages. There'll be no problem in obtaining invitations to the same social events. It gives us the perfect excuse to be seen together without the gossips or your brother jumping to wild conclusions."

Dorian studied him doubtfully.

"Perhaps you are concerned about the accusations against me," Nicholas said, regarding her with sudden skepticism.

"Oh, no, not that," Dorian said with dismay in her voice. "You are right, of course, about the practicality. It's just that I never expected to become engaged under such unromantic circumstances."

"Actually, I never expected to receive such a forthright offer of marriage," Nicholas said with a wry smile.

Dorian tried valiantly to smile. "You understand, I could have no duel between you and Davis."

"No duel," Nicholas said, understanding perfectly the reason for her proposal. She might be warm and pliant in his arms, but she had not asked him to wed her out of love or desire. She'd asked him in order to protect her brother. "No duel is what you wanted, isn't it?"

Dorian nodded. "Oh, yes, above all else."

"So you see, there are all kinds of reasons for alliances between a man and a woman that have nothing to do with true love,'' Nicholas said, pulling her up from the chair. ''Now, I want to kiss my fiancée.

Nicholas could feel that the magic of the earlier moment, before Davis had burst in on them, was gone. Dorian pressed her hands against his chest, and her lashes fluttered before she looked up at him. ''Please, don't kiss me like before.''

''Was that so terrible?''

''On the contrary, my lord, it was delightful—too delightful,'' Dorian said, a blush rising in her cheeks. She looked away in apparent embarrassment.

Pleased, Nicholas smiled. ''Perhaps you would prefer to forego such delightful kisses until we have made the official announcement of our betrothal.''

''Yes, I would.'' Dorian remained with her face upturned to his. He could feel her studying his features.

''Just a token?'' Nicholas bent to kiss her.

He touched her lips lightly at first, but as Dorian responded, leaning into the length of his body, he deepened the kiss. The heat rose in Nicholas again and he was ready to take up where they'd left off when Davis had interrupted them.

Dorian pushed away from him, then steadied herself with a hand on the table.

''I'm leaving now,'' he said, his voice thick. ''I shall make some show of it so your brother will know.''

''Yes, I think that best,'' Dorian said, pressing a hand to her flushed cheek. ''We can decide about the announcement later.''

''Yes,'' Nicholas agreed, longing—aching—to stay, but knowing that he'd already accomplished more this evening than he could ever have hoped. ''Good night, sweetheart.''

Dorian closed the door behind him and leaned her brow against the cool wood to stop her head from spinning.

She'd agreed to become the Countess of Seacombe for reasons that had nothing to do with true love. Though that had seemed reasonable at the moment, she must not forget that the idea had come from her out of necessity. Though Nicholas had agreed to it readily enough, he had called their betrothal an alliance.

As much as she'd come to care for Nicholas, as much as she admired his gallantry and his resourcefulness, she dare not forget that he wanted the fragment of music as much, if not more, than she did.

Nicholas never remembered making the decision or questioning what must be done next. As soon as he returned to Uncle George's town house, he sent his most trusted groom off to Seacombe Manor in Lincolnshire for the Derrington betrothal ring.

If he was going to be promised to Dorian St. John—if the *ton* and her brother were to believe that they were headed for the altar—the betrothal announcement had to be done correctly. Everything must appear proper and aboveboard. Dorian St. John would wear the amethyst-and-pearl ring that every Countess of Seacombe had worn down through the generations.

When the groom returned with the ring twenty-four hours later Nicholas showed it to Uncle George and told him what he intended to do with the heirloom.

"Dorian St. John is the only lady I can think of who wouldn't turn up her nose at your treasonous reputation," Uncle George said as they sat in the garden waiting for dinner to be announced. The old man eyed the ring in the last rays of daylight.

The evening was peaceful and the sky clear. The rumble of carriages destined for the theaters or balls or the gardens like Vauxhall would not commence for two more hours.

"Dorian St. John is probably the only member of the *ton* who can get you back into Society without anyone thinking the more of it. Of course, there's the St. John fortune to consider. Half of it is hers."

"I'm so glad you approve of my selection," Nicholas said, hoping to have heard a little more enthusiasm for the match from his uncle. "But I agreed that her money will remain her own."

"Is that wise?" Uncle George dropped his feet from the stool where they'd been resting and straightened in his chair. "Not that you have any great need of the ready but—"

"Dorian possesses other things that I'd rather have," Nicholas said, surprised to find himself remembering how soft and responsive she'd been in his arms, rather than the fact that she held a fragment of music he wanted.

"Well, you know what you want," Uncle George said with a shrug of his shoulders. "I remember you always did. Your father wanted to make a cavalry officer of you, but you went to sea instead. Told your father—I remember the defiance in your eyes—'A good ship is as reliable as any warhorse.' Left my brother with his mouth hanging open, you did. That didn't happen often."

Nicholas silently agreed. He didn't like to look back; he didn't believe in reviewing history. Lessons were best learned as you went and the rest forgotten. The treasonous accusations against him and the Derrington name was the only part of his past he could not put aside.

"Then your brother Gilbert died unexpectedly of fever," Uncle George prattled on, shaking his head. Gilbert had been the middle Derrington son, a fair, happy-go-lucky young man who was the heir apparent if anything happened to Charles, the oldest. "Who would have thought that Charles and his son would die in a stable fire trying to save the horses?"

"Charles was the horseman father wanted his sons to be," Nicholas said without bitterness. He had never been jealous of his older brothers. He'd had no ambition to be the heir to Seacombe in those days, and now that he was the earl the title set uneasily on his shoulders.

"Any lady would be pleased to wear this," Uncle George said, returning the ring to Nicholas.

He accepted it, peering into the sparkling purple depths that reminded him of Dorian's eyes.

"You do care for her?" Uncle George asked.

Nicholas glanced up at his uncle in surprise. "Of course I do. Why do you ask?"

"It's just that I thought you were intent on clearing up these accusations against you first," Uncle George said, suddenly concerned with the cuffs of his coat.

"That will come in time," Nicholas said. "But it's having those marks against me that makes it imperative that everything about this betrothal be done absolutely correctly."

Uncle George nodded. "I understand, Nick. If it's my blessing you want, you have it. If Davis St. John will accept his sister marrying into the questionable Derrington family, then the Derringtons can accept an upstart merchant family."

Nicholas smiled and slipped the ring into his pocket.

Just then the butler announced that dinner was served.

Pleased to have his uncle's blessing, Nicholas followed George from the garden satisfied that he could appease Davis with the marriage agreement papers ensuring that Dorian's fortune remained her own. Society would admire the ring he would present her and be placated. But most of all Nicholas wanted to please Dorian. Her cooperation had become essential in his plan to clear the Derrington name.

The lady would not be fooled by the mere gift of a betrothal ring, centuries-old heirloom or not. But bestowing the ring would be one step toward winning her over. Win her he would, Nicholas decided. Of all the people's minds he wanted to change, he wanted to see any doubt and mistrust disappear from Dorian's eyes.

"I can hardly wait to meet the Earl of Seacombe again," Aunt Charlotte said, installing herself in a chair near the fire. Dinner was over and Davis had escorted the ladies to the drawing room, where they were to receive the earl.

"Such an attractive man, as I recall." Aunt Charlotte's eyes were bright with excitement. "We met the night of the musicale here at the house."

"Yes, he is an attractive gentleman," Dorian repeated distractedly.

Davis leaned toward Dorian. "You're not having second thoughts, are you?"

He didn't like the faraway look in her eyes or the dark circles beneath them. His resentment of Derrington sharpened. Perhaps his hasty challenge had been a mistake; surely that was what had made Dorian say rash things—things the earl could use to his advantage.

"Nothing has been said yet by the gossips about your escapade at Tewk Abbey," Davis said, speaking softly to Dorian so Aunt Charlotte wouldn't hear him. "They are too busy prattling something about the duke sleeping in the tower because there was nowhere in the house for him to sleep but in the duchess's bed and they weren't sleeping together any longer.

"However, I did see a number of curious glances cast in your direction the day we left. It's not a moment too soon to make the announcement of your betrothal."

"Certainly not," Dorian said, studying her hands, folded in her lap. "But I want you to know that Nicholas and I did nothing wrong. We shared a simple kiss."

"Simple kiss!" Davis rolled his eyes at the ceiling. "Dorian, I saw you and him on the bed."

"Saw who in whose bed?" Aunt Charlotte regarded them with a lively interest. "House parties have always been a delightful source of romantic tales."

"Nothing, no one, really, Aunt Charlotte," Davis said, "a lady of your years should not be troubling herself with these things."

"One's never too old for romance, Davis," Aunt Charlotte said, seemingly unoffended. "You'll learn that soon enough."

Dorian blushed.

Davis paced to the window. After the mantel clock had ticked away a few more seconds he turned to Dorian. "You don't suppose the fellow has had second thoughts? He wouldn't dare."

"Nicholas will be here," Dorian said, conviction ringing in her voice.

Dorian's uncharacteristically docile acceptance of the situation unnerved Davis. "*You* are having second thoughts."

"No, none," she said without looking at him. "Nor are you allowed any second thoughts. Remember, it was betrothal or a duel."

"A duel?" Aunt Charlotte twisted around in her chair to face Davis. "Did you challenge the Earl of Seacombe? So he was the gentleman you found in Dorian's room?"

Dorian groaned softly. Davis felt a blush rise in his cheeks.

Aunt Charlotte peered across the room at Dorian. "You and the Earl of Seacombe are lovers?"

"It's not like that, Aunt Charlotte," Dorian said, with hardly enough outrage to satisfy Davis.

"No, not like that at all," Davis repeated. "Everything is going to be proper and the betrothal will be announced in the newspapers."

"You don't have to protect me from anything," Aunt Charlotte said. "I understand about youth and love and passion."

Davis turned back to the window. How could his spinster aunt say such things? He remembered the scene in Dorian's room all too well. The man had thrown Dorian down on the bed. What else could he have done? Davis wondered. As her only male protector, he had to see that her reputation was defended. But the other side of the troubling question was, would Seacombe really make Dorian a good husband?

While Davis had always thought that a husband with a firm hand would benefit his headstrong sister, he couldn't in all good conscience turn her over to a villain.

If rumors were to be believed, Seacombe might well be a villain of the worst kind. A man who could betray his countrymen in battle; what kind of husband would such a man make? Yet Davis couldn't quite bring himself to cast Nicholas Derrington into that cold-hearted and sinister role. During the house parties the earl had shown Dorian every courtesy and had at times even been charming, in a quiet, sober way. When pressed over the matter of his liberties with Dorian he had readily agreed to marriage—and refused her fortune. Hardly the actions of a villain.

But the most confounded part of it all was that Dorian had accepted Seacombe's marriage offer. His sister, who had vowed to marry for true love or not at all, had practically asked the earl to wed her.

Davis was so wrapped up in his reflections that he started when Barton, their butler, announced the Earl of Seacombe.

He turned in time to see Dorian rise when Seacombe entered the room, but she did not go to him. The two regarded each other without expression for a long moment.

"Lord Seacombe, welcome," Aunt Charlotte said, looking up at the earl. "You're taller than I remembered, broad-shouldered. And dark hair with blue eyes. Oh, you and Dorian will make a lovely couple at the altar."

Dorian coughed.

"I'm so pleased that my appearance meets with your approval, Miss St. John." Nicholas grinned and bowed over Aunt Charlotte's hand.

"And charming, too. Do call me Aunt Charlotte," Charlotte said. "You'll be a member of the family soon."

Sherry was brought and the conversation flowed well enough, considering the awkwardness of the circumstances, Davis thought. Aunt Charlotte soon excused herself and the interview took a more serious turn.

Nicholas held out a sheaf of documents to Davis. "The betrothal agreement we discussed the night of our—discussion regarding's Dorian's inheritance. I know you will want to have your solicitors look it over, but I wanted to deliver it personally."

"Very thoughtful of you, Seacombe," Davis said, taking the

agreement from the earl. "I will have a look at the agreement in my study and leave you two to make your plans," Davis said, satisfied that the Dorian's pallor and the dark smudges under her eyes must be from bridal nerves.

He was finding it more and more difficult to think of this man as a villain and a traitor. Surely Seacombe would only have Dorian's happiness at heart. Dorian must have some feeling for the man. Why else would she agree to all of this?

Chapter Nine

As soon as Davis had shut the salon door behind him, Nicholas eyed Dorian. He had never seen her looking so pale—or so somber.

"You are well, I trust," Nicholas began uneasily, longing to see her laugh and dance around the room with the pleasure of her betrothal. Wasn't that how most young ladies behaved upon becoming promised? But then, he had learned that Dorian seldom reacted like most young women.

"Yes, I am quite well. Thank you," Dorian said, studying her hands in her lap.

"I know our betrothal happened rather unexpectedly." Nicholas paced to the fireplace to stare with unseeing eyes at the fire; then he glanced at Dorian once more. "But I see no reason to view it as any less significant than any other alliance between aristocratic families."

"Yes, it is an *alliance.*" Dorian's head came up slowly, her brow furrowed and her eyes dark with questions. "I've been giving it much thought since we've returned from Tewk Abbey. Betrothal and marriage are very serious steps."

Nicholas nodded in agreement.

"There are many people to please when two people become betrothed, especially the families to be united," Nicholas continued with the speech he'd mentally prepared during his carriage ride to the St. John town house. "In our instance, there is your brother and my uncle to satisfy. I believe we have done that."

Dorian hesitated. "Davis appears placated. I assume that was your intention in presenting him with the marriage agreement."

"It was," Nicholas said, certain she understood his motives. "And Uncle George gave his blessing to our union."

"That is most kind of your uncle." Dorian never looked up from her hands.

Nicholas toyed with the ring in his pocket again. This was more difficult that he'd anticipated. "Then there is Society to appease also."

"Yes, I suppose that to be true," Dorian agreed without looking at him.

"We must announce this betrothal and seal it with a token for all of Society to see."

Still Dorian did not look up at him. Eager to see her face, Nicholas crossed the room and sat down on the sofa next to her. He took her hands in his and found them cold. At last she raised her gaze to meet his. Her eyes were wide and troubled. Nicholas pressed on, refusing to let her doubts, whatever they might be, deter him.

"I have brought you a gift, a token to seal our pledge to one another." He pulled the ring from his pocket and held it out for Dorian to see.

The large oval amethyst captured the candlelight in its facets and shattered the light into rays of blue and purple and wine. Around it a dozen tiny, perfectly round pearls set in gold glowed lustrous white and pink.

"The first earl brought this ring back with him from the Crusades. It has been worn by every Countess of Seacombe since."

A tiny gasp of wonder and admiration escaped Dorian, but she made no move to take the ring from him.

"Do you like it?" he asked, certain that she did, but perplexed when she did not reach for it.

"I think it's the most beautiful thing I have ever seen," she said, without taking her gaze from the stone. "My lord, it is rich. Elegant. Exotic. And noble. Everything the betrothal ring of a countess should be."

"Then allow me to slip it on your finger," Nicholas said, tugging at her left hand. "Everything will be official and the *ton* will know that we are betrothed."

Dorian pulled her hand away. "Oh, no, I can't wear this."

Nicholas frowned. What the deuce was she up to?

Dorian spoke hurriedly. "My lord, I know you don't offer this ring to me lightly, but I can't possibly accept it. Surely you understand that."

"I do not." Nicholas struggled to keep the indignation and annoyance from his voice. Did she not understand the significance?

"I mean no offense," Dorian said, sounding most contrite. "But we both know how this betrothal came about and why we are willing to let it stand."

"Refresh my memory," Nicholas snapped, offended and hurt in an odd way he didn't quite understand but was determined to mask. He rose abruptly from the sofa.

"You understood I could not bear to have you and Davis face each other on the dueling field. And we both still want Franz's music," Dorian explained. "So you offered betrothal, the one thing that Davis would have to accept. You also knew that as a couple we would be invited to all the crushes and won't have to go through elaborate machinations to make sure we both attend the same parties."

When she paused Nicholas noted that her hands had curled into tiny fists, her knuckles white and her fingernails biting into her palms. It occurred to him that this interview might be no easier for her than it was for him.

"As you said earlier," she added, "Davis is satisfied, and the *ton* will have nothing to gossip about."

Her cool appraisal of the benefits of their betrothal annoyed Nicholas even more than her refusal of the ring. "What happens to our alliance when we have located the music?"

"When we accomplish our purpose one of us will cry off."

"Cry off the betrothal?" Nicholas repeated evenly, mastering his complete amazement.

"I shall do it. Everyone knows how difficult to please I am. There will be no negative reflection on your reputation, and if I cry off, Davis can't challenge you again."

"I'm glad you have this all worked out," Nicholas said. He returned the ring to his pocket and crossed to the window without caring that it was too dark to see the garden beyond. Her cool rationale annoyed the hell out of him. He wanted to shake her until she agreed to take his family's ring.

"You know who you should give this ring to," Dorian said.

Nicholas turned on her. Was there no end to her presumption? "Ah. Have you decided who my bride should be?"

"No, of course not." Dorian looked quite astonished. "I would never presume to do that. But this token of betrothal rightfully belongs to the woman to whom your are willing to commit you life and your heart."

He should have known. "My true love."

"Precisely." Dorian gave him a soft smile, and an expression of immense relief. Charming though it was, the expression exasperated Nicholas.

He frowned. It was on the tip of his tongue to inform her of how little she knew of true love. She was a virgin brought up by a spinster aunt. Her knowledge of marriage was nonexistent. Her knowledge of men consisted of leading her brother around by the nose. She was a pampered, protected young woman who had never worried over anything more serious than which gown to select for the next ball.

"When the time comes," Dorian continued, obviously unaware of his annoyance, "and you have found the woman you love and cherish, you will be able to put the Seacombe ring on her finger in good conscience.''

''How thoughtful of you to consider my conscience,'' Nicholas said drily over his shoulder, but his sarcasm seemed lost on Dorian.

''My lord, I want you to know that I am aware of the honor you have just offered me. And I am so very grateful for the way you protected my reputation and saved Davis from a nasty encounter on the dueling field.''

''I was not being entirely unselfish,'' Nicholas said, unashamed to be honest. ''I am not fond of unnecessary bloodshed, especially if it might be my own.''

''I quite agree with you,'' Dorian said. ''As it turns out, I think this betrothal is the wisest course for us.''

Nicholas scrutinized Dorian's innocent face. ''Then, as you see it, what is our next move?''

Dorian's aspect brightened, giving away the fact that she'd been laying plans all along. ''There are several collectors I think we should question here in Town. We can call on them and ascertain whether they have any of Franz's work.''

''And if we find they have nothing?''

''At the end of the month the Marquess of Fernham is having a huge house party at Floraton Court,'' Dorian said. ''He has a fabulous collection of manuscripts.''

''The marquess collects music, too?''

''He began acquiring music recently,'' Dorian said, seemingly lost in her plotting. ''I learned of it from one of Franz's former pupils, who came to visit Aunt Charlotte the day before last. Everyone is bringing us any bit of news they hear.''

''Do you believe we should attend this party?''

''Yes, if we've found nothing among the collectors here.''

Nicholas nodded, studying the touching earnestness in Dorian's face and reminding himself that she possessed one of the pieces of music he sought. He suddenly regretted nothing about their betrothal, regardless of the strange terms Dorian had imposed on it. Between them, they had two pieces of the music.

Possessing the third was very nearly within his reach. "Have you considered that, as my betrothed, the *ton* will be looking for a ring on your finger."

"I suppose so," Dorian agreed thoughtfully, then added with an airy wave of her hand, "They tend to be rather shallow about such things. But we shall be attending parties together so I suppose we must do something for appearances. However, the ring I wear need not be such a valued family heirloom. Nor need it be a symbol of your commitment. Oh, no, for our betrothal any bauble will do."

Seething with something that wasn't quite outrage—but violent irritation at least—Nicholas dismissed his carriage when he left Dorian and walked to Uncle George's town house unconcerned about the fog. He was armed this evening and after his discussion with Dorian, he was too angry to fear anyone. He wanted time to himself to think. He needed the exercise to ease his indignation.

Any bauble will do, she had said. *Any bauble?* Did she not understand that he would not have offered the Seacombe amethyst to her if he had not wanted her to have it?

The tolling of the ships' bells rolling in from the river on the fog consoled him. Each time Nicholas pictured Dorian's face as she refused the ring, a hurtful pang of astonishment returned, renewing and refreshing an odd pain that mystified and stunned him.

Dorian had already plotted their course, steering clear of any awkward emotional snags like commitment, love, or marriage. He should be relieved. He should be thankful—what man in his right mind would want to marry such a headstrong woman?

Shaking his head, once more Nicholas found himself surprisingly in sympathy with Davis St. John, who had to deal with Dorian's willful nature daily, and also because the young man had suffered a similar rejection from Elizabeth. No doubt Davis had thought it impossible that the lady would refuse him, just as Nicholas had never expected Dorian to refuse the Seacombe ring.

By the time Nicholas had reached home the evening chill had dampened his anger.

In light of Dorian's independence, he had to wonder if he wanted to go through with this ridiculous charade. The lady was self-willed beyond belief. The pretense of being betrothed could quickly become more trouble that he'd ever anticipated. In fact it already had.

No one knew of their betrothal yet. No announcement had been made. It was not too late to reconsider this absurd but convenient plan to search out the third piece of music.

At the door Nicholas gave his cloak to Uncle George's butler, Rogers, then went straight to the dining room and poured himself a brandy to take the sting of Dorian's rejection. He was about to imbibe his first sip when he felt the pull of someone watching him from behind.

When he turned around he spied Uncle George and Gavin sitting at the table with their own brandy glasses. They were staring at him with surprise and expectation.

"I didn't know you were here," Nicholas said, chagrined to have been so unaware of his surroundings.

"We wasn't expecting you home so early," Uncle George said. No doubt he had explained to Gavin the nature of Nicholas's business with the St. Johns.

"You seem a bit preoccupied," Gavin said, clearly grinning with the pleasure of catching his friend off guard. "Is there some trouble?"

Still a trifle outraged, Nicholas told them what had happened without revealing his emotional turmoil.

"Dorian St. John refused the Seacombe amethyst!" Uncle George cried, nearly upsetting his brandy.

"I never heard of any lady turning down a betrothal ring," Gavin said with a wry laugh. "You do seem to have fallen upon some strange luck, Nicholas."

"What exactly was her excuse?" Uncle George demanded.

"There are scores of young ladies who'd give their eye teeth for that ring."

"Did it not suit her taste?" Gavin asked. "Ladies can be odd about these things. Eleanor was very specific about the sort of ring she wanted."

"Davis St. John did not like the marriage agreement?" Uncle George ventured. "He may be young, but I hear he's a shrewd businessman."

"I believe she liked the ring well enough," Nicholas said, taking a chair near the fire, the awe in her voice and the gleam of wonder in Dorian's eyes vivid in his memory. "Davis took no issue with the agreement. And Dorian was very pleased that you gave us your blessing, Uncle George."

"Then is she crying off the betrothal?"

"On the contrary," Nicholas said. "Miss Dorian St. John agreed that I should send out the announcement to the *Post*, *Gazette*, and *The Times* tomorrow, though it includes no date for the nuptials. I am the one debating about crying off."

Nicholas caught Gavin and Uncle George exchanging glances. He sipped his brandy once more, wondering what Davis would do if he decided to withdraw the offer to marry his sister. Not that Nicholas was afraid of the young man, but he didn't want to distress Dorian. Lord, how had he gotten himself into this mess, dancing a pretty jig to a stubborn lady's tune?

Uncle George leaned forward in his chair. "Has she shown you her piece of the Chamier music?"

"No. I could hardly ask to see it before the lady accepts the ring," Nicholas said, lounging back in his chair and extending his feet toward the fire.

"What's this?" Gavin asked, setting his snifter down on the table and leaning toward Nicholas. "Are you saying Dorian St. John possesses a piece of Chamier music?"

"Yes. And I have one, now, after the auction last week," Nicholas said.

"You have access to two pieces of Chamier's famous love

song to his mistress?'' Gavin half rose out of his chair. ''So you've not struck your colors on this?''

''I've never struck my colors before, at sea or at home,'' Nicholas said, still proud of his reputation as one of Nelson's best captains. ''You know that. Why should I start now?''

Gavin regarded him a moment longer before settling back in his chair. ''You've told me none of this.''

''You've been at sea, my friend,'' Nicholas said, a bit surprised at Gavin's assumption that he would give up his search for the truth.

''But if the story that was smuggled to you from the prison is true,'' Gavin said, ''and the traitor's name is written on the back of the music, you will soon know who betrayed you and Nelson's fleet.''

''If the many assumptions you've just made are true, Gavin, it's possible I will know the truth before long.''

Uncle George frowned. ''Nicholas, you're not leading this poor girl on for the sake of the music, are you?''

''No, I'm not leading the lady on.'' The irony of Uncle George's question amused Nicholas, especially after Dorian's lecture about the Seacombe amethyst and his true love. No one led the lady anywhere. ''I believe Dorian and I understand one another reasonably well. She is eager to complete the piece of music for her own reason—as I am.''

''So you are working together as a betrothed couple?'' Gavin said. ''For the purpose of finding the music. Then your intentions are not honorable?''

''No, it's not at all like that,'' Nicholas protested, not actually certain himself how it was. Dorian had offered the perfect out— she'd cry off when the time came—in other words, when the music had been found. Yet Nicholas found himself oddly uncomfortable with her solution, convenient though it seemed.

Of course he could cry off *now* and save a lot of aggravation—and never know what Dorian was doing or what she'd found in her search. The next sip of brandy burned uncomfortably all the way down to the pit of his belly.

"The *ton* and her brother will expect to see a ring on her finger," Uncle George said, echoing some of the thoughts that had been on Nicholas's mind. "Won't do the Derrington name much good to clear it of treason, then smudge it by compromising a lady—music or no."

"Precisely," Nicholas said, beginning to think that it might be better if he cried off now and saved himself pain and embarrassment later. He tossed off the last of the brandy.

Any bauble, indeed!

Chapter Ten

Davis decided a few days after Dorian's betrothal that he needed to make a trip to see his tailor. It was late in the spring to be ordering a new wardrobe, but he needed several things nonetheless. For one thing, despite his valet's miraculous talents, which he had boasted of to Susanna, Davis's hunt coat was beyond resuscitation.

For another thing, he wanted to be prepared when Elizabeth realized the error of her ways and looked in his direction again. She had always been impressed by a smartly dressed man. He wanted to look his best when his day arrived.

So, driving his curricle, he took himself and his valet off to his tailor in Conduit Street one warm partly sunny afternoon when nothing more promising appeared on his calendar.

As he drove through the streets, he was annoyed to find every red-haired woman of low station or high along the way caught his roving eye. The truth was, Lady Susanna had haunted his dreams and his waking hours since the house party at Tewk Abbey more than Lady Elizabeth ever had. Shockingly, his dreams had been filled with deliciously lusty images of Susanna Sunridge's fair bosom and narrow waist.

Davis didn't know what to make of his preoccupation with the widow, but he didn't like it one wit. He was put out with himself for being distracted by a woman of little social standing with tasteless fiery-red hair and an unfashionably voluptuous body—the thought of which had the power to make his groin ache.

For the next hour at the tailor's Davis was able to banish Susanna Sunridge from his mind. He fingered cloth samples, viewed the newest designs in waistcoats and coats, and selected what his tailor advised. Meyer was seldom wrong; only Dorian was more expert. Davis made his selections and was soon ready to be on his way home.

By the time he and his valet climbed into the curricle, dreary clouds had closed over the partly sunny spring sky and a slow rain had begun to fall. The cobbles were slippery and carriage sides glistened with moisture. They had driven several blocks and were nearing Covent Garden when traffic came to a standstill.

"Be a good man," Davis said to his valet, "and find out what the delay is."

The fellow took the umbrella they always carried in the curricle and did as he was instructed. Within a few minutes he returned. "It's a breakdown, sir. Lady Sunridge's hired carriage."

"Lady Susanna?" Davis groaned inwardly. Of all the people—what on earth was she doing in Town? He thought he'd overheard her say at Tewk Abbey that she was bound to visit some country cousin or other. "Did she recognize you?"

"Yes, sir," the valet said. "She and her maid are in a bit of a spot with all their boxes and packages and such. I'll offer my assistance if you like."

"No, stay here with the curricle," Davis said, resigning himself to doing the gentlemanly thing, though he wished some other gentleman had been about to come to her aid. Still, his body's wayward lust was hardly the fault of the lady; her deportment had been proper and above reproach.

Davis could not leave an acquaintance in distress. He handed the reins to his valet, took the umbrella, and started down the street.

"Mr. St. John, I am so glad to see you here," Susanna cried when she saw him. The rain had soaked through her parasol, spotted her pale blue bonnet, and caused the jaunty silk flowers on the brim to droop over her ears. The rain had streaked the thin stuff of her gown.

"Lady Susanna." Davis bowed. Her brilliant smile of relief actually made him feel small for his annoyance. "How may I be of assistance to you?"

"I do seem to always be in need of rescue when you are about." She shoved the dripping silk flowers aside and curtsied.

Then she proceeded to explain that one of the carriage wheels was broken and that the driver had gone off to see about a replacement. But in the meantime the carriage was clogging traffic. And she and the maid she'd brought along were being drenched while all the lovely things she had purchased were also in danger of being ruined by the rain.

" 'Tis very simple, dear lady," Davis said, with a sweep of his hand toward his waiting curricle. "I shall drive you to your abode and my valet and your maid will see to hiring another vehicle to bring your things along."

"Oh, that would so kind of you," Susanna said, a smile of adoring gratitude warming her amber eyes.

Davis had to smile in return, suddenly less sorry that he had stopped to help.

Within a few minutes Susanna was seated in the curricle and Davis had adjusted the calash top to make certain that they were both protected from the rain. The covering also obscured them from the inquiring eyes of others. Deftly, Davis maneuvered the little curricle around in the street and set out in the opposite direction to avoid the traffic.

"I didn't know you were in Town," he said, making conversation as they drove.

"Oh, my sister who lives in Russell Square was just delivered of a lovely baby girl. She wrote to ask if I would help her with the household and all. I could hardly refuse."

"Then we are destined for Russell Square?" Davis asked, recognizing the direction as a respectable part of Town.

"Yes. I do so hope that is not too far out of your way," Susanna said.

"Not at all, dear lady," Davis said. "How do you find Town this time of year?"

"Oh, it has been so long since I was here, I'm quite enjoying seeing it with new eyes." Susanna prattled on about making social calls and going to the theater and enjoying the street performers and the markets and the shops. New fashions. New fabrics. New furnishings. "Country life is all well and good for the mind and body, I suppose, but city life is so invigorating."

"And so it is," Davis agreed, touched by her enthusiasm for the crowded, dirty streets of London. "Also, perhaps you find it safer than fox hunting in Sussex."

"Oh, my." Susanna covered her blushing cheeks with her hands. "I was so embarrassed by that episode. I do hope you will let me forget that miserable moment."

Davis immediately regretted that he'd reminded her of her harrowing horseback ride. "Nothing to be embarrassed about, dear lady. All of us have instances when things seem to leap beyond our control."

"Mr. St. John, I can't imagine that ever happens to you."

Davis eyed her, observing how the curricle jostling over the cobblestones made her breast sway beneath the thin blue muslin of her gown. Stirred but conscience-stricken, he immediately turned his gaze to the street ahead of them. "I'm afraid I must admit to some weaknesses, dear lady."

Next to him, sitting close in the confines of the curricle, he felt her shiver.

"Are you chilled?" he asked, mortified that he had not thought of the possibility before now. "Here, take my coat."

Keeping one hand on the reins, he struggled awkwardly to get out of the tight-fitting garment.

"No, that's really not necessary, sir," Susanna protested. "I'm really all right."

"No, believe me, it's necessary," Davis insisted, continuing to struggle with his coat while he drove the team.

"Here, let me help you," Susanna offered, leaning forward so that Davis could see the tautness of her nipples against the delicate fabric of her gown and glimpse the deep valley between her breasts as she reached to help him. He looked away. Finally he was free of the garment and shoved it at her. "Put this around you."

She quickly did as he instructed. Davis heaved an audible sigh of relief.

They talked then of safer things, like how quickly her sister's baby was growing and how the weather would surely clear in another day or so.

"Oh, I recognize where we are now," Susanna said when they were within a few blocks of Russell Square. "My sister will be wondering what happened to me in this weather. I shall tell her I was well looked after by Mr. Davis St. John."

Davis smiled wryly. He hardly deserved such praise.

"You must come in and let us warm you with tea and sandwiches, or at least have a dram of port before you start back in this weather."

Davis shook his head as he drew the curricule to a halt in front of the number Susanna had given him. The street was deserted in the rain. To his relief, a groom dashed out of the ground-floor door to take the horses' heads and a footman jogged out to the curricule.

"Bring the lady a cloak and an umbrella to get her into the house dry," Davis ordered. The footman dashed back to the house to do his bidding.

"Yes, I must return your coat," Susanna said, beginning to slip the garment from her shoulders.

"No," Davis said, but the scoop of her gown was already visible. Davis stared at the dark, lovely valley between her breasts once more and sucked in a deep breath. "Susanna, may I kiss you?"

Susanna stared at him, her lips parted in delicious invitation. "Oh, yes."

She was reaching for him before her reply had registered in his lust-filled brain. Lacing her fingers through his hair, she pulled him down until his mouth fused with her hot lips.

Davis groaned, unable to hold back any longer. He dropped the reins, pulled her back into the shadow of the covered curricle, and slipped his hands inside his coat, up along her ribs, until he could enjoy the fullness of her breasts against his palms. He thrust his tongue deeply into her mouth where he was teased and tantalized with a sweet knowledge beyond anything the ladybirds of Whitechapel had ever offered him.

None of his intimate forays frightened her. None were rejected; all were met with her own questing tongue. Finally Davis had to release her, gulping for air as she kissed his cheek, trailing tiny, feathery kisses along his jaw. He could feel a feverish perspiration breaking out across his forehead. Those little kisses could drive a man mad.

He nibbled her ear, then her neck. His coat fell away from her shoulders, baring the warm, creamy skin of her throat and her breasts above the scooped neckline of her gown.

Davis hesitated, wanting to resist the temptation. But when she placed a breathy kiss against his ear he was lost. Cupping his hands beneath her breasts, he lifted them to bury his face against her white bosom. His nose pressed in that sweet valley, he inhaled her warm cinnamon scent. He feasted on the creamy smoothness of her skin and, through her sheer gown, he took aching delight in teasing her nipples with his thumbs until they grew hard and pebbly.

Susanna gave a shuddering sigh and stroked his hair. For

the moment Davis reveled in the sweet heaven of her bosom and the painful hell of his skin-tight pantaloons.

Somehow the sound of the footman splashing through the puddles on the pavement penetrated Davis's passion-drugged consciousness. He sat up and immediately began to pull his coat around Susanna again.

"Here's your footman," he said as evenly as possible, trying to clear his head of the lust that had so easily overwhelmed him. He was afraid to look into Susanna's face. What must she think? "You must go inside and sit before a warm fire and refresh yourself with some hot tea."

"Oh, of course," Susanna said, straightening her bonnet, which had been knocked askew against the side of the curricule.

He could feel her peering at him, but he refused to look directly at her.

Without further delay she alighted from the curricle on the arm of the footman. She stood for a moment under the umbrella the fellow held for her, looking up at Davis.

"I will be at the Floraton Court house party at the end of the month," she said in a small, hopeful voice. "Shall I see you there?"

"No, not I," Davis said without hesitation, taking up the reins once more. He'd seen the invitation to Floraton Court among the many that arrived at the house daily and had been undecided about accepting it. Now his decision was made. "I am committed to another engagement."

"Oh, well, then," she said, looking up at him rather like a forlorn, lost little girl instead of the seductress she'd just become in his arms. "Thank you again for your help, sir. Good day."

"Think nothing of it. Good day." Davis hastily slapped the reins on his team of matched bays to make quick his departure. There was nothing that could make him go anywhere near Floraton Court this season. Not now. If he couldn't keep his hands off Susanna Sunridge, he could at least be certain that he did not see her again.

*   *   *

Had she made a mistake? Dorian wondered the next morning as she sat at her writing desk trying to concentrate on answering her correspondence. All she could think of was last night's scene with Nicholas. Had it been wrong of her to refuse the Seacombe ring because she knew she was not the woman he loved?

His face had been so inscrutable, his gaze so noncommittal as she'd explained to him how beneficial their engagement was that she had no real idea of what he felt. Undoubtedly she had offended him.

Dorian toyed with her quill pen and shook her head. The books on deportment never explained how one should handle a predicament like this one. Uncertain what to do, she tried to concentrate on her letter writing.

The morning stretched on forever. Dorian jumped every time someone rapped on the door, hoping that Nicholas would send a note or some token that he was not angry with her. But no message came.

Dorian gave up on her correspondence, laying aside her pen and writing paper. What would she do if she lost his goodwill? If he suddenly was no longer a part of her life? Would his fragment of Franz's music become impossible to acquire?

Dorian didn't even want to think of that possibility.

To keep her mind off her worries she spent the afternoon reviewing the household accounts. She had taken the duty over from Aunt Charlotte last year when it had become obvious that the lady's health could not tolerate the stress and strain. A large household staff and the associated crowd of tradesmen was a constant source of small conflicts and irritating misunderstandings that had to be dealt with evenhandedly.

By the morning of the second day without a word from Nicholas, Dorian was certain that she'd lost his esteem. He must have changed his mind about their betrothal. The thought of not being able to have access to the piece of Franz's music tied an uncomfortable knot of fear in her stomach, for Aunt Charlotte's sake. The thought that she no longer stood in Nicholas's good graces made her heart grow heavy.

But she was too busy with Dr. Fisher's weekly call on her aunt to dwell on her concerns.

"What do you think?" Dorian asked as soon as they left Aunt Charlotte in her bedchamber, where the doctor had conducted his examination. She was not surprised to find Davis loitering there. He always seemed to remember when the doctor was due.

"How is she, Dr. Fisher?" Davis pressed.

"I think she is holding up very well," Dr. Fisher said, smiling up at Dorian and her brother through his thick spectacles. He was a small man, with a bald head and a clean-shaven face. He was unfailingly impeccable in his toilet and unfashionable in his dress. "Whatever it is that you're doing for her, continue to do it. She is as well—no, she is even better than I had expected."

"Then we have more time?" Davis asked, lowering his voice as they walked down the stairs.

"I wish I could say that," the doctor replied. "But I cannot. As I have told you before, I can make no promises, Mr. St. John. Despite her appearance I cannot change my prognosis. I allowed six months—and that was three months ago. I see no reason to change that. But by all means continue what you are doing for her."

Davis nodded, his mouth set in a grim line of disappointment.

After Dr. Fisher had departed Dorian squeezed her brother's arm. "But it's a good report, Davis, and we should be encouraged, don't you think? I am."

"I am encouraged," Davis said. "It's the compilation of Franz's music that keeps her going, isn't it?"

"I believe it is," Dorian admitted.

"Then we must pursue all our efforts to keep her occupied with the project."

"My plan exactly," Dorian said, unwilling to admit to her

brother that she had probably offended the one man who owned the most important piece of Franz's work. Mentally she began wording a conciliatory note to send to Nicholas Derrington, the Earl of Seacombe. Under the awkward circumstances, it seemed the prudent thing to do.

But why wait the torturous hours that the exchange of notes carried by footmen would take? Dorian thought as she watched Davis take himself off to his study.

She would just call on the earl and beg for his forgiveness. Why not? She never allowed herself to think of the impropriety of it. She just reached for the bell and ordered the carriage brought around.

Chapter Eleven

"I'm sorry, Miss St. John," the Derrington family butler said, bowing ever so politely to Dorian as she stood on the doorstep of the Derrington town house accompanied only by her coach driver and her tiger.

The butler was a tall, distinguished servant who obviously took great pride in his station and knew better than to offend a caller, however strange her errand might seem. "Neither his lordship, the Honorable George Derrington, nor Lord Seacombe are receiving callers today."

"Would you be so kind as to inquire if that applies to me, please," Dorian insisted, her heart pounding so rapidly at the audacity of her persistence that she was certain the butler and her tiger could hear the thuds.

"Yes, miss," the butler said, looking doubtful.

For a moment she thought he was going to make her stand on the doorstep while he did so. But he stepped back from the entrance and allowed her and her servant to enter. "Wait here while I inquire."

As they waited, her tiger, a servant hired by Davis, stared

off into space as if he had no wish to be associated with this lady who called upon gentlemen without a proper chaperon. Dorian was certain that he would report back to Davis about this call. But she didn't care. Soothing any ruffled feathers she might have caused was of primary importance. She prayed that Nicholas was at home because she feared if he wasn't, he was out looking for Chamier's music—without her.

Dorian stared at the ceiling, refusing to allow herself to entertain that unsettling thought.

The town house smelled faintly of cigars and leather and was decorated in a masculine, old-fashioned style befitting a country gentleman who preferred comfort—wooden paneling, brass fixtures, ancestral portraits, and military prints.

Dorian strained her ears for the sound of male voices anywhere in the house but heard nothing.

She was beginning to regret her hasty decision to confront Nicholas when he appeared, shrugging into his coat, a look of concern darkening his face. "What are you doing here?"

Dorian was so relieved at the sight of him that she ignored his brusque greeting. "I, uh, well, my lord, I came to see you."

He strode down the hall toward her, the butler in his wake. "Nothing is amiss, is it?"

"No. Well, yes." Dorian couldn't seem to decide what she wanted to say. She'd been so intent on seeing him that she hadn't rehearsed any particular speech.

Nicholas stopped before her. "Does Davis know you are here without a chaperon?"

"No," Dorian admitted. "I thought your uncle would be here."

"Uncle George is out at the moment." Nicholas took her arm and led her into the drawing room. He instructed the butler to send up the housekeeper with a tray of tea and cakes. A smile never touched his lips. "And what brings you to me under such questionable circumstances?"

Dorian took a deep breath and plunged into something like

an apology. "I felt perhaps I did not make myself very clear the other evening when you called."

"You made yourself quite clear," Nicholas said without meeting her gaze. He took her pelisse from her shoulders, then gestured toward a chair by the window. Dorian refused to be seated.

"That's what I was afraid of," she said quickly. "I did offend you."

Nicholas stopped in the midst of handing her wrap to the butler. "Offend me?"

"I pray you, forgive the way I tend to overstate things," Dorian said. "I'm certain that I must have said things very badly the other evening. Your generous offer took me by surprise. Though I know we do not care for each other as a betrothed couple should, I hope my insensitivity did not—I did not mean to seem ungrateful to you for your thoughtfulness—with Davis's challenge and all."

Nicholas regarded her for a long, quiet moment. "Do you wish to amend your response to my offer?"

Dorian hesitated. Much as she wished to win her way back into his good favor, she could not be dishonest. "No, my lord. I meant what I said about the ring belonging to the lady who captures your heart."

Nicholas nodded. "I thought as much."

"I just—when I did not hear from you I thought I should call to be certain you understood I was not indifferent to the honor that you did me by offering the Seacombe ring."

At that moment the housekeeper came into the room with a tray of refreshments. Nicholas led Dorian to the sofa. After they were served the servant retired to the corner near the fireplace and took up some sewing.

Dorian sipped at her tea. "Thank you for seeing to a chaperon."

A wicked grin flashed across Nicholas's face, dazzling Dorian and creating flutters in her belly. Perhaps not all was lost.

"Mrs. Estes is a fine lady, a loyal servant, and deaf as a gate post. We are free to discuss what we wish. I'm sorry if my lack of communication distressed you. It seems that neither I nor you had any idea how difficult it might be to come to terms over a betrothal masquerade—or to find a suitable bauble."

At the repetition of her careless words, Dorian felt the color rise in her cheeks.

"However, I did late yesterday have some success," Nicholas said, reaching into his waistcoat pocket. "I purchased this for you and you only."

With an inscrutable expression, he held out a fine emerald-cut sapphire set in gold and flanked by a cluster of diamonds on either side. "Will this do for your betrothal ring?"

Dorian stared at Nicholas, completely ashamed of herself for thinking that he was out searching for the music without her. He'd merely been shopping for a ring—for her. "My lord, this takes my breath away."

Nicholas smiled as if he was quite pleased and reached for her hand. The heartache that had been troubling her for two days eased. She allowed him to take her trembling fingers in his hand. He gently slipped the ring onto the third finger of her left hand. It fit perfectly.

"Are you chilled?" he asked, looking up at her suddenly. "Your hand is cold and you are shivering."

"Oh, no," Dorian protested. "Not at all. I'm—I'm just overwhelmed by the generosity of this gift."

"Now, am I allowed the privilege of kissing my betrothed?"

Dorian smiled at him nervously. "Of course, my lord." She closed her eyes and offered up her lips.

His lips touched hers briefly, airily, lightly brushing against them. When Dorian opened her eyes, disappointed with the shortness of the contact, she found him peering into her face, studying her mouth.

"Well, if that's all—" Dorian began, pulling away and thinking it must be time for her to leave.

" 'Tis not all, sweetheart," Nicholas murmured. "Come close again."

He clasped the back of her head in his hand, and with a low moan he pressed his lips to hers, urgently this time. Pulling her into the circle of his other arm, he skillfully used his tongue to tease her lips, seeking entrance.

With a thrill of excitement tickling in her belly, Dorian opened to him. All the fear that she'd lost him seeped away. She applied herself to kissing him with all the yearning and care she truly felt. She pressed against him, tasted his lips, explored the corners of his mouth.

He took all that she had to give, drawing her into him. The shock and thrill of it coursed through Dorian. She trembled and caught hold of his lapels to prevent him from pulling away. He only .pulled her closer. She could feel his heart beating rapidly beneath her hands and knew her heart was beating just as fast.

The clearing of a throat sliced through Dorian's senses. Nicholas abruptly released her.

"Excuse me, my lord," said the housekeeper, looming over the back of the sofa, rattling the lid in the teapot she'd recovered from the tray. "Do you and the miss require fresh hot water for your tea?"

Nicholas withdrew his arm from around Dorian, annoyance marring on his handsome face.

The housekeeper regarded him, nonplussed. "Your uncle would be most unhappy with me if I did not see to the proper care of his guests."

Dorian couldn't meet the lady's eyes, or those of Nicholas. She would have gladly gone on and on with the kiss whether the housekeeper was in the room or not. She still wanted to. The thought shocked her.

"Quite right, ma'am." Nicholas shifted uneasily on the sofa. "We want no spots of scandal on our betrothal, now do we?"

"No, of course not," Dorian admitted.

''I thought not,'' the housekeeper said, then returned to her chair and her sewing.

''I'll take you home,'' Nicholas said. ''I've had word from a cleric at a small church across town that he may have something of Franz Chamier's in his collection.''

''A new lead?'' Dorian sat up straight and tried to shake the lethargy of the kiss from her mind. ''You could have gone without me.''

Nicholas grinned. ''I considered it. But what good would it do me to gain one piece of Franz's music and lose the other?''

A week later Dorian dropped another stack of old manuscripts onto the table. Dust plumed into a cloud around her. Desperately, she grabbed her handkerchief just in time to catch the sneeze, a great noisy eruption that no lady would ever wish to admit to.

''Bless you.'' Nicholas looked up at her from across the church attic where he was also sorting through papers. This was the third church they had searched in the last week to no avail. Dorian had been glad to have his help. ''I'm not finding anything here either.''

''I don't believe it's here,'' she snuffled from behind her handkerchief.

''It surely was good of the old curate to allow us to search through his collection,'' Dorian said, fanning herself with a large page of music. She and Nicholas had spent over two hours in the warm, dusty attic room, looking through piles of music that made up the collection of the old churchman. The stacks were only minimally organized. ''But everything here is church-related. I hardly expect to find Franz's love song to Aunt Charlotte among these hymns.''

''I've seen nothing but hymns,'' Nicholas said. ''And I honestly believe that after all this time I finally know what I'm looking at when I study a page of music.''

''We've spent enough time here to establish that it's highly unlikely that the fragment of Franz's music is here,'' Dorian said with a weary sigh.

''I agree.'' Nicholas dusted off his hands and walked around the table to stand beside her. ''Let's go. I'm sure we can find a sunnier and cooler place than a stuffy church attic to spend the rest of the afternoon.''

''Let's have lemonade with Aunt Charlotte in the garden.'' Dorian smiled up at him, aware that there was more to her innocent invitation than he would perceive. Aunt Charlotte had asked to meet the Earl of Seacombe again, now that he was to become part of the family.

Although the betrothal allowed them to spend a good deal of time together without questions being asked, Aunt Charlotte had not felt up to receiving guests or meeting Dorian's betrothed until recently. Now Dorian found herself regretting a few things that she had told Aunt Charlotte about Nicholas.

But she decided that it was time to make the most of Nicholas's calls at the St. John Mayfair town house. Surely if he knew her aunt better, he would reconsider his determination to keep Franz's music from her—if they found it.

''Lemonade in your garden sounds like a splendid idea,'' Nicholas agreed. He smiled as he reached for Dorian's hand and started down the attic steps. ''I should like very much to meet your Aunt Charlotte, the woman for whom Franz Chamier used his last piece of paper to write her a love song.''

By the time Dorian and Nicholas arrived at the town house Aunt Charlotte had risen from her afternoon rest. But she had not yet descended from her room. Nervously, Dorian instructed that the garden table be laid with a pitcher of fresh lemonade, small sandwiches, fruit, and iced cakes.

When all was ready she sent the butler to fetch her aunt. Then she turned to Nicholas. She had no other choice but to trust him in this.

''There is one thing I think you should understand before Aunt Charlotte arrives.''

Nicholas turned to her, looking incredibly handsome in his

dark blue coat, snowy white shirt and shiny black boots. "What's that?"

"Aunt Charlotte has lived a rather unconventional life." Dorian's courage flickered uncertainly. She took a deep breath and began again. "As a musician, and a lady interested in the arts, she has associated with people who think differently about love and marriage. She entertains some rather unorthodox but strong beliefs about men and women."

"Yes? I've heard something to that effect." Nicholas nodded, but his expression revealed nothing but interest in her words.

"Well, she seems to believe that because we are betrothed we are lovers," Dorian said, avoiding Nicholas's gaze. Then she hurried on. "You see, she believes that love is a gift and a treasure to be given wholly and generously. It is not an emotion to be fettered by ceremonies or contracts. Rather an unusual notion, I agree, but—there it is."

Surprise flashed in Nicholas's blue eyes. The smile disappeared from his face.

Dorian's face burned with embarrassment. "I inform you now so that you will not be surprised by the assumptions she may make about our relationship."

"I see," Nicholas said. He clasped his hands behind him and turned away, pacing along one of the gravel paths between the flower beds.

Dorian glanced down at the betrothal ring on her finger, still hardly believing that he had presented it to her when she'd called at his town house. "I realize this may require a little more effort in making the pretense of our betrothal credible, but I thought you should know what Aunt Charlotte will expect of us."

He stopped his pacing and turned to her once more "You wish me to not only act the part of an attentive fiancé in public, but also to portray the part of your lover to your family?"

Dorian gulped in a rather unladylike manner and tried to smile. "You sum it up very well, my lord."

"Of course, as my betrothed, you will reciprocate?"

"Of course," Dorian agreed. How difficult could that be?

"We will never know when we are being observed," Nicholas reminded her. "We will have to be consistent in our treatment of each other at all times. If we are to be convincing, that is."

"Only when we are with Aunt Charlotte."

"Still, I must be thoughtful of your wishes, indulgent even," Nicholas said.

Dorian nodded nervously.

"You must heed mine," he added.

Dorian hesitated, suddenly feeling she was being led somewhere. "Just how do you mean, my lord?"

"Well, as the future Countess of Seacombe you must give second thought before you go gadding about without a proper chaperon or me as your escort."

"You sound suspiciously as though you've been talking with Davis," Dorian snapped, unhappy with Nicholas's attempts to curb her independence. "I shall endeavor to avoid impulsive 'gadding about,' as you call it, my lord, but I treasure my freedom to come and go as I please."

"And I would never think of interfering with that," Nicholas said. "Your independence is even charming at times, but do consider your safety if appearances are not of importance to you."

"So I shall," Dorian said, turning away with a frown on her face. Being betrothed was going to require some adjusting.

Nicholas reached for her hand and pulled her toward him again. "There is responsibility in truly loving one another," Nicholas said, stroking her knuckles with his thumb and smiling at her patiently. If a certain softness had not come over his face, his words would have made her feel trapped. "When one truly loves another he or she can no longer be careless with her welfare. She has become an important part of another's life and she owes it to her lover to take every care of herself."

Dorian listened, wondering where he had learned so much about love, wishing he felt that way about her.

Then, in a spontaneous and disarming gesture, Nicholas bent and brushed a light, warm kiss across her fingers.

"That is the part we are to play, is it not?" he said, peering into her eyes with a smile that seemed to mock her. "The rôle of true lovers?"

Dorian sucked in a breath. Her belly fluttered and tears welled in her eyes.

Instantly she withdrew her hand from his and swallowed her rash tears. She reached for the lemonade pitcher, eager to put the subject of love behind them. "Yes, that is our rôle, but 'tis a rôle only. Shall I pour the lemonade?"

"Indeed," Nicholas said. She could feel him studying her.

Yet as she poured from a crystal pitcher, the truth Nicholas had spoken about the responsibilities of love raced through her mind. "I've often thought that if Franz Chamier had truly loved Aunt Charlotte, he would never have allowed himself to get murdered while he was in prison."

"A man rarely *allows* himself to get killed for any reason," Nicholas said, standing over her as she filled the glasses. "But in Chamier's case I regret to say the poor man had already decided that his first love was his country."

"I'm afraid you're right," Dorian agreed, handing a glass to Nicholas. "The man was a patriot first, a composer second, and—well, but I would never hint of any of this to Aunt Charlotte."

"No, of course not."

"However, I understand that loyalty to country and homeland is an important thing to a man," Dorian continued, wondering what Nicholas's first love was.

He quirked a brow at her. She understood that she was treading into sensitive territory. She only wanted to tell him that she understood how important clearing his family name was to him, but before she could say more she heard Aunt Charlotte's voice.

"My dears," Charlotte called from the threshold of the conservatory, where she stood patting the violet turban atop her head. She wore a violet gown and her soft white hair was dressed in a wreath of curls about her face. She smiled at them girlishly. "Forgive me for taking so long to come down. My maid was fussy with my hair today. I said 'Just tuck it under the turban, Mary,' but she insisted on a few curls for his lordship."

"You look lovely," Dorian called loud enough for her aunt to hear. In an aside to Nicholas she muttered, "Remember, we are betrothed and we are lovers."

"How could I forget?" Nicholas murmured in return and slipped a possessive arm around her waist. His touch made Dorian grow warm and weak. Then he spoke more loudly.

"Indeed, Miss St. John." Nicholas clicked his heels together and gave the hint of a bow. " 'Twas worth the wait."

Aunt Charlotte's shy smile broadened. She stepped onto the garden path, headed right for Nicholas, and offered her hand. "I do adore gentlemen of the sea. They are so gallant and in such a dashing way."

Nicholas accepted her hand and bowed courteously over it. Aunt Charlotte bobbed a curtsey.

"So, my lord, now you are Dorian's betrothed," Aunt Charlotte said, looking him over as if she had not met him once already at the musicale. "My niece is an unusual young lady and will require a husband who is undaunted by her originality."

"I'm well aware of that, ma'am," Nicholas said.

"I'm so pleased," Aunt Charlotte said. "Dorian despaired of ever finding a husband who would tolerate her temperament, but I knew she would. She is too lovely and special not to be snapped up by an extraordinary gentleman like yourself."

"You are too kind, Miss St. John."

"Oh, you must call me Aunt Charlotte now," she said. "You are part of the family, or will be soon enough. Have you two set a date?"

"Ah, well," Dorian stammered, casting an appeal for help in Nicholas's direction. "We thought perhaps in a year or so."

"Why so long?" Aunt Charlotte exclaimed. "The days slip by more quickly that you expect. Now that you have found each other, don't let unimportant things keep you apart."

"I have some business I wish to conclude first," Nicholas said. "But that should not take long. We might be able to wed in a matter of months. Wouldn't that be wonderful, sweetheart?"

Nicholas pulled Dorian close and smiled at her; the light of mocking sincerity flashed in his blue eyes.

"Oh, I'm so glad to hear that," Dorian said with a weak smile. The man clearly intended to be as difficult to deal with in the guise of lover as he could possibly manage.

"Yes, and then I could be present at your wedding," Aunt Charlotte said. "I would so like that."

"And so would we, of course," Dorian agreed, eager once more to change the topic of conversation to something more neutral and less connected with the future—hers or Aunt Charlotte's. "Let's have our lemonade, shall we?"

For a few moments they exchanged comments about the weather and the flowers coming into bloom in the garden. Nicholas turned his full charm on Aunt Charlotte. He dusted off the garden bench for her. They sat side-by-side, discussing nothing of any great importance. Dorian was encouraged at first—until she overheard Nicholas bring up the subject of Franz's music.

"I would like very much to see the work you've done in compiling Mr. Chamier's music, ma'am."

"Wonderful," Aunt Charlotte said. "I'm always pleased to discover another lover of Franz's music. I'd be delighted to show you what I have."

Apprehensive, Dorian sipped her lemonade and dropped into the garden chair. Cold fear coiled deep inside her: tight, icy, and sharp. Why did she feel she'd unwittingly invited the fox into the dovecote? Of course, this was what Nicholas had wanted from her all along—access to Aunt Charlotte and her collection.

All she could do now was pray that once Nicholas saw how gentle and loving Aunt Charlotte was, how devoted and adoring, he would be won over to her side.

Chapter Twelve

Nicholas no longer had any doubt that he was complete master of himself. How else could he have remained civil and sane through the last hour while Aunt Charlotte showed him Chamier's work, page by page?

The parlor where they were seated, and where Aunt Charlotte worked—judging from the stacks of music on the pianoforte— was stuffy despite the French doors opened onto the garden. Nicholas longed to remove his coat, loosen his neckcloth, and dig into the stacks himself. But convention required that he politely allow the lady to show him her collection.

All the while he was keenly aware of Dorian drifting restlessly around the room. She did not trust him; he was sure of it, and that fact annoyed him. Like his colleagues who had been so quick to believe the tales of his betrayal, she lurked in the room, ready to believe the worst of him.

Still, he did not have time to deal with her and her doubts now. He was about to see the second piece of the love song that could prove him innocent of charges of treason.

"Here, it is: the fragment Dorian said you were interested

in seeing," Aunt Charlotte said, at last opening a dark red folio. Tenderly, the lady took the fragment from the folder and laid it on the table before him.

Nicholas was almost afraid to touch the piece of paper at first. Other than the fact that it was faded, it appeared to be a perfectly ordinary piece of music manuscript with bars marked into measures and spotted with stemmed notes. Nonetheless, it held a clue to the truth.

"His other work is hardly as faded as this," Nicholas said, curious about the condition of the manuscript.

"That's because he wrote it in prison, where he had to make his own ink," Aunt Charlotte said. "You see, being locked away from the world and even from musical instruments could not keep Franz from his composing."

Movement across the table made Nicholas glance up to see Dorian sit down across from him, her eyes studying his face, questioning his motives.

"He worked in the cold, half-starved," Dorian said.

The dark concern in her eyes touched Nicholas, but he could not afford to indulge himself in soft feelings at the moment—no matter how much he might want to help Dorian and her aunt.

Dorian continued. "Despite our efforts to get food and water to him, little of what we sent got through. But that could not keep him from composing this last song dedicated to Aunt Charlotte."

"He was a man of great energy and determination." Aunt Charlotte leaned closer, as if she was confiding something that Nicholas should know. "And he believed in justice above all things."

Nicholas stared down at the fragment and wondered if justice had been on the composer's mind as he wrote this music for the woman he loved.

"You may look at it more closely," Aunt Charlotte urged. "I understand you have another part of this music."

"Yes, I do," Nicholas said, unsurprised that Dorian had

informed her aunt of the facts and feeling a bit uneasy, knowing he had no intention of giving up his portion to Aunt Charlotte. "I have the top portion where Franz Chamier wrote the title, 'A Whisper of Violets,' and signed his name."

"'A Whisper of Violets,'" Charlotte repeated and sighed. The wistful sound knifed through his conscience.

Dorian huffed and leaned across the table. "Then you understand how important this piece is to Aunt Charlotte."

"Now, Dorian, there is no reason to become upset with his lordship over this," Aunt Charlotte said, reaching out to pat her niece's hand. "I have a lot of empathy with anyone who values Franz's music."

"I know, but—"

"It's all right, Dorian," Aunt Charlotte said with the serenity and patience that Nicholas suspected her niece would probably never achieve. "His lordship may look his fill and no harm done."

Dorian huffed once more but remained silent.

"Please, my lord, examine it closely if you like," Aunt Charlotte urged again.

Carefully, Nicholas turned over the fragment, only managing to steady his hands through sheer force of will. He found on the back what he expected to find; the last few letters of the name that could clear his reputation. The jagged rip split one letter, but the last two were relatively clear—Greek letters.

"I have no idea what the writing on the back means," Aunt Charlotte said. "All I know is that paper was scarce in prison and Franz, or someone else, wrote on the back of the music, but I can't imagine for what purpose."

"Do you read Greek?" Dorian asked, her eyes narrow with suspicion.

"Some," Nicholas said. "I was a navy man, a ship's captain, not a scholar."

"I believe the last letter is—" she began.

"Sigma," Nicholas supplied for her. "I think the other letter is an epsilon . . . or another sigma. One has to allow for writing style, and then it's difficult to be certain because of the tear."

"What does it mean?" Aunt Charlotte asked.

"I don't know," Nicholas admitted.

"Are there also Greek letters on your portion?" Dorian asked.

Nicholas nodded. "Delta, then an alpha. The third letter is obscured by the tear."

"So the third or middle portion holds the essential letters," Aunt Charlotte said, leaning forward to study the characters more closely. Nicholas looked up to see that she was almost as captivated by the puzzle as he was. Then she asked, "Do you suppose they are the initials of a secret society?"

"I hadn't given that a thought," Nicholas admitted. "I was thinking it is the name of a master spy or a spy ring."

"Spy ring? Of course, a definite possibility," Charlotte said, tapping her finger on her chin.

"May I remind you that the third piece bears the heart of Aunt Charlotte's song," Dorian told them, scowling as if they were wayward children.

"Oh, I do not forget that," Aunt Charlotte said. "I was merely trying to help his lordship. These letters seem to be important to him."

"But we are not giving up our portion," Dorian said, glaring purposefully at Nicholas.

"Certainly not, dear," Aunt Charlotte said. "Please notice that his lordship has not asked that of us either."

"Indeed, I would never think to ask you to do so," Nicholas added quickly. He wanted nothing to provoke Dorian's suspicions and fears further. "I do appreciate the opportunity to examine your fragment and to admire the work you've done in compiling Chamier's work. 'Tis a prodigious effort you have mounted here."

"It means much to me," Aunt Charlotte admitted.

"And your pride in the work is evident." Nicholas watched Charlotte carefully tuck the fragment back into the red portfolio.

The healthy color that had glowed in her cheeks when she'd first come into the garden had drained from her face. "I fear I have overstayed my time here."

"Oh, no, my lord," Aunt Charlotte protested.

But Nicholas rose and took his leave. Dorian followed him into the passage, beyond Aunt Charlotte's hearing.

Nicholas turned to her. "I trust you keep this work in a safe place. It has become very valuable."

"I daresay it has," Dorian said. "We have offers for Franz's work daily. We keep the original pieces of the collection locked away, except when Aunt Charlotte is working on it."

"Good," Nicholas said, disappointed that he had not learned more that was of help to him but certain now that someone knew the truth. "Pray keep the house locked. Whoever the third piece of music identifies will be eager to have it."

"I understand." Dorian sounded annoyed with him for believing her foolish enough to behave otherwise. "The house is always secure."

"Very well," Nicholas said, still nettled by Dorian's suspicions, though he was determined to keep that from coming between them.

"Now that you have seen for yourself how important this music is to Aunt Charlotte," Dorian said, wringing her hands, "I hope you will reconsider your demand to have the originals of each piece."

The soft look of appeal in her eyes nearly made Nicholas capitulate. But he couldn't, even if he wanted to.

He stopped short of the door and eyed the butler.

Dorian appeared to understand his gesture. "That's all, Barton. I will see Lord Seacombe out."

Barton bowed and smiled knowingly. "As you wish, Miss Dorian."

"I wonder what that was about?" Dorian asked as the butler disappeared belowstairs. "Barton never smiles. He considers it bad form."

"He thinks we wish a private moment for a farewell."

"He does?" Dorian lifted her startled gaze to Nicholas's face. "Do we?"

"Naturally." Nicholas moved closer and spoke in a low voice. "Kiss me, sweetheart. The upstairs maid is watching us from the landing and the parlor maid can see us in the drawing-room mirror. We must keep up the guise of our engagement."

Dorian pressed her lips together in irritation. "You are shameless, my lord."

"I know," Nicholas admitted as he bent to claim his kiss. Wary though she was, he found her mouth soft and warm. To his satisfaction, she kissed him back, stretching up on her toes and placing her hands briefly on his coat lapels.

Nicholas wrapped his arms around her and pulled her close, cherishing the feel of her soft contours against him. A shiver ran through Dorian's body, delighting him. He nibbled at her lips and drank in the soft whimper she uttered. More than ever he longed to find the proof he needed to clear his name, not just for the honor of his family, but to prove himself to Dorian.

"I am not a traitor," he whispered against her ear. "Believe me. Trust me."

She smiled weakly. "I want to, my lord. Oh, how I want to."

Nicholas leaned over his uncle's shoulder, peering once more at the fragment of music he had laid out for them to study. As soon as he'd arrived home from the St. John town house, they had adjourned to the study and ordered the lamps lit though it was still daylight. They needed every advantage as they viewed the fragment again.

"Alpha, iota or mu, then omicron followed by mu." Uncle George wrote out the Greek letters Nicholas recited for him. He was seated at the desk with Nicholas behind him. They had both spent hours over the small, faded piece of manuscript.

Now, armed with the information Nicholas had gained from seeing the St. John fragment, they hoped another look at their own piece would reveal some new clue unseen before.

"The meaning is not obvious," Uncle George said without looking up from the fragment. "Oh, by the by, I forgot to ask; does your lady like the bauble you found for her?"

Nicholas smiled to himself, recalling the pleasure—and relief—he'd seen on Dorian's face when he slipped the sapphire ring on her finger a week before. Her kiss had been unforgettable, too. "She seemed pleased enough."

"I should think so," Uncle George said. "Though I can't imagine any young woman refusing the Seacombe amethyst. You are officially betrothed, then?"

"Officially," Nicholas repeated, musing over Dorian's request that they treat each other as lovers before her aunt. He rather liked the idea.

"Frankly, Nick," Uncle George began, "I'm surprised you decided to take a wife before this mystery is solved."

"I had no intentions of doing so, Uncle George," Nicholas admitted. "I would much rather wed after this shadow is removed from the Derrington name, but betrothal to Miss St. John offers certain unique advantages."

"Such as having the opportunity to view the second fragment," Uncle George suggested. "I hope you know what you're doing, Nick."

Nicholas offered no reply. Things were not exactly progressing as he'd first planned, but a good battle plan always left room for maneuvering. Victory came with preparation, planning, and the ability to make the most of new opportunities as they presented themselves. He could find no reason to be dissatisfied with the commitments he'd made so far. But he didn't expect Uncle George to understand that. He wasn't certain he understood his feelings for Dorian himself.

They both contemplated the fragment in silence.

"Damme if I know what these Greek letters could mean," Uncle George said with a shake of his head. "I thought we would find the name of a man. With the beginning letters and the last ones you learned, surely between us we could recognize a name. But this?''

Nicholas took a cheroot from the box on his uncle's desk, lit it from the lamp, and sat down by the cold hearth. ''I expected a surname, too, or a spy's code name. Aunt Charlotte suggested something interesting, a secret society.''

''Now there's a possibility,'' Uncle George agreed. ''Clever lady. I hadn't thought of that. Admiral Nelson had a number of enemies here at home as well as among Napoleon's officers. They might have banded into some society to accomplish his end, or at least his embarrassment.''

Nicholas shook his head. ''Somehow I still think that is a remote possibility. One man was responsible. The more people involved, the more likely the truth would have been revealed already. You know the old saying—three men can keep a secret if two of them are dead.''

''I see what you mean,'' Uncle George said. ''Then there is another possibility.''

Nicholas glanced at his uncle, wondering what he might have missed.

''Perhaps this composer fellow didn't actually know the information that it has been rumored he knew,'' Uncle George offered. ''Maybe this note is just a scribble.''

Nicholas drew on his cheroot. ''I thought of that, too, but if Franz Chamier didn't know something, why was he murdered? Even his fellow countrymen who found his rebellious ideas so dangerous had little reason to kill him. He was in jail, out of the way, where he could cause little trouble in his homeland.

''No, I think he knew something that incriminated an Englishman, just as the rumors have said. Somehow he sent the message out on the pieces of music before his enemy could end his life. We are left to interpret what he wrote.''

''That seems sensible enough,'' Uncle George said. ''But

even knowing what is on the second portion is not enough to solve the puzzle.''

"No, we have to have the third fragment, wherever it is,'' Nicholas said. ''The problem is, whoever this piece of music names is looking for it, too, and will probably do anything to keep it out of my hands.''

Chapter Thirteen

Dorian was hardly prepared for the furor—or the complications—the announcement of her betrothal to the Earl of Seacombe brought into her life. Daily the silver salver on the hallway table was piled high with notes of best wishes and invitations from curious members of the *ton*, and she shared the invitations with Nicholas, who called every day. He was a most attentive fiancé.

Twice an unpleasant surprise appeared among the invitations. Both times Dorian had been so unprepared that she was unable to keep them from Nicholas. Especially the first one.

It had appeared to be just another bit of social correspondence. The stationery was of a high quality, though the handwriting appeared a bit strange.

"Oh," Dorian said when she read the first one.

"What is it?" Nicholas dropped the invitation he had been scanning and reached for the note that had startled her. "You just turned as white as a ship's sail."

Dorian fumbled with the note, wanting to hide the thing, but it was to late. He'd already snatched it from her hand.

He read it, a dark expression of displeasure passing over his face before he glanced up at her. "You don't believe this, do you?"

"Of course not," Dorian said, despite the fact that she was so shaken that her hand trembled. The note, written in an obviously disguised hand, accused Nicholas of the vilest of treasonable acts, betraying his king, his country, and his navy. The author claimed to be informing Dorian of these things "for her own good." "The writer won't even dignify his claims with a signature. It's nothing to take note of."

"Have there been other notes such as this?" Nicholas asked, fixing Dorian with a gaze that would instantly recognize a lie. "Anything at all like this?"

"No, nothing," Dorian said with perfect honesty. "Burn it. I won't have such nonsense in the house."

Nicholas frowned. "You must tell me if you receive more of these."

"Of course I will my lord," Dorian said, turning to the other invitations, eager to be rid of the thing.

Without another word, Nicholas tossed the note onto the small fire that had been lit to take the chill off the morning room. The paper caught flame and disintegrated into ashes. Dorian forgot about it.

Ordinarily once they sorted through their social obligations, Nicholas would take her for a drive in the park. She had the distinct impression he liked very much to be seen with her. And she rather liked being seen with him. Almost without exception, people looked twice when they saw them together. Dorian liked to think it was because they made a fine-looking couple.

Dorian's days were filled with sending out acceptances, fittings for new gowns—she could hardly appear in her old wardrobe now that she was to become a countess—and with an assortment of engagements in Nicholas's company.

She had little time to look in on Aunt Charlotte as often as she liked or to wonder why Davis had suddenly dedicated himself to his work at the import business. That her brother accepted only invitations to events where he knew Lady Elizabeth would be present was no surprise to Dorian, but his lack of interest in anything else was a change.

Still, her schedule was too full with Nicholas and social activities for her to question Davis about his mood. No doubt once Lady Elizabeth looked his way again he would become himself once more.

What seemed more curious to her was Nicholas's behavior. Dorian thought his sudden interest in the social scene strange for a man who, until a few months ago, had practically lived the life of a hermit.

Now he wanted to be seen everywhere. He insisted on accepting invitations to musicales, soirees, the theater, and balls.

One night, as they drove home in the carriage from one of the countless engagements they attended, Dorian decided to question him about accepting so many invitations.

"Someone has the third piece of music," Nicholas said. No lamp burned inside the carriage and Dorian could not see his face in the shadows. "The more people we see and talk to, the more likely we are to hear some clue that will help us."

"But I barely know some of the people who are sending us invitations, and I fear they want us at their ball or soiree only as a curiosity," Dorian protested.

"A penalty we must suffer for the sake of our investigation," Nicholas reminded her, seemingly unperturbed by her questions. After a pause he asked, "Have you not enjoyed our outings?"

"Well, no. I mean, yes, I have enjoyed most of them," Dorian stammered honestly, sorry that he had reminded her that their betrothal was only a pretense. In private moments with him she found herself longing to believe that their engagement was real.

She'd come to quite enjoy the advantage of dancing at a ball with gentlemen who knew that Nicholas lurked somewhere about. She had the same number of dance partners as before;

she was an heiress, and there had always been plenty of gentlemen to partner her. Most had been eager to create a favorable impression; some had been overbearing in their presentation of themselves; others, mostly penniless aristocrats, had been quite arrogant.

Now her partners were unfailingly polite, occasionally curious. She couldn't say whether this behavior was out of respect for her betrothal to a peer of the realm or their fear of a man thought to be a traitor. Neither prospect enthused her.

Whichever the case, balls became more of a pleasure for Dorian, and the musicales also proved more entertaining. It was clear Nicholas was learning more about music than he'd ever known before or cared to know. He had developed quite a good ear for music and even seemed to enjoy some of it.

"I was quite proud of you at the musicale this evening," Dorian said.

Nicholas turned to her, surprise on his face. "How so?"

"You sat through that ghastly solo by Lady Weston without turning a hair." Dorian found herself taking an unreasonable amount of pride in his accomplishment.

He grinned. "I displayed no less fortitude than the company I was in. I saw no one cringe when she reached for high C. But I must admit that I had to wonder if someone should suggest to the lady that she take up painting."

Dorian chuckled. "I fear she is quite devoted to her music. I must admit that I am amazed by your patience, my lord. Even I who love music and have spent much time listening to all levels of accomplishment found myself impatient with the performance this evening."

"But not the company, I hope." Nicholas took off his hat and moved from his place opposite Dorian to sit beside her.

Dorian's heart beat faster. His thigh was hard and warm against hers. The citrus scent of his shaving soap reached her as he slipped his arm around her shoulders. Nicholas had been a gentlemen at all times in all things when they were in public or in the presence of Aunt Charlotte or Davis. But every touch of his, no matter how proper and casual, even his scent, often left her weak-kneed and light-headed. While she knew he meant nothing by these simple displays of familiarity, she found she was not indifferent to them.

The memory of his intimate farewell kiss in the town house hallway had made Dorian's heart race each time she thought of it. No kiss of his since then had offered the same passionate intimacy. She wondered breathlessly when he might advance on her so again.

"No, my lord," Dorian whispered, with the heat of a blush rising in her cheeks. "I have enjoyed the company as much or more than the outings."

"I'm glad to hear that. So have I." He leaned close, touching her chin and guiding her mouth to his.

Dorian accepted the kiss eagerly and boldly ventured to stroke Nicholas's thigh. He groaned deep in his throat, caught her errant hand, but deepened the kiss. It was wet and hot, yet not urgent or awkward like the stolen kisses she'd allowed her other suitors.

Passionately, his lips rubbed hers apart. His tongue probed and explored, thrusting deep into her mouth on daring forays. Dorian reached for his close-cropped hair, clutching handfuls, clinging to him and pressing her mouth to his. He pulled her closer, stretching his thigh across hers and slipping his hand down her back to turn her until her breasts were pressed against his waistcoat.

Dorian whimpered. Nicholas released her lips, then kissed his way down her throat and chest and nuzzled her breasts.

"Give me more, Dorian," he murmured against her throat. It was not a demand or a plea—just a request that Dorian knew a lady should not honor. Her breast tingled and grew heavy in the palm of his hand. She knew only his mouth would relieve the restless pressure.

Beneath her pelisse she slipped the shoulder of her low-cut gown down her arm far enough to bare her breast. She had never done such a thing before for any man. He made her ache with need. When her breast was bare, she was surprised to find she felt no embarrassment, just the desire to please him and to find her own pleasure in his touch.

"More," Dorian whispered, lacing her fingers through his hair again and offering herself to him.

She barely had time to feel the chill of the night air against her bare skin before his open mouth sought the raised nipple of one breast and closed over it. It beaded against his flicking tongue.

Dorian arched her back. The tugging of his mouth drew a splendid heat from deep inside her. She sighed with the thrill and the satisfaction. He moved to her other breast, freeing it and then tugging with the same need and giving the same pleasure. The first ached with cold and loss.

As if he knew, he covered it, cupping her breast in his hand, teasing the nipple gently with his thumb. Uttering a soft cry of exquisite pleasure, Dorian longed for him to push her down onto the seat and lie with the full length of his body pressed against hers as he'd done on the bed at Tewk Abbey.

She held him back, allowing herself to slip down onto the cushion. He followed her down, his mouth tender and persistent on her breasts.

The carriage jolted over something in the street. She heard the voice of the driver calling to the horses over the clatter of their hooves on the cobblestones.

Nicholas released her breast, his face pressed against her throat, breathing heavily.

The carriage moved on, seeming to hit every rut along the way.

Nicholas cursed. He sat up and pulled her with him. "This won't do."

Annoyance flared in his eyes. He began rearranging his waist-coat, then he reached for her.

"No, I'll do it," she protested, already pulling at the shoulders of her gown.

"No, let me," he said, his voice husky, the command of a captain in his tone. Dorian let her hands drop away.

Patiently he eased the fabric up over her shoulders, tenderly tucking her breasts away in a fashion that only renewed all the heat that had been flowing through Dorian. Then she realized that just enough light from the street lamps seeped into the carriage for him to see the white outline of her breasts and the rosy buds of her nipples, which he studied as he worked.

When he was finished Nicholas kissed the fullness her neckline exposed. "I only regret there was no lamp in here."

"I think you saw enough, my lord."

Dorian pulled her pelisse close around her shoulders. "Nicholas?"

"What is it?" In the darkness, he seemed intent on rearranging his clothing again.

"Do all betrothed couples do things like this in the dark?"

"I have no idea what all betrothed couples do," Nicholas said. From the sound of humor in his voice he obviously found her question amusing and naive. "My only concern is what happens between us. And as tempting as it is to be alone with you like this, the carriage is not the right place."

"Not the right place for what?"

"For what nearly passed between us."

Dorian glared at Nicholas, confused and frustrated by the way he always cut short their intimacies. Did these stolen kisses and caresses not affect him at all?

"Oh! I see what you mean." She made no attempt to hide her irritation. " 'Twas much more comfortable to seduce me in my bedchamber at Tewk Abbey. Wouldn't you agree, my lord?"

Even in the darkness of the carriage she saw the sudden flare of his nostrils and the telling desire that smoldered in his eyes. He wanted her; she was sure of it. The knowledge thrilled her.

Instead of her words goading him into continuing as she'd hoped they would, Nicholas threw himself into the seat across from her. "Indeed. Don't thrust out that truculent lip at me, Dorian. It will win you nothing."

In one swift movement he braced his foot on the edge of her seat. Dorian started, then stared at the Hessian boot pressing her legs so close to the carriage wall she could not move. The black leather gleamed in the dim light that penetrated from outside the carriage. His instep rubbed suggestively against her silk-covered knee—the gesture possessive and insolent.

She glanced back at him. But shadow fell over his face so she could no longer read his expression as he slouched in the seat across from her.

"The fact remains, sweetheart, that I do not deflower virgins on the jostling seat of a carriage."

Disappointment—and jealousy—curled uncomfortably in Dorian's belly. She opened her mouth to protest her maidenly condition but could not. Nor could she help but wonder what other virgins there might have been in Nicholas's life. What other women had offered themselves to him? And had he been so infuriatingly noble and virtuous with them?

"*Now*—tell me what you know of the Marquess of Fernham."

"Lord Fernham?" Dorian repeated, confused by the sudden turn in the conversation. Nicholas wanted to talk of Fernham as if nothing had happened between them! As if she hadn't almost surrendered her body—and her heart—to him.

She took a deep, shaky breath. "Let's see."

Determined not to make more of a fool of herself, she pulled her pelisse closed at her throat and worked to discipline a mind still wayward with desire. "I believe Fernham inherited his father's collection of musical instruments and is continuing to add to it. He decided to collect music to go along with his inventory of instruments."

"Then he is a good candidate," Nicholas said.

"Yes, indeed," Dorian agreed, resigning herself to this new topic of discussion. "Lady Fernham considers herself something of a botanist. I hear the flowers in her conservatory are

"Lady Susanna, the widow?" Dorian blinked at him in surprise. "I've heard she's going to be at Floraton Court."

"I know." Davis nodded. "What else?"

"She's just out of mourning for her husband, who possessed a baronetcy in Devonshire."

Davis nodded. "Children?"

"No, I don't believe so, but doesn't she seem the sort who would be a wonderful mother? So warm and gentle."

Davis cleared his throat and shifted on the carriage seat across from Dorian. "Family connections?"

Dorian eyed her brother more critically now. So many questions about Susanna Sunridge. "I believe her father is a vicar."

"A vicar?" Davis groaned.

"Not just any vicar," Dorian baited. "The third son of the Hamilton-Joneses. You know, the fifth Earl of Heathfield."

Davis head came up. "The Hamilton-Joneses?"

Dorian kept a smile of satisfaction from her face. "And I believe her mother was the fourth daughter of the Viscount of Sarsden. Fine old connections, somewhat prestigious but not particularly profitable. Nothing for an ambitious man to build on."

"The Viscount of Sarsden," Davis repeated with just a touch of awe in his voice. "So that is how she comes to be invited to all the parties."

"Indeed, that and, you must admit, she is delightful company."

"Yes, oh yes," Davis agreed quickly. "Despite her red hair, she possesses a certain charm. A luscious figure."

"You noticed?"

Davis slid her a look that told her he was ignoring her sarcasm. "Is she being courted by anyone, or is she partial to some gentleman?"

"I've heard of no one," Dorian said, secretly delighted by her brother's interest but aware that she must not show it. There was no quicker way to send Davis off in another direction than to show her approval of what he was doing. "Whoever weds

Susanna will have to be satisfied with her treasure of virtues and attributes, I'm afraid. But I'm certain she will be snapped up by some lucky, discerning gentleman by the end of the Little Season.''

Dorian paused for effect, knowing from Davis's scowl that he was listening very closely. ''Yes, by the end of the season, I'm sure of it, if not sooner.''

''Hmm.'' Davis turned away to watch the ponies grazing across the Floraton Court park.

Dorian studied his face. His eyes had grown dark with some sort of concern. His lips were pressed together in a grimace. She thought his interest in Susanna reassuring. Still, she couldn't be certain just what Davis thought of Susanna Sunridge.

No matter how hard she tried, her own mind was preoccupied with questions about Sir Gavin's wife, Lady Eleanor. She prayed for a dowdy, countrified woman.

Lady Eleanor was a gracious beauty.

Dorian silently berated herself. Of course the lady would be attractive; nothing less could hold a man like Nicholas. But she had not been prepared for the perfection of the lady's person: dark chestnut hair with huge brown eyes, a long graceful neck, white shoulders, and a willowy figure endowed with just enough bosom to be flattered by the high empire fashions of *en vogue*.

Dorian and Davis were the last to arrive at Floraton Court, so they joined the tour of the house late. Nicholas came to Dorian's side immediately. Hasty introductions were made so as not to interrupt Lord Fernham's lecture on the wonders of Rome and the way his father and the architect had worked to bring them to Floraton Court.

Lady Eleanor smiled distantly as she made Dorian's acquaintance. Dorian's own smile froze on her face. The lady was so much more handsome than she had anticipated, she felt quite put out. Nicholas kept them near Sir Gavin and Lady Eleanor throughout the entire tour. The realization of Nicholas's attraction toward the lovely lady—wife of a friend or not— left Dorian feeling oddly uncertain of herself.

Lord Fernham led the way through the house, proudly pointing out the state bed that had been installed for the king's visit of a decade ago. Dorian stared at the red coverings and matching draperies without seeing them. Everyone in the company admired the room and its fine decoration, but Dorian hardly heard a word. She was busy studying Lady Eleanor's shining curls, piled artfully atop her head.

Surreptitiously, Dorian touched her own hair, blond, thick and heavy and refusing to curl. It insisted on hanging down her back—sometimes even into her face—despite the most securely placed combs or her maid's best efforts with pins and curling irons.

They filed through the great marbled hall once more and into the library. Lord Fernham pointed out his collection of letters from famous men of history. His pride and joy was a letter signed by Peter the Great of Russia.

As he chattered on, Dorian studied Lady Eleanor's complexion. She judged the lady's pale and flawless skin to be the envy of every woman in the party. No roses bloomed in her cheeks, as they always did in Dorian's. Dorian wished she had taken the time to powder the color from her face when she freshened up instead of rushing through her toilet in order to find Nicholas.

Leading them down another long windowed corridor, Lord Fernham launched into a lecture about his musical instrument collection. Dorian barely brushed her hand along the edge of the pianoforte.

Lady Eleanor's mouth was perfection itself. Her lips formed the perfect small bow that fashion dictated as the stamp of true beauty.

Self-consciously, Dorian chewed on her lips and glanced up at Nicholas, who remained at her side. What did he think of her mouth? She had always known her lips were too full, and too distinctly wine-colored, and her mouth too wide. Pressing her fingers against her lips, she wondered why she'd been born with this mouth, and why she'd never been troubled by its lack of perfection before now.

As they left the music room, Lady Fernham led them along another corridor to the greenhouse.

When they entered the room, filled with sunshine and plants, Dorian could see that it was something of a marvel. Unlike the old-fashioned orangeries that were little more than long, high-ceilinged passages with windows facing the south, the green-house was a building of three masonry walls with glass windows to the south and to the sky and the sun above. The large room was tiered with beds of vibrant violets, fragrant lilies, and exotic orchids. In the center sat a sofa, cushions, tables, and chairs.

"I often take tea here among my flowers," Lady Fernham said with a sweeping gesture. "Plants are such fine company, except, of course, when I have a house full of my good friends as I do today."

The group laughed as expected. Lady Eleanor smiled at her hostess, then turned the same lovely expression on Nicholas.

Shy and uncertain of herself for the first time in her life, Dorian latched onto Nicholas's arm. He was watching Lady Eleanor, admiring the lady's smile, no doubt.

Nicholas turned to her at her touch, yet his smile seemed a bit cool, distracted.

"Is something wrong?" he asked.

Dorian realized how sober she must appear to him. She shook her head. "Oh, no. I just wanted to share the loveliness of the greenhouse with you."

"Full of flowers the color of your eyes," Nicholas said.

Though she knew his words were mere flattery, Dorian couldn't resist returning his smile and feeling the smallest glimmer of hope flutter in her heart.

"You are too kind, my lord," Dorian said, but when she looked up at Nicholas again to call his attention to a singularly beautiful lily he was staring at Lady Eleanor once more, a sad longing in his eyes.

HERE'S A SPECIAL INVITATION TO ENJOY TODAY'S FINEST HISTORICAL ROMANCES— ABSOLUTELY FREE! *(a $19.96 value)*

Now you can enjoy the latest Zebra Lovegram Historical Romances without even leaving your home with our convenient Zebra Home Subscription Service. Zebra Home Subscription Service offers you the following benefits that you don't want to miss:

- 4 BRAND NEW bestselling Zebra Lovegram Historical Romances delivered to your doorstep each month (usually before they're available in the bookstores!)

  - 20% off each title or a savings of almost $4.00 each month

  - FREE home delivery

  - A FREE monthly newsletter, *Zebra/Pinnacle Romance News* that features author profiles, contests, special member benefits, book previews and more

- No risks or obligations...in other words you can cancel whenever you wish with no questions asked

So join hundreds of thousands of readers who already belong to Zebra Home Subscription Service and enjoy the very best Historical Romances That Burn With The Fire of History!

And remember....there is no minimum purchase required. After you've enjoyed your initial FREE package of 4 books, you'll begin to receive monthly shipments of new Zebra titles. Each shipment will be yours to examine for 10 days and then if you decide to keep the books, you'll pay the preferred subscriber's price of just $4.00 per title. That's $16 for all 4 books with FREE home delivery! And if you want us to stop sending books, just say the word....it's that simple.

It's a no-lose proposition, so send for your 4 FREE books today!

Chapter Fourteen

Davis decided on the third evening at Floraton Court, as the string quartet struck up a country dance, that it had been a terrible mistake for him to have come. For the first two days every time he tried to catch Susanna Sunridge's eye she turned away. He had told himself it was mere coincidence, but by the third day, when she left the room as he entered, he could no longer think of her evasive actions as happenstance.

Susanna Sunridge wouldn't even nod a greeting to him across the room.

Not that he didn't deserve a bit of a cut after his behavior in Town, Davis silently acknowledged as the informal dancing began. His actions had been appalling. And he had lied to her about coming to Floraton Court—with the best of intentions—but he had lied. Undoubtedly she was offended.

The evening was warm, perfect for country dancing. The mood of the company had mellowed after imbibing fine wine with an early supper. Davis decided that he would at least ask Susanna to dance. She could hardly refuse before the amiable company. She would have to allow him to touch her with everyone in the house watching. Oh, how he wanted to touch her.

But, most importantly, he would apologize for his unforgivable behavior. She at least deserved that, though he didn't expect it to ease the ache that grew in his groin every time he remembered the warm womanly scent of her that he'd found in the valley between her breasts.

The truth was, he didn't know exactly why he had come. Part of the reason was because he'd begun to realize that Elizabeth was serious in her intentions to find another suitor. A rumor had reached him that Herby Dashworth, a viscount and the heir to a dukedom, was calling on her. Davis said nothing of it to Dorian. An I-told-you-so was the last thing he needed to hear from his twin sister.

What he did need—and desired desperately—was a live, breathing, soft, responsive woman in his arms. He had no desire for a Cyprian, regardless of how skilled and seductive she might be. He wanted Susanna Sunridge. Since he'd forgotten himself that day in the rain, he'd been unable to think of anyone else. He'd relived that moment every day—of the way he'd filled his hands with her generous breasts, of the way they'd swelled in his hands, of the way she'd sighed and kissed his ear.

He'd tried to tell himself that seeing her again would get the need out of his system. She was hardly the first woman he'd been intimate with.

Now that she stood across the room from him, wearing a pale yellow gown, her vibrant red curls swept off her neck and her arms bare—begging to be touched—his desire for her only grew. Maybe she wasn't the first woman he'd been intimate with, but she was the only woman he'd ever wanted to pleasure as well as seeking his own gratification.

As he watched her, she accepted another offer to dance. The music was lively, and the country dances were rowdy. She laughed at something her partner said as she moved gracefully through the steps. Davis frowned, envying the pleasure the fellow must be experiencing with Susanna in his arms.

Davis suddenly had second thoughts about approaching her for a dance. What if she did refuse him in front of all the guests?

He started when someone tugged at his sleeve.

"That shade of yellow looks quite nice with her hair, doesn't it?" Dorian said, watching Susanna as closely as he. "You're going to ask her to dance, aren't you?"

"Ask who?" Davis said, not wanting his sister to know how much Susanna Sunridge had come to occupy his thoughts. "I don't know who you're talking about."

"Yes, you do." Dorian grinned. "I've seen how Susanna looks at you when she thinks you won't take notice, and how you watch her when you don't think she will observe you. You want to dance with her. I'm certain she'll be delighted to dance with you."

"You don't know any such thing," Davis said, knowing it would do useless to deny what Dorian said. But he had strategy of his own. "I see Seacombe enjoys dancing with Lady Eleanor. Her husband doesn't seem to mind one wit. In fact, Seacombe seems to be quite enchanted with Lady Eleanor."

" 'Tis only natural. They were childhood friends." Dorian's generous mouth thinned into a grim line, as it did whenever something pained her. Davis turned to see Lord Seacombe and Lady Eleanor laughing as they executed some complicated step in the dance. "Is he neglecting you?"

"Of course not." Dorian twisted the sapphire ring on her finger.

"But what?"

"Lady Eleanor is so lovely, Davis." Her voice was low and troubled. "So demure and compliant. So perfectly fashionable."

"No more fashionable than you," Davis said, surprised by Dorian's uncharacteristic self-doubt.

The music came to an abrupt end and the dancers applauded the string quartet's performance.

Dorian gave Davis a gentle shove in Susanna's direction. "Go ask Susanna now. No second thoughts. Do it."

Davis decided she was right. He struck out across the marble hall that was being used as a ballroom and strode across the floor right up to Susanna before he had time to think again and lose courage.

"Lady Susanna." He bowed before her.

She looked up at him, her amber eyes darkening with some emotion about which he didn't care to speculate.

"Mr. St. John," she greeted without offering her hand.

"May I have the next dance?" Davis blurted.

Susanna glanced around the room as if she hoped to find someone coming to her aid. "So kind of you to ask, but—but I have promised the next dance to Lord Fernham."

"There you are, Lady Susanna," Lord Fernham called, as he bustled out of a crowd of his guests. "Dear lady, we do have the next dance, don't we? Would it disappoint you overmuch if I begged off? So naughty of me, I know, but Sir Gavin has asked to see the musical instrument collection more closely. St. John, be so good as to dance with the lady for me, won't you?"

Lord Fernham leaned close to Susanna, as if to confide in her, but spoke loudly enough for all to hear. "You'll enjoy the footwork of a younger man more than my tripping about, I assure you. There's a good man, St. John."

Just as suddenly as he'd appeared, Fernham was gone, leaving Susanna committed to dancing with Davis, whether she liked it or not.

Susanna looked up at Davis once more, an expression of vexation pinching her pretty mouth. "It would seem you may have the next dance."

"Lord Fernham's misfortune is my good luck." Davis reached for her hand as the music began. Perhaps she was reluctant to dance with him, but at least he would have his opportunity to say what he wanted to say.

The first few complicated figures of the dance did not allow for him to say much to her, and she moved through the pattern without looking at him. Her hands were warm and her movements easy and supple. As they paraded around the floor arm-in-arm, to Davis's surprise Susanna opened the conversation.

"I had not expected to see you at Floraton Court," she said.

"A change of plans," Davis said. "And I wanted to see you."

She indicated no surprise; they danced on.

Davis gulped down the second thoughts that threatened to render him silent. "I wanted to apologize for my behavior in the curricle. It was uncalled for. You were the perfect lady and I—I don't know."

"I had wondered what I did to invite you to take such a liberty," she said, though she appeared to be concentrating on the dance steps.

"Nothing, nothing at all," Davis hurried to assure her. "But I find you so attractive and I'm afraid I—well, my baser nature got the better of my good manners. Though I know my actions were unforgivable, I've come to Floraton to beg your forgiveness."

The next part of the dance separated them. Davis could only wonder what Susanna was thinking as she danced in the line of ladies across the floor from him. She smiled politely, as though she was enjoying the dance, but her expression revealed nothing.

Finally they were reunited for the last figure of the dance. Davis had nearly given up hope that she would give him a response.

"I must confess, Mr. St. John, that I also find you attractive," she said, with hardly a change in her polite smile. "You need not apologize for your actions in Town. Nor ask for forgiveness, for I don't believe you committed any offense requiring it."

Davis paused, lost in astonishment. *She found him attractive!* he marveled. He completely lost the rhythm of the music. She tugged on his arm and helped him move into the next pattern.

"You are too kind, Lady Susanna," he stammered, his head

swimming with the possible implications of her words. *She found him attractive;* he could not free himself from that wondrous discovery.

"Not at all, Mr.—Davis?" she whispered. "May I call you Davis?"

He nodded. "May I call you Susanna?"

"Yes, please, Davis."

They smiled at each other, enraptured. Her smile was no longer merely polite but warm and inviting. Davis gave himself up to the golden amber of her eyes as the dance came to an end.

"Lady Susanna, dear." Lady Floraton seized Susanna's arm. "The men are deserting us for the billiards tables, so the ladies are setting up a game of cards for ladies only. Sorry, St. John. You'll have to content yourself with billiards. Come, dear."

"Of course." But before allowing Lady Floraton to drag her off to cards, Susanna turned to Davis once more and gazed up at him with a wistfully shy smile. "If you should care to know, my room is southernmost on the third-floor passage on the right, overlooking the pony park. Thank you, Davis, for a most enjoyable dance."

She offered her hand. Davis seized it and kissed it, boldly stroking her palm with his thumb. Her gaze held his as he told her, "The pleasure was mine, dear lady."

After she had gone Davis stood rooted in the middle of the ballroom, too shocked, amazed, and delighted to move. *Southernmost room on the third-floor passage on the right,* he repeated to himself silently over and over again to burn it into his memory—as if he could ever forget where to find Susanna Sunridge.

Lord and Lady Fernham insisted on including the children in many of the amusements, which Dorian thought a delightful change from the adult sophistication of most house parties.

Sometimes the after-supper games were led by the children—

five girls and three boys—who were delightfully precocious. Other times they would perform songs or readings for the company, just as the ladies did. Sometimes the adults joined in the children's games of crossquestions or jackstraws.

Despite the good-natured merriment of the house party company, Dorian felt as though she'd been cut adrift. Davis was distracted by Susanna Sunridge and Dorian was glad of that. But he was also too preoccupied to listen to her fears and doubts.

Nicholas seemed to have eyes only for Lady Eleanor, his childhood friend and now the wife of a former colleague. While the other ladies of the party were very nice, Dorian hardly knew any of them well enough to confide in them.

She could only look on in frustration while Nicholas danced with Lady Eleanor, or joined her in a foursome to play whist. Yet she could not complain that he was an inattentive fiancé. Without fail, he appeared at her side when he was needed to escort her into supper or to offer his arm whenever the social situation required it of him.

But then, since she'd arrived at Floraton Court, she'd found that Nicholas's gaze frequently drifted in Lady Eleanor's direction. Though Dorian could find no fault with his treatment of her when he was at her side, she sensed that his thoughts lingered elsewhere. Even when she brought up the subject of the music, he treated it with a certain careless indifference. It was almost as if he'd forgotten why they were there.

She couldn't help but wonder what Sir Gavin thought of the attention Nicholas was paying to Lady Eleanor.

The one tradition at Floraton Court that the Fernhams insisted on observing each afternoon was the feeding of the ponies. Lady Fernham and the children were inordinately fond of their ponies, and neither drove nor rode anything other than the shaggy beasts. To the Fernhams, the four-legged creatures were more than a mode of transportation; they were pets. And the ponies loved their privileged position, taking full advantage of the favor they enjoyed.

Each afternoon after the park was cleaned so the ladies wouldn't soil their slippers or the shine be dulled on the gentlemen's boots, the children led the company out to feed the ponies. This event was followed by a tea with sandwiches; then everyone retired to their room to dress for supper.

The informality of the daily outing allowed the company to mix more than it might in the confines of the house, which lent itself to the segregation of the sexes: men in the billiards room or smoking over the dining-room table, ladies in the drawing room, performing in the music room, or reading in the library.

Dorian watched Nicholas wander off toward Lady Eleanor, who was feeding a white mare and foal alongside one of the children. Davis and Susanna seemed to be making a shy effort to speak to one another. Casually, Dorian followed Sir Gavin toward a gray gelding one of the Fernham boys favored with some apples.

Sir Gavin turned and handed her an apple. "Here, you feed him. He is a greedy one."

Dorian reached for the apple. The gray snatched the fruit from Dorian's hand almost as soon as she'd taken it from Sir Gavin.

Surprised, they both laughed.

"See what I mean," Sir Gavin said, taking more apples from the Fernham boy. "Let's find a more docile creature, one more appreciative."

Obligingly, the Fernham boy led his favorite gelding away from them. A golden filly ambled forward, casting a hopeful look in their direction.

Dorian offered the pony the apple. "Are you enjoying the party, Sir Gavin?"

"Yes, I am," he said, as if he was surprised by her question. "Lady Eleanor and I have not had much opportunity to move in social circles, with the war and my naval career keeping me at sea so much of the time."

"Yes, I'm certain that must be disappointing for Lady Eleanor," Dorian sympathized.

"Oh, she has made no complaint," Sir Gavin said. "I'm just glad for this opportunity for her to be out and about in the right places. She is lovely, is she not? She deserves to be on display."

"Indeed, unique," Dorian agreed, following Sir Gavin's gaze in the direction of his wife, who was still chatting with Nicholas. "I understand you, Lady Eleanor, and Lord Seacombe were childhood friends."

"Yes, we were," Sir Gavin said, turning back to Dorian. "That was long ago, but in the old days I used to think Eleanor loved Nicholas, and he returned her feelings."

Dorian's heart beat a little faster, but she tried to remain calm. She slipped another apple to the golden filly, who seemed to have attached herself to them.

"A childhood infatuation," she said. "How dreadful for you."

"I was young and my feelings where resilient," Sir Gavin said. "But Nicholas was only a third son. Eleanor's family disapproved of the time she spent with us, especially with Nicholas. With two older brothers, no one ever thought he'd become the Earl of Seacombe one day."

"I suppose not," Dorian said. "So Lady Eleanor looked higher?"

"No, but her family did," Sir Gavin said. "It was my own good fortune that Eleanor developed an interest elsewhere on her own. She told me once that she thought Nicholas was too ambitious. Too competitive. I sometimes wonder what would have happened if Nicholas weren't quite so driven. Ambition can be a cruel thing."

"Ambition?" Dorian repeated, a little shocked at Sir Gavin's insight. He'd seemed so supportive of Nicholas when he'd been confronted by Captain Kenwick at the musicale in Town.

"I suppose Eleanor will always have feelings for Nicholas," Sir Gavin went on. "And so shall I, for that matter. There were good times together.

"And you, Miss St. John," Sir Gavin began after an embarrassing pause. "Are you enjoying the festivities? The Fernhams certainly are a unique family, are they not?"

"Yes, and I enjoy their warm hospitality," Dorian said.

Sir Gavin leaned closer. "And have you and Nicholas found what you are searching for?"

"We've not had an opportunity to look for it," Dorian said, a bit surprised by the question. She'd expected remarks of a less personal nature from Sir Gavin. "Nicholas has asked if we might see the music library, but Lord Fernham has been too busy leading his guests through other activities to show us his collection yet."

"I know why Nicholas wants the music," Sir Gavin said. "He believes it holds some clue to prove his innocence of the treason he is purported to have committed. But I'm not certain I understand your interest in acquiring the music and why you are helping Nicholas."

"It's for my Aunt Charlotte," Dorian said, uneasy about revealing so much to this man whom she did not know well, no matter if he was a close friend of Nicholas's.

"Ah, yes, she is a collector of Chamier's music," Sir Gavin said, appearing to have been enlightened. Dorian suddenly realized that he assumed that her betrothal to Nicholas was based on her aunt's connection with the music he wanted.

"I'm on a search of my own," Dorian said, lest Sir Gavin think her a fool for allowing Nicholas to draw her into a meaningless betrothal.

"How so?" He studied her, seeming truly interested.

"I want the complete music for my aunt," Dorian began to explain. "You see, it is a love song that Franz composed for her, his last work as far as we know. It's just coincidence that on the back is written the proof that Nicholas searches for. But I must have the love song for Aunt Charlotte before she dies."

Sir Gavin frowned. "The lady's health is in danger?"

"Dr. Fisher only gives her a few more months," Dorian said, suddenly overwhelmed by the reality that she usually could keep at bay. Tears threatened, but she gulped and blinked them away. Nicholas would never understand her fear that she wouldn't be able to produce the music before Aunt Charlotte left them.

"I'm sorry to hear that," Sir Gavin said, scratching the pony behind the ears. "I feel there is one more thing that I must say to you. Nicholas is a very single-minded man. He will stop at nothing to get what he wants. Eleanor knows that."

The golden filly nudged Dorian's knee, begging for the other apple she held in her hand. Numb with the doubts and fears that crowded into her mind, Dorian gave the apple to the pony.

"I know you think me a disloyal friend for telling you these things about Nicholas," Sir Gavin said. "I'm eternally grateful that Eleanor realized her mistake when she did. But I thought you should know so you can protect yourself and your aunt. You are a strong woman. You know your own mind, and you have your brother to protect you, but beware of Nicholas."

When Dorian turned back to ask Sir Gavin something more she found that he'd left her side. Nicholas was still talking with Lady Eleanor, who regarded him with an enraptured smile on those perfect, bow-shaped lips.

Nicholas looked so handsome in the dark blue he always wore, the nankeen pantaloons and shiny black boots. A lock of dark hair had fallen across his brow and his eyes were light with laughter at the ponies. Her breath caught in her throat. She tried to vanquish the doubts that Sir Gavin had just planted, but shadowy uncertainties lingered. She knew as well as anyone that Nicholas was a very determined man.

She wondered if Sir Gavin had listened to his own words of warning. Perhaps he trusted his wife, but could he trust his own competitive, ambitious childhood friend?

"This one likes you," Nicholas said of the dappled pony that insisted on nuzzling Eleanor's skirt. This was his first opportunity to talk with her privately since they'd all arrived, and he was glad of the informal setting.

"Do you have another apple?" Eleanor asked, fending off the persistent equine. "Quick, he's going to stain my gown."

"I can remember when you cared little for what happened to your skirts." Nicholas immediately distracted the pony with an apple snatched from the basket carried by a servant. The image of Eleanor climbing an apple tree flashed through his head. There had been moments, when they were children, that he'd thought Eleanor might be the most daring of the four Lincolnshire friends. "I remember when you were the first to the top of the apple tree."

"What a memory you have. That was a long time ago," Eleanor said with a laugh. "We've grown up, or have you not noticed?"

"I noticed," Nicholas said, admiring her graceful figure and long, elegant neck.

"Oh, Nicholas, I'm so glad you are here and that you've decided to appear in Society again," Eleanor said, with a swift glance at the others to see if they were being observed. "We've not had a chance to talk in private since before Trafalgar and Jonathan's death and all that followed."

"There isn't much to say about those things," Nicholas said, more interested in knowing how her life had been with Gavin than discussing his own past.

"How terrible you must have felt, losing command of the *Dauntless,* and then seeing Jonathan and the men of the *Daedalus* go down as well—and not be able to do anything but bear the blame for all of it."

"It was difficult." Nicholas blocked thoughts of all the memories her words evoked and took an apple from another passing servant's basket. "Let's see if this little black fellow would like a treat."

Obediently, Eleanor offered the apple to the pony, who sniffed it discriminatingly and then with a switch of his elegant tail snatched it from her hand. Nicholas and Eleanor laughed at the pony's haughty greed.

Eleanor cast Nicholas a regretful smile and touched his arm.

"I'm sorry. I brought up painful memories for you, didn't I? But I have thought of you so often, of your career in ruins, of your family dead. Oh, Nicholas, I can only guess how painful these past two years have been for you."

"I have survived well enough," Nicholas said, feeling his back stiffen with annoyance at the tenor of pity in her voice. Pity was the last thing he wanted from Eleanor or anyone else. "I have thought of you often also, and wondered if that oaf of a husband of yours is making you happy."

"Oh, Gavin and I are very happy." A glowing smile lit Eleanor's face. "Never fear on my behalf."

But then a new thought seemed to occur to her. "Pray do not hold winning command of the *Dauntless* against Gavin. True, he longed to command a ship of the line, just as you did, but he never intended for it to be *your* ship."

"Of course not," Nicholas said, astonished that she should think that he'd hold Gavin's good fortune against him.

"But, of course, you have the title now, Earl of Seacombe," Eleanor said with a pleased smile. "Who of us would have thought all those years ago you'd inherit? You do have a talent for landing on your feet, Nicholas."

The black pony moved in closer, nudging Nicholas's leg this time. He gave the creature another apple, all the while wondering how anyone could believe that seeing his career in ruins and losing his father and two brothers could be called "landing on his feet." "The sea was always my dream, Eleanor. You sailed in my little sloop with Gavin, Jon, and me when we were children often enough to know that."

"But even if a naval career is lost to you," Eleanor said, her voice sympathetic as she scratched the pony behind its ears, "you have the riches and the power of a nobleman. Be thankful, Nicholas, that no one could ever prove anything against you."

"I am grateful for many things, Eleanor, but lack of proof is not one of them."

Eleanor frowned at him, clearly not understanding what he meant. Nicholas knew she, like many others, misunderstood his determination to learn the truth about what had happened to his good name and Jon Collard's life.

"I'm glad for your happiness with Gavin," Nicholas said, satisfied he'd learned what he wanted to know. "I think I'd better see how Dorian is doing with these wheedling little creatures—and your husband."

Dorian smiled uncertainly at Nicholas as he approached. Gavin had already moved on to feed some other ponies with the Fernham children. Her sudden pallor troubled him. He wondered suddenly what Gavin had told her. "Are you all right, sweetheart? Is something wrong?"

Dorian shook her head, forcing a smile to her lips. "I'm very well, my lord."

She lied; Nicholas knew it from the way she avoided his gaze as she took his arm. He put his hand over hers and squeezed it, sorry that he'd failed her somehow. Eleanor might be happy, but his own betrothed wasn't. He promised himself he'd remedy that very soon.

Chapter Fifteen

"Here's the key to the music library, Seacombe," Lord Fernham said, handing a long skeleton key to Nicholas. "Deuced spooky mourning ring you wear there. For Lord Nelson's untimely death, I suppose."

"No, actually, not," Nicholas said, reluctant as always to explain the ring and acutely aware of Dorian's watchful gaze on him. The reasons why he wore the ring were too personal to reveal. "But I wear it in memory of a friend, a true, loyal midshipman of mine who died at the Battle of Trafalgar, as Admiral Nelson did."

"What was the midshipman's name?" Dorian asked, her eyes dark and serious.

Nicholas shook his head at her. Now was not the time to unearth old obligations and deeply buried sorrows.

"Damnable shame and bad luck, losing Nelson, but then, we won the battle," Lord Fernham said with a shake of his head. "What's done is done. Take the key and show the lady the music library. I ain't too keen on this outing to the village fair with the children and the ladies, but what can a gentleman do, what? Though there might be a good horse race to put some ready on.''

''I'm not much of a gambler on the horses, my lord,'' Nicholas said. ''Miss St. John and I have been looking forward to exploring your music collection.''

''Good, then have at it,'' the marquess said. ''Glad to have someone enjoy it. The children would rather spend their time out of doors with the ponies than with the music.''

''Thank you,'' Nicholas said, taking Dorian's hand and leading her away.

''You never told me you wear that ring for one of your midshipmen,'' Dorian said, annoyance and hurt in her voice.

''I did not believe it of interest to you,'' Nicholas said, satisfied that Dorian was ignorant of the details of his alleged treason.

''And why not? We are betrothed,'' Dorian said, quiet indignation in her voice. ''Shouldn't everything about you and how you feel be of concern to me?''

Nicholas stopped in the middle of the corridor leading to the music room and stared at Dorian, wondering if she really understood what she was saying.

She halted also and stammered, ''I mean, if we were truly betrothed, everything about you would be of concern to me.''

Nicholas smiled at her. ''And if we were truly betrothed, I would feel likewise, I'm sure.''

Dorian pursed her lips in annoyance. ''Of course, if we were truly betrothed.''

Nicholas cast her a sidelong glance. Had their charade worn as thin with her as it had with him? he wondered. She'd been petulant and pouty since the afternoon in the pony park. Stepping aside, he gestured for her to precede him. She swept past with a twitch of her skirts and Nicholas followed, admiring the sway of her hips.

''Is everyone going to the fair?'' Dorian asked, wondering if they were going to be able to work alone together.

''At first I thought Lady Eleanor and Sir Gavin might like

to join us,'' Nicholas began. ''That would make our examination of the library completely proper and above suspicion, but then the marquess seemed so unconcerned that I thought it unnecessary to invite anyone else.''

''Lady Eleanor was eager to go to the fair,'' Dorian said, chewing on her lip as if she must solve some mystery.

Nicholas grinned. ''Eleanor likes country fairs. She'll have Gavin buying every trinket and oddity that strikes her fancy.''

They arrived at the locked door of the music library and Dorian turned. Her eyes had grown large as she stared up at him. Nicholas realized she wasn't being petulant or pouty at all. Something genuinely troubled her. ''What is it, sweetheart?''

''Do you envy Sir Gavin?'' she asked.

Nicholas tried not to show his surprise by proceeding to put the key in the lock. ''What brings this on?''

''He told me that you and Lady Eleanor planned to marry once.''

''Whatever possessed Gavin to tell you that?'' Nicholas said, mystified and annoyed by his friend's behavior. ''That was a long time ago.''

''So it's true.'' Dorian sounded agitated. ''Do you envy him now that he's married to Lady Eleanor?''

Nicholas turned the key in the lock and the door swung open. If he didn't know better, he'd think she was behaving like a jealous woman. ''Would it trouble you if I did?''

''Of course not,'' Dorian said, walking past him through the door. He caught the scent of violets in her hair. ''I was just curious about why you have spent so much time with Lady Eleanor.''

''She is a friend,'' Nicholas said evenly to hide his surprise. She *was* jealous. ''Have I neglected you?''

''Not quite,'' Dorian said, turning her back on him, her spine straight and rigid with pique. ''But very nearly. I understand that this engagement is for your convenience as well as mine, but I prefer not to be treated as anything less than your true betrothed.''

"I'm sorry if you feel that I have treated you as anything less," Nicholas said, mildly annoyed with her announcement yet pleased with her obvious envy. "That was never my intention. Dorian?"

She turned to him, her bottom lip thrust out.

"I see that I have annoyed you," Nicholas said with an obvious sigh of regret. "I suppose, if we were *truly* betrothed, you'd be jealous of my attentions to Lady Eleanor. But of course you are not."

Dorian became very still. Nicholas could see her considering the idea. "If we were *truly* betrothed, wouldn't you expect me to be jealous of a woman you once loved? I would wonder if you still loved her."

"But I don't," Nicholas said. Her feminine ire amused and touched him. He suspected the petted and spoiled Dorian St. John, the toast of Town, had never had reason to be jealous of anyone in her life. The glittering green monster was a stranger to her. Nicholas couldn't resist the grin spreading across his face.

"That idea of our betrothal was a childhood game. It all happened a very long time ago and we were little more than children. So if you and I werĕ true lovers, you would have no need to be troubled by my attentions to Lady Eleanor."

Hope glimmered in Dorian's violet eyes. "So a reunion with an old friend is the reason you were so eager to see her?"

Nicholas sighed and wondered if he could explain to Dorian what he wasn't certain he understood himself. "I think it has to do with the responsibilities of love. We talked about that once before."

Dorian nodded, her face softening a little. "But I don't see the connection here."

"I suppose some might think it a misplaced responsibility," Nicholas began, "but it seems to me that if you loved someone once, you have an obligation to make certain that person is happy and safe."

Dorian frowned. "You mean you still feel responsible for

Lady Eleanor's happiness? That doesn't make any sense. Her happiness is Gavin's responsibility now.''

''As it should be,'' Nicholas agreed, sorry that he'd ever attempted this explanation to someone who thought true love was a matter of writing love songs. ''But I wanted to talk to her and be certain that she is content with her life. Whatever her choice, I loved her once and have an obligation to help her if she should need it. That is not the same thing as being in love. I would do no less for a friend. It is nothing for you to be jealous of.''

Dorian studied him a moment longer, then shook her head, her lower lip still full and petulant. ''I'm not jealous. Why would I be jealous of a friend? That's what you and Lady Eleanor are now: friends. And we're not really betrothed. Why should I be jealous?''

''Exactly. Then there is no reason to continue this conversation,'' Nicholas said, troubled by her disavowal of the jealousy that was clearly eating at her. He was annoyed with the game Gavin was playing.

Dorian strolled into the music room, which was filled with shelves and cubicles for manuscripts and books. ''Things seem to be very orderly in here.''

Nicholas listened to the quiet of the enormous house and noted the bellpull in the corner of the music room. Servants lurked everywhere, but the marquess, his family, and the guests were gone. He knew how to solve one of his problems—Dorian and Eleanor. The other, the missing evidence, he was uncertain about.

''We have the remainder of the afternoon and this evening to search. We should be able to find out whether Lord Fernham has what we're after.''

''Yes, we can work here.'' Dorian pulled a chair over to a long table in the middle of the music room.

Nicholas drew a chair up next to hers, glad to see that she was compliant, for once. ''Yes, let's work right here, side by side.''

* * *

Dorian glanced at Nicholas as he worked next to her.

I know we have an agreement, but are we friends? The silent, selfish question chased its tail through her mind as she sorted through the stacks of music on the table. But she never uttered the words aloud. From beneath her lashes she gazed at Nicholas, who was intent on the manuscript before him.

He sat paging through boxes of music for the next several hours, his face intent, his eyes keen and focused on his purpose. When darkness closed in they lit two branches of candlesticks and placed them on either end of the table to light the work area.

By then Dorian realized what a silly question it was. Childish, even. *Are we friends?* But the words had loomed in her head ever since Nicholas had told her that he cared no more for Lady Eleanor than he did a friend.

Of course, he and she were not friends. They weren't exactly enemies either, but they each had their own reasons for wanting Aunt Charlotte's love song—and there was no room for compromise.

"I'm not finding anything." Abruptly, Nicholas shoved aside the manuscript box he'd been examining and turned toward her, placing a hand on the back of her chair.

"Nor I. I'm becoming discouraged," Dorian lamented.

His hand slipped to her shoulder. His warmth burned through her gown. She feared she would melt right there in the chair next to him—and the horrible part was, he'd never notice. He was probably thinking of his tête-a-tête with Eleanor.

"Don't fret. We shall find what we're searching for." He withdrew his hand to close the box and latch it. With it he took his warmth and the reassurance he'd offered with his words. Dorian felt cold and lost and very much like a little girl again. They would never be friends, only friendly competitors.

"Let's go into the greenhouse next door," Nicholas suggested. "I can smell the flowers from here."

"Yes, I can, too." Dorian thought his suggestion a delightful idea. "I would like to see Lady Fernham's plants again."

She rose and reached for a branch of candles. Nicholas stayed her hand with his and, leaning over her shoulder, blew out all the flames.

"The moon is full. We'll see the flowers by the moonlight, of course," Nicholas said, his lips nearly brushing her ear. "Isn't that what lovers do?"

"Lovers?" Startled by his suggestion, Dorian felt her face grow warm in the darkness. Surely she had not heard him correctly. His blue coat sleeve brushed against her bare arm, making her skin tingle with her awareness of him. She did not move again until he did.

"Isn't that what the marquess thinks we are? Lovers? And your Aunt Charlotte, too, of course."

"I suppose so," Dorian admitted halfheartedly, allowing him to lead her out of the room. She was weary of playing the part of the happy fiancée.

"Then we must not disappoint them." Nicholas led her through the darkness and along the short hall to the greenhouse that occupied the other half of this wing of the house.

The minute they stepped through the door the sweet scent of orchids and violets assaulted them.

"Oh, this is a wonderful change from the music room," Dorian said, delighted to smell something besides musty manuscripts. But visions of the pages of music still lingered in her head, despite the beauty of the flowers. "I must admit, I'm discouraged that we've not found even an early work by Franz. I wonder if Lord Fernham realizes how incomplete his collection is."

"But if we'd found something of Chamier's, you would want to relieve Lord Fernham of it, leaving his collection incomplete once more. Am I right?"

Dorian laughed at her own contradiction. Some of her tension eased away with the laughter. "Well, yes, you're correct. But enough of music and manuscripts today. I'm going to sit down right here and watch the moon over the trees in the pony park and smell the flowers.''

''Do that while I order some food.'' Nicholas rang for the footman. When the servant arrived Nicholas ordered a picnic cover and a basket of food to be brought to the greenhouse, to Dorian's surprise. If the servant was shocked, as she was, the man never raised an eyebrow.

As soon as the footman had been sent on his way, Nicholas strode across the slate floor and threw open the French doors, admitting the cool night air.

''A picnic cover?'' she ventured.

Soft moonlight filtered through the windows into the greenhouse. Beyond the glass the garden gleamed silvery and shiny wet with the evening mist. Shattered rose blossoms dropped, littering the grass with soft petals, and rosebuds bobbed under the weight of glistening dewdrops

He gestured to the floor. ''We'll picnic in here.''

''What a novel idea.'' Dorian had never thought of such a thing as an indoor picnic. ''But I thought picnics are always held outside in the sunshine on the grass.''

''Do you think to partake of picnics only in the shade of a tree, my lady?'' A mocking smile played across Nicholas's lips. ''There are all manner of meals al fresco. For this one the moon will be our sun.''

''Indeed, the moon will serve well enough,'' Dorian agreed with a smile, not so taken aback by the idea of the picnic as she was by his whimsy. ''Pray tell me, what other manner of picnics are there?''

''I've been known to picnic on the quarterdeck.''

''The quarterdeck? Does a navy captain often entertain so aboard his ship?''

''Occasionally, but only for ladies of note.''

''Ladies of note?'' Dorian asked, instantly thinking of Eleanor. Nicholas's smile turned to one of private amusement. Dorian sensed that he was pleased with the jealousy that plagued her.

"During the particular picnic I'm thinking of, I entertained the charming Lady Hamilton, Admiral Nelson's lady friend—and the admiral himself, of course."

"You know Lady Hamilton?"

"You've heard of her, I see?"

"Hasn't everyone?" Dorian blurted. Who had not heard of Nelson's married mistress? "Some say she's very charming, and that she was quite distraught over the admiral's death."

"She is charming." Nicholas paused and frowned. Dorian realized that he was sorry he had brought up the subject. "I believe she was genuinely fond of Nelson, though I never understood the relationship."

"What do you mean?" Dorian asked, perching on the edge of her chair and longing for intimate details of one of the most scandalous love affairs of the decade.

"I admired Admiral Nelson. He was a brilliant navy man and a superb leader, but I simply never understood how Emma Hamilton's husband could allow . . . ah, here is our picnic now."

The stoic footman entered with two assistants in tow.

"Arrange things over there, before the doors," Nicholas directed them.

Dorian watched in silent wonder as the three footmen spread a clean, heavy cloth on the slate floor and set out a huge willow basket of food.

"That will be all. Thank you," Nicholas said when they had finished. "We'll wait on ourselves."

With a polite bow, the servants disappeared from the greenhouse, softly closing the door behind them.

"Welcome, my lady." Nicholas bowed and with a sweep of his arm encompassed the greenhouse and the garden beyond. "Welcome to our late-night picnic supper."

He pulled the cushions out of the garden chairs. "Please be seated. The floor will be a little harder than the earth."

"Thank you, my lord." She accepted his steadying hand as she seated herself on a cushion.

To her surprise, Nicholas began to shrug out of his coat. "Will you forgive me for making myself comfortable? 'Tis a bit stuffy in here."

"Of course, my lord; make yourself comfortable," Dorian said, warming to the informality of his suggestion. She kicked off her black velvet slippers. "May I do likewise?"

"There's the spirit." Nicholas grinned at her as he settled himself on a cushion with the picnic basket between them. "Do see what the kitchen has packed for us."

Dorian reached into the basket. "We have bread, cheese, fruit pies, cake and a bottle of wine."

"And an orange," Nicholas said, taking the last delicacy from the basket. "I confess a weakness for this particular fruit."

"You, too?" Dorian smiled at him. "When we go to the theater I always insist that Davis buy me an orange."

"Shall we share this one?" Nicholas suggested, taking a knife from his pocket.

Deftly he began to peel the orange, tracing his blade round the contour of the fruit.

"Tell me about growing up with Sir Gavin and Lady Eleanor," Dorian ventured as she unwrapped the linen napkin from the cheese.

"There's not much to tell." He continued to peel the orange carefully. "We shared a tutor in the early years. Father brought in a very learned man from Oxford who was quite a good teacher. I think he truly liked instructing young minds. That was to our benefit. Gavin's family, and Eleanor's, too, were invited to take advantage of the man's presence, along with my brothers and I. The five of us spent many hours in the schoolroom together, as well as roaming the countryside—and sailing. Jon Collard, our steward's son, always sailed with us."

A wistful smile played across Nicholas's face as he told Dorian about those happy years.

"Did you always love Eleanor?" Dorian smiled up at him innocently, all the time hating herself for being unable to let go of the subject.

"Actually, in those days I believed she would wed one of my brothers." Nicholas put aside the orange to accept the bread and cheese Dorian offered him. "When she turned her attentions to me I was surprised but pleased."

Dorian's bread and cheese turned dry as dust in her mouth. She reached for a glass of wine to wash it down.

"I suddenly found I was the envy of my older brother, Gilbert. And of Gavin, too." Nicholas laughed and took up the orange again. "Gavin and I competed for everything, so that was no surprise."

"And Gavin eventually won her heart?" Dorian asked, aware that she might be treading into sensitive territory.

"So I believed until recently." Nicholas continued to cut a spiral of the aromatic skin from the juicy flesh. "But I've begun to wonder if perhaps I allowed him the victory."

"You gave up?"

"Let's just say that I did not pursue my quarry as diligently as I have pursued other things in my life."

"Then she must not have been your true love," Dorian said, trying to hide the smile of satisfaction that threatened to spread across her face.

"You may be right about that," Nicholas said. "Nevertheless, she made the best choice."

"How so?"

"She does not possess the strength to stand by a man accused of treason."

The candidness of the observation caught Dorian by surprise. A rush of gladness flooded through her, eroding the lump of jealousy that had lodged in her aching heart. If he knew and understood Eleanor that well, then surely he could not love her. If he had not fought for her, perhaps he'd never loved her. "But you are still friends?"

"Yes, friends," Nicholas said, intent on the orange and the peeling that spiraled away between his long, strong fingers. The scent of citrus tickled her nose, and a bit of juice sprayed from between his fingers. "Nothing more than friends."

Dorian sighed and sat in relieved silence, listening to the night sounds beyond the open windows and waiting for Nicholas to offer her a piece of the orange.

As Nicholas cut the fruit into sections, he glanced at Dorian. She smiled at him briefly, and he knew he'd set her mind at ease about Eleanor. He continued to peel the orange. She watched his hands with rapt attention, then licked her lips, moistening her mouth with a dainty pink tongue. Desire stirred deep in his loins.

In the beginning he had never intended to use an orange as part of a seduction. Yet, curious as to how innocent Dorian really was, he took the first slice and offered it to her. He thrust it close to her face, almost pressing it against her lips.

She stared cross-eyed at the fruit he held under her nose. Daintily, she licked her lips again. Her gaze flickered uncertainly over him for a moment, surprise and confusion written in the depth of her eyes. Then, with a defiant toss of her head, she snatched the fruit from his hand.

Nicholas hid his disappointment.

"Thank you, my lord." Her words were crisp and frosty. She shifted on her cushion, putting a cool distance between them. The white lace of her demure afternoon gown stretched across her throat, pressing into the smooth swell of her full breasts. Nicholas ached.

He watched her, unwilling to look away and unable to hide the smile of regret that formed on his lips. He would have enjoyed her docile submission in accepting the food from his hand. Yet her cool possession was perfectly in keeping with her nature, and it pleased him.

As she ate a drip of sticky juice trickled from the corner of her mouth. Nicholas thought of licking it away, then tasting her lips. But she grabbed a napkin first, covering her mouth. Her gaze grew suspicious as she wiped away the droplet. He realized he was staring too boldly and quickly returned to carving the orange.

She swallowed the bite and wiped each of her long, delicate

fingers with care. Nicholas tried not to notice but finally had to put down the knife before he did himself harm. He shook his head to free himself of thoughts of sucking sweet orange juice from her fingers, of tonguing away the stickiness from the tender place between each digit and licking clean her palm.

"And what about yourself, my lord?" she asked, innocently unaware of his fantasy.

"Me?" Nicholas asked, struggling with lusty images that refused to leave him. He had no idea what she was asking about.

"Are we not to share the orange?" Dorian snatched a slice from his hand and put it to his mouth. Nicholas smiled and took the bite, purposely nipping her fingertips.

She sobered, her pretty wine-colored mouth pursing into a frown. Nicholas knew this kind of play was new to her. Suddenly her eyes widened; then mischief glinted in their violet depths. She was an apt pupil. Plucking a slice of the orange from his hand, she shoved it playfully under his nose again. "Here; indulge yourself."

Nicholas drew a deep breath. "Temptress."

Indeed, he would indulge himself—and her. He seized her hand with such force that she dropped the fruit. He pulled her palm to his mouth and kissed the warm, sensitive inside of her hand and wrist, purposely tasting the delicate white skin that pulsed with life. She yielded to his strength and whimpered. He tasted her again, savoring her sweet tanginess, though hardly finding enough to satisfy his painful need.

Grasping her slender shoulders to prevent her retreat, he pulled her toward him over the picnic basket. Willow snapped under their weight. He pressed his lips to hers, moving across her mouth to savor the last of the orange—and taste the essence that was Dorian. Sweet heaven, she tasted him back.

Nicholas released her and peered into her face to behold her response, uncertain that she was really ready for him. Her sigh whispered against his jaw. Lashes fluttered against her flushed cheeks. When she looked up she eagerly offered her mouth again. Nicholas took it, slipping a hand down her back and pulling her closer, longing to press her against his body to ease his discomfort.

He offered her a taste of his tongue this time and she accepted it—relished it. Nicholas groaned. He wrenched the damned basket from between them and tossed it aside. Bread and cheese rolled across the slate floor. Then he drew her closer, intent on dragging her down onto the picnic cover. He would spend the entire evening tempting her, seducing her, pleasuring her into the complete surrender he desired.

A surrender that would bind and obligate her to him in a way mere betrothal could not.

Awash in a sea of emotions she had never experienced before, Dorian allowed Nicholas to pull her down onto the picnic cover. She sighed and slipped her arms around his neck. The kiss lengthened until she was desperately in need of breath. Her heart threatened to flutter away; or worse—she would turn blue and faint. But she clung to him.

This time his mouth worked across hers in a relentless, demanding way. Fierce. Unlike any kiss he'd offered her before. His obvious passion thrilled her. Warmed her from the inside out. She tried to offer him the same ardor, fervor, yearning.

Just as she was thinking she could not bear to sever this new link between them, he released her.

A cool draft blew between them. Her gasp for air echoed throughout the greenhouse. She shivered, yet clung to him. He was not going to push her away again as he had in the carriage.

With her lips feeling scandalously bruised, almost swollen, she leaned her head against his shoulder.

"Wait here, just a moment, sweetheart." Gently, Nicholas removed her arms from around his neck and rose from his cushion. "I'll be right back."

Before Dorian could protest he got to his feet and threaded his way through the plants and flowers to the greenhouse door. She heard him turn the key in the lock.

"There now, all is secure," he said when he returned. He

threw himself down on the cushion and pulled Dorian along with him so they lay face-to-face, side-by-side. ''Privacy and no carriage bouncing along beneath us, as we had a fortnight ago.''

Dorian realized with a shiver what Nicholas intended. The time had come to surrender to her desire and his demands. Now that the moment had truly arrived she found herself frightened. She pulled away from him, uncertain of what to do next. What if she disappointed him?

''So a greenhouse is an acceptable place to deflower a virgin?'' she asked, surprised at the harshness of her own voice.

Nicholas pulled her close again and whispered into her ear. ''Sweetheart, love deserves its own seclusion and comfort.''

He slipped away the shoulder of her gown and kissed her bare skin. The warmth of his lips flowed through her once more, stirring sensations delicious and unfamiliar to Dorian. Her fear weakened.

''No distractions should come between us,'' he murmured as his lips moved teasingly along her collarbone and his hand caressed her breast through the sheer cotton of her gown. ''Only me touching you and you touching me.''

He kissed the base of her throat. Dorian's fear dissolved, leaving her helpless and vulnerable—and completely trusting.

The next few minutes were filled with tender caresses and gentle strokes that somehow resulted in the removal of Dorian's gown and petticoats. Though she felt somewhat embarrassed, the desire and intensity she saw in Nicholas's gaze made her bold. She brazenly shimmied out of her underdrawers, aware of the building heat in his gaze. Her inhibitions and embarrassment fell away as she lay down naked beside him, her passion growing and flowering under the warmth in his eyes and the gentle persuasion of his hands.

She tugged at the collar of his shirt. Nicholas sat up with his back to her. Dorian heard first one boot and then the next drop on the slate floor. The rustle of fabric told her he was shedding his shirt. She watched the moonlight turn his skin to silver and limn the muscles of his broad shoulders and the powerful chords of his back. He stood and turned toward her. His belly was hard and flat, and a mat of dark hair covered his chest.

Standing over her, he stepped out of his pantaloons, revealing long, hard thighs, narrow hips, and a distinctly aroused male body. Dorian stared. Except for the dark hair, he was as well-proportioned and supple as any of Floraton Court's smooth, nude Roman statues. However, her covert appraisal of the male anatomy in marble had never suggested to her that the private parts of a man's body could grow so large.

"Oh, goodness," Dorian breathed as she watched him lay down beside her again. His size fascinated and shocked her. He was hard and swollen. His masculinity appeared quite enormous. "I had no idea. What if . . ."

Nicholas touched her chin with his thumb. "We will work together just fine as long as we take our time."

He kissed her throat. Then he bent his head to take one nipple carefully between his teeth.

Dorian tensed, then gasped at the thrill that spiraled through her. She threaded her fingers through his hair and clung to him. Wantonly, she arched her back, offering herself so that he could take more of her into his mouth.

Nicholas obliged her, tugging at her breast in the same way that had left her weak and mindless in the carriage. Needing to relieve her own aching desire, Dorian pressed closer to him, bringing up her knee to rest on his hip, opening herself to his caressing hands. He touched her, lightly at first, then more intimately, slowly exploring her unfolding body. Each bold foray of his fingers set her aflame. She gasped with shock—and delight.

"So warm and wet." Nicholas's voice was deep and rich with praise. His long fingers moved over her, thrilling and teaching her, making her grow willful in her need. She stroked his shoulders, tracing his spine downward to his firm hips. He sucked in his breath and seized her hand.

"I want your touch, too, but we must be careful—of my control." He guided her hands to the fullness of his manhood and prompted her with dark, heated words. "I've never known a touch as heavenly as yours."

Inspired, Dorian caressed him and brushed her fingertips across the tip of his engorged shaft, surprised at its smoothness.

He sucked in another sharp breath. "Be merciful, sweetheart."

Fearful that she might have hurt him, she pulled away. He grasped her fingers.

"Oh, no," he whispered and drew her hands back to him. "Again."

Obediently, Dorian closed trembling fingers around him once more. He closed his eyes and moaned in pleasure. His response awed her. She'd never dreamed she might have such power over a man. But he allowed her no more liberties.

Swiftly, he moved on top of her, nudging her legs apart and settling himself between them. She lay open, quivering and exposed beneath his powerful body, but he did not force her to accept him yet.

Instead, he lowered his mouth to hers and whispered against her lips, "It will be wonderful." He kissed her nose, her chin, her ear, then brushed his mouth across her lips once more. "I promise. Wonderful."

He slid his hand between their bellies and found the swollen petals between her legs. Dorian shivered, but trustingly opened herself to his seeking fingers. Each stroke fanned the flames burning deep inside her.

She clung to Nicholas, pressing herself against his hand, knowing instinctively that only he could quench the flames burning inside her.

His exploration grew more intimate, reaching deeper into her dark, dewy recesses, warming and stretching her for a purpose she remotely understood—and ached to have fulfilled by him.

''Nicholas, please,'' she begged between her gasps of delight and moans of desire.

''Tell me if you want me, sweetheart.'' He pressed the broad head of his shaft against her aching opening.

The solid size of him daunted Dorian, but she wanted and needed him, regardless of the price or the pain.

Without thinking, she raked her fingernails across his back and confessed. ''Yes, my love, I want you. Yes.''

Nicholas moaned. Perspiration broke out on his brow as he attempted to enter her with excruciating care.

Dorian stiffened, unprepared for the painful pressure of his invasion. The bright hot aching need for him ebbed as the force against her body built. Still, she wanted him, and she understood that his control was strained. There was no going back now— even if she wanted to.

''Am I hurting you?'' Nicholas asked between clenched teeth.

''No,'' Dorian lied against his shoulder.

Nicholas withdrew immediately.

''Then why are you stiff as a board in my arms, sweetheart?'' he murmured against her temple.

''Oh, Nicholas, don't stop now,'' Dorian whimpered and kissed his neck to reassure him.

Nicholas reached between them again, seeking the dewy nub that rendered her helpless. At the same time his lips moved down her body to take her taut, aching nipple into his mouth.

Under his renewed assault flames flared inside Dorian again. She gasped and clutched his hair. Settling deeper into the cushions, she spread herself open to his touch, knowing nothing of the world but the sensations of his mouth tugging on her breast and his fingers gently preparing her—one, two, three at a time.

The fire storm swirled and burned, sweet and bright, threatening to break over Dorian and consume her. She lifted her hips beneath his hand and whispered pleas for release. When she opened her eyes to peer into his face, Nicholas only smiled at her, a masterful, sensual smile, his hand moving relentlessly.

The release came, sudden and fiery, in a sweet, shattering wave. Dorian arched her back, reaching and exalting in the blinding exquisiteness.

Nicholas took her then, swiftly covering her body with his, plunging deeply into the virginal passage that he had prepared so carefully for his coming.

Dorian cried out as he filled her completely, then filled her again and again. Another wave broke over her, mingling pleasure with pain. She reveled in the gloriousness of it. She moved with Nicholas, gripping his shoulders until her fingernails left imprints on his skin.

Still inside her, he rose up, taking her hands in his and stretched their arms out over their heads. Only then, Dorian realized, when Nicholas was assured of her release, did he seek his own in one last urgent thrust.

In the waning throes of her own fulfillment, Dorian felt Nicholas's shuddering climax overtake him, his strong hands nearly crushing hers as his body convulsed with pleasure.

Their hands remained clasped. His head sank against her shoulder. When he stirred again, he kissed her ear and whispered in a voice rich with male satisfaction, ''Now, sweetheart, we no longer need to pretend to Aunt Charlotte that we're lovers.''

Chapter Sixteen

At midnight, after all the guests had returned from the fair and retired to their respective chambers, Davis decided it was time to accept Susanna's invitation.

He stood in the third-floor passage, hidden by the shadow of a classic sculpture of a well-endowed satyr. A shaft of moonlight fell through the window at the end of the corridor, lighting the way to Susanna's room.

Two nights had passed since the country dancing. Davis feared Susanna would think he did not care to accept her invitation. During the days they had exchanged a few words—the most casual of comments in appreciation of the activities—words that were perfectly acceptable in company. Each night one activity or another had kept him from stealing to her room.

The first evening the billiards game had turned into a late-night hunter's story-telling session, complete with brandy and cigars in the library. The second night Davis had found himself engaged in a game of Hazard in which Sir Gavin had lost a considerable amount of ready.

With a steely glint in his eye, the sea captain had laughingly demanded that all stay until he won it back. Not a man rose from the table, though Davis was sure some thought Trafford rather unsportsmanlike about his losses. Eventually the captain won his money back, but not until the cock crowed. Then Davis and the other gentlemen had gratefully fallen into their beds and into a sound sleep—until Lady Fernham had ordered them roused to accompany the ladies to feed the ponies.

Now, two days later, Davis skulked in the shadowy hall, feeling as callow and foolish as a village swain. What if he'd been mistaken about Susanna's meaning? he wondered, worried that he was thinking with the wrong part of his body again. Perhaps she hadn't intended an invitation at all? Worse, what if she had changed her mind and did not wish him near her? Women did that.

But what else could her words have meant? He frowned as another thought occurred to him. What if she had intended an invitation and thought him ungrateful and unmanly for not accepting it?

Then he was wasting time, he told himself. This was his chance to rid himself of this silly obsession with her once and for all. Learn the truth. Knock on her door.

Resolutely, Davis stepped out of the shadow and headed toward the door on the right.

The floor creaked behind him. Alerted, Davis ducked into the cover of the statue's shadow once more.

Around the corner crept a pretty little maid, a girl Davis recognized as one of the upstairs servants who changed linen, pressed clothes, and helped the ladies with their toilets. She was a shapely thing, with fair hair and ivory skin, wearing only a night rail and a wrapper.

She stopped at the corner, giggled, and turned to wave to someone in the darkness behind her, then scurried along the passage to the doorway on the left. She paused at the door and knocked softly. A deep voice bade her to enter, as though she was expected. Davis recognized the baritone of an old, bewhiskered bachelor whom Lord Fernham had invited to the party. He watched the door open and the maid disappear inside. Then all was silent once more.

Davis exhaled a long, slow breath, relieved to have remained undiscovered. The last thing he wanted was to cast a shadow on the St. John name or on Susanna's reputation by being caught prowling outside her room. Perhaps he was being a fool and this idea was a terrible mistake.

While he was still caught in his dilemma, a door on the right of the passage opened slowly. A shaft of candlelight mingled with moonlight fell on the carpeted floor.

Susanna appeared in the opening, her bright hair loose about her shoulders and the light revealing her curvaceous nakedness beneath the thin gown. The sight stirred Davis's loins.

"Hello?" she called softly. "Is someone there? I thought I heard something."

Davis cursed silently but stepped out into the passage.

"There you are," she whispered with the loveliest smile of relief—and of welcome. "I thought you would never come."

Davis said nothing. He closed the distance between them in a heartbeat, brushing past her into the room and pulling her in with him. Closing the door, he pressed her up against it, tilted her face up to his, and kissed her passionately. He made no secret or excuse for what he wanted from her.

She returned his kiss, opening her mouth to his demands and emitting soft whimpers of surrender. Their contact grew hot and wet. With his mouth, Davis demanded, and she allowed him every intimacy. Without releasing the kiss, he caressed her shoulders, so delicate and fragile, her breasts so full in his hands, her ribs tapering to her waist, then her hips, firm and round against his palms.

He pressed her lower body against his erection; willingly, she rubbed against him. He released her briefly. It was his turn to voice his pleasure in a long, low moan. Then he took her mouth again. His hands brushed up along her body once more, playing briefly with her swollen nipples, then reaching the throat of her gown.

"Yes," she whispered against his lips. "Ooooh, yes."

"I want you," Davis murmured, a tiny part of him still afraid she didn't understand.

"Yes, I know," she whispered. "Take what you desire."

Davis lost all control. He gripped the front of her gown in both hands and ripped it open, exposing her luscious breasts. She sighed and pressed her head back against the door, as if being bared before his eyes was exactly what she needed and wanted. Davis took only a moment to admire the lovely sight of Susanna naked before him, her nipples already hard.

Then he tongued her lips once more and began to move down her throat, kissing and tasting and grasping every part of her that gave him pleasure. Her shoulders, her breasts heavy and budded for him, her ribs, her navel, her flat belly.

She laced her fingers through his hair and took shallow, excited gasps, whispering his name with each indrawn breath.

The tattered gown clung about her hips. Davis grasped the remnants of it and ripped it open to the floor. The sheer cotton pooled at her feet, leaving her hips, her downy red delta, and her smooth white thighs bare to Davis's sight, his hands, his lips.

Like a starving man invited to a feast, like a man lost in the wilderness who stumbles upon an oasis, Davis knelt before her and availed himself of her gifts. Why had he ever thought her silky titan curls were too bright and ugly?

Once more he felt her fingers laced through his hair. He kissed her white thighs; then, daringly, he touched her with his tongue. She gave a soft cry and shivered. That was all the encouragement Davis needed. He tasted her again and again, delirious with the pleasure of feeling her body quicken beneath his intimate assault.

She murmured his name over and over. She tugged on his hair as if she was trying to pull him away, but it was a weak effort. Davis knew as her breathing came quicker that he was going to be victorious. Her sighs accelerated to soft, rapid coos of pleasure. She shuddered once more. With her long last shrill sigh she fell quiet, and Davis felt her body sag against the door.

He got quickly to his feet just in time to catch her in his arms. Her eyes were closed, her cheeks flushed with excitement. Pleased with his performance but concerned at her swoon, Davis swung Susanna up in his arms and carried her to the bed. Gently he laid her across the linen sheets and sat down beside her.

At his touch on her cheek her eyes fluttered open. "What happened? I was enjoying the most exquisite things you were doing—then—it happened—again and again."

"I did my best," Davis confessed with sincere humility. "You're all right?"

Susanna's eyes fluttered closed again. "I'm all right, I think. I'm feeling absolutely too sublime to be certain."

Her eyes snapped open and she studied his face, then let her gaze rove downward over his body. "What about you?"

"I'm staying," he said, reaching for his neckcloth and rising from the bed to undress. "The night is young—unless you don't feel you are ready for more."

She sat up, the candlelight limning her beautifully naked body, her amber eyes wide and dark. "Oh, you must stay. I can't let you go away like ..."

"Like what?" Davis asked, conscious once more that her gaze had drifted to the front of his pantaloons.

Slowly she looked up at him, her face soft and pleading. "You know what I mean."

"I do," Davis admitted, though he would have liked to hear her say she wanted to satisfy him, too. Perhaps those words would come later. He tossed aside his neckcloth and pulled off his boots with more ease than he'd ever expected to manage without a valet.

When he stood up and glanced at Susanna she was watching his every move. He shrugged out of his shirt, tossing it aside to reach for his pantaloons.

Susanna rose gracefully to her knees and reached for the buttons. Davis hesitated.

"Let me," she whispered, shyly avoiding his gaze.

Davis dropped his hands to his sides, staring at the canopy above and allowing her to unbutton one set of buttons and then the other. Slowly; she worked too slowly, he thought.

As she pulled open his pants, she tenderly took his arousal in one hand and stroked him. Davis gasped and looked down into her face, surprised by the naughty, seductive expression in her eyes. In that moment he understood what she intended.

When she lowered her head he grabbed a handful of red curls. He didn't intend to hurt her, but he couldn't let her go on.

"No, no, not our first time together, sweet vixen," Davis said, though he hardly had a voice with which to speak. He ached to have her—or be taken by her—in any fashion she pleased. "Time enough for special favors later. Move over."

Susanna didn't argue with him, but moved to the far side of the bed while he stripped off his pants. He blew out the candle and climbed in beside her.

He pulled her into his arms and kissed her again, long and slow, with tenderness and care. She obligingly wrapped her arms around his neck and kissed him in return, her tongue as demanding and passionate as his own. Finished with risque games, Davis rose over her, and in the manner he thought intended by God, completed their mating.

Chapter Seventeen

When Dorian drifted off to sleep in his arms Nicholas pulled the corner of the picnic cover over them. He studied her face, so soft and innocent in slumber, and longed to take her again but could not—not after she'd just experienced her first time with a man.

Gently, he pressed his cheek against the top of her head, surprised at the tenderness and possessiveness that over-whelmed him. He had not expected to feel so protective toward her after their moments of intimacy. Sweet Dorian who could drive a man mad with her headstrong independence and willful ways; she had surrendered to him at last. He would not give her up, nor would he allow anyone to harm her.

Whether Dorian would permit him such an entitlement was another question but he would face that with the new day.

He pulled her close. They slept in each other's arms until almost dawn. Rousing her gently, Nicholas helped her dress decently enough for them to get back to their individual rooms before the servants were up and about.

He would have preferred to spend the day in Dorian's company, but a round of shooting had been planned for the male houseguests. To deny the marquess the joy of showing off the abundance of game on his estate would have been bad form.

By midmorning Nicholas found himself in the field with Sir Gavin and the other men, shooting grouse and most anything else that flew up before the onslaught of the beaters.

At first the conversation between them was sporadic and general, full of the typical courtesy of asking after each other's relations and the quality of the performance by the mummers and fair games in the village the day before.

Neither Nicholas's thoughts nor his heart were in the shooting. Memories of Dorian's sweet responses in his arms were still vivid enough to stir him. Though he believed firmly that gentlemen didn't kiss and tell, for the first time in his life part of him wanted to crow to the world that Dorian had found her first woman's pleasure in his arms.

On the other hand, it wasn't any of the world's damned affair what transpired between Dorian and him. So he conspired to put on a hunter's face and trudge through the fields with the other men.

As the morning wore on, the shooters broke into groups of twos and threes. Conversation turned more personal.

Gavin took his turn at downing two more birds.

"Another good shot," Nicholas said. "Your eye is keen today."

"My eye is keen every day," Gavin said, handing off the smoking gun to the gun bearer. "But I doubt you could hit the side of an elephant today. How many have you downed this morning?"

"One or two," Nicholas admitted reluctantly. Everything was a test between himself and Gavin—always had been. A friendly rivalry, but Nicholas cared little about it today.

"Actually Nicholas, I wanted to talk to you privately about your betrothed."

Surprised that Gavin should bring up Dorian, Nicholas nodded for him to speak his mind.

''You really should explain to Dorian about you and Eleanor.''

Nicholas frowned as he took a reloaded gun from the bearer. ''I thought I had.''

''She was asking me questions about you and Eleanor just the other day while you two were feeding the ponies,'' Gavin said. ''She had some very interesting things to say.''

The beaters in the field ahead of them flushed another pair of birds. Nicholas shouldered a gun and took aim, but his concentration was gone.

''That's your third miss this morning, Seacombe.''

''I know how many that is,'' Nicholas said, suddenly annoyed.

He handed the gun back to the bearer. ''Exactly what did Dorian have to say?''

''She told me about the search for the music for her aunt's compilation of Chamier's work.'' Gavin took a reloaded gun from the bearer, but no more birds took flight.

''Yes. We each have our reasons for wanting that piece of music.'' Nicholas signaled to the beaters that he wanted to move to another area.

''She may be more determined than you know.'' Gavin walked the field at Nicholas's side. ''Her aunt is not well.''

''I am aware that Charlotte's health is delicate.'' Nicholas watched the beaters move through the woods ahead of them and on into another meadow.

''Delicate? I understand she is dying.''

Nicholas halted. ''What do you mean? Dorian wouldn't be here if Charlotte were on her deathbed. She and Davis insist on reports being delivered from the town house every other day or so.''

''Oh, nothing so imminent,'' Gavin said, stopping to face Nicholas. ''She told me her aunt's heart is very weak. The doctors don't expect the lady to live past fall.''

Nicholas drew a slow, deep breath. Dorian had never told him that. Of course, something like that would feed Dorian's steely determination. His gaze flicked across Gavin's face. The satisfaction he read in Gavin's gray eyes annoyed him.

"You didn't know?"

"I don't imagine it's something Dorian or Davis care to have bandied about in Society," Nicholas snapped and turned to walk on into the next meadow.

Gavin followed. "Of course; I agree. I have no intention of spreading the news, but I'm surprised she did not tell you. You two being betrothed, I'd assumed there were no secrets between you."

Nicholas carefully hid his anger from Gavin. "There is no reason why she should tell me."

"I say, this looks a likely place for a bird or two." Gavin stopped and looked about the meadow. "I would have thought the lady would have used every ploy she could think of to get what she wanted from you."

Nicholas whirled on Gavin. "Dorian may be headstrong and a bit overindulged by her brother, but she's not manipulative. She's not like that."

Gavin's smirk disappeared; he shook his head. "You don't have to defend your lady to me, Seacombe."

Nicholas didn't understand his own anger, but he made no more effort to hide it from Gavin. "Don't start on Dorian as you did on Eleanor. Do you understand me?"

Gavin's face hardened. Fearlessly he stepped up to Nicholas. "You never wanted Eleanor, so don't start acting the betrayed suitor now. I won Eleanor and you lost."

"Hello?"

Gavin started.

Nicholas recognized Dorian's voice and turned to see her walk up behind them, a tentative smile on her face.

Nicholas cursed silently and prayed Dorian had overheard nothing of their conversation. "Dorian."

Gavin doffed his hunting cap. "Miss St. John."

"I thought I'd come out to see how the shooting was going."

Dorian's uncertain gaze searched Nicholas's face. He realized there were things that had gone unsaid between them last night.

"How's the sport today?" she asked when she reached Nicholas's side.

"We've bagged enough birds to assure a full course of game at supper tonight." Gavin proudly gestured toward the game bag carried by the beaters.

"How wonderful." Dorian glanced at the beaters, but her gaze once more sought out Nicholas.

"My shooting is a bit off today, actually." Nicholas handed his gun to the bearer and began to peel off his shooting gloves. "If you don't mind, Gavin, I believe I'll pack it in for the day."

"Fine. I believe I'll flush out the marquess and see what he's doing." Gavin waved to them as Nicholas took Dorian's arm and started back toward the house.

"I didn't mean to interrupt," Dorian said the minute they were out of Gavin's hearing.

"You didn't." Nicholas slowed his pace so they wouldn't reach the house too soon. "I'm glad you came out here. It made me realize we have things to discuss after last night."

"Yes, well, I thought so, too."

"First, obviously, the music is not here," Nicholas said.

"I quite agree. It's not here and, judging from the type of music the marquess has collected, I think we can cross him off the list of possibilities altogether."

"Agreed," Nicholas said. "Secondly, I want to know why you didn't tell me the truth about your aunt's illness."

Dorian's eyes widened slightly, as though she was surprised by his question. "What truth?"

"You told Sir Gavin all about the doctor's prognosis, but not me. She will not live beyond the fall." Nicholas stopped on the path in a shaded area where they were hidden from the house and from the hunters in the field. He turned Dorian toward him.

A frown puckered her pretty brow. "Why are you angry

because I told Gavin and not you? You've met Aunt Charlotte and seen how easily exhausted she is. Is her prognosis such a surprise? I don't say much about it because we need no one's pity.''

In his annoyance Nicholas paced a few steps away from her, then back. ''But I had to learn the truth from Gavin, a mere acquaintance from your brother's club.''

''That's why you're angry?'' Dorian cocked her head at him. ''If we are going to discuss things that annoy—may I mention that I came out here to join you this morning only to find you and Sir Gavin talking about Lady Eleanor.''

Nicholas's annoyance rapidly shifted into frustration and he looked away, aware that Dorian's jealousy of Eleanor meant she cared about him. But the green emotion was a serpent not to be trusted or relied upon. He knew it was the same one that made him angry over her confession to Gavin. He ground his teeth, feeling trapped in a maze of circumstances that he was unable to explain to Dorian and by emotions he dare not examine too closely.

Dorian's hand on his arm drew him back to her, and he found himself gazing down into the earnest depths of her violet eyes. ''Nicholas, after last night I don't want to doubt you. And I don't want you to doubt me either.''

Compelled by a visceral urgency that the morning spent with Gavin had stirred, Nicholas grasped her hands in both of his. Her fingers were cool and dry. In the sunlight rich blue lights glittered inside her betrothal ring.

''Then let's lay all these doubts, ours and Society's, to rest by setting a wedding date,'' he urged. ''As early as possible. In fact, I shall get a special license as soon as we return to Town.''

''What?'' Dorian shook her head in confusion and attempted to pull away. ''No, Nicholas, that was never part of our agreement.''

''Agreement be damned. Think how pleased your aunt will

be to see you wed." He tightened his grip on her. "Davis can have no objections."

"No." Dorian tugged her hands from his grasp. "No, I don't believe marriage will establish trust or anything else between us. Not under these circumstances."

Suddenly Nicholas knew what she wanted to hear. In a theatrical gesture he thumped his right hand over his heart. "Would it satisfy you if I swore my undying love?"

Dorian paled. Her eyes turned dark, almost black, and her mouth thinned in outrage—and pain. Nicholas knew he'd made a terrible mistake. She backed away from him.

"Don't mock me, Nicholas Derrington." Her voice was low and icy. "However foolish you find my ideals of love. However worldly and cynical you think you are. Don't mock me. Not after I gave you my body *and* my heart last night."

"Dorian?"

She whirled on her heel and left him standing in the middle of the path feeling as though he'd just suffered a savage blow to the gut.

Dorian was so angry she saw none of the beauty of Floraton Park as she hurried down the path toward the house.

With fists tucked in the folds of her skirt she marched along blind to the leafy trees and deaf to the wild call of the peacocks. All she could see was Nicholas's dramatic thumping of his chest. How dare he? All she could hear was his hollow declaration of love. How could he? She'd just overheard him talking of Eleanor. He'd been with Gavin; perhaps the topic of the man's wife was understandable. But she could hardly believe after she and Nicholas had lain in each other's arms that he would be so callous as to take advantage of her vulnerability where Aunt Charlotte was concerned.

"Undying love, indeed," Dorian muttered to herself. The sweet, pleasurable remnants of their nocturnal picnic faded away. A sudden chill made her shiver and her heart began to

ache. She had not been seduced; she would never be so hypocrit-
ical as to accuse Nicholas of that. She had wanted him. But
what, then did he want? She spoke the answer aloud. ''He
wants our piece of the music. That's what.''

When she reached the house she found a message from Aunt
Charlotte's doctor waiting for her. Worry immediately dimmed
her indignation as she read. Her aunt had suffered a mild attack,
Dr. Fisher wrote, but nothing for Dorian to be troubled about
he reassured her. She was not reassured. Without hesitation
Dorian made her excuses, ordered her bags packed and said
her thanks to the marquess and marquessa.

Davis insisted on remaining another day or two, even after
Dorian showed him the note from Aunt Charlotte's doctor. He
seemed to have found something at Floraton Court that amused
him. Dorian was not her brother's keeper, anymore than she
considered him hers. She did not argue with him.

But, to her dismay, when she left the house and was about
to step into the carriage, Nicholas appeared on horseback
intending to accompany her back to Town.

The sight of him annoyed her. She longed to be out of his
company and free of the powerful feelings that his presence
stirred in her. But accompany her he did.

In the days that followed he called daily at the town house,
making himself a congenial companion to Aunt Charlotte—as
well as an attentive fiancé to Dorian in the lady's company.
But when they were alone together Nicholas became polite and
distant in a way that relieved Dorian. She hoped he understood
at last the depth and breadth of their relationship.

''Aunt Charlotte is looking well today,'' he said to Dorian
one afternoon after the lady had gone upstairs for her nap.

''Yes, I believe her doctor overreacted a bit about this last
spell of hers.'' Dorian rang for the servants to clear away the
tea.

Davis, who had returned home only the day before, threw
himself down in a chair and stared out the window. ''I hope
they continue to be wrong.''

"We all do." Nicholas picked up a stack of mail that Dorian realized contained the invitations that had arrived in the last two weeks.

"Miss Dorian? Mr. Davis?" The butler appeared in the doorway of the music room, looking rather puzzled.

"What is it, Barton?" Dorian couldn't imagine what would fluster the unflappable butler. He'd been a part of the St. John household since she and Davis were in the nursery. He was imperturbable.

"Lady Elizabeth Eastleigh and her companion wish to know whether you and Mr. Davis are at home to callers."

Dorian understood Barton's confusion. It was much too late in the afternoon for Quality to pay polite social calls. She glanced at Davis. His mouth had dropped open. In his slack-jawed state he appeared to be even more surprised than she.

"I'm not at home to callers, Barton," Dorian said. "But Davis will be delighted to receive Lady Elizabeth and her companion. Show them into the drawing room."

Davis frowned and shook his head, but it was too late. Barton had already disappeared on his errand.

"This is what you were hoping for, isn't it?" Dorian couldn't understand why Davis was sitting there as if he was reluctant to receive Lady Elizabeth.

"I'm not certain any longer."

"You're not certain?" Dorian stared at her brother and decided he must be ill. "I don't understand."

The stunned surprise had passed from Davis's face. He stood, smoothed the front of his waistcoat, and checked the knot of his neckcloth. "I'm not certain that I like being second best in Lady Elizabeth's estimation."

Dorian glanced in Nicholas's direction, hoping that he might be able to shed some light on this mysterious male behavior. He shrugged and shook his head.

Davis strolled out of the room as if he had all day to reach the drawing room and greet the duke's daughter, the very lady whom he'd vowed to marry not so long ago.

Dorian turned to Nicholas again, but he held up a hand to silence her.

"Don't ask. I don't know what Davis is thinking. He's your brother."

"But he's of your gender." Dorian wrung her hands.

"Just the same, I'm only responsible for my own actions." Nicholas held up the handful of mail. "Don't worry about Davis. I believe he's becoming quite capable in his relationship with the ladies. While we're waiting for the outcome of this social call, let's see what delightful entertainments await us among these invitations."

Davis stopped outside the door of the drawing room and took a deep breath. It was hard to believe there'd been a time when he would have given a goodly sum of money if it would have brought Lady Elizabeth to his door. But since he'd become acquainted with Susanna he'd found he was willing to wait quite some time for Elizabeth.

But she'd called on him at last and he should be thankful, he reminded himself. If all went well, if Elizabeth was here for the reason he suspected, he'd be able to pick up where they'd left off. By Christmas he might be the newest member of the Duke of Eastleigh's family.

"Barton?" Davis turned to the butler waiting near the drawing-room doors. "Send up some sherry and cakes."

"Very good, Mr. Davis."

Davis plastered a smile on his face and nodded to the butler, who immediately opened the drawing room doors.

"Elizabeth, how good to see you." Davis strode into the room, reaching for the hand Elizabeth held out to him. She rose from her chair, giving Davis an opportunity to take in the slenderness of her figure in her tasteful green gown with puffed sleeves and embroidered hem. Tight silver-blond curls framed her face, while green ribbons tied the length of her hair high on her head. On her feet he glimpsed green slippers.

She smiled her restrained, elegant smile as she allowed Davis to press her white hand to his lips. "Davis, so good to see you. I missed you dreadfully. You remember my companion, Miss Marels."

"Of course, Miss Marels." Davis gestured to the chairs. "Please be seated, ladies. And I missed you, Elizabeth. I had no idea you were back from Brighton. How did you find it?"

That was all the prompting Lady Elizabeth needed. She launched into a detailed list of whom she'd met in the Prince of Wales's favorite seaside resort.

"Father and I promenaded on the Steyne each evening and there were delightful lofty discussions of all sorts at Fisher's circulating library."

A servant carried in a silver tray of sherry and cakes and served each lady.

"I'm so glad to hear that you enjoyed yourself." Davis was surprised to find that he did not envy her the stay in Brighton. The relaxed pace of country house parties had been much more to his liking than the frantic see-and-be-seen atmosphere of the coastal village. "Did you see the prince?"

"But of course." Elizabeth smiled indulgently, as though Davis had asked a foolish question. The expression annoyed him. "We dined with Prinny on several occasions. I daresay, he is the most considerate host. He escorted me into the dining room one evening. The meal was superb and the entertainment divine. You and your sister must join us sometime."

"I'm certain Dorian would find it amusing." Davis sipped his sherry and decided to turn the conversation in a direction he would enjoy. "And did you find bathing in the sea as rejuvenating as they say it is?"

Elizabeth sobered. Her back stiffened, and she took a dainty sip of her sherry. "You would ask about that."

"I'm simply curious about the benefits of bathing." Davis managed to keep a teasing grin from his face. Elizabeth didn't like to be teased. "Can you blame me for asking?"

"No doubt you've heard of the scandalous things some of

the young blades get up to,'' Miss Marels said, clearly more interested in the topic than Lady Elizabeth.

''What scandalous things?'' Davis baited, though he did know. One of the gentlemen at his club had admitted to spying on the ladies bathing at Brighton with a telescope. Over a bottle of hock and with a little prompting, the young man had described in titillating detail the delightful way *wet* bathing shifts clung to a lady's body.

''But it's all done so properly and the bathing machine is so carefully built that it's really quite private when a lady bathes,'' Miss Marels explained.

Davis listened to her description of the horse-drawn bathing wagon that was pulled out into the sea so ladies could bath in privacy. Guiltily, he found his bathing fantasies turning to Susanna—not Elizabeth. His mind's eye dressed Susanna in a thin white bathing shift. His mouth went dry with the image of dripping wet, transparent fabric clinging to Susanna's ripe breasts and cupping her firm, round bottom. Davis shifted uncomfortably in his chair.

''I don't believe those detestable young men can possibly see anything from the shore, even if they *are* using telescopes,'' Miss Marels concluded righteously.

Davis shook his head, more to rid himself of Susanna's image than in agreement with the lady. ''I'm certain you are correct about that, Miss Marels.''

''That was the only unpleasant thing about the stay.'' Elizabeth finished her sherry and set the glass on the tray the servant offered. ''Father and I discussed it, and we think you must consider a Brighton visit at the end of the summer.''

The pointedness of the invitation was not wasted on Davis. He sat up in his chair, the tantalizing image of Susanna vanquished immediately. Lady Elizabeth, daughter of the Duke of Eastleigh, was requesting his company at Brighton. But it was bad form to appear too eager.

He paused. ''Indeed. Dorian and I must consider it.''

''Good.'' Elizabeth rose. Miss Marels gulped down her

remaining sherry and jumped to her feet also. "I shall be at the Draytons' ball tomorrow night, and at the Mansfields' soiree next week."

"What a delightful coincidence." Davis stepped to Elizabeth's side to escort her to the door, signaling to Barton to call around the lady's carriage. "I'll be attending the same events. May I call on you soon for a drive in the park?"

"Yes, please do." Elizabeth smiled, a glimmer of warmth coming into her delft blue eyes for the first time during the call.

Davis's heart warmed at the hint of affection from her and patted the hand she'd placed on his arm. They exchanged a few more pleasantries; then Lady Elizabeth was climbing into her carriage and waving her farewell to Davis. When her carriage disappeared around the corner he strolled back into the house feeling quite on top of the world. *He still had a chance to win Elizabeth!*

Barton met him at the door.

"Mr. Davis? This letter just arrived for you."

"Thank you, Barton." Davis ripped open the note without thinking, without even looking at the seal.

Susanna's signature jumped off the page at him. His heart skipped a beat at the sight of her graceful handwriting. He'd heard nothing from her since they'd parted at Floraton Court.

Before he read any of the letter he put on as casual a face as he could manage and strolled into his study.

The hour had grown late and the servants had already lit the candles. Davis shut the door and leaned against it, too weak-kneed to go far. Without further delay he put the paper to his nose and drew in a long breath, seeking Susanna's scent. The paper was not scented, but the aroma of apples and cinnamon came to him—delicate as always, but underscored with a hint of a woman's musk. He closed his eyes. His entire body reacted as if she was standing in the room with him. As if she was pressed against him, warm and soft, vital and passionate and incredibly responsive.

With a concerted effort he made his brain function apart from his body and opened his eyes to read the missive. It was a polite letter—perfectly proper and ladylike in its phrasing—informing him that she was in Town staying with her sister once more and would be pleased to receive a call.

Davis groaned. The prospect of seeing Susanna sounded better to him than any of the dazzling invitations that arrived daily. How he longed to see her, even if only for a few brief minutes in a roomfull of whey-faced relations. Even if it was only to touch her hand and bask in her sweet, quiet smile.

She'd taught him much during those wildly passionate nights at Floraton Court. He'd discovered more treasure in one woman than he thought possible to find. Susanna not only gave him complete, lusty physical satisfaction, but her quiet smile and husky voice soothed his temper and lightened his mood more thoroughly than any amount of Elizabeth's impressive name-dropping.

He walked to the desk, tapping the note against the palm of his hand. But he dare not see Susanna, not now—not with Elizabeth back in Town and hinting for him to join her and her father at Brighton. It was too likely that someone would learn of the call, tell tales, or jump to the wrong conclusion.

With trembling fingers he thrust Susanna's note into the candle flame. The ivory paper caught fire. Flames licked away at the words Susanna had so thoughtfully penned.

Davis ignored the guilt and regret beating rapidly in his heart. Only when the flames scorched his fingers did he drop the burning note onto the hearth. As he watched, the flames died and the charred remains crumbled into ashes.

Chapter Eighteen

"I've heard strange things about Lord Sindby." Dorian sat in the theater box next to Nicholas, still unsettled about which direction their search should take.

Nicholas had planned the evening at Covent Garden to see the farce *The Quaker,* to be followed by *Macbeth*. During the break between the two performances the subject of Sindby's invitation had come to Dorian's mind again. The Earl of Sindby had requested the pleasure of their company at a house party on his ancient estate, Stalker Keep. Dorian shivered. Just the name of the place was enough to discourage any visitor.

"What have you heard?" Nicholas was watching the crowd in the pit below, his expression inscrutable. She sensed he knew more about the sinister earl than he was willing to reveal.

"He collects death masks, for one thing." Dorian frowned and nervously flipped open her fan to stir the air, though the thought of death masks chilled her. "Don't you think that a bit morbid? And then, he is a bachelor. Who is going to be his hostess?"

"I've met the man, long ago at some reception or other.

He's an indefatigable sportsman.'' Nicholas never took his eyes from the pit, but leaned over the balustrade and waved at someone whose eye he had finally caught. Only then did he face Dorian. "Sindby is indeed a strange person. I believe a cousin of his serves as his hostess. His invitation is not one I would consider accepting, except that I have heard that he collects the music of obscure dead composers."

"How cheerful. Just where did you get your information?"

"I have a contact who has been very helpful." Nicholas studied her a moment longer. "Is it too warm in here for you? Would you like to go outside?"

"No, I'm fine." Dorian flipped the fan closed and thrust it into her lap. For some reason she could not explain she did not want to go to Stalker Keep. "Did this informant tell you Aunt Charlotte and I had a piece of the song?"

Nicholas paused, his eyes narrowing. Dorian wondered if she'd strained his patience with her too far at last. "My contact informed me that a piece would turn up in the auction house. How did you hear about it?"

Dorian relented with a shrug. "From a rather disreputable music dealer. Do you trust this informant?"

"As much as you trust your disreputable music dealer."

"Then I suppose we must consider this invitation seriously." Dorian followed Nicholas's gaze this time and realized that he was watching a rather attractive dowager in the box almost directly opposite theirs. The lady glared at Nicholas in return, her face hard and cold.

"Do you know her?" From the expensive but old-fashioned style of her dark purple dress Dorian took the lady to be country gentry, in Town to enjoy Society and the theater.

"Yes, as a matter of fact I do." Nicholas turned back to Dorian. "She's mother of a friend from long ago."

"There you are, my lord." An orange girl with rosy cheeks and snapping dark eyes appeared at the door of the box. The basket she carried against her hip was heaped with oranges, and apples polished to their tempting best sheen. A citrus fragrance filled the box. "You was the one what waved to me, was you not, my lord?"

"Indeed, I was." Nicholas cast a sidelong glance at Dorian, then grinned at the girl. "Once on a picnic, not so long ago, I promised my lady that I would take her to the theater and buy her the best oranges in the place. I trust that's what you have."

The gesture surprised and touched Dorian. She couldn't keep herself from laughing. "Nicholas, 'tis not really necessary."

"But I always keep my promises."

"And aren't you fortunate, my lady." The girl set down her basket and pointed to her fresh, shiny goods. "For I have the very best oranges to be had here in the theater. And I know they are just what his lordship wants for you."

Nicholas slipped the girl a coin. She peered at it, her eyes growing round. "And you may keep the basket, too, my lord and my lady, seeing as you'll need it to carry all them oranges away with you."

Then the girl was gone, calling out to one of her friends in delight, "I've sold all my supply for the night."

"Nicholas, what are we going to do with so many oranges?"

"*We* are going to eat them." He took out the knife he carried and began to peel an orange, just as he had the night of the greenhouse picnic.

Dorian felt her breath grow shallow and quick with the memory of his hands on her that night. The heat of a blush flooded her cheeks.

"Nicholas, please." She pushed away his hand when he waved a succulent slice under her nose. "No, I will not allow you to feed me here in front of all these people."

Nicholas grinned at her again and put the slice of orange into her hand. "Suck on it and let me watch you."

Before she could make a suitable reply to that seductive remark, she was saved by the beginning of the second play.

Dorian would have rather seen *Romeo and Juliet; Macbeth*, though well presented and performed, seemed far too dark and ominous for her mood. The audience received the play well, then filed out of the theater in a relatively orderly fashion compared to other performances Dorian had attended.

The basket of fruit was given over to Nicholas's tiger to carry as they threaded their way through the crowd to the street.

While they waited for the carriage they exchanged few comments. The noise and bustle of the crowd discouraged conversation.

Dorian allowed Nicholas to lead the way to the edge of the crush without taking particular note of the people around them. Suddenly Nicholas came to a halt. Dorian walked into his back before she realized that something was wrong—someone stood in their way.

A strident voice rang out. "How dare you go about in public like this, Nicholas Derrington, as if all's right with the world and you have nothing to be ashamed of?"

Every fiber of Nicholas's body tightened beneath his cutaway coat. Dorian could feel his anxiety. She recovered from colliding with him and peered around his arm at the dowager in purple whom she'd seen Nicholas watching earlier in the evening. Her middle-aged face was white with rage. On closer examination Dorian saw that the lady's features were ravaged by grief.

"Good evening, Mrs. Collard." Nicholas spoke calmly, but the tension in his body belied his courteous greeting.

"Is that all you have to say for yourself?" Mrs. Collard demanded, her fury so intense, it drew a gasp from Dorian .

Fortunately most of the theater crowd had dispersed and they were alone on the street.

"You think you can fool the world by wearing that mourning ring for my son? Pretending you are sorry for Jonathan's death when the truth is, you had no care about wasting his life."

"I assure you, ma'am, there will never be enough words to express the depth of my grief for your son and all the other midshipmen and sailors who died at Trafalgar."

"And you think that absolves you? You were his idol. He believed in you. He would have done anything for you, gone anywhere for you and His Majesty's Navy. And you threw his life away for what—for a few gold coins? For a place in Napoleon's army?''

''That's not the truth of it, Mrs. Collard. I don't know who tried to pass the information to the French. I don't know who wasted so many precious lives, but I intend to find out.''

''You expect me to believe that?'' Mrs. Collard snapped. The lady's companion touched her arm and murmured something in her ear. Clearly she was trying to draw Mrs. Collard away.

Dorian saw the carriage bearing the Seacombe crest drive up the street. Rather unbecomingly, she jumped up and down and waved to the coachman.

''Nicholas, the carriage is to our left.'' Dorian prodded and pulled him in that direction.

''Believe me, I do not wear this ring to fool anyone.'' Nicholas refused to be budged. ''I wear it so I won't forget the waste. Rest assured, I will find the villain.''

''Do not lavish meaningless promises on me,'' Mrs. Collard shouted over her shoulder as her companion drew her toward their carriage.

For a moment Dorian thought Nicholas was going to follow them. She tugged on his arm. ''Nicholas? She won't hear anything you tell her. Come away.''

After some hesitation, Nicholas allowed Dorian to lead the way to the carriage. He climbed in after her and sat down on the opposite seat.

The tiger snapped open the communicating door. ''Where to, my lord?''

Dorian peered into Nicholas's stern white face, worried about the anguish in his eyes. ''Just drive, please, and keep driving.''

''Yes, miss.'' He snapped the door shut and the carriage rumbled down the cobblestone street.

Nicholas's eyes were dark and glazed with a pain Dorian realized he'd never allowed her to see. She'd known early on in their relationship that he wanted the music for a reason connected with his family's darkened reputation. He was a prideful man and a naval officer; he could never let such an offense pass without doing everything possible to rectify it.

Yet when he'd examined the letters on the back of the music Aunt Charlotte possessed he'd revealed so little emotion. Dorian had felt they were doing nothing more important than solving a puzzle—a very personal puzzle—but merely a puzzle nonetheless.

Now she berated herself for never stopping to think how much the false accusations and the death of a friend must have hurt Nicholas. More than his pride was injured—his heart was torn and bruised and raw.

"That was Jonathan Collard's mother?" Dorian asked.

Nicholas stared into the darkness, still lost to her for the moment.

"Nicholas?"

"Yes, yes. That was Jonathan's mother."

"You wear the ring for him?" Dorian felt as though she was extracting information from a dazed child.

"We grew up together. His father was my father's estate steward." Nicholas took off his hat and ran his fingers through his hair.

"So Gavin knew him, too?" Dorian prodded.

"We all went to sea together, Gavin and I as midshipmen and Jon as a seaman." Nicholas thumped his head back against the carriage seat. "We were green boys of fifteen. We thought life on the high seas would be adventurous, exotic, and daring."

"And so it must have been."

Nicholas shook his head. "Life at sea is hard. But in Lord Nelson's navy the three of us managed to survive and prosper—until Trafalgar."

"Is Mr. Collard still steward at Seacombe Manor?"

"No. He died years ago, before Jon's death." Nicholas was quiet for a moment. "I had wanted to call on Mrs. Collard two years ago when I returned. She has a pension house in the village and still works sometimes at the home farm. I wanted to offer my condolences, but Gavin discouraged me. She has not taken her son's death very equitably."

"Apparently not." Dorian sensed there was much more to the story of the three young men who had gone to sea, but she dared not pursue it now. "Though I can't blame a mother."

"Nor can I." The faraway look gleamed in his eyes.

Dorian fidgeted, uncertain what to do. Suddenly his gaze focused on her, his face still white with pain. He was with her again, though his mood was profoundly altered. The darkness of it frightened her.

Nicholas tapped on the tiger's door. "We must get you home."

"No." Dorian grasped his knee, obeying an urgent instinct to shelter him the only way she could think of. "Let's spend the entire night together."

"What would your brother say?"

"I don't care what Davis says. Besides, he's at the Earl of Drayton's ball, dancing with his beloved Lady Elizabeth. He won't be home until three or four himself. He'll never know I'm gone."

"I am not good company after that encounter, I fear."

"Where do you intend to go after you take me home?" Dorian scowled at him. "Don't tell me you are going back to your uncle's house."

"You know me too well." Nicholas eyed her as though he was contemplating his answer. "I might go down to the docks. The sights and sounds of the ships soothe me sometimes."

The tiger finally pulled open the door. "Yes, my lord?"

"Then take me with you," Dorian pleaded. "Show me the ships."

"Sweetheart, 'tis not the place for a lady. Nor is it proper, with no chaperon along."

"But surely I'd be safe with you, my fiancé," Dorian countered. Propriety be damned. Whatever the cost, she knew it was vital not to leave Nicholas to his own dark thoughts tonight.

Nicholas turned to her, surprise on his face; then he grasped her hand firmly. ''To the London docks.''

Fog rolled in off the river and clung close to the street as Nicholas helped Dorian from the carriage. Heavy and gray though the stuff was, it was not the impenetrable mist that had clogged the streets the night he'd visited the Blue Mermaid and been attacked. Nicholas felt a curious affinity for the drizzle; it matched his mood. He knew this darkness too well. Though he'd never banish Dorian from his side, tonight he wished she'd gone home and left him to his dark thoughts.

As soon as she had alighted from the carriage, she turned to him. He could just make out her features in the dim light falling from the street lamp. Her eyes were large, luminous, and dark; her lips were solemn. He hoped she didn't expect much of him.

''We don't have to talk if you don't want to,'' she said, as if she'd read his thoughts. Then she added, as she linked her arm through his, ''But I don't believe in brooding. You can tell me about the ships, if you're so inclined.''

Grateful for her understanding, Nicholas led them along the dock, pointing out the merchant ships he recognized. But these seemed small and insignificant to him. The giant first- and second-raters such as his ship, the *Dauntless,* and Admiral Nelson's *Victory,* the real fighting machines of His Majesty's Navy, were anchored downriver in deeper water, at Woolich.

Before long he fell silent. The scene with Jonathan Collard's mother replayed itself in his mind. Mrs. Collard's pain and grief had awakened his own. He listened to the lapping of the water against the ships' hulls and the clanging of the watch bells.

Life aboard the *Dauntless* seemed only yesterday. He couldn't fathom how it had all come to such a disreputable end. What if he couldn't prove the truth? He didn't even know what the truth was himself. Where was he to go from here?

''Nicholas?''

''We've come to the end.'' Nicholas stared down into the black flowing river water at the end of the dock.

''Let's go inside.'' Dorian tugged him away from the edge. ''Is there someplace where we can get something to warm us?''

Nicholas realized he was being remiss in caring for his lady. ''There's a respectable tavern and inn just up the hill, if you don't mind a humble establishment. Come along. Let's get you something warm to drink.''

The Tower House Inn was as respectable as Nicholas recalled; the owner was a polite pigtailed man, and his wife was tall, proper and decorous. The inn's patrons included a better quality of seaman and their ladies than found in establishments closer to the dock. Only a few curious glances were cast in their direction.

Nicholas found a table for them and ordered two hot buttered rums. ''Something to warm your blood, my lady, and ease you into slumber.''

As soon as the proprietress hurried away to fill the order before closing, Dorian leaned toward him. ''We are going to stay out all night, aren't we, Nicholas?''

''Dorian, Jonathan Collard is my ghost,'' Nicholas said, beginning to realize what she was up to. He appreciated her gesture. He did not think many women would have any idea of what he was feeling. ''I have to live with what happened. There is nothing for you to do. There is nothing you need do.''

Dorian leveled a sober violet-eyed gaze on him. ''A ghost is poor company for any man.''

Nicholas's groin throbbed with a sudden fierce need to possess her. He needed to be sure of her in a world where it seemed he could be sure of nothing. ''We will not roam the city in a carriage all night.''

''Perhaps there are private accommodations here where we might enjoy the warmth of a fire.''

Nicholas hesitated.

''It's what I want,'' Dorian said, ''if you will suffer my company.''

"Any time," Nicholas said. He called the innkeeper to the table and arranged for private rooms.

He wanted to pretend that he was a gentleman at least. But as soon as the innkeeper had lit the fire for them and closed the chamber door, Nicholas was consumed with a desperate urge to take Dorian into his arms and lose himself in her softness.

When she'd given herself to him in the greenhouse he'd felt completely certain of her. During that hot, wet time when he'd sunk deep inside her, he'd known she was his. He'd exalted in the pure physical pleasure. But now he'd laid the whole sordid disappointment of his life before her.

Nicholas touched her shoulders as she stood by the fire. "Let me take your cloak."

She shrugged out of it. He put it on a chair with his greatcoat. When he turned back to her, she faced him.

"What do you believe, Dorian? Does any part of you believe what Jonathan Collard's mother accused me of?"

Dorian reached out for him, slipping her arms around his neck. She kissed him with quick artless tenderness. "I believe in you. And there's nowhere I'd rather be than here with you— be you haunted and morose and damned poor company."

Nicholas swept her up in his arms. A small cry escaped Dorian as he carried her into the dark bedchamber. He eased her back down against the pillows. She did not protest when he stood over her and began to undress. He pulled off his shirt and dropped heavily on the bed to pull off his boots.

Dorian remained silent.

He rolled toward her, his fingers angling her head. Nicholas kissed her mouth, then her throat, then her mouth again. Dorian made small whimpering sounds of surrender and pleasure.

He allowed his hand to roam over her body, finding that as before she wore no stays. The silk of her dress slid soft and sheer beneath his hand. It was as if nothing separated his fingers from her hot, bare skin. She gasped as his hands moved down the front of her dress.

"We undressed too quickly the first time," he whispered. "It should happen slower."

"How slowly?" Dorian asked, as if she would not agree to just anything he desired.

He bent his head to kiss her mouth and reached for the crystal buttons of her dress. Ending the kiss, his eyes followed the vements of his hands as he carefully released each button from its hole. When they were all undone he parted the bodice and kissed her breasts through the sheer cotton of her chemise.

"Nicholas!" Dorian cried out as she ran her fingers through his hair.

He wasted no more time and untied the ribbons of her chemise, baring her breasts. Cupping them in his palms, he teased her nipples with his thumbs. Dorian chanted his name and raised her arms over her head, giving herself over to his touch.

Her nipples turned hard and pink as exotic pearls. He bent his head to suckle her, drawing one turgid crest and then the other into his mouth, tonguing her until she cried out and arched herself off the bed.

Things were moving too fast, but Nicholas could not force himself to hold back. He pressed her face between his hands and kissed her. When he released her and stood up to finish undressing she was gasping for breath.

Her eyes were solemn and watchful as he unbuttoned his pantaloons. She took in the sight of his naked, heavily aroused body without comment, then she sat up to wiggle out of her chemise and drawers. Her swollen breasts swayed deliciously.

"Come here, sweetheart." Nicholas stretched out on the bed and reached for her, grateful to find the fire of desire that had flared between them that night in the greenhouse still existed. He needed to know that Dorian would respond to him tonight as she had before.

A deep sense of relief shot through him as Dorian's arms went slowly around him. He touched the soft swell of her breasts and warmed with satisfaction at their swollen weight in his palms. He kissed each bud lightly, teasingly, this time reminding himself to take her slowly. He wanted her aroused as much as he was.

She moved restlessly beneath his hands, beneath his mouth. The blood roared in his heart. It was useless. The frantic need to possess her overwhelmed Nicholas's self-control. His willpower dissolved in the face of the raw need raging inside him.

"Sweetheart, I need to know that you believe in me."

"I believe in you," she whispered and stroked his hair. "And I'm here."

Nicholas was burning with desire as he lowered himself between her white thighs. Slipping his hands beneath her bottom, he drove into her, uttering a husky, joyous exclamation.

Dorian sucked in a breath, her body instinctively clutching him deep inside her. Nicholas peered into her face and saw that her eyes were open. He was glad. He wanted her to look at him, to see him. With their gazes locked, all that mattered was slaking the overpowering need that clamored within him.

He began to move quickly, driving again and again into Dorian's tight, dark warmth. As he moved, he watched her face, needing to see her responsive beneath him. She reached out and touched his cheek with the back of her hand.

A long sigh escaped Nicholas. The gentle and reassuring gesture eased the pain inside him—but the driving need to possess her grew more urgent. He reached between them to find the small, sensitive bud of delicate female flesh.

"Nicholas."

Her soft cry put him over the edge. Every muscle in his body strained as he reached the peak. He drove deep one last time, arching his spine and flinging his head back, crying out as he poured his seed into her.

She lifted herself against him, accepting all that he gave her, holding him close as he shuddered in her arms. He felt tiny convulsions rip through her, and then he was lost.

Nicholas lay awake for a long while afterward. He gazed into the shadows and put his mind to the task of how to learn the identity of the man who had caused all the useless deaths and ruined the Derrington family name.

"There is a way to find the truth," Dorian whispered in the darkness as she stroked his hair. "Someone has the answer. Someone has the evidence and may not even know it. We'll find it, Nicholas. We'll go to Stalker Keep and see what the Earl of Sindby has collected."

Nicholas kissed her, glad that he had not sent her home after the theater. She was the small, soft white light in his darkness. He'd be a fool to let go of that. "Yes. We'll go to Stalker Keep and solve this riddle together."

Chapter Nineteen

Dorian had always liked the moors, the ancient windswept hills covered in purple heather sprawling under a wild blue sky. But she could not bring herself to be enthusiastic about the trip to Stalker Keep, though she tried for Nicholas's sake.

In addition to the strange reputation of the earl himself, she dreaded the long, exhausting carriage journey—two days over a rough road with sleepless nights in less than adequate inns. But she would not complain of the trip.

Their passionate night together had made it clearer than ever that this trip was necessary. Nicholas needed to know who had betrayed him and his friend, if not for the good of his family's name, then for his own peace of mind. She could not deny him help. Not after he'd made love to her as she felt certain no other man could.

Nicholas might need and want her comfort, and she was glad to give it, but needing comfort was not the same thing as loving. She knew instinctively what all women know: engaging a man's body was not necessarily engaging a man's heart.

She couldn't make him love her, but she could help him

learn whether the Earl of Sindby was the collector who held the third piece of Franz's love song for Aunt Charlotte.

The pleasant part of the trip would be the company. Dorian had encountered Susanna Sunridge at the modiste and, in the course of their conversation, had asked the young widow to go along to Stalker Keep as her companion and chaperon. Now that Lady Elizabeth was back, Davis had shown no interest in pulling himself away from Town. And Nicholas had asked that she bring a companion.

"There's only so much propriety we can flaunt, my lady," Nicholas had told her in a voice that brooked no argument. For the most part his dark mood had dissipated with the dawn after their night together. Dorian had seen no hint of the empty darkness in his blue eyes that had frightened her so. She intended to keep that emptiness at bay.

Susanna had looked doubtful at Dorian's invitation to accompany her to Stalker Keep. "Isn't your brother going?"

"Oh, no; Davis has accepted other invitations and will be staying in Town," Dorian had said.

"The wild Scottish borderland," Susanna had exclaimed. "What a wonderful adventure! I'd love to go."

The next day, over tea with Nicholas, Davis, and Aunt Charlotte, Dorian had told them of her good fortune in having such delightful company along. Nicholas and Aunt Charlotte had agreed immediately.

Davis had paled and sloshed tea into his saucer. "Do you really think you should take her?"

"Why not?" Dorian couldn't understand what troubled him. "You're not going with us. I need a chaperon, and we will have enough room in the carriage."

"But Stalker Keep is such a far-off, wild place." Davis looked genuinely upset. He appealed to Nicholas. "You've heard the stories, Seacombe. I can't imagine why you are going at all."

"I've heard the stories, and I know why you are going," Charlotte volunteered.

That silenced them all.

Startled, Dorian turned to her aunt. "What do you know?"

"It's an old tale." Aunt Charlotte slowly took up her cup and finished her tea. Dorian glanced at Nicholas and realized he was as impatient as she to hear what her aunt had to say. "It's been circulating since I was a girl. The Griffins have long been thought to be devil worshippers."

Dorian opened her mouth to protest, though she'd heard the same tale and more.

"Devil worship!" Davis rose to his feet.

Charlotte held up a finger to silence her niece and nephew. "A good deal of the story centers around the fifth earl, known as 'Mad Jack,' who called the devil forth from a bottomless whirlpool called Hagberry Pot.

"It doesn't sound like a very nice place to visit. But I know you and Nicholas are making the trip because you've heard that the Earl of Sindby, Jules Griffin, collects Franz's music."

Nicholas leaned forward in his chair. "Yes, that's what we've heard. Have you heard otherwise?"

"Pray tell us, Aunt." Dorian moved to the edge of her chair, setting her teacup on the tray. "Is there more we should know?"

"It's true, Griffin does collect." Charlotte nodded. "I hate to think of such a man taking pleasure from Franz's work. But I heard it from one of Franz's early students. Lord Sindby had shown him some of the work he'd collected."

Nicholas and Dorian exchanged glances. The information Nicholas's source had given him was now confirmed.

"I still don't think you should take Susanna with you," Davis asserted, resuming his seat.

"Why? You don't seem to mind if *I* go." Dorian studied her brother, wondering the reason for his distress.

" 'Tis not the same thing. Nicholas will be with you." Davis set his teacup aside. "Susanna has no protector."

Dorian lifted a single brow. "Susanna?"

Davis blushed, his face turning rosy red. "She has been at

several parties we have attended. She has permitted me to call her by her Christian name.''

''Of course.''

''I shall be glad to look after Lady Susanna,'' Nicholas assured Davis. ''As I told Dorian, I met the earl some years ago through Sir Gavin. Gavin called on Uncle George and I yesterday. He and Lady Eleanor are going to be at Stalker Keep.''

Dorian tried not to show her surprise. Nicholas had not told her before now that he knew of the Traffords' attendance at the house party. It didn't reassure her.

Nicholas went on. ''Though I can say Sindby is quite an Original and a enthusiastic sportsman, I detected nothing sinister about him beyond his family's unique reputation—spread, I might add, by superstitious tenants on his estate.''

The information did not seem to mollify Davis. ''Nevertheless, I believe I should go along.''

''What?'' Dorian stared at her brother. ''But I've already sent your regrets.''

Davis waved away Dorian's concern. ''Surely one more guest won't make much difference at a large party. I've never known a hostess who wasn't delighted to have another gentleman at her table.''

Dorian could not argue with that fact of social life, but her brother's interest in this party mystified her. He much preferred fox hunting and dancing to a sportsman's tromp through the heather to shoot birds. ''But I thought you were going to the Mansfields' ball and hunt breakfast next week.''

''The more I think of it, the more certain I am that I should go with you to Stalker Keep.''

Two days later the four of them—Dorian, Davis, Nicholas, and Susanna—shared a carriage headed north.

The first blast of the pipe organ shook the walls of the medieval hall and sent a shudder through Dorian. The guests who had gathered to hear the Earl of Sindby demonstrate his prize possession reacted with a start.

"What a frightful noise," Susanna murmured in Dorian's ear. "The place seems quite old."

Dorian was thankful for the widow's company when they arrived. Of all the guests, they had come face-to-face with Sir Gavin and Lady Eleanor first thing. Eleanor was elegant and beautifully feminine in all the ways that made Dorian feel so inadequate. But with Susanna at her side Dorian felt as though she had an ally—a friend. She only wished her brother would behave more kindly toward the widow.

On the trip north Davis had paid the barest attention to Susanna. And the lady herself seemed reluctant to accept what little courtesies he'd offered her. The awkwardness between the two only served to make a long trip seem longer than it was. Dorian had been relieved to reach Stalker Keep without any delay—until she stepped out of the carriage to the Earl of Sindby's welcome.

A long, gaunt face and gleaming eyes belied Lord Sindby's smooth voice and gracious manner. He wore all black—coat, shirt and neckcloth all as dark as his hair. His complexion was parchment white. With a smile that sent chills down Dorian's spine, he took her hand in his cool, dry fingers.

"At last I have the opportunity to meet the darling of the *ton.*" He bowed over Dorian's hand but did not take the liberty of kissing her fingers. Nicholas stood right behind her. Nevertheless, the earl's eyes raked her in a way she found most disconcerting. Perhaps Nicholas had found nothing sinister in the man, but she thought him cold, unnerving, and distinctly odd.

His hostess was a white-haired, faded woman the earl introduced as Lady Haddo, his cousin, though she behaved toward him with the deference of a servant.

"Do come in and rest yourselves after so long a journey," the earl invited, gesturing toward the open door. "Most of the other guests are here. I trust you know everyone."

He had led her right to Sir Gavin and Lady Eleanor, and she had greeted the Traffords as graciously as she could. Then they had all submitted to the tour of Stalker Keep.

A shrill organ note pierced Dorian's thoughts, and she realized Susanna was awaiting a comment from her.

"Old, indeed, yes. I believe the earl said the original keep was built by the second lord of Stalker in 1560." Dorian recalled a few details from the letter the earl had sent with his invitation. The hall where they stood appeared to have undergone little change since the year it was built—except for the blasted organ. She went on speaking in Susanna's ear to be heard over the organ music. "There have been several additions since the 1500s, including a garden, stables, and a courtyard."

"And one pipe organ," Susanna added unnecessarily.

Nicholas and Davis moved in closer to hear their conversation.

"Quite a fortress," Nicholas observed. "A Sindby lord could hold off a sizable army from those walls. They must be six-foot thick. No doubt the clan held off the king's army sometime in the past."

"Well, it's not difficult to see why Sindby is a sportsman," Davis added, staring at the trophy head of a magnificent stag hanging over the giant fireplace at the other end of the hall. "Fine woods for deer in the river valley, and open moors for grouse rolling out in every direction."

Dorian looked at Nicholas, wondering whether he'd seen any sign of the earl's music collection.

Nicholas seemed to know what she was thinking and whispered in her ear, "It's probably in the same room with the death mask collection."

"I do not find that amusing." Dorian turned away, well aware of how Nicholas liked to bait her. But his teasing secretly pleased her. As he moved past her, he caught her hand and squeezed it in a quick, affectionate gesture that made her heart skip a beat. Then he was gone, already conversing with Sir Gavin.

She could not catch Nicholas's eye again. His touch had come and gone so swiftly, Dorian almost wondered whether the sweet affection in it had been just her imagination—her longing for something more from him than the respect he would accord his fiancé or the desire he felt for any female body.

By then the earl's blessedly brief organ recital was over. He led them up the wide stairs to see other wonders of the keep.

Though the earl had assumed that she and Davis knew everyone, several of the younger gentlemen were unknown to her, as were some of the older ladies, who turned out to be mothers of the gentlemen: the Allerbys and the Corsleys. Their lilting accents told Dorian they were border families. Something about the company seemed odd, but she couldn't quite put her finger on it.

Dorian soon realized Nicholas was correct about the music. It was displayed along with the death masks—in a dungeon room the earl had had converted for that purpose.

"Don't you think it appropriate to show my collection in the dungeon?" The earl grinned a long-toothed grin, taking obvious pride in his morbid showroom.

"There are more windows in here than I expected to find in a dungeon," Dorian commented, suddenly out of gracious things to say about Stalker Keep.

"Yes, the windows face west, to catch the evening sun," the earl explained. "Actually, this is the upper dungeon, and a rather pleasant place. The lower dungeon is something of a hole-in-the rock. Too dark and entirely too damp for preserving a collection of any kind."

"Certainly dampness would be bad for a collection."

"Most assuredly," the earl agreed, taking Dorian's hand and leading her away from the group that had gathered around a death mask of a Scottish rebel. "I understand from Sir Gavin that you and Lord Seacombe are interested in Franz Chamier's music."

"Yes, we are." Dorian glanced in Gavin's direction, wondering how much Nicholas had told his friend about their search and about the fact that their engagement was a charade that allowed them to work together without raising eyebrows. She prayed Nicholas had not shared anything about the nights they had spent together in each other's arms.

The earl nodded. "Then I have several things to show you. But not now. Later in your stay, when the others are occupied and entertained with other things. We will slip back here."

With that tempting but cryptic promise the earl left her side, clapped his hands to attract the attention of his guests, and led them all upstairs to supper.

Dorian told Nicholas what the earl had said as soon as they had a moment to speak together alone. Nicholas escorted her upstairs. Several of the guests had retired already, but others remained downstairs, drinking and playing cards.

Nicholas frowned as they stopped outside the door of Dorian's room. "What do you think Sindby has to show us?"

"I'm not sure." Dorian tried to think of exactly what they knew about Franz's death in jail. "We've always known that Chamier was killed because he'd overheard or learned something he wasn't suppose to know. Now I realize it must have been the identity of the man you seek."

Nicholas opened the door and slipped inside behind Dorian. "A sailor and a ship's carpenter from my ship, the *Dauntless*, were caught in the act of attempting to pass information to the Franco-Spanish fleet in Cadiz while we were awaiting them off Cape Trafalgar. The information about Nelson's battleplan they carried was too detailed to be something they had learned on their own; they were couriers for someone else. Someone highly placed. Someone who was privy to Admiral Nelson's meetings with his captains. Neither man would reveal the identity of their source. The ship's carpenter had some connection that saved him from the yardarm; the sailor hung. Then the rumors began to surface that I was the source."

"As a decoy for the real traitor?"

"I believe so. But it was also a logical conclusion. The two men were under my command, though no other connection between us could be proven."

Dorian nodded. "Let's continue along this path. If the carpenter was in jail with Franz, would he be foolish enough to reveal his source and admit that he was a traitor to the other prisoners?"

"No," Nicholas said. "His fellow prisoners would probably take exception to him trafficking with the French. However, he might reveal his role to a foreigner, expecting sympathy. Does that make sense?"

"Yes, but the Franz Chamier I knew, the Hungarian expatriot, would take a narrow view of disloyalty to homeland."

Nicholas picked up on her speculation. "Franz writes the identity of the source on the only thing he has, the back of 'A Whisper of Violets.' And to disguise it, in case it fell into the wrong hands, he writes the name in Greek."

Dorian continued. "Then he smuggles it out as best he can, in three small pieces. Aunt Charlotte and I received one."

"One went astray, probably the one I have. The third was snapped up by the villain, who had by then realized Chamier knew his identity and intended to reveal it. Dare we hope we've come to the last call in our search for the third piece?"

"Oh, I hope so," Dorian said on a prayerful breath.

They stared at each other for a moment, astonished that they had put so much together. Suddenly Nicholas swept her up into his arms, his mouth covering hers in a quick, hard kiss.

"We're so close to the end I can feel it," he murmured in her ear. "Sweetheart, let me stay the night."

"No, I can't," Dorian said, pushing herself away from him.

"Oh." Nicholas studied her, then seemed relieved as some new thought occurred to him. "That's nothing to be concerned about. We'll just sleep in each other's arms. I think I can manage that."

"No, I don't mean that," Dorian said, blushing as she realized he thought she refused him for some physical reason.

A soft knock on the door interrupted them.

"Dorian?" Susanna pushed open the door.

Nicholas released Dorian immediately.

"Come in, Susanna. Nicholas and I were just saying good night."

"Oh, I'm sorry. I didn't mean to interrupt."

Dorian grinned at Nicholas. "It seems accommodations are a bit crowded, my lord. Susanna and I are sharing a room."

"I see." Nicholas bid Susanna a polite good night, then drew Dorian out into the hallway with him. "If you'd married me as I asked you to at Floraton Court, you and I could be sharing a room tonight."

Then he took her jaw between his thumb and forefinger and kissed her again.

Dorian protested, struggling against his hold. She did not care to be seen kissing him in the hallway.

"Admit it." He lifted his mouth from hers only long enough to speak. "You'd rather sleep with me than Susanna."

"You'd like to think so, wouldn't you?" She would not give him the satisfaction of knowing how she longed to have him touch her in all those secret places again.

"Don't tease me, my lady. We can always seek out the accommodations in some other place—the dungeon, perhaps?"

He kissed her again before she could object. He pressed her against the wall, inserting his knee between her thighs and exploring her mouth in the most intimate manner. Her whimpers of protest turned to sighs of surrender.

She hadn't intended to capitulate. He didn't need her now as he had the night they had walked along the docks. Several days had passed since their last intimate encounter. Every hour in his company, she'd relived the pleasure she'd found in his arms.

Still, she couldn't allow him to think she had no will of her own every time he put his hands and mouth on her. She succeeded in tearing her mouth free. Her lips felt swollen and bruised. When she dragged her tongue over them she tasted port and tobacco. She tasted Nicholas.

She took a deep breath to steady herself and leaned against the stone wall. Without opening her eyes, she could feel Nicholas studying her face.

''Good night, my lord.'' She prayed he would leave her now to compose herself before she went back into her room to face Susanna.

''I'm not finished.'' He lowered his head again. This time his lips ate at hers, nibbling and sucking, rubbing and caressing. Her fingers clutched at him, forming deep furrows in the fine fabric covering the hard muscles of his upper arms.

When the kiss ended she rolled her head to one side. ''No more.''

He left her mouth and began on her neck.

A low groan escaped her as they kissed ravenously, engaging in an orgy of kissing that was blatantly erotic and carnal. He swept her mouth with his tongue, as though to rid it of pride and protest.

Dorian's knees went weak. She braced herself against the wall for support, afraid that if Nicholas stepped away from her she would slump into a puddle on the floor.

He brushed one more light kiss against her lips. ''Now I'll say good night,'' he said, his hands at her waist, barely steadying her, his lips brushing against her ear. ''Just remember that you could have slept with me tonight.''

He left her aching for him. She opened her eyes just in time to see him disappear into the shadowy darkness at the end of the passage.

Chapter Twenty

Davis frowned at the playing cards in his hands and wondered why he'd felt so compelled to come along on this boring weekend on the Scottish border.

Like a fool he'd passed up an opportunity to ride to the hounds and dance at the Mansfields' prestigious hunt ball. Elizabeth was there—and Herby Dashworth, too.

But here he was at Stalker Keep, where his host was surely mad. The company, for the most part, was regrettably common. Aside from Sir Gavin and Lord Seacombe, the gentlemen lacked polish, drank too much, gambled too heavily, and in general behaved rather coarsely.

Susanna had all but cut him dead again—no more than he deserved, perhaps, but the slight stung nonetheless. He was feeling rather sorry for himself; justifiably so, he thought, as he stared at his poor assortment of cards.

Here he sat at the card table, following in the less than illustrious footsteps of the other gentlemen guests—drinking and gambling and chuckling at the ribaldry that passed for humor.

The evening had grown late. The ladies had retired, leaving the men to their cards and stories in the great hall. Davis couldn't quite dismiss the drunken notion that the boar's head over his shoulder was eyeing his cards rather disapprovingly. He'd like to see how the bloody creature would play them in this blasted game.

"That was a damned fine shot you took at the stag this morning, St. John," said Corsley, a big-nosed young man with brown hair. He puffed away on a cigar. "Going to hang that magnificent head in your drawing room?"

"In my study, I think," Davis said, knowing Dorian would never permit the mounted stag's head in the drawing room. "I want it hanging where I can admire it at my leisure."

Lord Sindby threw the winning card on the table. "I believe the game is mine."

"Right you are, my lord," agreed Allerby, another young gentleman with dark hair and a ruddy complexion. He'd been draining his brandy regularly as they played.

"That is all the cards for me this evening," Sindby declared, rising from the table. "I'm going to join Trafford and Seacombe over by the fire. But you three play on if you wish. The night is young."

After their host had left the table Corsley picked up the cards and began to shuffle them. "Another game, gentlemen?"

"Fine with me," Allerby said. "I think that's damned smart thinking, St. John, hanging that stag's head in your study."

"Right." Davis rather liked the idea, too, now that he thought of it.

"Can't deny the hunting has been good here." Corsley dealt out the cards and spoke around the cigar clamped in his teeth. "I hear he has to work at it, though. The poachers around here are smart and deuced bold. Carry your game off from right under your nose."

He leaned forward to confide in the other two. "His lordship told me about his problems last night after everyone had retired. He's even had to resort to man-traps."

"That's a bit extreme, isn't it?" Davis eyed the other two at the table, surprised that they weren't as shocked as he by the mention of the medieval method of discouraging poachers. He blinked away the fuzziness of his inebriation. Now that Corsley mentioned it, Davis recalled seeing one of the eighty-pound, horseshoe-jawed monsters with inch-and-a-half-long teeth hanging on the wall of one of the outbuildings. At the time he'd thought it was for bears or wolves. But the damnable thing was a man-trap.

"Gives the thieving, poaching bloke a better chance than a spring gun," said Allerby, sorting through his cards. "If he trips a wire, the gun shoots off his head. If he steps into a man-trap, he only gets a mangled leg for his trouble."

"And a free trip straight to Australia for seven years or so," Corsley added with a chuckle.

"Zounds, St. John. Don't look so shocked." Allerby gestured to the footman to pour more brandy. "I'm sure Sindby had his gamekeeper remove all the traps before we arrived for the hunting."

"No doubt," Davis agreed, staring at his cards without seeing them. He'd lost what little interest he had in the game.

Corsley threw out the first card. Davis resolved to make this his last game of the evening.

"What do you two think of the lady guests?" Allerby tossed down a winning card and took the round, the ruddiness of his face deepening with victory. "By the by, St. John, I find your sister quite charming, and so attractive. Seacombe hardly leaves her out of his sight long enough to give a fellow an opportunity for a little flirtation."

"Seacombe is rather possessive." Davis watched Corsley take the next round. He didn't much care that he was losing at the game; he just wanted it over so he could retire for the evening. "But Dorian needs a firm hand."

"Do you know her companion very well—the redheaded widow, Lady Susanna?" asked Corsley, lowering his voice as he spoke.

"The pretty little lady with the big bosom?" Allerby snickered.

Davis immediately disliked the men's tone of voice. "Well enough."

"Then tell us, is it true?" Allerby asked, his eyes glittering with salacious curiosity.

"I don't know what you mean." Davis finally won a round.

"You know." Corsley glanced over his shoulder to be certain the servants weren't lingering close enough to overhear them. "Her husband was an older man, but healthy enough. Then he just ups and dies."

Davis was bewildered but suspicious of their inquisitiveness. "Older men do that sometimes."

"Don't be a dunce, St. John." Allerby squirmed in his chair impatiently. "Surely you've heard the story. They say she kept him very busy—in the bed. Word is she's a lusty little piece. In fact, the story goes that she humped him to death. Nothing intentional, mind you. Just ordinary marital duty, over and over again."

Davis went cold and still.

Corsley grinned at Allerby. "What a way to go, eh? He died in the saddle."

Allerby shook his head. "The story goes that she was doing the riding. The old man died in the traces."

Corsley brayed.

Allerby crowed.

Davis threw down his cards, rose from the table, and slammed his fist squarely into Corsley's face. The cigar flipped into the air. Blood spurted across the game table. Corsley gave a nasal squeal and clutched his nose as he tumbled from his chair to the floor.

Coolly, Davis turned on Allerby. Cards flew in all directions as the young man knocked over his chair and scrambled to get beyond Davis's reach.

"Here, here. What goes on here?" Sindby, who had been sitting by the fire with Trafford and Seacombe, jumped to his feet. "I don't mind a rowdy game, gentlemen, but no fisticuffs in the house, please."

Davis calmly rubbed his sore knuckles. "I'm settling a matter of honor, my lord. But nothing worthy of a challenge." He glared pointedly at Corsley and Allerby. "The comments do not merit the dignity of the dueling field."

Sindby looked from one wide-eyed young man to the other, who still clutched his bloody nose. "Corsley? Allerby? Do you have anything to add?"

"We were just discussing the accomplishments of the ladies," Allerby said. "Nothing for anyone to take offense at."

"Well, I took offense." Davis kicked his chair out of his way. "I will hear no gossip about any of the ladies in the company. Now, if you will excuse me, I shall retire for the evening."

Davis turned his back on them all and climbed the stairs. He doubted that anything he'd done or said would stop Corsley's vile stories from circulating.

Outside Dorian and Susanna's chamber door, Davis hesitated, listening for the sound of their voices, but all was quiet.

Of all the house parties they had attended, why did this one require his sister and the one lady he truly cared about to share a room? How he longed to knock on the door and question Susanna about the story. They had not discussed her husband beyond the few casual references made during their first breakfast together at Tewk Abbey. If there was any truth at all to the tale Corsley had told, what an awful thing for Susanna to have to suffer through. The guilt. The embarrassment. The loneliness. The *need*—through all those months of mourning. How Davis knew about need!

For the first time during the long, tedious hours of the week he was glad he'd made the trip—for Susanna's sake.

"This has been the strangest house party we've ever attended," Lady Eleanor confided to Dorian as Lord Sindby led the ladies to the dungeon on the fifth day of their visit to Stalker Keep.

He'd come to the ladies at the breakfast table, hours after the gentlemen had gone out at dawn to do their daily shooting, and offered to show them his extensive music collection.

Dorian had almost protested on the spot. She wanted Nicholas to accompany them, but Sindby had been so coy about his collection, she decided not to object.

So the ladies followed Sindby, who carried a torch, down the winding dungeon stairs. The company included all the ladies: Lady Eleanor, Lady Susanna, Dorian, Lady Allerby, Lady Corsley, and the Gordons, a mother and a daughter from a neighboring estate. When they reached the bottom Sindby and his footman went around the room lighting the torches mounted on the walls.

"It's rather a dark day, and I don't want us to be without the light we need to appreciate the fine works that I'm going to show you."

As Sindby and his servant began to lay out the manuscripts on the long table, Dorian nodded sympathetically to Lady Eleanor. "Indeed, this has been an unusual week. Have you been here before?"

"Oh, no, though Sir Gavin and the earl have been acquainted for some time." Lady Eleanor smiled politely. "Gavin has been longing to come up for the shooting. But I confess, I find it rather monotonous. Did you enjoy the outing to the Hagberry Pot yesterday?"

"Lord Sindby is an excellent story-teller," Dorian said. "I quite expected the Fifth lord of Sindby to rise out of the water of the pool hand-in-hand with the Devil himself."

Lady Eleanor smiled, a lovely, winning smile this time.

"Do you have an interest in music, Lady Eleanor?" Dorian ventured.

"I play the pianoforte a little," Lady Eleanor said. "Still, that does not keep me from appreciating the talents of those more skilled than myself. I understand you and your aunt are quite masterful at the keyboard."

"Music has always been a big part of our lives," Dorian said. "And my aunt was a student and great admirer of the composer Franz Chamier."

"Yes, so I've heard," Lady Eleanor said. "Sir Gavin told me about you and Nicholas searching for some missing piece of his music for your aunt, who is ill, I'm sorry to hear. It sounds very adventurous and exciting, if a little worrisome."

"Oh, I'm afraid it's been nothing like that," Dorian said, reluctant to say more because she had no idea how much Eleanor knew about Nicholas's determination to clear his family name of treason charges.

"Here we are: the best of my collection from dead musicians the world over." Lord Sindby gestured to the materials laid out on the table.

Dorian had realized on their second day at Stalker Keep that Lord Sindby had a penchant for sending the men off to shoot game so that he could have the ladies to himself. He loved a female audience. He beamed with pleasure under the onslaught of appreciative smiles, fluttering eyelashes, and murmurs of gratitude. He was hardly as sinister as Dorian first thought him to be.

"For you, Miss St. John, I have something special."

Dorian turned from Lady Eleanor to see Sindby descending on her with a large leather-bound portfolio tucked under his arm. He plopped it down on the table, untied the ribbons binding it, and threw it open.

Dorian gasped. In front of her lay a sheaf of Franz's work that she and Aunt Charlotte had given up for lost when his landlord had thrown the near penniless composer out of his lodgings only weeks before he was dragged off to jail for inciting a riot.

"Where did you find these?" Dorian demanded, shuffling through the pages of Franz's music. Some of it was first draft, while other pages were final copy that had never been published or sold. The portfolio was a treasure trove that she had to have for Aunt Charlotte. She opened her mouth and turned on Sindby.

He held up his hand before she could speak. "No, dear lady, not a word until you have been through all of it. There are even some pieces composed for my pipe organ in there. You did not know that Chamier composed for the organ, did you? When you have finished we will talk, if you wish. But go through it and enjoy."

Then he was off to show one of the other ladies a copy of a song that bore her Christian name.

Hands trembling, Dorian sat down at the table and began to go through the music more thoroughly, taking stock as well as she could with a mind still dazzled with this discovery.

So absorbed was she in the materials, she quite forgot about the damp eeriness of the dungeon. She turned page after page of beautiful work and hummed to herself. How she longed to try it on the pianoforte, but she'd not seen one at Stalker Keep. Lord Sindby favored the pipe organ and a little Celtic harp that sat near the fire in the great hall.

With the turn of every page she prayed she'd find the fragment she and Nicholas sought. The find would be too good to be true, but she prayed for the miracle nevertheless. At last she turned over the final page in the portfolio without finding the fragment. She sighed with the joy of what she'd found and the disappointment of not finding what she needed most.

When she looked up she found Lady Eleanor sitting down in the chair beside her. "Did you find what you are searching for?"

"No, I'm afraid not. But this is a great find, a large amount of Franz's work that Aunt Charlotte and I feared lost forever," Dorian said. "My aunt will be thrilled. This will keep her working for months to come."

"What do you think, Miss St. John?" Lord Sindby began as he appeared at her side. Lady Eleanor tactfully excused herself.

"I think it's the most marvelous thing I've seen in years," Dorian confessed. "I do hope we can come to terms regarding acquisition of this wonderful collection."

"I was afraid you might have desires along that line," Lord Sindby said with haughty regret. "But I cannot give up this portfolio. Chamier composed those organ pieces just for me and the organ here at Stalker Keep."

Dorian drew a deep breath and hid her disappointment as well as she could. "You must be thrilled and feel honored to have had such a talented artist as Franz Chamier compose for you."

"Indeed; so you can see why I cannot give up this work."

Dorian gestured to the chair Lady Eleanor had left. "Have I told you about my aunt, Lord Sindby?"

His lordship sat down and Dorian told him about her search for Franz's music and Aunt Charlotte's dedicated work in compiling as complete a portfolio as possible. She did not mention her aunt's illness or her attachment to the composer. The less said of personal matters the better, she decided.

"A charming story." The earl cast her a cool smile; he was clearly unmoved. "But I intend to keep the music I have. I'll be glad to have some of the music copied for you, if you like."

"Perhaps I might begin transcribing some of it now," Dorian suggested, unwilling to return to London without at least part of this work for Aunt Charlotte.

"Well, of course, if you like," Sindby said, appearing to be a little miffed. "Such boring work, copying, when we are here to enjoy ourselves."

"It would mean a great deal for me to be able to do this for my aunt, since you've been so generous as to offer me the opportunity," Dorian said, determined to be polite and respectful, though she was very annoyed that her host refused to come to any kind of terms with her.

"But, of course, copy whatever you like," Sindby said. "I'll have paper and ink brought immediately."

Nicholas listened to Dorian's story closely, watching her eyes sparkle with excitement as she recounted the wonders she'd found in Sindby's portfolio of Chamier music. "But you're certain the fragment of your aunt's love song was not among the works you saw?"

"Unfortunately it wasn't there." She shook her head, and her bottom lip took on its full stubborn look. "But I must have the collection for Aunt Charlotte."

Sir Gavin and Lady Eleanor had joined them for sherry in the great hall, awaiting the announcement that dinner would be served. Davis sat near the fire morosely studying the flames, and Lady Susanna lingered near the window, watching the sun drop beyond the hills. Nicholas had noted that the two had hardly spoken to each other during their entire stay at Stalker Keep.

Sindby stood with Corsley and Allerby near the fireplace, discussing the day's fishing. The earl seemed to take great vicarious pleasure in hearing the hunting stories, though he seldom went out with his guests. Over the past few days Nicholas had come to rather dislike the man. He seemed to take pleasure in setting people at odds with each other for his own amusement. It was just like him to torture Dorian with his collection of Chamier music. Surely there was a way around Sindby and his acquisitiveness, Nicholas thought as he finished his sherry.

"It was quite interesting to look at a composer's work firsthand," Lady Eleanor observed. "His lordship did offer to have copies made. But I quite understand your disappointment on behalf of your aunt, Dorian."

"Perhaps if you spoke to Sindby, Nick," Gavin said. "And the mention of the right price might make him reconsider. But it's too bad he doesn't have the piece you're both looking for."

"I don't believe money is what he wants," Dorian lamented. "I believe he truly loves the pieces and wants to continue to possess Chamier's music just for the sake of having it. Oh, how Aunt Charlotte would love to see these works. You should have seen them, Nicholas.

"Some of the songs had Hungarian lyrics written on them, while others were things he'd attempted to set English words to. I must make copies to take home to Aunt Charlotte. He will have to permit me to do that."

"I'm sure he will be glad to cooperate with you," Nicholas said, intending to bend the earl's ear over cigars and port after dinner.

The meal was elegant and delicious, as always. The earl kept a good cook, a well-stocked kitchen, and a select wine cellar; and he set a fine table. Fishing stories abounded about the big trout that had gotten away.

Two hours later, after five courses and three wines, the ladies departed for the great hall. The men settled themselves comfortably at the table to enjoy the fine cigars the earl had imported from the Carolinas.

Nicholas got up and strolled down the dining room to take an empty chair next to the earl. Allerby turned, as if to object to Nicholas taking his chair; then he seemed to think better of it.

"Seacombe, nice catch today, that six pound trout."

"Good of you to say so, Sindby." Nicholas accepted a light for his cigar from the butler. "I say, Dorian is quite excited about coming upon your portfolio of Chamier's music."

"Yes, that did put quite a spark in her eye, didn't it?" Sindby puffed on his cigar and seemed pleased with himself. "She wanted to purchase it, but I had to refuse her offer, of course. Some of those pieces were composed for my very own pipe organ here in Stalker Keep."

Nicholas leaned back in his chair and puffed on the cigar. It was a fine, flavorful piece of tobacco. "Well, the thing of it is, Dorian's aunt is compiling a complete collection of Chamier's work for posterity. As a former student of Chamier's, she has a special personal interest in his work. She surely would like to have that portfolio of the composer's work.''

''Yes, I understand the circumstances.'' Sindby leaned forward. ''Dorian already told me of her aunt's interest in Chamier. Quite a romantic tale. I always love romanic stories.''

''Time is of the essence. Her aunt is ill. Perhaps Dorian didn't make that clear,'' Nicholas said, his words crisp, despite his languid slouch in his chair.

''How unfortunate.''

Nicholas sat up in his chair, his dislike for Sindby turning into real distaste.

''Of course,'' Sindby said, clearly wary of Nicholas's shift in position. ''It was never my intention to keep the work from the world. Dorian is welcome to whatever copies she wishes to take with her, but I must have the originals for my collection.''

''I understand that you are an avid collector, but think of what you might be able to add to your collection with a profitable sale of Chamier's music.'' Nicholas puffed on his cigar and waved his hand indifferently in the air. ''Just something for you to consider. I could make giving up Chamier's music to Dorian for her aunt very lucrative for you.''

''As a man of means you understand, of course, that money is of no matter to me,'' Sindby said, clearly offended.

''Of course. I didn't think it would be. Just an idle offer on my part,'' Nicholas said. ''But under the circumstances I'm certain you'd be glad to share the name and address of the dealer from who you purchased these works.''

''Dealer?''

''Well, I know the organ music was yours from the beginning, commissioned by you and therefore yours without question.'' Nicholas suppressed his impatience; he didn't give a damn about the organ score. ''Just give me the name of the dealer from whom you purchased the other works you possess.''

Sindby regarded Nicholas solemnly for a moment before he nodded. ''Yes, I can do that. I'll have it for you tomorrow at breakfast.''

"Have you talked him into selling the Chamier collection to you yet?" Gavin asked, sitting down next to Nicholas.

"Not yet," Sindby said. "But he is giving it a bloody good try."

Nicholas merely smiled and let the subject of the music drop. He set aside his frustration. He couldn't help but wonder if Sindby had this portfolio of Chamier's work, what other works of the composer might be stacked away in some idle lord's collection.

A frisky young hackney gelding broke away from its groom and decided not to be recaptured. It was the most interesting event to have occurred in the six days at Stalker Keep.

Susanna had been the first to call the ladies' attention to the chase. She'd spied it from a window of the great hall. Dorian, who'd spent the morning copying music for Aunt Charlotte, and all the other ladies, rushed to the windows to watch with glee as the freedom-loving equine eluded his captors.

The bay gelding romped across the courtyard and galloped through the garden, leading the grooms and coachman a merry chase over azaleas, through rosebeds, down a graveled path, across a bit of closely mown lawn, and through the lily pond.

The ladies cheered as the drenched grooms staggered back from the flying water. Why it should be so thrilling to see a runaway horse was impossible for Dorian to explain. It was just exciting to see some creature running free and enjoying itself, Dorian thought.

"Excuse me, Miss St. John."

Dorian turned to find Lady Haddo standing behind her.

"The butler informs me that one of the beaters is here with a message for you. He insists on delivering the message to you personally.

Dorian sobered. Her first thought was for Aunt Charlotte's welfare, but Lady Haddo said the man was one of the local beaters. Did Nicholas or Davis want something of her? "I'll come right away. Is he at the entrance?"

"Yes. Please follow me," Lady Haddo said.

Just inside the entrance, Dorian found the messenger waiting for her: a burly giant of a man. He was so tall, in fact, she had to tip her head back to meet his gaze. Dorian had never seen him before. Nor had she expected to recognize him, though he seemed to know her.

"Thank you, Lady Haddo," Dorian said. Her hostess politely moved away down the hall. "What is it?"

"Miss St. John." He carried his wide-brimmed hat and wore a loose farmer's smock over an ordinary shirt and trousers with uncommonly fine boots. He spoke in a baritone voice with a surprisingly citified accent. "I'm sorry. I didn't mean to alarm you, miss. I've come with a message from Lord Seacombe."

"Yes, what is it?" Dorian asked, smiling encouragement at the man. "First, what is your name?"

"Uh, Otis." He grinned self-consciously and clutched the hat in both hands. "I been helping the beaters. His lordship asked me to ask you to walk down into the woods and have lunch with him out of the basket Cook sent for the gentlemen."

"What a perfectly delightful idea," Dorian said, touched by Nicholas's thoughtfulness. "I'm sure some of the other ladies would be delighted to come."

"Oh, no, miss," Otis said, his dark brown eyes round with surprise. "His lordship said I was to ask only you. That he is alone and didn't think the other gentlemen wanted the ladies along."

"I see." Dorian knew that Nicholas's patience with hunting each and every day was wearing thin. She knew how he loved picnics under all sorts of circumstances. And he knew how disappointed she was about not being able to convince Sindby to give up the music he owned. He was trying to revive her spirits. "I'll be just a moment while I get my cloak and change into walking shoes."

"Yes, miss." Otis held his finger to his lips. "But don't say nothing to the other ladies."

"I understand."

Dorian hurriedly prepared for a walk in the woods, looking forward to fresh air and new scenery. The day was a bit dreary, but the men usually stayed out until midafternoon at least. The afternoons in the great hall could become endless.

Back downstairs, Otis led her across the courtyard, where the bay gelding was still loping through the flower beds and creating general havoc. Dorian thought briefly about asking one of the footmen to go with them should they need help in carrying anything back to the castle, but the servants seemed to have their hands full with the horse.

Soon Dorian and Otis were walking down the hill at a brisk pace away from Stalker Keep and into the dense woods that filled the river valley below. She followed her guide without minding where they were going. The air was cool and crisp, and the trees and wild plants fresh and green. She drew in a deep breath. It was good to be free of the confines of the old castle and the chatter of the women. Was that why the men were so content to traipse off to the woods every day? she wondered. Did Stalker Keep oppress them, too?

They walked in silence for some time, the giant Otis leading her deeper and deeper into the woods. The day grew darker as they walked into the deep woods, where the trees soared tall and thick overhead. The forest were quiet. She heard neither birds nor the sound of gunshots nor of beaters scaring up game. Had the men decided to stop hunting for the day? she wondered.

"How far is it?" Dorian asked at last, not because she was tired, but because it seemed they had come a long way—much farther than she'd expected.

"Not much farther now, miss." Some ways down the path, Otis halted and turned on Dorian. He pointed in the direction of a thicket some yards away. "There. His lordship is in there. You can just follow the path into the thicket and find him."

Dorian turned to the thicket. It seemed a strange place for a picnic. "Nicholas? Are you there?"

"Shhhh." Otis put his finger to his lips to shush her. "You don't need to call to him. He knows you are coming and your voice might scare away the game for the other sportsmen."

Something about this whole moment suddenly seemed wrong. "Where is Nicholas?" Dorian demanded.

"He's in the thicket, I tell you." Otis appeared quite vexed and motioned in a shooing movement to urge her down the path. "Go; you'll find him there. Just go. He's waiting."

"Is Nicholas all right?" Dorian swung back to the thicket. "What's going on here?"

Otis looked startled; then he nodded emphatically. "Yes, his lordship hurt himself, but he didn't want me to say nothing to distress you. He's there waiting for you to come help him."

The glibness of the answer did not satisfy Dorian. She was more certain than ever that something was desperately wrong and that the giant could not be trusted.

"Well, why didn't you say so?" Dorian said, forcing a brave smile onto her face as her heart froze into cold crystals of fear. The man was at least three times bigger than she. "Of course I'll go to his aid. In the thicket, you say?"

"Yes, miss."

She knew that whatever she did she should not go into that thicket—first. "The path is so narrow, would you mind leading the way?"

Confusion passed over Otis's face. "It's just there; you can see that the way is clear."

"Which side of the thicket?"

"Just go down the path," Otis snapped. "Go; his lordship is waiting for you."

Dorian gathered up her skirts and started around to the side. "I'll surprise him," she whispered.

"No, no." Otis grabbed her by the arm and pulled her back. "You must go down the path."

She latched onto his arm and started down the path, dragging him along as best she could. "This way, then."

Reluctantly, he followed her, attempting to pry loose her hold as he stepped down the path with her.

"I'll probably need your help," Dorian said, somehow certain that his company ensured her safety.

Otis grumbled under his breath. With immense effort, he pulled himself free of her grasp and flung her down the path. Off balance, Dorian staggered and thumped to the ground square on her bottom. A cry of pain and dismay escaped her.

Otis stared at her as if debating what to do. Then, suddenly, he came down the path toward her before she could get to her feet. Anger hardened his enormous fleshy face. When he reached down for her, Dorian scrambled away, but her skirt and cloak thwarted her escape.

Just before he reached her, Otis's foot snapped a vine or something on the ground. Instantly he halted, a look of obscene dismay crossing his face.

Dorian stared up at him, confused and terrified, all the time struggling to get to her feet. He cursed her.

From the corner of her eye she caught the flash, then from behind the tree came the deafening blast of a shotgun.

Chapter Twenty-one

"You quite ruined our good fun," Lady Corsley said when Davis showed his face in the great hall that afternoon.

The ladies were gathered around a tea tray, looking as graceful and colorful in their afternoon gowns as a flock of brightly plumed tropical birds.

"Did I?" Davis's gaze scanned the group, seeking out Susanna. Dorian was nowhere to be seen, but Lady Eleanor was there with the other lady guests. At last he spotted Susanna. She sat in a chair near the window dressed in a pretty apricot-hued gown that cupped the lovely roundness of her bosom. "How did I ruin your fun, Lady Corsley?"

"You captured that poor coach horse," Lady Allerby interjected for her friend, her smile belying any real upset. "We were all cheering for the poor spirited creature; then you arrived and instructed the grooms to corner him."

"That 'poor creature' has done a great deal of damage to Stalker Keep's gardens," Davis said. "I believe the stablemaster plans to return it to the home farm for additional training."

"And what brought you back to the keep so early in the

afternoon?'' Lady Corsley asked with a raised brow—of either curiosity or disapproval, Davis couldn't be certain which.

"I was rather off my mark today and thought to return and ask Lady Susanna to go out for a drive with me."

The ladies went silent. In unison they turned to stare in Susanna's direction. Her amber eyes widened as she realized that she'd become the center of attention. A crimson blush rose in her fair cheeks. He'd never singled her out in company before, except for a polite, almost required dance that would cause comment from no one.

Davis held his breath, awaiting her answer, all the while praying she would consent to his invitation. She must hear him out in private.

Susanna rose, her expression sober, doubtful, far from reassuring to Davis. "Yes, a drive would be pleasant."

Wise enough not to question her affirmative reply, Davis held out his hand for hers and clasped it firmly in front of all the ladies in the room.

"Very well," Lady Haddo said primly. "I'll order the pony cart brought around."

Davis couldn't have selected a better vehicle for the drive if he'd chosen one himself. The pony cart was small, easily maneuverable, and permitted only two passengers to sit close—side by side, elbows rubbing.

"What shall be our destination?" he asked as he guided the brown-and-white-spotted pony through the courtyard gate and out onto the moor road. Behind them rode a young groom at a respectful distance.

After punching Corsley in the nose—which, judging from Lady Corsley's cordiality, the young man had neglected to mention to his mother—Davis was unwilling to risk any behavior less than proper with Susanna. "I'd advise that we stay out of the woods, where the sportsmen are still shooting today."

"Let's drive to Hagberry Pot," Susanna suggested.

Davis thought that a devilishly good idea. "Excellent. I

haven't seen that wonder of Lord Sindby's demesne, though I understand he took you ladies to see it the other day.''

"Yes, and told quite a dramatic tale about the fifth earl and the devil and treasure.'' Susanna smiled. "The man is definitely an Original. The *ton* has no idea how original.''

"I quite agree." Davis made no effort to hurry the pony along. The road was rutted, and to hasten the creature's pace would only make their ride bumpier.

Susanna gestured toward the pony. "I do hope this little brown-and-white fellow is no relation to the troublesome coach horse.''

"Oh, I doubt it." Davis glanced at Susanna just in time to catch her smiling about the horse chase. "Did I also ruin your fun when we caught the horse?''

"Oh, no, nothing like that.'' Susanna turned away to watch the passing moor. "I believe you quite saved the day for the servants. I imagine the gardener is near weeping. All his roses are trampled and the lily pond laid to waste. And the stablemaster red-faced with embarrassment.''

"The garden and the gardener will recover." Davis smiled to himself, feeling absurdly heroic again in Susanna's company. He liked the feeling. "The stablemaster will recover, also, and he best think of tipping the gin bottle less frequently.''

Their conversation turned to other things, less exciting but worthy of comment in a discussion between two people still learning to be comfortable in each other's company.

They found Hagberry Pot, a dark rock-edged pool filling the low ground between the rolling hills of the moor. Off to one side stood an ancient grove of stunted trees.

Davis brought the cart to a halt. The groom hurried forward to take the pony's bridle. Davis climbed out of the cart and came around to help Susanna climb down.

"Now you're going to tell me the earl's story, aren't you?'' he prompted, though he had little interest in the tale. It sounded like so many of the yarns the Scots liked to spin. But he endeavored to listen with half an ear as they strolled around the glassy black pool on the moors.

When they had reached the far side, away from the groom, who had sat down under one of the trees and appeared to have gone to sleep, Davis turned to Susanna.

"I want to ask you something," he said, feeling his heart rise into his throat.

"Yes, Davis, I thought there must be a purpose to this invitation." Susanna tried to withdraw her hand from his, but he refused to release her.

"I'd like to ask you to allow me to pay you suit during this season in Town." There; he'd said it.

A small *oh* escaped Susanna.

When she said nothing more Davis hurried on. "I know I have behaved badly. Most ungentlemanly. Quite disrespectfully. Oh, damme, Susanna, it seems I'm always apologizing to you for my appalling behavior. But I want to set it all right. What do you say?"

"Well . . ." The word was uttered more as an anxious sigh than a comment. Susanna straightened her shoulders and fixed him with an unwavering gaze. "And what does Lady Elizabeth think of your intentions?"

"Lady Elizabeth plays no role in my life," Davis said, unsurprised that she knew about the duke's daughter. It would be impossible for her not to have heard, since she'd been staying in Town. "I've decided that we are not at all suited."

"But, honestly, Davis, how can you consider me? I have nothing to offer you but myself."

That damnable, infernal lust that kept him awake at night and aching for her during the day seized him. "Yourself is exactly what I want. We will wed at the end of the Season."

Clearly speechless, Susanna stared at him, her mouth shaped in a small delectable *O* that Davis longed to seal with his lips.

But he would not rush her. He got down on one knee.

"Davis, stop that." The moment she realized what he was doing, Susanna tried to pull away again. She cast an uneasy glance over her shoulder in the direction of the sleeping groom. "Get up from there. What do you think you're about? The groom will see you kneeling like that."

"I hope he does. I'm proposing marriage," Davis said, squeezing her dainty hand in both of his. "I swear, we will wed at the end of the Season—or sooner, if you like."

"Oh, Davis, I'm not certain . . ."

"We can announce our engagement at Lord Sindby's ball before we leave here." An unpleasant complication occurred to him. "Unless—is there some relation I must speak to about requesting your hand?"

"No. It's just that—well . . ." Susanna stammered and frowned, a bewildered and unhappy expression. "Davis, you declare these lofty intentions to me now, and you have love for me when we are in—well, you know, in private moments— but when you are back in Town will you regret your actions, as I'm sure you have in the past?"

The painful truth of her words sliced through Davis's heart. He didn't like himself very much. He squeezed his eyes shut against the shameful ache and humbly bowed his head, pressing Susanna's hand against his brow. He could not look at her. "How I wish you did not know me so well, darling, but how I love you all the more for it."

When Davis finally had the courage to look into her eyes he found her wiping away silent tears with gloved fingers.

Shocked, he jumped to his feet. "I did not declare myself to bring you unhappiness, Susanna. If you do not know what to say, then at least consider my proposal. Take as much time as you like. I promise nothing improper will pass between us. And know that should you do me the favor of agreeing to be my wife, I can keep you in as comfortable a style as you wish. No expense will be too . . ." He stopped when he saw the offense on her face.

"I care nothing about your fortune, sir. She blushed and looked out over the pool. "But must you withdraw your, uh, your prodigious favors?"

At first Davis did not believe he'd heard her correctly. "My what—oh, you mean . . ."

She faced him this time and whispered, "I've been dying for your touch and your kiss for weeks."

Davis needed no second invitation. He took her in his arms and kissed her. Her lips were warm and sweet. They parted beneath his. His tongue gently explored the inside. She teased the corner of his lips. He combed his fingers through her silky red hair, bending back her head, knocking off her bonnet. He let his hands drift over her shoulders and down the length of her body, briefly caressing her breasts. Groaning with heartfelt pleasure and carnal satisfaction, he seized her waist and pulled her close enough for her to feel his arousal against her belly.

"I love you, Susanna," he whispered against her lips, "and I promise to share everything I have with you."

The concussion of the shotgun blast deafened Dorian and stung her cheek. The shot shattered Otis's arm and shoulder. Blood spattered across Dorian's face and gown. He spun around, away from the explosion, and stumbled into the underbrush. But somehow he remained on his feet, clutching his arm and roaring in pain—and rage.

Dorian attempted to scramble farther away from him. For a moment she feared he was going to come at her again. Once she gained her feet she hesitated, torn between the urge to flee and to help an injured fellow human being. All the time her awareness grew that if she'd been standing where Otis was when the gun fired, her head would have been blown off.

From a distance she heard the cry of the beaters.

Otis's pain-glazed eyes shifted in the direction of the calls. His face contorted and he screamed angry, unintelligible words at Dorian. Then he turned and fled, loping down the path with remarkable agility. His wounded arm flopped uselessly at his side.

In moments Lord Sindby's gamekeeper appeared with several of his men. They stared at Dorian, their mouths agape.

"Where is Lord Seacombe?" Dorian demanded immediately. She'd noticed that not a soul appeared from the cover of the thicket.

"He's way on the other side of the men," the sandy-haired gamekeeper said. "What happened, miss? We heard a shot."

"It came from over there." Dorian pointed to the tree. The gamekeeper's men went to investigate. "Please send for Lord Seacombe. And send someone after Otis so we can question him."

The gamekeeper sent one of his men after Nicholas but did nothing about Otis. Without taking his gaze from her face he gestured toward a tree stump. "I think you'd better sit down while we wait, miss."

"But what about your man Otis?" Dorian waved in the direction in which the wounded scoundrel had fled. "I want to know just what he was up to. Besides that, he's going to need help or he'll bleed to death."

"Miss, I don't have a man named Otis."

Dorian stared at him in disbelief.

The gamekeeper, a neatly dressed man for an outdoorsman, took a reasonably clean kerchief from his pocket. "Mayhap you'd like to put this against your face."

"Otis is not one of your men?"

The gamekeeper shook his head and held out the kerchief to her.

Dorian realized she must look a fright, with blood spattered all across the front of her cloak and gown. She accepted the cloth. Her cheek stung when she touched it, and when she took away the cloth to look at it she was shocked by the amount of blood.

"I don't think it's bad, miss," the gamekeeper comforted. "Here comes Lord Seacombe. Over here, your lordship. The lady needs your help."

Suddenly Nicholas was there, sweeping onlookers aside,

reaching her, taking in the sight of her, and examining the side of her face without asking unnecessary questions. Within a few moments he'd ordered a physician to be sent for immediately and a bottle of medicinal spirits and fresh water to be brought instantly.

Dorian sighed with relief, content to leave Nicholas to take charge with all the calm authority of a ship's captain.

When the hunters' luncheon basket of spirits, food, and water arrived Nicholas knelt at her side and began to look more closely at the side of her face.

"It looks worse than it is," he said, washing away some of the blood. His big hands were warm and gentle.

"How bad is that?" The shock of the experience was wearing off and Dorian was more alarmed now. Her hands began to tremble. No one knew who Otis was.

"Give her some brandy, gamekeeper." Nicholas continued to work on the side of her face. "It appears that a couple of pellets grazed you near the hairline. Dorian, what were you doing out here?"

The gamekeeper thrust a cup of brandy into her hands and she obediently took a sip of the stinging liquor. It burned her throat all the way down to her stomach.

"You sent for me, didn't you?"

Nicholas stopped and peered into her face. "I did not send for you today. Tell me what happened."

Dorian told him the story of Otis coming to the keep with a message for her, an invitation to share the luncheon basket. "He was a huge man, dressed just like the other beaters, except for his boots."

"We have no man named Otis," the gamekeeper repeated. "There's no one by that name living in these parts."

"How big, Dorian? How big was this man? My size?" Nicholas asked, his blue eyes suddenly dark and narrow.

"Oh, no, much larger. He could almost be a giant in a penny show at a country fair. He wanted me to walk down this path. By then I was beginning to think something was amiss."

Nicholas made no further comment nor asked any more questions. He ordered two of the beaters to follow the trail of blood that led off through the woods. The two men set off immediately.

By then Lord Sindby had appeared, hurrying down the path from the keep with Lady Haddo following in his wake. His slicked-back black hair was flying loose around his head. "What is all this about a shooting and Miss St. John? Seacombe! I'm glad you're here already."

Just then a beater came out from behind the tree carrying a spring gun—a shotgun with a wire hanging from the trigger.

Lord Sindby's pale complexion went livid. He whirled on his gamekeeper. "What is that doing here? I told you to clear the woods of all the poacher traps. And I thought we'd agreed to never use the spring guns again."

"I did have them cleared, my lord. I walked the woods and paths myself. I swear it." The gamekeeper had paled, and Dorian felt sorry for the man. She believed he was telling the truth, and that he was as shocked to see the weapon as his lord was. Otis was the man they should be questioning.

Lady Haddo took over tending to Dorian's injury, though the lady's touch was less tender and compassionate than Nicholas's had been. Lord Sindby issued orders to the gamekeeper and the beaters.

Nicholas said little except to speak with Dorian. As soon as she was found to be steady on her feet, they walked back to the keep, where they arrived just as the physician drove into the courtyard.

Dorian's wounds were tended and found to be minor, as Nicholas had thought. The beaters returned, reporting that they'd lost the trail of blood somewhere up on the moors and found no other evidence of anyone named Otis.

With Nicholas still at her side, the physician gave Dorian some medication that sent her straight to sleep. But even as the drug wrapped her in a cloak of warm fuzziness and she drifted off to sleep, she was aware of Nicholas hovering nearby.

Feeling safe, she still wondered to herself who Otis was and why he could possibly want to do her harm.

"Before you say anything," Sindby began as he faced Nicholas and Davis in his study, "you must remember that Dorian really isn't seriously injured."

"I'm aware of that, Sindby," Nicholas growled. The reminder did not lighten his mood.

Davis, who had just returned from his drive with Susanna to hear the news of Dorian's misfortune, cast a quick glance in Nicholas's direction. "Is that true? Is she all right?"

"Yes. The physician attended her and she's asleep now." Nicholas spoke quietly; his rage was cold and dark. Now that Dorian was safe asleep upstairs he considered indulging himself in the fury of it. "Thank God above she is not seriously injured, but no thanks can be offered to you, Sindby, for your abundant supply of man-traps and spring guns."

"A spring gun! What are you thinking, sir?" Davis shouted at Sindby.

"Seacombe, you heard my gamekeeper swear he had removed them all. You can't imagine the problem we have up here with the tenants and farmers supplementing their income by selling game birds on the black market in Town."

"Blast your damned tenants and you." Davis barely raised his voice this time, but the angry glare in his eyes left no doubt about the intensity of his feelings.

"And who is this Otis that Dorian spoke of?" Nicholas demanded, unmoved by Sindby's tenant problems. "Do you allow strangers to come into the house and lure your guests away?"

"How was I or Lady Haddo to know that your fiancé would go traipsing off into the woods with any stranger who came to the door?"

Nicholas had to grab Davis's arm to keep the man from going after Sindby.

Hastily, Sindby retreated behind his desk. "I can assure you that Lady Haddo and I are just as outraged as you are."

Nicholas would not allow himself to be drawn away from where he was going. Nor did he intend to reveal that he'd probably had some experience with the giant Otis. "This stranger apparently knew about the spring gun behind the tree."

Sindby's face went blank. "I don't understand. What are you saying?"

"I'm saying that if he isn't one of your own or from this neighborhood, he is a stranger who not only found his way into your home but into your barns and stables. If your gamekeeper had removed all the traps, then this stranger set one up for the purpose of harming Miss St. John."

"Good God, man," Davis ranted. "My sister has never hurt a soul in her life, and now there's been an attempt to murder her on the grounds of Stalker Keep. How safe are your other guests?"

Guiltily, Nicholas released Davis's arm. They were giving Sindby a lot of grief over this incident when Nicholas knew he himself was the reason behind it. But he'd never dreamed his giant pursuer would follow him to the borderland—much less attack Dorian. Still, Sindby needed to run a tighter ship, and that didn't mean setting more man-traps. Nicholas intended to make the man pay for whatever part he had played—intentionally or not—in the attempt on Dorian. "We must leave as soon as Dorian feels well enough to travel," Nicholas said.

"No, no, not before the ball." Sindby came out from behind the protection of his desk. "All of the gentry and Quality for miles around have been invited. The ball is going to be the event of the year in this county. You can't possibly take one of the most fashionable guests away before my ball."

Nicholas looked to Davis as if to ask his opinion.

"I think she must go home and rest." Davis shook his head and frowned, but not before Nicholas caught the gleam in the young man's eye. "Unless, Lord Sindby, you think there might be something that could be done to make up for the shock to my poor sister's delicate system.''

''I don't know what that would be,'' Nicholas lied, covering his admiration for Davis. He was, indeed, Dorian's twin brother.

''Well, then, you will stay a few days longer, at least until we are certain that Miss St. John is feeling well again, and I can find some way to make up for this shocking business.''

''For a few days,'' Davis acquiesced with all the wounded dignity of a concerned brother. ''Now, if you don't mind, I'd like to look in on my sister.''

As soon as Nicholas and he had left the study and started up the stairs, Davis asked, ''For Aunt Charlotte's sake, do you think it's going to work?''

''For Aunt Charlotte's sake, I thought it was worth a try,'' Nicholas said. ''Now, time will tell.''

In his room, Nicholas washed up and changed into clothes suitable for dining, though he did not feel very sociable. He wanted a bottle of good brandy, a cigar, and a chair next to the fire in Dorian's bedchamber, where he could see to her safety. Only a the cigar seemed possible. Sindby preferred whisky over brandy, and Davis would never accept Nicholas spending the night sitting next to his sister's bed. At least Susanna Sunridge would be there with her.

The gleam of white paper caught Nicholas's eye as he lifted his coat off the bed. The footman, who'd been serving several of the gentlemen as valet, had laid out his clothes. Tucked beneath the garments lay a note.

The obviously disguised handwriting reminded him of the script used in the anonymous note that had arrived at the St. Johns's town house after the betrothal announcement. Nicholas snapped it up and ripped it open.

Dear Traitor,
   Next time your lady, whom you loved so well in the greenhouse, will not be as fortunate. Give up your fruit-less search.

Dorian awoke the next morning feeling well and quite certain that she was going to be able to put the horror of what happened in the woods behind her without any ill effects. But as the morning wore on she found that her hearing in her right ear was greatly reduced. The physician had warned her that might happen but told her that over a period of days her hearing probably would return. The pellet wounds on the side of her face were sore but seemed to be healing already and were easily covered with tendrils of hair.

"Perhaps the man mistook you for someone else," Susanna suggested at the breakfast table. Dorian had refused to take breakfast on a tray in her room.

A lovely pink blush glowed in Susanna's cheeks. There seemed to be an ease between her and Davis, who sat beside her, that had not existed earlier.

Nicholas had taken the place next to Dorian. She sensed in him a growing gloominess that she did not like at all.

"I don't think so," Dorian said. "He asked for me by name. I'm sure Lady Haddo will tell you the same thing. In fact, I had the distinct sense that he knew me—I mean, he recognized me."

Nicholas shifted in his chair. "I believe we should consider returning to London."

"But that would ruin Lord Sindby's plans for the ball," Davis said with a grin; then he peered more closely at Dorian. "Unless, of course, you wish to go, Dorian. But you do look chipper this morning."

"I'm quite all right," Dorian said, "though I believe I won't walk much farther than the gardens today. The ball is only a day away."

"If we are to stay, you won't go out without Davis or me as an escort," Nicholas said, sipping from a cup of black coffee. His voice rang with a finality that no one at the table cared to refute.

Though Dorian found herself a little jumpy about someone approaching her from behind, which she thought only natural, she had no intention of returning to Town. In fact, she had every intention of continuing with the copying of Chamier's music that she had begun only the day before.

The new complication in her plans was Nicholas.

He'd lost interest in hunting and fishing and proceeded to follow her around Stalker Keep, so that she couldn't even seek out a chamber pot without him sending a maid to accompany her. Though she enjoyed Nicholas's company, and had longed for it when he was out hunting, she found this new attention smothering.

Not only that, but he was no longer the old Nicholas, who baited and challenged her, then grinned like a schoolboy. Though he still smiled, and the expression was genuine—even almost indulgent—something about it was unaccountably grim and withdrawn. His eyes had become unreadable once more, as they had the night she had feared to leave him alone. But what she saw in them was not moroseness; she saw something hard and cold that frightened her.

If she thought about the change in him too long, a chill slithered down her spine. So she ignored reflection, preferring to think that her odd perceptions of Nicholas's changed mood were merely the result of her close call with a shotgun.

Chapter Twenty-two

The ball at Stalker Keep was a great success. Lord Sindby made no secret of his delight. Any family of standing in the county was there, filling the old keep and the garden with bejeweled ladies in rich gowns and gentlemen in elegant black evening dress.

Dorian enjoyed herself, finding the ladies friendly and curious about the latest fashion and the gentlemen gallant and blatantly gossipy about each other and everyone else, including Prinny. But no one knew of a giant of a man named Otis.

She danced with nearly every man there, including Lord Sindby, Allerby, Corsley, Sir Gavin, and Davis—the latter being mostly occupied with Susanna.

Nicholas danced with her once, as convention required, and danced once, also, with Lady Eleanor. Though his good manners beautifully disguised his remoteness from Sindby's guests, Dorian knew it was there, deep and dark and brooding—more intense than she'd ever perceived before. There was no more fooling herself into thinking she was misreading his mood.

Nicholas was changed.

By the morning of their departure, the day after the ball, Dorian was relieved to learn that Nicholas intended to ride on horseback rather than with them in the carriage.

"Why?" Dorian asked Davis, as the footman carried the last of her luggage down the stairs. They were standing in the entry hall waiting for the last of the trunks to be loaded and for Lord Sindby and Lady Haddo to make their appearance so farewells could be taken.

"He said something about highwaymen," Davis said. "After what happened to you I think it's a realistic concern."

"Perhaps, but—"

"There you are, Dorian, my dear." Lord Sindby hurried toward them with Lady Haddo, a footman, and Nicholas in tow. "I am sorry to see you rush off so soon after the ball, but I understand from your brother that there is the matter of your aunt's health to consider."

"Yes, we do wish to see that she is well," Dorian said, eager to show Aunt Charlotte the new works of Franz's that she'd discovered and copied. "But we do so appreciate your hospitality."

"Ah, but I'm afraid that your stay was not all that I would have liked it to have been," Lord Sindby said with a regretful frown. "In light of that fact, I would like you to have this to take to your aunt."

The footman stepped forward and offered the portfolio of Chamier's works to Dorian.

Speechless, she stared at the leather-bound folder of music.

"Please, you must take it," Lord Sindby said with some anxiety. "I should be ever so offended if you didn't."

Dorian glanced at Nicholas, who stood behind the earl. He gave an imperceptible shrug.

Dorian took it from the footman's hands, certain that somehow Nicholas had managed to persuade Sindby to relinquish the pieces. "On behalf of my aunt I am delighted to accept this music, my lord."

Sindby pursed his lips. "I have kept the organ music Chamier composed for me, but all the other pieces of music are there. I hope they are useful to your aunt in assembling her compilation of Chamier's work.''

''Indeed, I'm certain she will find it most helpful,'' Dorian said, surprised to find tears threatening but careful to hide them. Neither Sindby nor Nicholas could possibly know what a wonderful gift this was. ''This means a great deal to me and to Aunt Charlotte, my lord. Thank you so much. I know she will wish to acknowledge your contribution in the published collection.''

''My pleasure, my dear,'' Lord Sindby said, allowing Dorian to give him a brief kiss on the cheek. ''I'm delighted to be able to contribute to her fine efforts.''

Farewells and thank-yous were exchanged and they were soon rumbling along the road south. Dorian sat in the carriage, clutching the portfolio against her heart and wondering just how Nicholas had managed to sway the earl into giving her this generous gift. He'd had a hand in changing the earl's mind; she had no doubt of it.

Yet, mile by mile, she could feel him pulling away from her. Riding alongside the carriage instead of inside with her was just the first step.

''Look at this. And this!'' Aunt Charlotte stood at her desk in the overheated room, flipping through the pieces of music Dorian had returned with. Color glowed in her cheeks. Excitement sparkled in her eyes. Dorian smiled to herself and sank into a nearby chair.

''And we'd feared this work was lost forever!'' Aunt Charlotte exclaimed, scanning a piece from the portfolio.

Upon their return, Dorian and Davis had found their aunt in bed, pale and weak, muttering that she'd done all she could do for Franz's work. Dorian had shrugged out of her cloak and spread the portfolio open on the bed immediately.

Davis had ordered tea and sandwiches without delay. "They have work to do," he'd explained to Barton.

Before long the lady had been propped up in bed and was paging through the music with a renewed interest in life. This morning Aunt Charlotte was on her feet, studying the new works and making plans for additions and arrangements to the compilation.

Dorian watched, pleased with her aunt's miraculous recovery. But she had slept badly her first night home and was still exhausted from the journey.

"Oh, dearest, this is wonderful," Aunt Charlotte declared without taking her eyes off the pages of music before her. "I never dreamed we'd have the opportunity to share this with the world."

"Nor I," Dorian agreed, stifling a yawn. Davis, apparently satisfied that Aunt Charlotte was on the mend, had already left to spend the day at his business office.

"And you say there was music for a pipe organ? I had no idea that Franz had ever composed for an organ." Aunt Charlotte's enthusiasm would have been contagious if Dorian hadn't been so tired.

There was a knock at the door.

Dorian turned. "Yes, Barton?"

"Miss Dorian, his lordship, the Earl of Seacombe has called to see you. He says it is most important."

Dorian's exhaustion slipped away. She sat up a little straighter in her chair. Every instinct she possessed told her that Nicholas had come with bad news. "Show him into the drawing room, Barton. I'll be right there."

"Lord Seacombe is here?" Aunt Charlotte looked up from the music. "He was instrumental in acquiring this portfolio, didn't you say? I must thank him."

"Yes, I think that would be an excellent idea," Dorian said, suddenly wanting someone with her when she faced him in his present dark mood.

And she was glad of Aunt Charlotte's company when she

saw the coolness in him melt away under Charlotte's warmth and excitement. With her cap ribbons aflutter, Aunt Charlotte hurried across the drawing room to take Nicholas's hands in hers and offer him her heartfelt thanks for his part in acquiring Franz's work.

"I had little to do with that. To share this music with the world is the best possible thing Sindby could do for music lovers everywhere," Nicholas said, glancing over Aunt Charlotte's head at Dorian, who had neglected to tell her aunt of the shooting incident. Dorian shook her head to tell him so.

In the conversation that followed he alluded to nothing amiss during the stay at Stalker Keep.

They sat and talked of the visit for a few moments: innocent conversation, pleasant and social.

Aunt Charlotte stood. "I have said enough and have much work to do, thanks to you, Lord Seacombe, and Dorian," Aunt Charlotte said, moving to the door.

"Do stay and have tea with us, Aunt Charlotte," Dorian pleaded, nearly desperate to make her aunt stay so she would not be alone with Nicholas.

"You are betrothed," Aunt Charlotte reminded her unnecessarily. "And you know I don't hold with those silly conventions of Society. Heavens, the servants are about, and I'll be in the next room. Do enjoy your tea, and thank you again, my lord." Then she was gone.

The withdrawal of her joy and energy deflated the atmosphere in the room. Dorian turned to Nicholas, dismayed by the cool remoteness she found lingering in his eyes.

She took a deep breath and decided there was nothing to do but face whatever was to come. "You've come with bad news?"

The planes of his face grew hard. He turned away from her to pace the length of the room and back again. Finally he stopped and stood with his feet braced, as if he were riding the deck of a ship in heavy seas. "I've come to say I think it time for *you* to cry off the engagement."

Dorian stared at his shoulder and tried to take a breath, but her lungs failed her.

Nicholas touched her arm. "Perhaps you should sit down."

She shook her head but refused to look at him. "I'm fine as I am. Really, I am. Is there more?"

He walked away from her, his back to her. "I wish that I could . . ."

"Ease the awkwardness," Dorian supplied for him.

He nodded.

She stared at his back, trying to memorize the achingly familiar breadth of his shoulders, the strong cords of his neck, the way his dark hair curled over the edge of his snowy white neckcloth. How she loved the curve of his ear. She savored the secret she knew: that a light kiss at the base of his neck just at the collarbone could make him suck in his breath and demolish his discipline.

Dorian swallowed the lump in her throat and searched for the courage she once believed was hers. "Have you found the fragment, then?"

Nicholas whirled on her, his eyes frostier than Dorian thought possible. She backed away from him.

"No, I have not found the music," he said, his voice icy. "Difficult as it may be for you to believe, I am not going back on our agreement."

"Then why?" Dorian's words nearly came out in a sob, but she mastered her voice and her face. She would never allow him to know how much he had hurt her. How much she'd come to care for him. How much she loved him. "I mean, this comes as something of a shock. I had no idea that you were dissatisfied with the alliance to which we'd agreed."

"I am not dissatisfied," Nicholas said, with a despairing shake of his head that Dorian found mysteriously reassuring. "Let's just say that I think our arrangement has served its purpose."

Dorian's blood turned cold. "And what purpose was that?"

"We learned all the places where Franz's music does not

exist. We found some works for your aunt and were able to acquire them. And for that I am profoundly happy.''

''But we did not find the love song for her. What will I tell her about us? She believes us lovers.'' It was the only thing Dorian had to cling to. The one snag with which she could still hold him, or so she hoped. ''We did not find the one piece of music that is most important to her—and to you.''

''I am saying that I no longer believe that you and I can find it together,'' Nicholas said, his voice harsh and authoritative. ''If you want to be the one to cry off as we first discussed, then so be it. It matters not to me.

''But our betrothal will come to an end. Make no mistake about what I am saying, Dorian. I want it made as public as possible that you and I are no longer engaged to be married. There will be no more house parties, or musicales, or balls, or drives in the park, or—'' He hesitated, and the tone of his voice dropped and became husky. ''Or trysts in dockside inns.''

Humiliated, Dorian turned her back to him, feeling like a fool. Surely she had been more than a dalliance, more than a means to an end for him. ''Your purpose has been served.''

She waited in silence, hoping he would deny her implication. But he did not.

''I believe we understand each other,'' he said at last.

''Apparently so,'' Dorian said, pulling at the sapphire ring on her finger. When she'd succeeded in slipping it off she turned to him. ''If I am crying off, then I must return this to you.''

When she held the sapphire to him, he shook his head. ''No, the ring is yours.''

''I don't want it. It would only serve as a reminder of too many things that I do not care to recall.''

Nicholas flinched. ''I certainly have no use for it. I bought it for you. Keep it. I shall take my leave and will expect to hear the word around town very soon that you have cried off our engagement.''

''How will you respond when someone asks you about it?''

"I will have no comment," Nicholas said. "As a matter of fact, I'm intending to go to the country for a long stay. You may tell Davis and Society whatever you wish; I will have no objection. I was not seeking a wife when this all began, nor am I looking for one now. What the *ton* thinks of me personally makes no matter to me."

What about what I think and how I feel? Dorian longed to ask. *Is this truly what you want, Nicholas? Tell me, was it all a charade?* But she watched him walk to the door in silence.

He turned to her one last time. "I do not expect that we shall meet again privately. I just want you to know that I do wish you happiness."

With that he left the room.

Dorian sobbed, a wail of pain, a cry of rage. She threw the ring at the door and dissolved into tears over a man she had promised herself she would never allow to trouble her.

The sapphire clattered to the floor, its yellow gold band, white diamonds, and blue gemstone glittering harshly in the cold morning sunlight.

It was midafternoon by the time Nicholas arrived at the Blue Mermaid after a long walk along the docks and a lengthy call made in Bow Street.

A group of sailors were already gathered at the bar and several tables were occupied. Nicholas settled into a corner table, ordered a pint of ale, and prepared himself for a long wait. He tried not to think of his parting with Dorian, but there was no escaping the desolation that crept over him as the details filtered back through his defenses.

Two years ago, when the unsubstantiated charges of treason had first been laid before him, he'd thought he'd lost everything. He'd been a walking husk of a man for weeks, even months afterward. He'd lost his good name. He'd thought there was no more for him to lose.

Then he'd overcome that misery and come back fighting.

He'd become a man bent on learning the truth at any price, even if he had to make his way in the very Society he resented. Even if he had to act out a charade as a devoted fiancé to a spoiled heiress. Restoring the Derrington good name was worth any effort.

But today he'd learned something more about what mattered in his life. Today he'd given up his world and his future; he'd thrown it aside because he knew now what was more important than reputation. It was the welfare of someone you loved with all your heart.

Better for them to live apart, for Dorian to laugh in another man's arms, than for her to be dead—because he'd thoughtlessly led his villain to her. Better that she never speak to him again, that they never touch hands or share a smile. That their breaths never mingle in a sweet sigh of sensual satisfaction.

How she must hate him now. He'd heard the ring hit the door as he walked away. At this very minute she was probably ripping the marriage agreement he'd given Davis into tiny shreds with vengeful pleasure.

Nicholas suspected she would loathe him forever. And he deserved it. He'd endangered her existence, her happiness and welfare with his determination for justice, for the Derrington name, and to avenge Jon Collard's death. But her pain would pass. She'd be alive and happy again someday.

There was nothing wrong with his cause, with his search for truth and justice, but he could not allow it to jeopardize Dorian. He would live the rest of his life branded a traitor if that's what was required, if that's what was necessary to ensure her health and happiness.

But that did not mean he would allow the villain to win.

Two hours, many dark thoughts, and a pint of ale later, Jamie Collard walked through the door of the Blue Mermaid. Close behind him followed Sir Gavin Trafford.

"I wasn't certain that you were still in Town," Nicholas said, shaking his friend's hand.

"Eleanor decided she wanted to stay for a while before

retiring to the country again—after I finish some business in
Town. She did so enjoy the stay at Sindby's place . . . except
for the incident with Dorian, of course.'' Gavin pulled up a
chair and Jamie Collard followed suit as the barmaid hurried
over.

"What are we toasting?'' Gavin asked when they'd all been
served and Nicholas had lifted his pint in the traditional gesture.

"Bachelorhood.'' Nicholas downed half of his third pint of
ale. "The bride has cried off.''

The other two men stared at him in silence.

"Then the story that Uncle George is spreading at the club
is true?'' Gavin's chair creaked as he leaned forward across
the table. "Dorian St. John cried off her betrothal?''

"What does her brother think?'' Jamie asked with a frown.
"Do you believe he'll challenge you?''

"I believe he'll be glad to be rid of me.''

"Even with your title?'' Gavin asked with a raised brow.
"I suppose his decision to challenge you will be based on what
his sister says.''

"Dorian won't incite a duel,'' Nicholas said with confidence.
That was the one thing he knew he could count on from her.

"Why did she cry off now?'' Gavin asked.

"If it was anything, it was because of the attack at Stalker
Keep.'' Nicholas glanced at Jamie. "Have you learned anything?''

"Learned what?'' Gavin looked from Nicholas to Jamie.
"You told Jamie what happened at Stalker Keep?''

Nicholas nodded, studying his friend.

"There is a man such as you described, my lord. He's abiding
with an old woman near the docks,'' Jamie said. "He's recovering from having his arm amputated. Some kind of accident.''

Gavin fell curiously silent.

"Name?'' Nicholas asked.

"Oswald Filbey, a big man who prefers nice clothes and
buys his boots from a bootmaker in Conduit Street,'' Jamie
said. "And there's more. A manuscript collector—the one

Sindby referred to you—told me of a lady who came to him with a piece of Chamier music. She was asking how much it was worth. He knew about the reward you and Miss St. John had offered for it, though he'd never met either of you. The whole of the Town dealers know about it. But when he told the lady how valuable it was, she seemed shocked and left with the music.''

"Did he get her name?"

"No, but he said she was a blond lady. Probably Quality, because she was elegantly dressed and was accompanied by a maid and a footman."

The news surprised Nicholas, though he tried not to show it.

"Sounds like Dorian." Gavin peered into his face. "Would Dorian be selling the Chamier music she possesses?"

Nicholas drained the ale from his mug. "No, it's not Dorian. I know it's not Dorian."

Chapter
Twenty-three

"It's nothing really serious, is it, Dr. Fisher?" Dorian asked as soon as she and the doctor left Aunt Charlotte's room. "Just another of her spells?"

The doctor strode down the hallway until he came face-to-face with Davis. "I need to speak with both of you downstairs, if I may."

Dorian did not like the grimness around the doctor's mouth or the low edge in his voice. Dr. Fisher was an excellent physician and a very kind man, but he was invariably cross when things were not going as he liked.

Davis and she exchanged uneasy glances. She allowed Davis to lead them into the drawing room.

"Well, Doctor?" Davis made no effort to be hospitable.

"I regret to say that this is the beginning of the end for your aunt."

Dorian tried to swallow but found she couldn't.

"But she's had these spells before," Davis protested.

"None of this duration, and she is weaker this time," Dr. Fisher said with a sad shake of his head. "I wish I could tell you otherwise. Your aunt is a lovely lady, and I would give anything to be more optimistic. But I cannot.''

''What can we do for her?'' Dorian asked, trying to be practical, trying not to think of the future.

Dr. Fisher prescribed medication and gave Dorian instructions that she vowed to follow strictly. When the doctor left she and Davis stared at each other in silence.

''I can't believe this is happening,'' Davis said, running his fingers through his hair.

''Nor I,'' Dorian said, still numbed by the doctor's news. ''So much is yet left undone.''

''Yes, so much,'' Davis echoed. He strode toward the door. He stopped with his hand on the latch. ''You'll say nothing to Aunt Charlotte about your broken engagement. She liked Nicholas so, I'm not certain how she would take it.''

Dorian nodded, grateful that Davis had taken the news about the broken engagement so calmly. She'd already considered the way it would affect Aunt Charlotte.

''Then I must be go. I must do what I can do.''

''Yes, but what is that?'' Dorian asked, mystified by his sudden energy and urgency.

Davis opened the door and ordered the carriage, his hat, his gloves, and his walking stick from Barton. ''I have a call to make; several of them, in fact. Don't wait up for me tonight.''

Dorian did not wait up for him. She spent the rest of her day seeing that the doctor's orders were followed and that Aunt Charlotte's medication was acquired and properly administered. At bedtime she was unable sleep, so she wandered into Davis's study and began to write.

By midnight she'd penned the last name she could remember on the long piece of parchment that she'd unrolled before her on the desk.

Stroking the end of her nose with her quill, Dorian studied the list of names—her own list of suspects. It was a long one, impressive, overwhelming with the names of people of importance. It represented lives, ambitions, resentments, jealousies, greed, and aspirations she could only begin to guess at—the sustenance of betrayal.

She'd begun the list with Nicholas's fellow captains: Thomas Kenwick and Gavin Trafford, Collingwood, Hardy, King, Moorsom, and Stockham. Then she'd added collectors' names, including Algernon Halthorpe and the Earl of Sindby. She even listed the few French and Spanish captains of the enemy's fleet that she could remember from newspaper accounts: Villeneuve, Garvina, Magendie.

Not a single name began with anything that could be interpreted as a Greek delta, which Nicholas said was the first letter in the clue on the back of the piece of music.

Suddenly the candle on the desk flickered. Dorian's heart fluttered with fear. Her ordeal with Otis had made her skittish. She started up from the desk, ready to flee, only to find Davis standing in the doorway, carrying his own candle.

"What on earth are you doing?" he demanded before a yawn overtook him. He was still dressed in his street clothes.

"I couldn't sleep," Dorian said, regaining her composure and sinking back into her chair.

"Doesn't that call for a glass of warm milk and a dull book?" Davis asked. A gleam of interest sparked in his eyes. He walked over to the desk and peered at the parchment. "What on earth are you doing?"

"I'm deducing who has the music," Dorian said, feeling a little foolish but more determined than ever to find the music for Aunt Charlotte before it was too late. "Seacombe and I may no longer be working together, but that does not mean I have given up the search."

"I never thought it would." Davis pulled up a chair to the desk and peered at Dorian's list.

"And so what have you deduced? What's this? You've even included some of the French captains at Trafalgar."

"They are the ones who would have paid good money for information from spies," Dorian said.

"Why would a British naval captain serve as a spy? Surely not for money?" Davis suppressed another yawn.

"I quite agree. Money alone is not enough to make a captain betray his fleet." Dorian studied her brother, waiting for him to come to the same understanding that she had. But his eyelids looked too heavy for him to reach it without her help. "Why would Captain Nicholas Derrington betray his navy? Up to the Battle of Trafalgar, he'd been a successful officer, moving right up through the ranks since he'd gone to sea as a midshipman at the age of fifteen. Then he inherited the Seacombe title, which is a well-endowed one, and the entailed estates as well as other farms and businesses that have always prospered and been well-run."

Davis agreed with a nod.

"Money has never been a concern to the Derringtons. Why do you think he was so willing to allow me to retain my fortune? He's not even particularly given to gaming."

"I noticed that, but he's damned good at it when he chooses," Davis commented, looking thoughtful. "So then, why would any ship's captain betray his navy?"

"For revenge or ambition," Dorian revealed.

"Or for love," Davis added, suddenly clear-eyed.

Dorian peered at her brother and blinked. "Would a man betray his country for love?"

" 'Tis a motivation at least as strong as ambition."

The thought was a new one for Dorian; she'd been so certain ambition was the culprit. Gavin's career had not moved upward as smoothly as Nicholas's had, and clearly a rivalry existed between the two men.

But Davis's insight offered new areas of speculation. Dorian had not missed the fact that her brother had lost all interest in Lady Elizabeth and had seemed to rebuild his world around Lady Susanna. He smiled frequently now and seemed to look forward to each day with an eagerness he'd never displayed before.

When he'd been attached to Elizabeth he'd been far too

worldly to act as if he was enjoying himself, displaying a mask of ennui that the *ton* seemed to require. He'd worn the face of boredom that he thought Lady Elizabeth would expect of him. But Davis was in love now, she hoped. He'd changed—for the better.

Perhaps there was something to what he said about the power of love. She could not forget the image of a youthful threesome: Nicholas, Eleanor, and Gavin.

Nicholas had admitted that he'd cared for Eleanor, and Gavin clearly had loved her; she was now his wife. Where had Eleanor's feelings lain? Had Gavin always been her choice of the two handsome men with whom she'd grown up?

"Tell me, Davis, how strong is the power of love?"

Davis peered at her list. "Very powerful. Don't you know that? You love Nicholas, don't you? Isn't that why you've been moping around the house ever since you cried off on the engagement?"

Dorian frowned at him. "That is neither here nor there right now. We are seeking the music for Aunt Charlotte's sake." ·

"*You* asked about the power of love." Davis rose from his chair, strolled across the room to the window, and tapped on the glass. "I can show you the power of love."

Dorian ignored him and looked down at the list again. No matter how many names she added, she came back to the same thought. As much as she wanted to find some new suspect, Gavin seemed to be the only one who might have had enough resentment to betray his king and country in an effort to destroy Nicholas.

Impatient, Davis stepped away from the window. "Come over here, Dorian. I want to show you something."

"It's three in the morning, Davis," Dorian said. "There's nothing out there to see."

"Come here, please. I want to show you something about the power of love," Davis insisted.

Puzzled, Dorian abandoned her list and joined her brother at the window.

"See that man there?"

"I don't see anyone out there."

"The man in a frock coat standing in the shadows over there; see him?" Davis pointed out the figure to Dorian.

At last she saw the well-concealed man. "Who is he? Why is he there? Do you know him?"

Davis sighed. "I spotted him lingering there off and on all day, as I was coming and going, so I went to speak to him just before I came home."

Dorian gasped. "You should have sent one of the footmen."

Davis shook his head. "He is a Bow Street runner. I thought as much before I approached him."

"A runner! Why is he watching us?"

"Nicholas hired him."

Dorian stared at the shadowy figure uncomprehendingly, her heart fluttering at the mention of Nicholas's name. "I don't understand."

"I won't go into the details of the conversation. It took a bit of time and one of my premium cigars to get out of him what I wanted to know. The man is a clever chap, but once I learned who his employer was, I understood better. It seems Nicholas hired that runner to protect you."

Dorian said nothing to that, too astonished by Davis's news and the knowledge that her brother had shared a friendly smoke with a runner.

Davis went on. "Of course, I know Nicholas is only thinking of you. In his place, after what happened at Stalker Keep, I would have done the same. But it took me a bit to get over the insult; as if I can't take care of my own sister. But I believe he was damned concerned about that incident with that Otis bloke."

The name sent a chill through her.

"The runner is supposed to watch who comes and goes here at the house and to follow you everywhere," Davis said.

"I don't much like the idea of having a runner following

my every move,'' Dorian protested, though her heart sang at Nicholas's concern.

''I don't have the slightest idea what passed between you two,'' Davis continued. ''I don't know whether you cried off or Nicholas called for the end of the betrothal. But he's damned apprehensive for your safety.''

Dorian shook her head. ''That's merely his sense of responsibility. You forget he was a ship's captain and took the welfare of his men as a serious obligation. Did you ever stop to think that there might be another reason for his having me watched?''

Davis let the drapery fall closed and peered into Dorian's face. ''Such as?''

''To find out whether I've found the music he wants.''

''That's very cynical, dear sister.''

''Perhaps, but I believe I know who is behind all of this, and I think there is enough of a rivalry between these two men to bring out the worst in them.''

Surprise crossed Davis's face. ''Who do you think it is?''

Dorian glanced at the list on her desk and decided to say what she truly thought. ''Sir Gavin Trafford.''

There, she'd said it aloud for the first time after all these days of suspecting Nicholas's life-long friend.

''He's Nicholas's best friend. Why would he—?''

''Because he wanted to be certain that Lady Eleanor would never turn to Nicholas again. How could she love a traitor, a man whose sparkling career was tarnished and his family name laid to ruins?''

''But at the expense of so many lives?''

''He probably didn't think of that before hand.'' Dorian wanted to give Gavin as much credit as possible.

''Has Nicholas ever suspected?''

''I don't think so. Nicholas would never think a friend of his would betray him purposely. He'd never want to believe that Gavin contributed to the death of their mutual friend, Jonathan Collard.''

"Collard. Collard. The Bow Street runner mentioned his name, too. No, it was Jamie Collard. A relation, you think?"

"Perhaps."

"What are you going to do, Dorian? Nicholas must be told."

"He'll never believe it," Dorian said. "I don't have a shred of evidence to back up my suspicions. We need proof."

"Such as finding the third fragment of music in Trafford's possession?" Davis finished for her.

"Precisely, and what are the chances of that?"

"If Trafford had it, why would he risk discovery by keeping it? If I were him, I'd burn it."

"Unless you needed the money you never received because the information you sold to the French never reached them," Dorian said. "I wonder how much Lady Eleanor knows. It's possible she may have no idea what her husband has been up to. But I'd love to talk to her and find out."

"Well, don't plan a social call to discuss something like treason with a traitor's wife," Davis said. "Whether she knows the truth or not, she'd never admit his guilt to you."

"I suppose not," Dorian said thoughtfully.

"Dorian, this is such a pleasant surprise," Lady Eleanor Trafford exclaimed, sweeping into the lavishly decorated drawing room with a strained smile on her lovely bow-shaped lips. Despite her good manners, the lady clearly had not expected or wanted callers.

"So kind of you to receive me so unexpectedly. When I heard that you'd decided to stay in Town, I thought the least I could do is call and see how you were recovering from our long stay at Stalker Keep." Dorian primly folded her hands in her lap and looked up at the lovely woman who had captured Nicholas heart once.

"But it is I who should be calling on you, to see how you survived your terrible ordeal at Lord Sindby's house party," Lady Eleanor said, perching on a chair opposite Dorian. "I regret that Sir Gavin is at the Admiralty today. How sorry he will be that he missed you.''

Dorian flashed her best smile. ''I merely wanted to say hello and tell you, lest you have not heard, that I have cried off my betrothal.''

Eleanor regarded her with a look of pity that made Dorian uncomfortable. ''Gavin told me. He learned of it directly from Nick last night. I do hope the unfortunate incident at Lord Sindby's was not the cause of it.''

''No, of course not,'' Dorian said, surprised by Eleanor and Gavin's knowledge of the broken betrothal. Nicholas certainly had wasted no time in letting people know. ''I find myself compelled to get to the bottom of that mystery some day. However, I've come today on another errand. I hope you can help us.''

''But you and Nicholas are no longer engaged,'' Eleanor said, furrowing her pretty brow. ''Of course, I would do anything to help Nicholas—or you. Gavin said Nicholas was as openly troubled as he's ever seen him over the end of your betrothal.''

The thought of Nicholas's unhappiness momentarily distracted Dorian from the purpose of her visit. But she could not believe his heart was as heavy as hers. Nevertheless she would not allow what had come between them to stop her from doing what she had to do for Aunt Charlotte's sake.

''You must be very proud of Sir Gavin and his successful career in His Majesty's Navy,'' Dorian said, wanting to steer the topic back to Gavin and his career.

''Indeed I am.'' A quick, genuine smile beamed on Eleanor's lips and shone in her delft blue eyes.

''And he looks so handsome in his uniform,'' Dorian said, admiring a small portrait of Sir Gavin that hung at the far end of the room. She noted that the furnishings were costly for those of a modest country gentlemen and navy captain. Over the fireplace hung a portrait of Lady Eleanor.

''Yes, I believe so. I would have put Gavin's portrait over

the fireplace, but he quite insisted that the prettier face belonged in the place of honor."

"How thoughtful and gallant of him," Dorian said, wondering if she'd been foolish to think that such a loyal wife as Eleanor would be any help to her.

"I understood from Nicholas that you and he and Sir Gavin and a young man named Jon Collard were childhood friends."

"Indeed we were," Eleanor said with a soft, nostalgic laugh. "I was such a hoyden in those days. I romped about the county as wild as the boys. That's what comes from being the only daughter and lady among the county gentry. As soon as Nicholas and Gavin and Jon went off to the navy, Papa sent me to school to learn proper deportment."

"It sounds as if you were great friends and had a wonderful childhood together."

"Yes. I do miss those carefree days sometimes." Eleanor leaned forward to speak more softly. "There is nothing like being the only female with three handsome male escorts."

"I can see that would be a heady experience for a girl," Dorian said, suspecting each of the three boys of being in love with the lovely young Eleanor. Her heart turned cold with envy at the thought of Nicholas in Eleanor's thrall. "Then you had the good fortune to win Gavin's heart."

A frown flitted across Eleanor's face, then vanished. "There was a time when I'd rather have given my heart to Nicholas, but Gavin won me over."

"How do you feel about Nicholas now?"

"Oh, we are good friends, of course." Eleanor's expression shifted as a new thought occurred to her. "I pray you don't think we are more than that? No need for any jealousy. Surely I was not the cause of the break between you two?"

"But you are so lovely, Lady Eleanor, you must understand that I might doubt Nicholas when I saw how he looked at you," Dorian ventured, pleased to see the lady look away, touch her hair, and smooth her skirts, preening.

"But all that is over with now," Dorian went on, dismissing

the past with a wave of her hand. "Nevertheless, I wish to find the missing music for my aunt. I wondered if perhaps you might have seen it."

"The Chamier music you were searching for at Stalker Keep?" Eleanor's eyes widened in astonishment. "The piece that Nicholas believes will clear the Derrington name? It's become very valuable, hasn't it?"

"Yes, it has." Dorian studied the myriad of emotions that crossed Eleanor's face. The lady understood exactly what Dorian was asking, and for some reason she wanted to avoid answering her question. "My aunt is gravely ill."

"I can't believe you think Gavin or I—?" Eleanor shook her head. "That's quite absurd. You are implying that it was my husband who—"

"I am implying nothing," Dorian said, more convinced than ever that Eleanor knew something. "I am merely trying to comfort my aunt and help Nicholas. If you know anything about the music, please tell me."

"I cannot help you, Miss St. John." Eleanor rose elegantly to her feet and reached for the bellpull. "If you'll excuse me, I believe it is time for you to leave."

Eleanor's rudeness encouraged Dorian. "I'm implying only that Sir Gavin might know something more about what happened at Trafalgar than he has admitted so far. If he does . . . if you know . . . you can help me and Nicholas, for the sake of your old friendship."

The butler appeared in the doorway, summoned by the bell.

"Jarvis, Miss St. John is leaving," Eleanor said and turned away.

Dorian gathered up her gloves and parasol. "Pray, think about what I have said, Lady Eleanor."

"I assure you, Miss St. John, there is nothing to think about."

Dorian found herself on the doorstep of the Trafford town house, staring at the street and wondering what to do next. Should she approach Nicholas and warn him about Gavin?

He'd never believe her. Or should she go to Gavin? If she took that step, it should be very carefully made.

Out of the corner of her eye she saw a man wearing a hat that hid his face disappear into the shadow of the alley. He turned briefly to watch her descend the town-house steps. Another man joined him, a sailor from the looks of his clothing and his wide-brimmed hat. Dorian recognized the man in the coat and gave a little wave to her new shadow—or shadows. She seemed to have two of them now: Nicholas's Bow Street runner and his sailor companion.

She climbed into the carriage and thought about what she should do all the way home. There was no escaping it; she had to talk to Nicholas.

Chapter Twenty-four

"I'm so sorry to hear that your aunt is ill," Susanna said as Davis turned the team of four perfectly matched blacks drawing his phaeton onto the Hyde Park path. They'd reached the park at exactly five o'clock, just at the height of the social hour. Davis smiled to himself, satisfied that everyone would see him and Susanna together. "Are you sure this is where you wish to be? I mean, in light of the state of your aunt's health."

"Aunt Charlotte insisted that we take this drive," Davis lied, gazing briefly at Susanna as he drove. His aunt would be, if she knew what he was up to.

Susanna looked beautiful in a royal blue gown, her glorious red hair tucked beneath a matching blue bonnet trimmed with white silk flowers. If Elizabeth and Herby Dashworth didn't spy him and Susanna together, some tale-carrying soul was bound to see them and spread the word. Not that this outing was to send a message to Elizabeth. No, Davis had quite another purpose in mind.

"Aunt Charlotte has never been one to make others suffer

because she does not feel well, and she told me she did not want us to miss out on the splendid sunshine and fresh air.''

"How kind of her," Susanna said. "But I do feel rather obvious."

"But *obvious* is exactly what I want," Davis said, grinning at her. "That's why I chose the phaeton and the team of blacks for today. I hope the whole world sees us together. It will make things easier for me later."

"You are being mysterious, sir," Susanna said, a soft smile on her lips, but a gleam of wariness in her amber eyes.

There was little time for conversation between the two of them, what for all the greetings that must be shared with the passing vehicles filled with lords and ladies.

They passed Lord Algernon Halthrope, accompanied by a lady neither of them recognized, and Captain Kenwick, driving with his wife and daughters. The Duke and Duchess of Tewk were seen enjoying the sunshine of Town. They even glimpsed Prinny's simple *vis-a-vis* drawn by an elegant team of matched bays.

"Do you think the Prince of Wales saw us together?" Susanna asked after they passed the plain vehicle with its purple shades drawn.

"I hope so," Davis said, grinning once more.

"You'd rather be seen with me than Lady Elizabeth?" Susanna pressed, looking straight ahead, not at Davis.

"Any day," Davis declared, his eyes on her rather than the path ahead. "And I brought you here to prove it to you, because all the social functions we've attended together have not seemed to convince you of my change of heart—of my love."

When she didn't respond Davis pulled the phaeton to the side of the path. The footman jumped down to take the horses' heads.

"If this drive is not enough," Davis said, pulling a document from his waistcoat pocket. "I have something more. Have a look at this."

Susanna took it from him slowly, unfolded it, and read

through the document, her eyes growing wider and wider as she scanned the words on the paper.

"Davis, this is a special license to marry," Susanna said, her voice a mere whisper. "You cannot possibly be serious."

Davis cupped her chin in his hand. "I'm more serious about this, Susanna, than I've ever been about anything in my life. Will you marry me?"

"But this seems rather hasty, particularly with your aunt ill," Susanna protested.

"Aunt Charlotte's illness is part of the reason for the haste," Davis admitted. "She has always declared that it was her wish to see Dorian and I happily married, and for love.

"Forgive my pressing you like this, Susanna. I would not do it for any other reason in the world. I'm more than willing to give you all the time you like, but for Aunt Charlotte—"

"Say no more," Susanna said, touching his hand and brushing her fingertips along his knuckles. Despite the fact that they both wore gloves, his hand tingled. "Your aunt is a lovely lady and I understand your desire to grant her wish. But let me get used to the idea."

"I know a clergyman who would perform the ceremony tomorrow—"

"Perhaps in a few weeks," Susanna suggested. "The timing just doesn't seem right, Davis. We'll be appearing at the Winsters' musicale together—then, maybe no one would be all that surprised."

Davis's disappointment was small. The day after tomorrow was not all that far away, though he'd hoped to convince her to go with him to the church this very evening. He could wait another day or two.

The Winsters' musicale was the solution to her problem, Dorian decided. She'd quite forgotten that she'd accepted the invitation weeks ago, and at first thought to send last-minute regrets. Aunt Charlotte was entirely too ill for her to be gadding about Town. But, on second thought, attending the musicale could be fortuitous now that she was certain that Nicholas would be there—Davis had heard that he'd not left for the country yet—and Gavin would be present as well. The Winsters were a fine old Lincolnshire family. Both men had to put in an appearance at least; to do less would be to snub one's neighbors.

And she would be there to confront both of them about the truth.

"You look lovely tonight, in a subdued sort of way," Davis said, casting an appraising glance over Dorian as their carriage waited in line to drop them at the Winsters' door. "The pearls in your hair are a nice touch."

Dorian looked down at her violet dress with its blue overskirt and shrugged. "Do I? Actually I haven't given dressing much thought, except—I thought Nicholas might like this color."

"If he is at the musicale this evening, I'm sure he will, but don't expect much attention from him." Davis touched his neckcloth to be certain the knot was straight. "*You* cried off your engagement, remember?"

Dorian frowned. Davis's baiting wasn't going to get hasty words out of her. Nicholas had honored their agreement and she would, too.

"Gossip will be running through the crowd and everyone will be watching the two of you, praying one of you will make a scene."

"Rest assured, I will not make a scene," Dorian vowed. She had given a lot of thought as to how to tell Nicholas that she believed his best friend held the key to the mystery.

At first she'd thought writing a letter would be the way to inform him, because to call at his town house would be unheard of after their broken engagement. And she was uncertain whether he'd receive her. She also had second thoughts about putting such accusations in writing. What if the letter went astray or, worse yet, Nicholas misunderstood what she was trying to tell him? Speaking to him personally was the only answer.

She was hardly in the mood for festivities as she stepped out of the carriage, but the opportunity to speak with Nicholas could hardly be ignored.

"Perhaps you could encourage Nicholas to ask me to dance," Dorian suggested to her brother as they walked up the townhouse steps.

Davis eyed her skeptically. "You want me to walk up to a man who has been rejected by you and say, 'By the by, old chap, Dorian wants to take a turn around the floor with you'? I think that would be received less than enthusiastically."

"Well, a dance would put a stop to the rumors of a feud between us," Dorian said.

"I'm not certain Nicholas cares to stop those rumors. From what I've seen and heard from his Uncle George, he's quite content with them."

"Perhaps not," Dorian said, battling the pain she felt every time she thought of the cool, indifferent way Nicholas had called off their engagement. "But I must speak to him somehow. Will you help me? Then I'll leave you to entertain Susanna."

"This smells of extortion, Sister," Davis said with an indulgent smile. "I'll do what I can, but I know he's not going to be very cooperative."

When Nicholas saw the black-clad Earl of Sindby and his foreign friend enter the Winsters' music room he rested a little easier in his chair. Gavin and Eleanor had already arrived and were chatting with the Winsters at the back of the room. Everything—everyone—was in place at last.

"Look who else is here," Uncle George said, nudging Nicholas in the side with his elbow. "Davis and Dorian St. John."

Nicholas nearly cursed aloud and turned to glare at the St. Johns.

Dorian gazed back at him solemnly. She looked lovely, if a

little pale. Her eyes seemed unusually large, and only the remotest of polite smiles lingered on those delicious wine-colored lips. He knew that Aunt Charlotte was failing, and clearly Dorian was troubled. He'd counted on Aunt Charlotte's illness to keep Dorian from appearing here tonight.

"You must snub them, you know—with her crying off on the engagement and all," Uncle George whispered.

Nicholas had no intention of snubbing the St. Johns. In fact, he really wanted to jump up, stride straight across the room, and throttle Dorian.

Why on earth had she called on Eleanor? When he heard of her call to the Traffords' town house from the Bow Street runner he'd almost gone to her Mayfair town house and demanded to know why she'd been so foolish.

"She's looking in your direction." Uncle George nudged Nicholas again. "Here's your chance to cut her dead."

Annoyed with Dorian's unexpected appearance, Nicholas frowned at her. The half smile on her lips disappeared. He plucked a glass of champagne off the tray carried by a passing footman and he turned his back while he took a sip.

"Oh, that was excellent." Uncle George chuckled. "A fine cut, and nearly everyone in the room was looking. You might have more talent for this Society thing that you thought, my boy."

The excellence of the display hardly gratified Nicholas. He drained his champagne glass and wondered how he was going to get Davis to take Dorian home as soon as possible.

The musicale proceeded with performances by several accomplished amateurs, followed by a bit of dancing and gossip, gaming and flirtations. Uncle George found friends with whom to talk of horse racing. Nicholas had little taste for any of it, but he danced with his hostess. To avoid the appearance of anything unusual, he danced with Lady Eleanor. Then he purposely gave the lady's hand to the Earl of Sindby. Except for Dorian's unexpected appearance, everything was going well.

When he saw Dorian occupied in the arms of Herby Dashworth he decided to approach Davis.

"Any chance of getting your sister away from here soon?" Nicholas asked without preamble. Time was beginning to run short.

Surprise crossed Davis's face. "Not before she talks to you."

"We have nothing to say to each other," Nicholas said as coldly as he could. "I explained that to her in our last meeting."

"Hear her out," Davis said, clearly puzzled by Nicholas's reluctance to speak to his sister. "What harm can it do?"

Nicholas shifted impatiently on his feet. How he had longed to see Dorian again. It had been only a week since he'd called at the Mayfair town house to break off the engagement, and the days had been full of laying plans and searching out facts. Yet denying himself the daily pleasure of Dorian's smile and voice, her presence and touch, had turned seven days into a cold, barren eternity.

"You might at least ask after Aunt Charlotte," Davis added. "Dorian would appreciate that."

Despite his better judgment Nicholas relented. Perhaps few words would send her on her way. "In the garden in a quarter of an hour."

Davis nodded. "She'll be in the arbor."

Nicholas didn't linger to watch Dorian finish the dance in Dashworth's arms.

Chapter Twenty-five

Nicholas had heard the Winsters' ormolu clock chime the passage of a quarter hour by the time he stepped into the garden. The sound of the chimes faded as he spotted Dorian lingering alone in the dark arbor. He approached her quietly, making only enough noise to avoid startling her. When she heard his footsteps on the gravel she turned toward him expectantly, slender and graceful as always.

Late summer moonlight cast leafy shadows across her face so he could not read her expression. Nevertheless, a small wave of pleasure brought a smile to Nicholas's lips. Dorian was never a lady to keep a gentleman waiting.

Despite the heavy aroma of wisteria on the night air he caught her violet scent. Her fragrance stirred a bittersweet longing for the past. Only a week ago he would have reached out for her, pulled her into his arms and kissed her. He would have stroked her body, combed his fingers through her heavy golden hair, and molded her against the length of him. But that had been a week ago.

He halted abruptly at the arbor entrance and clasped his

hands safely behind his back. "Davis said you wished to speak to me."

"Yes. Thank you for coming." The silk of her gown rustled as she stepped toward him, a bit of moonlight falling on her face when she did. She appeared unsure of herself. Though she moved toward him, she did not completely close the distance he'd left between them. "I'd like you to listen to me about who the true culprit is."

"So you think you know the truth?" Nicholas asked, his pleasure instantly turning to annoyance that she was so certain she knew more than he—annoyance that she had defied him by calling on the Traffords. "I believe I asked you to abandon this search of yours last week."

"Do you honestly think I could turn my back on the mystery of who caused Franz's death so easily?" Dorian paused. "Franz was a friend and you are—are a friend."

"You simply won't give up your interference because Aunt Charlotte is ill and you want the music," Nicholas said, barely controlling the anger that blossomed in him every time he thought of the danger he'd unwittingly led her into. "See to your aunt's comfort, but forget about 'A Whisper of Violets.' "

"It's not as simple as that and you know it," Dorian snapped, her patience clearly as short as his. "I was searching for Franz's music and murderer long before you became involved in this, Nicholas Derrington. If you think you can order me to give up now, you have a great deal to learn."

"Say what you have to say," Nicholas ordered, glancing over his shoulder toward the house to satisfy himself that no one else had entered the garden yet. "Be brief."

Dorian glared up at him and spoke with a defiant thrust of her chin. "The attempt to betray Nelson's plans to the French Combined Fleet happened just before the Battle of Trafalgar; within hours, isn't that true?"

"Yes. Because the plans had only been laid the night before, after we'd had word that the Combined Fleet had set sail, at last. We had lain in wait for them off the coast of Spain for weeks.'' Nicholas turned a shoulder toward Dorian. Trafalgar was an event he'd painfully relived more times than she could ever know. ''I see no reason to go over this with you.''

''When the couriers were caught what happened?'' Dorian asked, as if she had not heard him.

Nicholas realized there was no putting her off, much as he wanted to. ''The couriers were from my crew. Therefore, I was immediately suspended as captain of the *Dauntless.*''

''And?''

''And thrown belowdecks with the gunners,'' Nicholas said, betraying as little emotion as he could. But the memories were upon him again, memories of air heavy with gunsmoke and a deck so slippery with blood that the men could hardly move fast enough to load and fire the cannon. ''Every man is needed in battle, even candidates for the brig. Later, after the victory, after Nelson had died—I was not even allowed to see him before the end. . . .''

Nicholas paused, the bitterness over that rebuff still fresh. He'd admired and liked his commander, and it pained him greatly that he had not been able to say farewell as the admiral's other captains had. Clearing his throat to be certain he could trust his voice, Nicholas went on. ''And when not enough evidence was found to bring charges against me, I was asked to resign my commission.''

''No, no.'' Dorian shook her head, as if that was of no importance. ''I mean, who took over? Who took your command?''

''Gavin, of course. Everyone knew he was next to be promoted to a ship-of-the-line.''

''Go on,'' Dorian insisted. ''With Gavin in command of the *Dauntless,* who took command of Gavin's ship?''

''This is an exercise in futility, Dorian,'' Nicholas warned.

''I want you to see and understand who the villain was at Trafalgar,'' Dorian insisted.

Nicholas turned a stony face to her.

She gasped, and her eyes widened with surprise and understanding. "You do know. You know! Damn you, Nicholas! How long have you known?"

"I think it's time for you to return to the house." Without meeting her gaze, Nicholas reached for her arm to escort her back into the ballroom.

"Not yet." Dorian pulled away from him. "Do I understand correctly then? The first in command of Gavin's ship was ill, so your mutual friend, Jon Collard, took over the frigate *Daedalus*. Then . . . ?"

"It went down with all hands," Nicholas said, surprised at his own stoicism, though grief still gnawed inside him. "If Gavin had been aboard the *Daedalus* as captain and I'd been on the *Dauntless,* damn few of those lives would have been lost."

"Oh, Nicholas, I'm so sorry," Dorian whispered, the beginnings of tears forming in her lovely eyes. "I feared you would never believe it was Gavin who was the traitor."

Nicholas looked away. He'd never heard the accusation against his friend spoken aloud. He'd never uttered the words himself, though the suspicion had been alive in his mind for weeks. "Part of my heart still doesn't believe it's Gavin. I've doubted every captain who sat around Nelson's table the night before the battle, listening to the admiral lay the plans. All of those men were honorable and all of them my friends. I always come back to the same problem—why?"

"Either to ruin you or for money from the French."

Nicholas shook that off. "There's always been a rivalry between Gavin and myself. It's not to be denied, but I swear it was nothing sinister enough to evolve into treason. We've been like brothers all our lives, Dorian. We share a friendly competition, nothing more."

He'd said enough, Nicholas decided. Taking Dorian's arm, he began to lead her back toward the house once more. To his surprise, she did not resist him this time.

"Was it friendly competition when Sir Gavin married Lady Eleanor?" Dorian asked, trotting along at his side.

Nicholas hesitated, stopping in the middle of the garden path. Their rivalry had not been friendly then. He and Gavin had probably come as close to killing each other the day Nicholas learned that Eleanor had chosen Gavin as two friends could come. They'd been young and foolish then. Blood flowed hot and tempers flared. Dorian didn't need to know that. He caught the determined gleam in her eye. "I will confess that there was an element of conflict in what happened between Gavin and Eleanor and me. He won the lady; I won the commission."

"But don't you see, he wanted the commission, too," Dorian reminded him. "Apparently enough to attempt to ruin you. Now he has to stop our investigation, lest we reveal him to the authorities. That's why he hired Otis to discourage me from the search."

"He hired Otis to discourage both of us." Nicholas laughed a humorless laugh. Sweet, determined Dorian—naive to the end. "If you had died at Stalker Keep, I would have been accused of your murder."

"How?" Dorian stepped back from him in surprise, and he released her arm.

"By all appearances I sent for you that day. Remember? If you had walked in front of the spring gun and died, if the gun had been removed before you were found, the world would have believed that I shot you."

Dorian paused, her lips pursed and tense. "So that is why you ended the engagement. You feared for my safety."

"I had learned what I wanted to know and your assistance was no longer required." Nicholas grabbed her arm once more. He could ill afford her more time. "Don't leap to any noble conclusions about me, sweetheart. You must return to the house."

"I don't believe you." Dorian pulled away from his grasp. When he turned to her, expecting some new confrontation, she stretched up to kiss his cheek. Her lips brushed his jaw, light and sweet.

Nicholas thought he'd steeled his heart against her; too much lay ahead of him to allow himself any weaknesses. But a kiss?

With a low moan, his mouth descended on hers. His arms went around her waist and drew her intimately close. All the while his tongue played at parting her lips. And once it had, he sent it deep.

Slipping her arms around his neck, Dorian returned his kiss. Their mouths melded together with hunger and heat. The more he tasted of hers, the more he wanted. To his satisfaction, she seemed eager to give.

For the moment he forgot all the reasons why they shouldn't be kissing in the Winsters' garden. He lost himself in the passion of a hot, wet connection with Dorian—her lips, her tongue, her soft warm curves alive beneath his hands. He heard her moan. He ached to sweep her up in his arms and carry her somewhere dark and secluded.

At the sound of voices at the garden door of the house Nicholas grudgingly released Dorian.

"Lord Sindby and his friend will meet us out here in just a moment," Eleanor was saying to Gavin.

"It's not a trap?" Gavin asked. "Are you certain?"

Dorian opened her mouth to say something, but Nicholas hushed her with a finger to his lips. Cursing under his breath, he drew her deep into the shadows. He'd wanted to return her to the safety of the house before his plan went forward. Hopefully, Eleanor and Gavin would be too intent on their own affairs to notice them hiding in the darkness.

"Baron Hajda is a Hungarian interested in his countryman's work," Eleanor was saying. She wore a flowing green gown with a fringed shawl elegantly draped across her arms. "He will have no interest in what is written on the back of the music. And the really fine thing is that he is leaving the country the day after tomorrow."

"He is prepared to pay cash for the music?" Gavin asked.

"Lord Sindby assured me so," Eleanor said. "It will be so good to have money again. Who would have thought the French would never pay us? Let me talk with Sindby. He has a weakness for beautiful women.''

At Nicholas's side, Dorian seemed to choke silently on something. Once more he put a finger to his lips to keep her quiet.

Pump heels crunched on the white gravel. With champagne glasses in hand, Sindby and the baron wandered into the garden.

Eleanor's gown fluttered temptingly in the summer breeze as she strolled toward the men, leaving her husband behind. ''Lord Sindby. Baron Hajda, are you enjoying your visit to London?''

''Indeed I am, my lady,'' the baron said, his English accented but well spoken. The tall, spare man gallantly kissed Eleanor's hand.

''The baron is very glad that you have a piece of Chamier's music to sell to him,'' Sindby was saying as the threesome drifted along the path toward Gavin.

''I understand that my countryman's music has become almost impossible to acquire here in England,'' the baron said. ''It is most generous of you to offer this, er, what did you call it?''

''It is only a fragment of a love song,'' Eleanor said, smiling up at the baron. ''But it is one of the last things Franz Chamier ever wrote.''

''Which makes it all the more valuable,'' Sindby added, his eyes raking over Eleanor.

''Don't overplay your part, my lord,'' Nicholas muttered.

''What is going on?'' Dorian demanded in a hushed voice. Nicholas shook his head at her.

''May I see the piece?'' the baron asked.

''Of course,'' Eleanor said. ''I have it right here. It is so very small, I was able to roll it up and carry it in my bag.''

At the sight of the fragment, Nicholas had to restrain Dorian from jumping out of the shadows.

''No, let this play out,'' he whispered.

From their hiding place Nicholas watched the baron and

Sindby examine the fragment. Gavin paced behind them, clearly eager to finish the business.

"What do you think of it, Baron?" Eleanor asked, laying a hand on his arm.

"Very interesting, Lady Eleanor." The baron turned over the fragment. "What are these characters on the back?"

"Just scribbles," Gavin said, suddenly coming forward to interfere. He waved away the importance of the Greek letters. "Odd notes. Wouldn't you like to add it to your collection?"

"I think the baron is most interested," Lord Sindby said. "But I believe he would like to reconsider the price."

The next few minutes were filled with some rather genteel haggling. Dorian fidgeted at Nicholas's side. He knew how she felt. But inside he was growing very calm. Now that Eleanor and Gavin had revealed everything, there was no more reason to let anger and frustration rule his life. His course was clearly plotted.

Soon a price was settled upon. The baron handed over the money Nicholas had provided. Upon receiving the fragment from Eleanor, he rolled it up and tucked it in his pocket.

"I understand you are leaving for Hungary soon," Gavin said.

"I am," the baron said. "The day after tomorrow."

"Then let me advise you to keep this acquisition to yourself," Gavin warned. "There are many who would like to have that piece of music."

"So I understand," the baron said with a wry smile.

The gentlemen all laughed and shook hands; then Sindby and Hajda turned toward the house. Nicholas waited until the two had disappeared into the ballroom before he drew Dorian out of the shadows. He gently shoved her toward the house.

"Find Davis and have him take you home."

"I will not." She turned on him as if she thought him mad.

Gavin and Eleanor, who had been congratulating themselves on their new wealth, fell silent, startled.

"Good evening." Dorian spoke in a voice tremulous with anger.

"Dorian? Nick?" Gavin was slack-jawed with astonishment. He looked around the garden as if he thought they had materialized out of nowhere. "I didn't know we had company out here."

"Obviously," Nicholas said, staring at the stranger who had once been his friend. A peaceful sense of satisfaction settled over him. At last he faced his nemesis knowing the truth. He had weathered many dark hours of pain and bewilderment to reach an understanding and a decision. The law would frown on his course, but be that as it may; he would do what he had to do. Now that the moment had come, now that he fully understood how completely he and Jon—and Dorian—had been betrayed, he had no misgivings.

"Gavin Trafford, I challenge you to defend yourself on the dueling field for your insult to your king and country, to my honor and to the Derrington family name, to our friend Jon Collard."

Nicholas's gaze never wavered from Gavin's face. But he heard Dorian's gasp and felt her quick look of surprise slide over him.

"No, Nicholas," she whispered.

Eleanor backed away from Gavin, her horrified gaze locked on her husband.

Gavin never flinched. "All right. I will give you that satisfaction." His gray eyes gleamed hard and cold in the moonlight. "As the challenged, the choice of time, place, and weapons is mine. My second will notify yours as soon as I've made my decision."

Nicholas shook his head. "No. This is between us, Gavin. No formalities. I will grant you the choice of weapon and place, but I see no reason to involve seconds, and I choose the time— *tonight.*"

Gavin's mouth twisted, but he shrugged indifferently, his

first display of anxiety. "Pistols at Battersea at four o'clock, two hours from now."

"Done," Nicholas said, grimly pleased to have the course fixed.

"Then there's no time to waste." Dorian turned toward the house. "I'll find Uncle George and Davis and order the carriage."

Nicholas grabbed her wrist. "You are not going. Nor is Eleanor."

"Yes, I am," Dorian said.

"So am I," Eleanor agreed, stepping forward.

"Let them come," Gavin said, apparently unconcerned at the thought of his wife attending a bloody duel. "No seconds or physicians. No crowd of witnesses. Just you and me and our women. After all, they have been our partners in this, have they not?"

"The dueling field is no place for ladies," Nicholas declared, eager to eliminate as many distractions as possible from the final deadly confrontation between himself and Gavin.

"I'm going," Dorian said, loud enough for all to hear.

"I will not have you witness murder," Nicholas uttered under his breath, "honorably committed or not."

"I will not desert the field now, Nicholas, lady or not," Dorian replied. "I have done my part in this affair, my lord. You owe me this."

Steely determination glittered in her violet eyes, and Nicholas knew she was right. He also knew that she'd be at Battersea, one way or another.

Nicholas lit the St. Johns' carriage lamp so Dorian could look at the music fragment Sindby had surrendered to her on their way out of the town house. Their leave-taking had been very circumspect; dueling was illegal, and it would be foolish to apprise many people of what was about to take place.

Dorian had insisted on taking the St. John carriage.

As soon as the light glowed bright, Davis leaned over his sister's shoulder to examine the music she held. Nicholas had managed to discourage Uncle George from coming, but Davis would not be parted from his sister. Nicholas agreed only because now Dorian would not be there alone.

"Nicholas, the letters complete the spelling of *Daedalus,*" Dorian exclaimed, examining the back. "The letters never spelled the name of a person; it was the name of a ship. That was all Franz heard."

The revelation did not surprise Nicholas. Once he'd realized the characters might spell out a ship's name, he'd feared that translation might spell *Dauntless,* his ship, and only serve as proof of his alleged treason. "Promise me you'll share this information with the authorities, regardless of what happens."

Dorian frowned at him. "You will show them yourself." She turned the fragment over. "And this middle section of the music incorporates quite an unexpected melody—"

"Aunt Charlotte will be thrilled with this," Davis said. "We must show it to her as soon as possible. Dr. Fisher sent a message that he is very concerned about her condition."

"Then what are you two doing here?" Nicholas turned to Davis. "As soon as we arrive, drop me off. Then you must take your sister home. You must join your aunt."

"No," Dorian said, her voice terse. She rolled up the fragment and tucked it into her bag. "Time enough for that. We shall see this thing through."

Davis looked at Nicholas and shrugged. "I'm not fool enough to argue with that."

Beyond the carriage window, Nicholas glimpsed the street lamps of Westminster Bridge as they crossed the Thames. From time to time he could feel Dorian's gaze on him, and he wished once again that she hadn't come along. Soon he could see open fields beyond the trees, dotted with scattered buildings. They passed the road to Vauxhall; then only moonlight lit the countryside.

When the carriage halted Nicholas was first out of the carriage. He wanted to see whether Gavin had shown up. He had—with a huge, one-armed giant of a man and a couple of liveried servants who looked more like foot*pads* than foot*men*.

The giant moved with amazing swiftness. He was upon Nicholas in a moment, leveling a gun in his face. Nicholas blocked the carriage door, keeping Davis and Dorian inside.

"Be so kind as to hand over that little knife you're so fond of carrying," Gavin said, appearing at the giant's shoulder. Eleanor strolled from the Trafford carriage to her husband's side.

Nicholas complied.

"Now stand away and let your lady and her brother alight from the carriage," Gavin said. "What a nice little party we're going to have here."

Nicholas stood aside for Dorian and Davis. "Do as he says."

In silence, Dorian and Davis climbed out. Otis and Gavin backed away, allowing the three of them to stand with their backs to the carriage. Nicholas realized that Gavin was also armed.

"What's this all about, Gavin?" Nicholas demanded softly, berating himself for thinking this traitor could be trusted. "We had an appointment to settle a challenge."

"I'd truly hoped that it would never come to this," Gavin said. "I'd hoped you would retire to Seacombe Manor and let the past go. I believe you would have, if it weren't for the meddling of Dorian St. John."

"This is between you and I, Gavin," Nicholas said evenly. "Leave Dorian out of it."

"But I can't. Unfortunately, her grasp of the situation became clear when she called on Eleanor," Gavin went on. "Oh, she was very clever and said nothing outright, but Eleanor understood, and I agree with her that we must not permit Dorian to go on with the search."

"We'd already decided that at Stalker Keep," Eleanor said. "The two of you had obviously become too involved, romping about among the flowers. But Otis had a little difficulty carrying off that plan.''

The giant frowned and made a low, growling noise in his throat.

Nicholas stared at Eleanor and wondered when she'd become so cold-blooded. ''*You* knew about the greenhouse at Floraton Court?''

''It was your only opportunity. Besides, I could see the lust in your eyes,'' Eleanor admitted, turning to Dorian with a sly smile twisting her lovely face. ''You were determined to have her and she was quite willing to be had.''

''I'll hear no more of this,'' Nicholas snapped, angry enough to slap a woman for the first time in his life. Yet he remained wary enough to know that this was no time to lose control— no matter how justified. ''What precisely do you plan, Gavin?''

''Isn't it obvious?'' Gavin's voice was oily and patronizing. ''My original plan was to kill you in a duel. You challenge me over the honor of your family's name and your fiancé. Then Dorian shoots herself out of grief for her loss—you. Such a sad affair. But no one would be surprised to see a traitor die in a duel.''

''What about me?'' Davis demanded. ''You think I'm just going to stand here and say nothing?''

''Ah, because of you I have to change my plans,'' Gavin agreed. ''But it's not so difficult. You and Nicholas will kill each other in a duel over your sister. And Dorian's fate is the same: suicide out of grief. I'll relieve her of the music, of course.''

''Fits together very nicely,'' Dorian said.

''What about Sindby?'' Nicholas asked. ''He knows the truth.''

''I think Eleanor and I can deal with Sindby,'' Gavin said.

''Yes, one way or the other,'' Eleanor agreed, preening.

''But why?'' Nicholas asked, though he'd lost interest in Gavin's motivation. Time was important now.

''Because we were sick of seeing you win everything,''

Eleanor said, wearing a wicked smile as hateful and deranged as Gavin's. "Nicholas Derrington, captain of a second-rater, a ship of the line, next to be promoted to a first-rater. Then post captain. Then the earldom is dropped on you. And no matter how Gavin worked he remained a mere frigate's commander. It wasn't fair."

"We decided you needed a little grief in your life," Gavin continued. "Especially if it promoted my cause. I never dreamed I'd actually win command of the *Dauntless* that day."

"Did you dream that Jon Collard and your men would die on the ship you effectively deserted?" Nicholas reminded his friend, anger threatening his composure. "They paid for your good fortune, Gavin. We're going to duel, make no mistake. Where are the pistols?"

"You don't think I'm going to put a loaded gun in your hand, do you, Nick?" Gavin laughed at the ridiculousness of the thought. "I know you better than that. No, Otis will do the shooting."

"Of course you'd prefer to keep your hands clean," Nicholas said, nudging Dorian, who kept looking over her shoulder. She was going to alert the Traffords if they realized what she was looking for.

"We'll begin with killing Dorian, just to let you watch your lady love die. You know, death seldom comes quick, even a ball in the head. You've heard the cries of men dying. Think how sweet the whimpers of your lover will be as she clings to life with her blood pouring out on the ground."

Anger flamed into fury. Nicholas stepped forward to shield Dorian from Gavin. Dorian opened her mouth to say something, but Nicholas nudged her into silence. All he needed was time. A bit more time. "How can you be a party to all this, Eleanor? To murder?"

"Why should I feel mercy toward a man who turned his back on me for the sea?" Eleanor asked.

Nicholas stared at her, baffled by her description of his commitment to his career. He wondered if there was a soul inside the graceful body that stood before him. "I never made you any promises, Eleanor. In fact, I was always under the impression you looked higher than a mere third son. I remember you flirting outrageously with my brother Gilbert, who never took a woman seriously in his life."

"You're right about Gilbert," Eleanor said with a proud lift of her chin. "He died and you went to sea. But Gavin never forgot me. There were letters and calls on my family. Gifts and favors.

"But you left me behind, Nicholas. You were always more interested in your career and your ship than me. Gavin is my husband now. I'll make certain his career advances, no matter what."

Gavin cast his wife an admiring glance. Nicholas saw his hand loosen on the gun. With lightning speed, Nicholas seized Gavin's arm with both hands. He shoved Gavin backwards and twisted his arm behind his back.

Eleanor screamed.

Nicholas pried the pistol from Gavin's fingers. With his arm doubled behind him, Nicholas pressed the barrel of the gun against Gavin's backbone.

Otis roared and stumbled forward, waving his gun. Davis struck the inside of the giant's wrist, and the gun flew into the air. All eyes followed the pistol, flipping end-over-end through the predawn mist. Dorian dived for it. Davis staggered beneath it. Otis shoved Dorian aside in his effort to catch it. But, miraculously, Davis snagged the weapon. For an eternal moment he fumbled with the pistol, the barrel glinting in the carriage lamplight. Nicholas thought all was lost when suddenly Davis turned the gun on Otis and pulled back the hammer.

"Don't move," Davis ordered. The pistol barrel trembled, but Davis's grip was firm, his finger on the trigger. Otis froze.

"That's right, men, throw down your guns." Jamie Collard appeared from behind the carriage, armed with a saber and a pistol aimed at the liveried footpads who were holding the St.

John coachman and groom prisoner in the carriage. Faced with a third man, the footpads complied without protest.

"Oh, my heavens," Dorian cried. With her hand clutching her heart, she sank down on the carriage step. "I was beginning to think you'd never get here."

She echoed Nicholas's thoughts precisely.

Chapter Twenty-six

Dorian sighed with relief as she watched Jamie Collard manacle Otis to one coach wheel while Davis tied the two liveried footpads together. The scene was curiously quiet.

Nicholas had released Gavin, who hurriedly stepped as far away as he dared from the man who held a gun on him. He rubbed the arm Nicholas had ruthlessly twisted behind his back. The two men glared at each other, hatred gathering like storm clouds.

With sickening dismay, Dorian realized the confrontation was not over. She rose from the carriage step, her heart once more taking up its rapid thudding. Nicholas intended to do just what he had said; he would have his duel with Gavin—though the traitor hardly deserved the courtesy.

"Nicholas, Davis and Jamie can turn the Traffords over to the authorities," Dorian suggested, unable to keep the pleading note from her voice.

"St. John, take your sister home," Nicholas ordered. *"Now."*

Davis looked to Dorian, who had eyes only for Nicholas.

"Go, Dorian. Do as I say."

"I told you, I'm not leaving until it's finished."

"I'm in, too," Davis said.

"No need, my lord," Jamie Collard prodded, moving to Davis's side. "This is for the cap'n and me to settle. The magistrate is on his way. Trafford will get his due one way or 'nother."

"What are you talking about?" Eleanor demanded, linking her arm through her husband's, as if she would whisk him away. The wariness around her eyes betrayed her growing understanding that the end was at hand. Desperation crackled in her voice. "Let us go and we'll not say a word. Gavin will resign his commission and we'll retire to the country. We'll never say a word about any of this, I swear."

"I think that's become quite impossible, my dear," Gavin said, his gaze never leaving Nicholas. "Nick wants something more, don't you, Nick?"

"I challenged you to an honorable duel, Gavin. I demand satisfaction."

"Oh, no, Nicholas. No," Dorian whispered.

Nicholas turned on her, his face grim and closed. "Stay if you must Dorian, but I will countenance no interference and no hysterics. Is that clear?"

"Yes," she murmured, afraid to say more. Afraid he would truly send her away.

Nicholas turned to her brother. "Make yourself useful, Davis. Bring me the pistols from the carriage."

Davis did as he was bid, holding the box open to Nicholas.

Dorian could do nothing but look on and remind herself to breathe, for her body seemed to have forgotten how.

"Give Gavin the first choice," Nicholas said. "If you've no objection, Gavin, Davis will load your weapon."

Gavin opened his mouth as if he was about to protest.

"I'd asked Jamie Collard to do it," Nicholas went on smoothly, "but I suspect Jamie's feelings about his brother's death, due to your ambition, might make him careless in loading the gun.''

''Davis is fine.'' Gavin's gaze darted wildly around the moonlit glade, as if he hoped some force would appear out of the shadows to aid him as Jamie Collard had aided Nicholas. But the field remained quiet. When Davis offered him the box Gavin selected a pistol. Davis took it and began to load the weapon.

Dorian ignored the chill of the morning air as she watched Nicholas take the other gun from the box and ready it for the duel. His hands were steady and his gaze intent. He knew perfectly well what he was doing, and it was exactly what he wanted and had worked for for so long.

She had been a fool not to see that a duel was what it would all come to—Nicholas facing Gavin across a dewy field. It was how men thought they could settle things. A trial, a test of courage, of fate, of physics. Watch the hammer fall. See the gunpowder explode. Mark the path of the ball. Weep for the blood that flowed.

How would either man's death right the wrongs that had been done? Ease the pain caused? Mete out justice where there was none to be had? But *honor* would be served.

''You can't do this, Nicholas.'' Eleanor's quavering voice shook Dorian from her morbid reflections. ''This isn't a duel. This is no matter of honor. It is vengeance. It's murder.''

''You didn't seem to think that a few moments ago when your husband held the weapons.'' Nicholas examined his pistol closely. ''Save your words, Eleanor. Jamie, restrain her.''

Dorian took the opportunity to step to his side. ''Nicholas, you know she is right.''

''This is the way it must be, Dorian,'' Nicholas said, intent on the pistol he was loading. ''I want you to sit in the carriage until the duel is over. It won't be long now.''

''If the magistrate will be here any moment, we can tell him everything—without more bloodshed,'' Dorian said, breathless but unable to resist making an effort to stop the madness.

"No. Gavin owes me and the memory of Jonathan the opportunity to meet him on the field of honor. We must settle this score face-to-face, man-to-man. Whatever happens, you must hold on to the music."

"Yes, I will." Suddenly time seemed to be slipping away. Dorian pressed herself closer, spreading her hands across the lapels of Nicholas's coat, and peering up into his face. Thankfully he did not push her away. "I won't argue with a naval officer about this matter of dueling and honor. But Nicholas, I must tell you something very important."

"Must it be now?" He was looking over her head at Gavin.

"Yes, now." Dorian tugged on his lapels, demanding his attention. "I only want to tell you one thing."

He peered into her face at last. "Yes?"

"Remember when you told me that when you love someone, you have an obligation to them to keep yourself safe?"

"Yes?" Suspicion resonated in his voice.

"I don't know if you love me, Nicholas—whether you care enough about me to reconsider this duel—but I love you. Do you hear me? I love you. If you love me, don't do this."

Dorian's words sliced through the darkness of his soul like the beam from a lighthouse. Nicholas's breath caught painfully in his chest. He looked toward the sky, forcing himself to draw a deep gulp of air—cool, sweet morning air. *She loved him!* How could those simple, sentimental words be so disarming?

Dear lord, help him to get her away from here. He did not want her to witness this bloody show. *He did not need her there to distract him.*

"You cannot stop this, Dorian, even with vows of love."

"I was afraid of that." Wetting her lips with a pink tongue, Dorian hurried on, seemingly fascinated by the fabric of his coat. "But I can't bear to think of you never knowing how I feel."

"Rest assured, I know." His voice nearly failed him.

She peered into his eyes again. "I will not make a silly, weepy scene of this. No hysterics. Just know that no matter what happens, you are loved, Nicholas. It's as simple as that."

She stretched up on tip-toe and brushed a kiss across his lips, then pulled away before he could capture her lips again. But her hand lingered in his for one last, telling moment.

"Nick? Are you ready?" A fighting gleam glinted in Gavin's eyes. He'd clearly recovered from his earlier defeat.

"I'm ready," Nicholas said. "St. John is going to count off the paces."

With a curt nod, Nicholas and Gavin took their places, back-to-back, each holding his pistol with the muzzle pointed toward the sky. Near the Trafford carriage Jamie Collard restrained Eleanor with a hand on her arm. Dorian stood near the St. John equipage.

Davis's voice rang loud and clear across the glade. As he counted off each pace, Nicholas took a step.

"Six. Seven. Eight . . ."

In the east moonlight was giving way to the pearly glow of dawn. The mist was beginning to evaporate around them.

Nicholas paced off the count, but his concentration had deserted him. Lord, he'd been cool and ready for bloodshed and vengeance until Dorian had thrown himself into his arms. *She loved him. Could it really be that simple?*

"Twelve. Thirteen. Fourteen . . ."

Nothing else in life had been that simple. Not his near betrothal to Eleanor, or his hard-won career, or his assumption of an earldom he'd never sought. Especially not defending the honor of his family name. The stain of dishonor could not be allowed to remain on the house of Derrington. But suddenly none of that seemed to matter as much as the simple words Dorian had spoken.

"Sixteen. Seventeen. Eighteen."

Nicholas gathered himself to turn quickly, to take careful aim and fire. He'd thought this duel out carefully over the past weeks. If he died on this dueling field, he would die honorably, defending Derrington honor. If he killed Gavin, justice would be served. He might be arrested for murder. English law declared dueling nothing more than murder, but he was willing to live with that consequence. His aim must be true. Nothing else would be good enough. Anything less would be failure.

"Nineteen . . ."

Dorian cried out.

Something stung Nicholas's neck. The air stirred near his ear. The sharp report of a pistol cracked across the glade. Grabbing at his neck, he whirled around.

From the corner of his eye he saw Davis hold Dorian back.

Gavin stood facing him, his pistol leveled at Nicholas, smoke curling up from the barrel into the still morning air. Nicholas stared at Gavin in disbelief. He had ignored the count and fired at Nicholas's back.

Nicholas's hand came away from his neckcloth sticky with blood, but the sight of it did not shake him.

"You bloody, scum-sucking coward," Jamie shouted.

Nicholas held up his hand to stop the seaman from jumping Gavin. He glared at Gavin, his opponent—his enemy—and wondered why he'd ever expected an honorable duel from this stranger.

Coolly, ignoring Eleanor's screams, Nicholas raised his weapon and took careful aim. "Finish the count, Davis."

Gavin's mouth dropped open. Eleanor began to sob.

St. John stood his ground. "Twenty!"

Gavin dropped his dueling pistol and staggered backward, preparing to run.

Skewering Gavin along the gun sight, Nicholas realized how simple it was. Simple and precious—far too precious to throw away.

He squeeze the trigger with great care. Gunpowder flashed. The report echoed across the field. The ball struck Gavin's shoulder and sent him spinning to the ground. He screamed and howled, his hand clutching a bloody shoulder.

Only then did Jamie Collard release Eleanor, who ran to her husband's side.

Nicholas strode quickly across the damp grass to stand over Gavin. Dispassionately, he watched the man writhing like a worm on the ground at his feet.

"You've murdered him," Eleanor wept hysterically.

Gavin started up at Nicholas, bitter accusation in his eyes. "Why didn't you kill me? You should have killed me. I would have killed you."

"I won't be your judge and jury, Gavin, traitor that you are. You're a worm. I will not murder you. I'll not throw away life for what you've become. Nor will I deliver you from a traitor's fate—though heaven knows hanging is too good for you. God help you when the magistrate arrives."

Nicholas handed his pistol to Jamie and walked away, deliberately forgetting the people who had once been his friends.

"They ain't going nowhere as far as I'm concerned," Jamie declared, waving his loaded pistol at Gavin and Eleanor.

Nicholas held out his hand to Dorian, whom Davis had been holding back. Her hand trembled in his and her fingers were cold.

"It's only a scratch," he said before she could throw herself at him. "No need to fuss over it. Now, you told me you had word from the doctor about your aunt."

"Yes. Davis and I should go now," she said, sparing a brief glance in Gavin's direction, then handing Nicholas a fresh neckcloth, which he recognized as Davis's. Her face was pale, but she seemed remarkably in control of her emotions. "Will you come with us?"

"Go on, Cap'n. Your uncle and the Bow Street runner will be here with the magistrate any time now." Jamie said.

"Then let's be off," Nicholas said, taking Dorian's arm and ushering her toward the St. John carriage. "You have some music to play for Aunt Charlotte."

* * *

The carriage rattled through the sleepy morning streets of Town. Dorian glanced at Nicholas, but his thoughts seemed far away from the three of them crowded in the coach on their way to what she feared was a death watch.

Davis pounded on the top of the carriage. "Drop me at Russell Square."

"Russell Square? Why?" Dorian protested. "With Aunt Charlotte—"

"I'm going to bring Susanna back to the house," he said. "I believe it's important for her to be with us."

"Davis—"

"Please don't argue with me," her brother said. "You've been dealing with this your way; I have mine."

Suddenly Nicholas caught her eye, and with an imperceptible shake of his head, he warned her to leave her brother alone. She decided to relent.

After they had dropped her brother at Russell Square Dorian found the courage to ask about Nicholas's wound. "You are feeling all right?"

"What?" He seemed to have been drawn away from other thoughts. "Yes, it's stopped bleeding, I believe."

"With Davis's neckcloth in place of your own, nothing is noticeable," Dorian assured him. Once she'd started talking, she found she didn't want to stop. "He wanted you to die, you know. He intended to kill you with a ball in the back. But you never intended to kill him, did you?"

"Believe me, I showed no mercy," Nicholas said with a cold, dark smile that chilled Dorian's blood. "Gavin will suffer. He will watch his wife lose her love and respect for him. Then he will hang as a traitor."

By the familiar sound of the horses' hooves on the pavement, Dorian knew they had turned into their street. She reached into her evening bag to find her betrothal ring and slipped it on.

When she looked up she found Nicholas staring curiously her.

She shrugged apologetically. "I never told Aunt Charlotte that we had parted. I hope you won't object to one last scene in this charade."

When he remained silent a moment too long Dorian added, "As soon as she is strong again, I'll tell her the truth."

"It looks beautiful on your hand." Nicholas held her gaze. Unexpectedly, he leaned forward, reaching across the distance between them to seize her hand and kiss it. His grasp was as strong and compelling as she remembered it. His lips were warm and firm against her fingers. Shivering heat cascaded through her in response to his touch.

"Trust me, Dorian," he said, holding her gaze once more. "Aunt Charlotte will never suspect that we haven't been lovers all this time."

A little breath of regret escaped Dorian's lips. How she regretted that they hadn't been.

At the Mayfair town house they found Dr. Fisher already at Aunt Charlotte's bedside. The atmosphere in the house was hushed, though servants scurried upstairs and down to do the doctor's bidding and to make Aunt Charlotte comfortable. No trouble was spared for the lady the whole household adored.

Barton took their things and, upon Nicholas's request, immediately dispatched a footman to retrieve the last piece of the Chamier music locked away in Uncle George's town house. Dorian rushed into the study to find Aunt Charlotte's piece of the music. Once it was laid out on the worktable, she reached into her bodice and retrieved Gavin's piece of the music.

She unrolled it carefully. "I think it survived reasonably well."

"Tucked so close to your heart," Nicholas said, observing over her shoulder. Dorian was suddenly very conscious of the ample display of bosom that her ball gown offered. "Of course it survived."

Nicholas helped her smooth the piece next to the fragment

she already possessed and the one he'd brought with him. When they turned the sheet of music over, they found the e-d-a-l of *Daedalus* spelled out in Greek letters clearly written in Franz Chamier's handwriting.

"This will be the proof I need," Nicholas said.

Dorian nodded, her heart aching. She was going to lose someone very dear to her. She knew it and turned away.

Without further delay, Dorian led the way upstairs.

Just as they reached Aunt Charlotte's chamber, Dr. Fisher opened the door.

"I'm so glad you are here," the doctor whispered. "Where is your brother? I fear it won't be long now. She hasn't much strength left."

"Is she in pain?" Dorian asked, peering at her aunt over the little doctor's shoulder.

"No. I don't believe so, but there may be some discomfort."

"Dorian? Is that you?" Aunt Charlotte lifted her head from the pillow.

"Yes, here I am." Dorian brushed the doctor aside and hurried to her aunt's bedside, vaguely aware of Nicholas following her into the room. "I have something for you."

"Dorian, you know you don't need to bring me things," Aunt Charlotte protested, her head falling feebly onto her pillow, but her gnarled hand reaching for Dorian's. "I'm always glad to have your company."

"Aunt Charlotte, we found the third piece of the music." Dorian dropped down on the stool the doctor had placed at her aunt's bedside.

"Franz's song to me?" Aunt Charlotte seemed surprised, and her faded blue eyes suddenly focused, resting on Dorian. "I had given up hope that we would ever find it."

"I have two of the pieces here, and Nicholas has sent for the third," Dorian said.

She heard a commotion outside the room and looked back to see Davis enter. Susanna followed him, along with a third person, dressed in church robes.

Dorian jumped to her feet and dashed across the room to meet her brother. "What are you doing? This is not a time for callers. Aunt Charlotte is very weak. She needs peace and quiet."

Davis stiffened and drew Susanna close to his side. "I have news I wish to share with Aunt Charlotte. I'd appreciate your leaving this to me."

Dorian looked to the doctor to explain the circumstances to Davis.

"But you must not overexcite her," Dr. Fisher warned.

Davis nodded his understanding. Susanna glanced at Dorian, appearing somewhat embarrassed but clearly devoted to Davis's purpose.

"Aunt Charlotte?" Davis approached the bed, pulling Susanna along with him. The clergyman remained by the door.

"Who do you have with you, dear?"

"This is Lady Susanna Sunridge," Davis said. "Do you remember her? I brought her by for tea last week."

Dorian frowned. She had not been present at tea with Susanna.

"Yes, my dear, sit down," Aunt Charlotte invited. "Please forgive us for receiving you so informally. I'm so glad to see you again. I hope this bodes well for what is growing between the two of you."

"Thank you, Miss St. John." Pink rose in Susanna's cheeks as she bobbed a curtsy.

Dorian stared at her brother in astonishment. He was actually blushing himself.

"Yes, well, Aunt Charlotte, you know how you've always told Dorian and me about the importance of true love, and of finding the person with whom our soul was meant to be joined?"

"Yes, dear, and I've always wondered if you and your sister have understood what I was trying to tell you."

"Well, I do now," Davis said. "I've learned with Susanna's help."

Under happier circumstances Dorian would have cheered her

approval, but her brother's reformation brought a smile to her lips nonetheless. Good for Davis—and Susanna.

Davis turned to Susanna. "We would like to wed with your blessing, if possible. That's why I brought the Reverend Churchstow with us."

"Oh, but of course. A wedding here in my room." Aunt Charlotte struggled to sit up. Dorian rushed to help the lady. "What a delight. It would make me very happy, Davis, to see you wed at last."

Dr. Fisher frowned, but Dorian's scowl prevented him from saying more. She turned to Barton and one of the maids. "Let's have some flowers for the bride."

In short order flowers were brought from the garden. Dorian tied the pink and white roses into a bouquet.

Nicholas was asked to be groomsman and he promptly tucked a rose into Davis's lapel. Dorian gladly stood at Susanna's side as the maid of honor. She thought Susanna a lovely bride, though the widow had become very quiet and very pale. Dorian hoped she wasn't having second thoughts.

The ceremony was soon complete. No sooner had Davis kissed his bride than she turned green. She clamped her hand over her mouth and rushed out of the room.

Concerned, Dorian followed her new sister-in-law down the hallway. Realizing that Susanna was about to be sick, Dorian ushered her into her own room and offered her the chamber pot. Susanna immediately lost her breakfast into it.

"Are you all right?" Dorian asked, dismayed to have two sick people on her hands. "Here, let me get a cool towel for your face. Dr. Fisher must have a look at you, too."

"No, no." Susanna protested, though she was still bent over the pot. She seemed horrified at the thought of having the doctor examine her. "I'm not ill."

Dorian stared at Susanna. "You are not *well.*"

Susanna sighed before explaining. "I think I'm with child."

Dorian almost dropped the pitcher of water she was pouring into the basin to dampen a towel. "Does Davis know?"

"No, oh no," Susanna cried, and tears began to run down her cheeks. "I could never had gone through with this wedding if he knew."

Dorian understood immediately. She would never want to wed someone who felt obligated to marry her—even though she loved him.

"I'll tell him—soon, of course," Susanna hurried to say. "I have not lied to him. I just haven't told him the news, but I couldn't—"

"Quite right," Dorian said, offering the damp towel to Susanna. "Dry your tears. I understand completely. Davis will be pleased when you tell him. I'm sure he will be. A marriage should be for love and for love alone."

The upstairs maid knocked on the door and peeked in. "His lordship's footman has arrived with the music."

"Thank God," Dorian whispered.

"See, Aunt Charlotte, here it is all assembled at last," Dorian said, sitting down by Aunt Charlotte's bed and holding open the portfolio with the three fragments of the love song placed together at last.

Aunt Charlotte squinted at it. Davis, Susanna, Nicholas, and Dr. Fisher gathered around the bed. With a tender hand, the lady reached out to touch the paper, her dry fingers caressing the notes so lovingly written for her by a man destined to be murdered in jail.

"Here is the title across the top, just as Franz wrote it for you, 'A Whisper of Violets.'" Dorian pointed out the words.

"I can't see it very well, dear," Aunt Charlotte said, letting her head rest back against her pillow again. "Will you play it for me? Leave all the doors open; I'll be able to hear."

Dorian jumped to her feet, ready to do anything to please her aunt, anything to keep her with them. "I'm going down right now."

Portfolio in hand, Dorian scurried downstairs to the pianoforte, instructing all the servants as she went to open all the doors in the house so the music would reach Aunt Charlotte's room. She opened the top of the instrument to set the music free and sat down at the keyboard, ready to perform as she'd never performed before.

At first her fingers trembled; then the melody caught her. She played with all the emotion and feeling she could put into the music, all the tenderness and love she knew Franz would have wanted to be there for his Charlotte.

When Dorian finished playing the haunting melody, she jumped up from the pianoforte and ran into the hallway. Nicholas stood at the top of the stairs.

Dorian paused looking up at him, searching his face for news of Aunt Charlotte's reaction.

"Come upstairs, sweetheart," he said softly, reaching out to her. "Come say good-bye."

A heart-wrenching sob escaped Dorian. "She's gone?"

"She slipped away while she was listening to you play her song. But you must say farewell. She would want that."

Slowly, Dorian started up the steps, remembering little after she put her hand in Nicholas's palm. She allowed him to take her into Aunt Charlotte's room. Remotely, she heard Susanna's quiet weeping. She saw Davis's back turned to the room as he stared out the window. She recalled realizing that the figure in the bed was motionless. Yet the room seemed filled with Aunt Charlotte's spirit, warm and loving, so life-affirming. She said her farewell, recalling few details but for the numbness and the immensity of her grief.

Later she remembered Nicholas holding her while she wept, his embrace gentle and compassionate. She seemed to recall him murmuring comforting words and placing a tender kiss on the top of her head.

But she did recall his request, made softly, without explanation or apology.

"I need the music, Dorian."

His entreaty came as no surprise. Acquiring the music was

what their relationship had been about from the outset. Without protest, Dorian handed him the portfolio. The music held little meaning for her without Aunt Charlotte.

She could feel him studying her face as he took the portfolio from her, but she avoided his gaze. Her heart was too empty and numb to deal with his questions.

''I'll return with it soon,'' he promised.

But he did not.

Chapter
Twenty-seven

The days that followed Aunt Charlotte's death were a blur for Dorian. Despite her deathbed instructions that there was to be no mourning in the house, a wreath was hung on the door and Dorian, like Davis, wore a black armband, though convention required a lady in mourning to wear black garments.

"Black is not your color, Dorian," Aunt Charlotte had said once. "I don't want to look down from above and see you looking dowdy in black. What kind of honor is that to the dead?"

The remembrance was enough to bring a smile to Dorian's lips.

Her days were full of arrangements of all sorts, notes to respond to, sympathetic callers to receive. She moved through it, grateful for the shield of numbness. At night she collapsed into bed and slept a dreamless sleep.

She saw nothing of Nicholas except for a glimpse of him and Uncle George at the funeral service. They were but two among a throng of mourners who remembered Charlotte and

Franz. She knew that Nicholas had been busy doing just as he'd said he would.

" 'Tis all here in the papers," Davis announced one morning at the breakfast table, several weeks after the funeral.

He handed two penny presses to Dorian, who scanned the headlines. The press loved the story. Gavin Trafford was branded a villain and Nicholas a hero. She thought he must be satisfied at last. She was as glad for him as she could be in her benumbed state.

Headlines proclaimed an old family name cleared of allegations of treason. A quick reading of the articles hinted at meetings at the admiralty offices and receptions at homes where he had not been received since the rumors had first come to the fore. A smile spread across Dorian's face. She was glad for Nicholas. He was reinstating the Derrington name just as he'd wanted to do. She hoped Captain Kenwick was eating his disparaging words about Nicholas now.

"Oh dear, excuse me," Susanna cried, pushing herself away from the table. She clamped her hand over her mouth and dashed from the room.

Dorian started to rise to go after her.

"'Stay where you are, Miss Dorian, and eat your breakfast," said the maid who'd been helping serve breakfast. "You take care of yourself. I'll see to Mrs. St. John."

Davis stared after his wife with a frown of anxiety. Dorian wondered if Susanna had told him about the baby yet.

"Mrs. St. John," Davis repeated slowly, as though savoring each syllable. "You know, Dorian, Susanna doesn't care one bit that she is no longer *Lady* Susanna."

"I'm not surprised," Dorian said, staring at the food on her plate with little interest.

She'd just discovered weeks since that she was not with child. Instead of relieved, she found herself strangely disappointed. How fortunate Susanna was to know that the man she loved, loved her in return, and that the fruit of that love was already growing inside her.

Davis cleared his throat. "I should tell you—Susanna told me several days ago—I've been trying to become accustomed to the idea. Well, you and I are going to be a father."

For the first time in a month Dorian began to laugh.

"It's not a laughing matter, Dorian." With a pained expression, Davis flicked his napkin from his lap and threw it on the table. "This is a solemn thing. I meant to say an *aunt*, of course. I'm going to be a *father* and you're going to be an *aunt*."

Dorian sobered. "And you are glad of it?"

Davis regarded her with a look of complete honesty in his eyes. "Yes, especially the way everything turned out. I really love Susanna, and I'm damned lucky she agreed to have me. And it seems right somehow that a precious new life is coming when a beloved one has gone."

Dorian looked down at her plate and fought back tears. "Yes, I know what you mean."

"If the baby is a girl, Susanna and I would like to name her Charlotte," Davis said, "if you think that's fitting."

"I like the idea very much," Dorian said, touched by Davis's sentiment. "And I think Aunt Charlotte would like it, too."

With breakfast over, Dorian wandered into Aunt Charlotte's work room. For the last month she'd put off doing anything to the room. At first she couldn't bear the thought of disturbing anything her aunt had been working on; then the funeral and the callers had occupied all her time.

Now, as she stood in the middle of the room and scanned the stacks of music and portfolios, she found herself mentally making note of what things should go to her aunt's friends and what things should stay to be shown to Davis's daughter, Aunt Charlotte's namesake.

Aunt Charlotte had given her some instructions, but she had always disregarded them, as if in doing so she could put the end off. Now it was time to move on and deal with things.

Without Aunt Charlotte. Without Nicholas.

* * *

A week later Dorian was just finishing the draft of a letter to the publisher Aunt Charlotte had been considering to handle Franz's work when Barton appeared at the door of the work room. Before the butler could speak, Nicholas appeared behind him.

"Miss Dorian, you have a caller. His lordship, the Earl of Seacombe."

Dorian frowned at her butler for not asking if she was at home. When she caught the uncertain look in Barton's eye she realized Nicholas had prevented him from bringing her any warning.

"Thank you. Barton." She rose from the table, staring at Nicholas, suddenly aware of the way he filled the room, tall, broad-shouldered, and elegant in an understated way.

She noted that there was something different about him. He was carrying a portfolio under his arm, but that wasn't the difference. He was no longer wearing the black and gold skeleton mourning ring.

"Shall I bring tea, Miss Dorian?" Barton inquired.

"No," Dorian said. "Lord Seacombe won't be staying long."

"A tea tray would be good, Barton," Nicholas countered, walking toward the worktable.

"Very good, my lord." Barton bowed and left the room.

Dorian glared after her butler in annoyance. When did he start taking his instruction from her callers? But Barton had already gone for the tea. She turned back to Nicholas. "You aren't wearing the ring."

Nicholas put the red leather portfolio on the table, his head bowed. "I took a brief trip to Lincolnshire. A sort of pilgrimage."

"Yes?" Dorian nodded, encouraging him to go on. Despite her determination not to be moved, her heart began to ache.

"I sailed where the four of us—Gavin, Eleanor, Jon, and I—had sailed as friends many times long ago. I returned the mourning ring to the sea there, in Jon's memory."

"That's very fitting," Dorian said, touched in spite of herself.

His head came up and he searched her face. "I've come to return your aunt's song."

"I see." Dorian stared at the portfolio, struggling not to show any emotion. "It's very kind of you to bring it yourself."

"It was part of our agreement, if you will remember." He untied the laces and opened the binder to reveal the music. "I took it to the best manuscript and book binding shop in Town and asked them to restore it as best they could."

Nicholas stood back from the table, gesturing toward the opened portfolio.

Dorian moved closer, eager to peer at the sheet of "A Whisper of Violets" and very aware of his presence.

She looked down at the music, forcing herself to concentrate on it. The single sheet lay flat and smooth, the seams so invisible that it appeared whole.

"It's wonderful," she exclaimed, glancing up at him with shy pleasure and gratitude. "It hardly appears damaged at all. Oh, how I wish Aunt Charlotte could have seen it like this."

"I know; I had the same thought," Nicholas said, standing near enough to see over her shoulder but not touching her.

Dorian suddenly realized how much she wanted him to hold her in his arms again. In those first hours after Aunt Charlotte's death his embrace had been the closest thing to comfort she'd known.

Barton appeared in the doorway carrying the tea tray himself, instead of sending one of the maids. Dorian and Nicholas fell silent as the butler arranged the tray on a tea table.

When Barton was finished he bowed one more time with a pleased smile on his lips. "Lord Seacombe, if I may say so on behalf of the staff, we are very pleased to see that your name has been cleared in the press. Of course we never doubted you, but it is good to see your family honor restored and your service to the crown acknowledged."

"Yes, it is, Barton. Thank you. Very kind of you to say so,"

Nicholas said, clearly moved by the butler's words. "And thank the staff for me for their good wishes."

"Yes, my lord." Barton withdrew. Though he left the work room door open, Dorian remained aware that she and Nicholas were otherwise alone.

"May I offer you some refreshment?" Dorian forced herself to walk away from Nicholas and sit down at the tea table.

"Actually, I did not come to be entertained," Nicholas said after a thoughtful pause. "I came to return the music, which was part of our agreement, and to offer you something more."

Dorian pressed her lips together and busied herself with pouring tea. "Nothing more is necessary, is it, Nicholas? We, you and I, each seem to have achieved our goals."

"I hope that will not be the end of our dealings with one another." Nicholas reached into his waistcoat pocket. "Once not so long ago I offered you this ring. Remember?"

Dorian blinked at the pearl-encrusted Seacombe amethyst in confusion. "I remember."

"You told me that I should offer it only to my true love." Her heart raced, but she tried to remain calm. "Yes?"

"Did I mention that evening that I'd never offered this ring to anyone else?"

"Not even Eleanor?" The words were out of Dorian's mouth before she could stop them, though she knew she sounded like a jealous woman.

"It was not mine to offer when I came closest to contemplating betrothal to Eleanor, but I never offered her any ring, let alone the Seacombe amethyst. You are the only woman to whom I've ever offered this heirloom."

"Nicholas, I know you are a man of honor, but I assure you, you have no obligation to do this."

Inwardly Nicholas cursed his ineptness. He longed to possess just a bit of Franz Chamier's romanticism and idealism—just an ounce of the man's poetic nature. Surely then he could propose in such a way as to make her forget about their previous alliance.

Nicholas took a deep breath and decided to go to the heart of the matter. "You told me to offer this ring to my true love. So I am doing just that."

Dorian sat back. Her eyes widened a bit. Nicholas realized he'd been speaking a little too forcefully. He sat down on the sofa beside her and softened his tone. "You are my true love, sweetheart. That's what I've been trying to tell you for some time now."

She stared at the ring in his hand but made no move to reach for it. "Nicholas—"

"No, wait . . . I think I should point out some things here. It may be rather ungentlemanly to count, but this is the second time I've offered you this ring and the third time I've asked you to marry me."

Dorian looked at him doubtfully.

"The first time you sent me away, saying I should only offer the heirloom to my true love."

"Well, yes."

"The second time, at Floraton Court, you claimed I mocked your ideals of love and marriage. And this time—I can only pray that you are running short of excuses."

"Well—"

"Sweetheart, you cannot say you don't love me because you told me you did on the dueling field at Battersea. Remember? I recall very clearly."

"Do you? I wondered. Because I remember it very clearly, too." Dorian leaned forward, searching his face with an earnestness that Nicholas didn't understand. "The question then is, do you love me?"

"I thought I just said so." Nicholas sighed. He really was very awkward at this, but it was vital that he make Dorian understand without any theatrical gestures. "I have loved you from the moment I saw your bonnet feather tremble at the auction house when you challenged my bid."

Dorian sniffed. "But that's nonsense. You knew nothing about me."

"I'd learned enough to know you were worth pursuing, but you saved me from that," Nicholas said with a smile. "And you captured my heart completely when you wept for your brother's failed marriage proposal. Remember, under the table in Thorpe Hall."

"But that was ages ago. Before you offered me the Seacombe amethyst."

"Indeed, it was. You were the one who denied being my true love, sweetheart, not I." Nicholas reached for her hand. "Though I will admit that I didn't make my feelings very clear at the time. I believe I was still a bit shocked at finding myself in love."

Dorian's failure to draw away from him encouraged Nicholas.

"There have been many times when I wanted to tell you how much I loved you, but I knew I could not do it as a poet or a musician. I can write no songs to you."

"Nicholas, I'm not asking for a song," Dorian whispered. "I've given you my heart and I'm asking for yours in return."

"Then it is yours, sweetheart." He quickly slipped the amethyst on her finger. "And you must wear this."

Nicholas pulled her toward him and their lips met in a hungry, urgent kiss. Her arms slipped around his neck and her fingers laced through his hair. He crushed her against him until he could feel her breasts pressing close. He trailed kisses down her neck, savoring the sweet feminine taste of her until he encountered a gold chain.

"What's this?"

Dorian pulled away just enough to tug at the chain, freeing it from the bodice of her gown. "Our betrothal ring."

Nicholas stared at the blue flashing sapphire, trying to make sense of the fact that she still wore it so close to her heart. "You, madame, are a soft-hearted fraud."

"I fear as much," she admitted, her dark eyelashes fluttering.

"I confessed when I fell in love with you," Nicholas said, feeling confident at last. "You tell me when you first loved me."

Dorian blushed and her mouth dropped open in surprise. "Don't you know? I thought you always knew."

Nicholas would admit to nothing; he had to know the truth from her own lips. "When?"

"When you kissed me the night of the musicale." Dorian looked away, as if embarrassed by the admission. "I knew then you had the power to seduce me and I was certain you knew too."

"I knew." Nicholas wrapped his arms around her, this time certain that he would never have difficulty telling her how much he loved her again. "And I knew seduction would only be the beginning."

Epilogue

A year later Nicholas took a promising-looking envelope from Barton. He and Dorian had only been back in Town for a week after a delightful stay of several months at Seacombe Manor. But with Dorian's time drawing near they had returned to Town. Nicholas wanted to be near the best doctors and midwives when their child was born.

"I'll take this to her ladyship," he said. "Where is she?"

"She's in the work room, my lord," Barton said. "Mr. and Mrs. St. John and their daughters are with her."

"Thank you, Barton." Nicholas strolled down the hall, looking forward to joining his wife and greeting his in-laws. He seldom thought of returning to the sea these days. He liked having a family.

Dorian was lounging on the sofa, her feet up just as she had been when he'd left her that morning, but he wasn't fooled. She hadn't been there all day. He knew most of her tricks for evading his lectures, one of which was to arrange herself on the sofa just as he entered the front door.

She beamed a smile at him when he entered. He went straight

to kiss her cheek. "Barton told me we had visitors. Davis, Susanna, how is parenthood?"

Davis, who was juggling one titan-haired, indigo-eyed daughter, merely laughed.

Susanna smiled indulgently at the other identical titan-haired, indigo-eyed daughter. "Exhausting, my lord."

Nicholas grinned at the adorable six-month-olds. "And how are my nieces, Charlotte and Cassandra?"

Charlotte, in her mother's arms, gurgled and grinned sweetly at her uncle. But Cassandra, already papa's girl, regarded Nicholas with solemn eyes.

"Absolutely precious, aren't they?" Davis bragged.

"Davis, they are so charming that I do not envy you in about eighteen years."

"Don't feel too smug, Seacombe," Davis said. "With two of them I may have to call on their uncle for assistance when the suitors begin to break down the door."

Nicholas laughed and returned to Dorian's side. "And how are the heir and his mother doing today?"

"Restless," Dorian said, shifting slightly to make herself more comfortable. "What have you there, Nicholas?"

"This was just delivered as I came in," he said and handed it to Dorian. "Open it."

After examining the seal Dorian hastily ripped open the envelope. "It's from the music publisher to whom I showed Aunt Charlotte's compilation of Franz's work. It has taken me so long to finally complete it."

Cassandra protested briefly as Davis handed her to the nurse and walked to Dorian's side. Nicholas walked around behind the sofa, watching his wife rapidly scan the letter.

Dorian looked up with happiness glowing on her face. "They are going to publish the collection."

"The entire thing?" Davis asked, a smile spreading across his face.

"The entire thing, even 'A Whisper of Violets,'" Dorian said. "You don't mind, do you, Davis? At first I wasn't going to include it in the collection. I thought it too personal to be a proper song for the others to see. Then, I decided Aunt Charlotte was never ashamed of her love for Franz, nor he for her.''

Davis nodded. ''You did the right thing.''

''I agree,'' Nicholas said, touching Dorian's cheek and thanking heaven that a composer locked up in jail had had the courage to write the love song that brought them together.

Dorian smiled up at him. ''Love and love songs are meant to be shared.''

''You are certainly right about that, sweetheart.'' Nicholas bent close to share a brief congratulatory kiss. ''And that is exactly what I intend to share with you and our children the rest of my life.''

ABOUT THE AUTHOR

Linda Madl lives with her family in Leavenworth, Kansas. She is author of six historical romances, including *A Whisper of Violets* and *Bayou Rose* (available from Zebra Books). Linda loves hearing from readers; you may write to her c/o Zebra Books. Please include a self-addressed stamped envelope if you wish a response.

ROMANCE FROM JANELLE TAYLOR

Scientists believe 2 held on UFO

PASCAGOULA, Miss. (UPI)—A Northwestern University astronomer says the "very terrifying experience" of two men indicates that a strange craft from another planet did land in Mississippi.

"Where they are coming from and why they were here is a matter of conjecture," Dr. Allen Hynek said, "but the fact that they were here on this planet is beyond a reasonable doubt."

Hynek and Dr. James Harder of the University of California interviewed by hypnosis two shipyard workers who told authorities they were fishing from an old pier in the Pascagoula River when a "fish-shaped" vehicle emitting a bluish haze approached from the sky.

Charles Hickson, 42, and 18-year-old Calvin Parker, both of the Gautier community, have maintained throughout a weekend of intense questioning that they were taken aboard the craft by three weird creatures with wrinkled skin, crab-claw hands and pointed ears.

Hynek was scientific consultant to Project Bluebook when it was conducted on UFOs by the U.S. Air Force in the 1960s.

chairmen, Sen. Howard Cannon (D-
and Rep. Peter Rodino (D-N.J.), have
o allow live television coverage of the

pro
gres
rece
the

sland P

OCTOBER 15, 1973

Entered as Sec
at Postoffice, Babylon, Bay

beat b
of infar